THE
FIRST
GIRL
CHILD

ALSO BY AMY HARMON

Young Adult and Paranormal Romance

Slow Dance in Purgatory
Prom Night in Purgatory

Inspirational Romance

A Different Blue
Running Barefoot
Making Faces
Infinity + One
The Law of Moses
The Song of David
The Smallest Part

Historical Fiction

From Sand and Ash
What the Wind Knows

Romantic Fantasy

The Bird and the Sword
The Queen and the Cure

THE

FIRST

GIRL

CHILD

AMY HARMON

47NORTH

Published by 47North, Seattle

www.apub.com

Amazon, the Amazon logo, and 47North are trademarks of Amazon.com, Inc., or its affiliates.

ISBN-13: 9781542007962
ISBN-10: 1542007968

Cover design by Faceout Studio, Tim Green

Printed in the United States of America

For as the woman is of the man,
even so is the man also of the woman.

—*1 Corinthians 11:12*

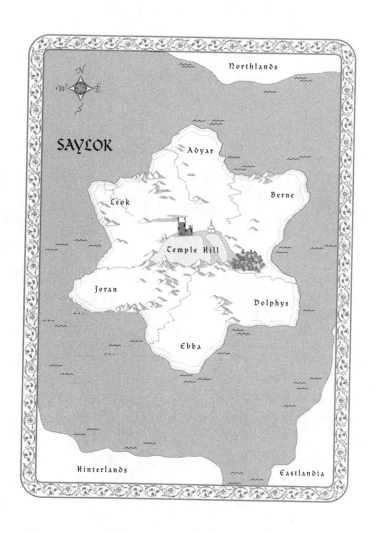

PRONUNCIATION GUIDE

Adyar: AD yahr
Alannah: a LAH nuh
Alba: AHL buh
Banruud: BAN rood
Bashti: BASH tee
Berne: burn
Bayr: bear
Dagmar: DAG mahr
Dalys: DAH lis
Desdemona: dez de MO nuh
Dolphys: DAHL fis
Dred: drehd
Dystel: DIS tahl
Ebba: EH buh
Elayne: ee LAYN
Ghost: ghost
Ivo: EYE voh
Joran: YOR uhn
Juliah: YOO lee uh
Leok: LEE awk
Liis: lees
Saylok: SAY lawk

PROLOGUE

They shouldn't have climbed for so long, but they'd been convinced that if they reached the top of Shinway, they would be able to look out over the sea, all the way to Eastlandia. They thought they might spot their father's sails—the sails of all the warriors of Dolphys—returning from raids on distant shores. Their father always brought them something, even though it often wasn't what either of them wanted. He gave Dagmar swords when he'd rather have scrolls. He brought Desdemona trinkets when she'd just as soon have a length of rope or a clever snare. Still, they watched for him, waited for him, and they'd climbed too high.

"It's going to storm, Des," Dagmar worried. "The fog has settled on the water, and we won't see Father even if he's almost ashore."

Desdemona scowled and kept walking, scrambling up the rocky path like the goats they kept and should be returning to. If Father did come home, he would wonder at the empty cottage and the hungry animals, the cow that hadn't been milked, and the wood that hadn't been gathered. They'd left at dawn, and it was midday, though the thickening clouds and the gray light made it seem much later. They had played along the way, collecting treasures only to discard them for new finds. They'd stopped for berries and climbed a towering oak that had lured them in with low-hanging branches. Now it was growing late, and they'd been gone too long.

"He isn't coming home today," Desdemona said, dismissive. "Yesterday, old Hilde asked the sea, and it gave her five shells in a pile on the sand. She said it would be five more days until the warriors return."

Mistress Dunhilde was charged with their care when their father was away, though she was drowsy and doddering, and Dagmar felt ofttimes that he looked after her more than she looked after them. But Hilde was rarely wrong about such things.

Dagmar stopped walking. "Then why did you insist on climbing to the peaks?" he asked, exasperated.

"I was weary of the cottage," Desdemona said, shrugging. She tossed him an impish grin and tugged at his hand.

"We need to turn back, Desdemona," Dagmar demanded. "A storm is coming and we'll be caught on the cliffs." His younger sister was constantly getting them into trouble, and she never listened.

"Don't worry, Dag. I will protect you," she reassured him, pulling her long blade from the leather sheath at her waist. She launched it with both hands at the unassuming pine tree directly in their path.

"I got him!" she crowed, racing toward the tree, and Dagmar realized she hadn't been aiming for the trunk at all. A gray rabbit, Desdemona's blade jutting out of his back, bounded away and disappeared among the rocks at the base of the highest crag. The three cliffs of Shinway were stacked like enormous steps, one atop the other, and were as stony and flat as the hills around them were green and rolling. They afforded nothing but a spectacular view and a long climb, and the people of Dolphys rarely made the pilgrimage to the top. Time was too short and life too hard for unnecessary journeys.

"Hurry, Dag," Desdemona called over her shoulder, tucking her skirt into the belt at her waist to keep it out of her way as she gave chase. She slipped once and caught herself on a jagged outcropping, but was up again immediately, clambering after her fat prey, who was bleeding but unbeaten.

"He went in there," Desdemona panted as Dagmar reached her side, pointing at a cavity tucked between the first two ledges.

"And he has your blade," Dagmar added, though he was certain the rabbit would be glad to be rid of it. The cave was not visible from the narrow path, and a curtain of ivy, spilling from one height to another, obscured the entrance.

"Let me see your hands," Dagmar ordered. Desdemona raised her palms, impatient. They were both abraded and bleeding from her fall.

"The bleeding will stop," she insisted. "They only sting a little. I'm going in. I want my blade and that rabbit. He'll make a fine stew and a pair of slippers."

Dagmar didn't bother to protest. The cave would be black as pitch; she couldn't go far. He studied the cliffs still rising above them and considered the distance they'd already come. Below him, to the left, lay the sea, though mist covered the water and the wind melded with the waves, muffling her sounds and her shores. But he knew she was there.

Behind him, the valley of Dolphys stretched in stubborn splendor, the silver line of the river Mogda snaking through it, winding around huts and homes that, from this height, appeared no bigger than bits of broken shell among the sands. Hills, lumpy, misshapen pyramids in green, dappled the valley, separating one community from another. There were many such hills in Dolphys. The people called them sleeping giants, though they appeared more like enormous, slumbering toads.

"It's dark in here," Desdemona called from the mouth of the cave, and Dagmar lifted his face to the skies. Clouds as dark and ominous as his father's temper swirled overhead, casting the world around him in the color of rain. He sighed and went in search of something to burn. It would be foolish to descend the mountain in a deluge, and the cave would be a good place to spend the next few hours, but they would need a fire.

A felled pine, its branches broken and brittle, would provide fodder enough. He hacked a few limbs free with the hatchet he wore at his waist and dragged them up the narrow path toward the opening in the rock. He had to stoop to enter, Desdemona holding the vines aside so he could drag his kindling behind him, but once inside, he could fully straighten. He could not see beyond a few steps, but the space felt as vast and unexplored as the night sky.

"We need light. Use my hatchet to clear some of the vines, and try not to cut off your toes," he ordered. Desdemona was a skilled huntress, but she was clumsy in the way of the overconfident and easily distracted. She obeyed him with an obligatory grumble, shearing the vines by the handful, allowing the tepid light to peer into the cave.

It didn't take Dagmar long to coax a flame, though the crack of Thor's hammer and the resulting torrent now lashing the cliffs threatened a longer stay than his fire would last. Desdemona crouched nearby, tying several twigs together with the stringy vines she'd cut, fashioning herself a torch. She made one for Dagmar as well but was too impatient to wait for him and went off to hunt the rabbit on her own.

Dagmar continued to tend the blaze, noting that the smoke from the branches did not gather but rose, whisked away into heights and places he could not see. There was an opening somewhere above him, he was certain, but he abandoned his musings when Desdemona called to him, her voice odd and distant like she too had risen with the smoke. He couldn't see her, but a ruddy glow smeared a section of the dark, and he walked toward it, the torch she'd crafted for him in his hand. Tunnels veered off the main section, man-size doorways that burrowed to places he would never explore, and Dagmar kept his back to the fire he had built as his eyes clung to the glimmer of light ahead. Desdemona had gone much farther than he would have ever gone alone, and he bit back sharp words when he finally reached her.

Framed by the arched opening of a separate cavity, Desdemona stood facing the wall, her torch lifted to illuminate something on the rock. As he neared, she turned slowly, lighting one section of wall at a time. The shadows breathed around her, expanding and disappearing

4

as she moved, and Dagmar noted the dimensions of the space. It was more a chamber than a cave, the rock encircling them like the dome of the temple he'd seen only once.

"What are they?" Desdemona asked as he stopped just inside the entrance. He copied her motion, raising his weak torch to see for himself.

He made three slow rotations around the perimeter before he answered her, his voice hushed, his heart loud. The chamber was filled with figures—hundreds of them—chiseled into the rock. Circles and obelisks, eyes and angles, a language of pictures and drawings Dagmar couldn't decipher but recognized all the same.

"They are . . . runes," Dagmar whispered, the fine hairs on his neck and arms rising in reverence.

"I thought the only runes were in the Temple of Saylok. I thought they were guarded by the keepers," Desdemona whispered. There was no fear in her face, and her voice echoed the thrill in Dagmar's own heart. He was wise enough to be afraid, afraid enough for both of them. But he was not afraid enough to leave. Thunder rumbled, hammering against the mountain above them. The reverberations made the cavity hum.

"What do you think they all mean? Are they stories?" Desdemona asked.

"Some of them. Look, you will recognize these," he said, pointing to the figures nearest the entrance. It was as if the runes began with them.

"It is a tale of the gods," she said, pleased with herself. "There is Father Saylok," Desdemona pointed out. "And Adyar the eagle, Berne the bear, Dolphys the wolf, Ebba the boar, Joran the horse, and Leok the lion." The chiseled renderings were remarkably detailed. The god, Saylok, son of Odin and father of their land, stood in the center of a six-pointed star, his animal children equidistant from him, each one occupying a section of the star.

5

Dagmar touched the uppermost point and moved to the right, saying the name of the clan—Adyar, Berne, Dolphys, Ebba, Joran, and Leok—as his fingers fluttered over each one. "This is how our land must look from the sky."

Desdemona, emboldened by his action, reached out a hand and pressed her palm to the rune directly in front of her, her eyes lit with curiosity in the jittery shadows.

"This rune has wings, Dagmar," she marveled, the lines hugging her fingers as she traced them. The rumble of distant thunder changed, rising in pitch until the drone became a thousand whispers. A fluttering swelled in the cave, like the wind outside was fleeing the rain.

Desdemona snatched her hand from the figure, but it was too late. From somewhere above them, a legion of wings descended, swirling around the chamber, striking the walls, clawing for space, tangling themselves in Desdemona's hair and tugging at Dagmar's clothes. Their torches were knocked free as they swatted wildly at the writhing bodies and papery wings. Muffled screams erupted from their throats as they buried their faces against each other, hiding from the swarm.

As quickly as they'd arrived, the bats found the opening in the chamber and rushed to depart, the swish and hiss of their flight echoing even after they were gone. For a moment the children huddled together, hands moving over their limbs and loose clothing, checking for blind trespassers.

The torches burned on, two small fires on the cavern floor, and Dagmar stooped to retrieve them, relieved that he and his sister wouldn't be left to find their way out in the dark. He shivered violently and shook out his clothes once more, but Desdemona had already moved on, torch in hand, her fear as fleeting as the bats.

"That rune had wings, but this one has a flame. Mayhaps it is a fire rune," she mused.

"No!" Dagmar yelled, and the sound split and jangled off the walls in a chorus of denial, but the carving Desdemona caressed whooshed

6

into flame, the lines of the symbol glowing like hot coals. Dagmar cursed, dropping his torch again. He shrugged out of his cloak so he could smother the fire licking the wall.

"Are you mad? You can't touch the runes," he bellowed, beating the flames. His cloak would be singed. It already stunk of bats. The rune blinked out as the fire was doused, and Dagmar stepped back, panting, waiting for the next calamity.

"Why can't I touch them? You did," Desdemona muttered, but she stooped to pick up his torch, chastened.

And Dagmar realized he had.

He had touched the walls first.

He had traced the star of Saylok and nothing had happened.

"Mayhaps . . . some of them are simply stories," he offered, feeling strangely empty.

"Then touch the fire rune," Desdemona challenged. "My torch has gone out."

He hesitated, knowing he was a fool and Desdemona was a tormentor. But he couldn't resist.

He expected heat and felt only the cold kiss of stone, the furrows tickling the tips of his fingers. He pressed harder, willing the rune to light, wanting the power his sister had so easily wielded. Suddenly— desperately—he wanted to call wings and fire, even if it meant the bats carried him away and the cave burst into flame.

But the rune denied him.

"Mayhaps I have rune blood," Desdemona marveled, oblivious to his disappointment. "Like the keepers."

"Rune blood and no bloody sense," Dagmar said, smiling at her to take away the sting of his words, smiling to take away the sting in his chest. He had always dreamed of being a Keeper of Saylok.

He froze, an idea dawning.

"There is . . . blood . . . on your fingers," he said. "You traced the runes in blood. Hilde says the keepers use blood to power the runes."

Desdemona held her fingers to the light. Blood stained the tips and lined the crevices.

"I *do* have rune blood," she marveled, gleeful.

Dagmar used the blade of his hatchet to nick his finger, wincing a little at the pinch. Blood welled, black in the poor light, and without allowing himself to fear, he traced a rune that enclosed an eye, wiping his blood in the furrows that formed lid, lash, and pupil. The rune seemed harmless enough, no wings or flames, no swords or headless men like some of the others.

Then he waited, hopeful and horrified at what he might see . . . or what he might *not* see.

Then darkness swallowed him whole and his mind was not his own.

Pictures formed and fell away, and distance narrowed as he rose above the cliffs. He was flying at dizzying speeds, soaring over the trees back to the cottage in Dolphys where he lived with his sister and his father, where he tended goats and fed pigs and read whatever he could scavenge, even if it was the scribblings of his own hand. He continued past his home, flashing over hills and vales, over forests and streams until he stood on the temple mount of Saylok, blood on his hands, eyes lifted to the rafters of the sanctum. He wore a keeper's robe—deep purple—and his head was cold. He touched it with wet fingers and felt the bare skin of his scalp.

The temple melted into a grove, giant trunks and heavy branches covering the sky and burrowing into the ground he knelt upon. He held a woman in his arms. She looked like his memories of his mother, but he'd been four when she died—so small—and he'd never held her this way. She had always held him. Her body was warm, but her eyes were cold, and he cried, great gulping sobs that tore at his chest and his throat.

"Dagmar, can you hear me?" his mother asked, but her gaze stayed fixed and her mouth did not move.

"Dagmar!" she cried, and Dagmar gasped, pulling long, deep breaths into his starving lungs. He breathed so deeply, the woman slipped from his arms, and he catapulted back across the distance, the landscape moving so quickly that the colors became a blur of greens and blues, light and dark, and he found himself back in the cave, lying on his back, his arms and legs flung wide, blood in his nostrils and a pulse behind his eyes. Desdemona knelt beside him, holding his torch, and he realized it was her voice that had called to him.

"You scared me," Desdemona whispered, wiping at her cheeks. She was crying. He was crying too. He sat up gingerly, and his stomach roiled.

"You fell to the ground like you were dead," she wailed.

He touched the knot forming on the back of his head beneath his braid. He had hair again.

"I want to go home, Dagmar. I want to be a warrior, not a keeper," Desdemona said, helping him stand. Her torch had gone out, but his had life enough to guide them from the chamber of runes back to his fire at the entrance of the cave. He felt disembodied—his feet moving, though he couldn't feel them, his hand in Desdemona's, though he felt nothing but stone. Stone, heavy and cold and dark. Stone all around him, stone beneath him, stone within him.

"The rain has stopped," Desdemona said as they exited the cave, but he would have kept walking even if the downpour continued. It was a while before he could speak, before his limbs warmed and his body felt like his own. Desdemona was silent beside him, as though she sensed his disorientation and grappled with her own. But when they finally staggered to the base of Shinway, he turned to her, his voice urgent yet hushed, afraid that even the trees would overhear.

"Promise me you will never go to the cave again," he begged his sister. "And promise me you will never tell anyone it is there."

"I promise," she said, but he saw her impatience and her fatigue. The experience in the cave had already faded for her, a bad dream easily pushed aside. She tugged at him, eager for the cottage, for supper, for rest. But he would never forget.

"Desdemona," he moaned. "Listen to me."

"I'm listening, Dagmar," she reassured him, and met his gaze.

"That cave is full of things not meant to be found," he whispered, and his voice quavered in fear.

Desdemona nodded, her blue eyes wide, and for the first time, Dagmar noticed how much she resembled their mother.

PART ONE

The Temple Boy

1

Dagmar preferred to pray outside. The walls of the temple were cool and quiet, but the stone was empty, lifeless, and he felt cut off from the wonder that made him want to pray. When he walked in the woods and touched the trees or picked his way up the grassy hills that rose up all around the land of Saylok, his soul was untethered, and the words in his heart loosened and rose to his mouth to spill from his lips. He prayed to Odin, the Allfather, though the word *father* always brought a pang of guilt to his breast. His father was a warrior—mighty and feared—and he'd been determined that Dagmar be a warrior as well. But Desdemona was the warrior, the best shield maiden in Dolphys, and she fought with a skill and a ferocity that drew admiration from the men of every clan. Dagmar did not want the admiration of men. He wanted the knowledge of the gods.

The Keepers of Saylok were revered and protected, something Dagmar had longed for all his life—peace, quiet, and safety. His father had not been able to refuse when Dagmar had petitioned the Chieftain of Dolphys to go to Temple Hill. Each year, one man from each of the six clans of Saylok was selected to supplicate the Keepers of Saylok. Not all supplicants would remain to be trained and eventually ordained. Some years none remained. The keepers had their own selection methods. But Dagmar had been chosen. He'd committed himself fully, and the Highest Keeper had seen his promise. He'd also taken note of his considerable strength, his size, and his affinity for the runes.

The Highest Keeper, a small, wizened man called Ivo, had asked him, his voice dripping with disdain and suspicion, "Why are you here, Dagmar of Dolphys? You are built like a warrior. You should be protecting your clan."

"I am built like a warrior, but I have the heart of a keeper," Dagmar had answered.

The Highest Keeper, his eyes rimmed in the black that also stained his wrinkled lips, had laughed at that. Spat.

"You do not have a keeper's heart. Yours is the heart of a defiant child."

"I refuse to be a warrior of Dolphys . . . or of any clan. That is the only defiance in my heart."

"And if I send you away?" the Highest Keeper had asked.

"I will walk to the cliffs of Shinway and throw myself from them," Dagmar answered. He'd been deadly serious.

The Highest Keeper had not sent him away. No other candidates had been chosen that year or the next from any of the clans. Nor even the year after that. But Dagmar had stayed. He was in his fifth year, and he was no longer called Supplicant. He was a keeper now.

Dagmar stepped across the creek, balancing on the slippery rocks, but his mind slid back to his sister. He had been her brother long before he was a Keeper of Saylok. He'd dreamed of her for three nights in a row. He'd woken at dawn sick with dread for her. If she'd been plain, her path might have been easier, but she was not plain, and Desdemona, for all her gifts, had terrible judgment. Mayhaps it was the absence of a mother and the example of a father who lived only to fight, who confused passion and hate, twisting them together so she couldn't separate the two.

He'd not seen her since he'd entered the temple. He'd written to her, but the letters he received back were few and far between. She was in love with a man. She'd never spoken his name, but Dagmar had seen the change in the way her words had leaned forward across the parchment, like she was falling into her future, eager and breathless. A match was being negotiated. The daughter of Dred, the most feared and powerful warrior in Dolphys, a woman of considerable skill in her own right, was of great value. Chieftain Dirth had wanted her for one of his own sons, but it made more sense to strengthen alliances with other clans. Desdemona would be promised to a man of another clan, it was almost certain.

Being among the trees was like being watched. No . . . not watched. Watched *over*. Being acknowledged, being seen, but not being judged. "We welcome you," the trees whispered. They welcomed him, yet they didn't impose upon him or ask to know his secrets.

Dagmar left the shadow of the towering pines and began to climb the hill that overlooked Berne to the east and Dolphys to the southeast. Between the two lands was a ridge of low hills—such hills existed throughout the country, separating one clan from another, as if the gods had intended the division. In the center, where the temple stood, the land was higher than at any other point, and from the temple mount one could look out over the lands of the clans. The rise north of the temple gave a glorious view of Adyar, the rise south, a view of Ebba. If Dagmar had wanted to see Joran or Leok he could have walked to the western side of Temple Hill and seen both—Joran to the southwest, Leok farther north. The view, no matter which direction he stood, took Dagmar's breath and added it to the sky.

Saylok was a beautiful country, shaped like a soft star with six rounded peninsulas, one for each of the clans. It floated in the middle of the North Sea, created when Odin himself had reached into the depths and clutched the seabed in his fist, pulling it up to the sunlight, leaving an island when he opened his hand.

"*Say lok*," Dagmar breathed, sighing each syllable, closing his eyes against the view so he could center his thoughts. *Saylok* meant "blessed," and in that moment, Dagmar knew he was, but he feared his own blessing did not extend to his sister. She had not been able to escape Dolphys. She had not been able to thwart her father's ambitions for her.

Dagmar removed his dagger from the leather cinch at his waist, and keeping his eyes closed and his thoughts centered on Desdemona's lovely face, he drew the blade across his palm. A thousand scars parted for the intrusion, and his blood welled warm and eager in the cup of his hand. Blood was the only thing the earth answered to. Blood represented sacrifice, and the earth would not trade her secrets for anything less.

Dagmar made a fist and, sinking to his knees, let the scarlet drops spill into the dirt. He spilled his blood for wisdom. Not power. But he knew other men—even other keepers—who wanted power more than anything else. It was forbidden, but the forbidden apple was too sweet for some to resist. If a keeper was discovered spilling blood—his or someone else's—for power, he was slain on Odin's altar. The Keepers of Saylok were charged with the protection of the forbidden runes and the succession of kings, not their own power, but it was easy to confuse responsibility with power. Dagmar struggled with it every day. Even now, as he traded his blood for insight into his sister's predicament. For he knew she was in a predicament. His dreams were quite clear on that point.

Taking his dagger, he dug into the earth, saying Desdemona's name as he did. Odin gave up one of his eyes for wisdom, and Dagmar drew the rune for sight, to see what his physical eyes could not. As he carved, he whispered the words, "I am a Keeper of Saylok, seeking a vision that I might bless and care for the one who calls me brother of the flesh."

Immediately, Desdemona's face filled his head, and it was not the memory of her face, pulled from the recesses of his own mind, but a new image. Desdemona's face was pale, her dark hair tumbling about her wan cheeks. She cried out, and it was his name on her lips. She raised a hand in supplication, and her palm, just like his, was smeared with blood. The image widened, as though Dagmar had stepped back to broaden his view.

Desdemona, clad in the colors of their clan, sat propped against a tree, her eyes closed, her chin tipped upward as though pleading for intercession. As he watched she began to scream, a small, agonizing wail that brought an answering cry to his own lips. The view widened again, until Desdemona was a mere blot of deep blue on a painting swathed in varying shades of green and brown.

Dagmar knew where she was, and it wasn't far. He could see the forest of his vision below the hilly rise. He rose and destroyed the rune with a swipe of his leathered sole, thanking the gods for their gifts as he did. His palm still oozed sluggishly, but he didn't bind it or even give it a second thought.

He shoved his dagger into its cinch and scrambled down the rise toward the wooded copse he'd seen in his vision. He moved swiftly, with purpose, but he didn't call out her name. He didn't want to take a chance that the other keepers would hear. He was still on temple grounds, and he wasn't the only man who enjoyed his solitude to meditate and commune. If Dagmar found Desdemona in the woods, he didn't know what he would do, where he would take her. The Keepers of Saylok were all men, and no women lived among them. But he wouldn't think of that now.

Dagmar searched quietly, his eyes scanning as he picked his way among the trees, knowing he should be close, wanting desperately to call out to her. He'd seen no one on his sojourn, seen no one all morning, but still he kept his silence. It was so quiet. No chirping or buzzing. No birds in the trees, no skittering of small creatures along the boughs above his head. He stopped and listened to the stillness. A low moan murmured through the trees to his left, and he rushed toward the sound.

She was exactly as she'd appeared in the vision, sitting against the tree as though she'd been propped there by Loki, the god of jest and mayhem, to trick him.

"Des?" he whispered, halting suddenly, not wanting to take another step. The skirt of her gown was soaked in blood, and her arms were crossed oddly over her chest. Her eyes fluttered open, closed, then opened again, weakly.

"Dag," she whimpered, and he approached as if he'd stepped into his own vision.

"You're wounded," he worried.

"No. Not wounded."

"You're bleeding!" The conversation was inane. He hadn't seen his sister in years, yet here she sat, in a pool of blood in the Temple Wood. He didn't ask her how she'd come to be there, and she didn't offer an explanation. Not yet. She simply watched him approach, her arms holding her chest, the way a woman does when she's trying to hide her breasts. He wondered suddenly if she'd been beaten and defiled. But as he grew closer, it became apparent that she wasn't covering her breasts. She was sheltering a child. An infant so small and bloodied, it hardly looked real. She'd loosened the ties on the front of her gown and pressed the child against her skin, drawing her clothing back over the small body.

"This is my son, brother," she said. "I've brought him to you." Her voice was weak, but her pale blue eyes, eyes so like his own, were fierce in her pallid face.

"To me? Desdemona, I am a keeper!"

"And I am your sister, and the only one who loves you." Her voice was harsh, cruel even, but it broke, and she shuddered, her head bobbing as though she fought for consciousness. "And you are the only one who loves me."

"Who is this child's father?"

A wail pierced the air, and Dagmar realized the wail he'd heard in his vision was the wail of this child, not his sister. The wail was lusty and loud and belied the size and condition of the infant who cried.

"His father is Banruud of Berne," Desdemona confessed.

"Why did you not go to him?" Banruud was the young Chieftain of Berne, promoted at his father's death, and already a powerful man. Dagmar and Desdemona had known Banruud since childhood. Their fathers had fought beside each other and against each other at times. Both were warriors. Both were widely respected. But Berend, Banruud's father, had been chieftain of his clan, and Dred of Dolphys had not. Dred had very little in life but his temper and his sword. Berend had a great deal more than that, and he never let Dred forget it. Dagmar wondered briefly if Banruud hadn't let Desdemona forget it either, if he'd made her believe he would make her a chieftain's wife, only to discard her like a soldier's whore.

"I did go to him. And I was turned away," Desdemona moaned, and Dagmar had his answer, if not the full story.

"How did you get here?"

"I rode. My horse is near. Somewhere. I couldn't go any farther. The babe was coming."

"You came alone?"

"Alone, but for the child inside me."

"Desdemona," Dagmar groaned. "Why, sister? Why here?"

"You must take him, Dagmar. And you must call him Bayr. Bayr for his father's clan. Bayr . . . because he will be as powerful as the beast he is named for."

Dagmar fell to his knees beside her and withdrew his knife, preparing to draw runes of healing into the earth, into the blood she had spilled to give birth to her child. He had to heal her. She had to care for her son.

"No, brother!" she hissed. "I have a rune of my own." A grayish tinge was spreading from her lips and up her cheeks, but she drew her own dagger from the belt at her waist. Dagmar wondered how she remained conscious. There was so much blood the ground was wet with it, encircling the exposed roots like the tree itself was bleeding.

"You must not, Desi. It is forbidden. Only the keepers can use the runes."

"I'm dying," Desdemona spat. "Who will punish the act?"

Dagmar winced, but she continued, and her blade moved in the earth as she spoke.

"I loved him," she confessed.

"Banruud?"

"I loved him, and it became inconvenient for him. He wants power more than anything else. He is just like his father. He wants to be king. He will marry the daughter of King Ansel. He thinks it will give him standing, and she will give him many sons. But my son will be the only child of Banruud."

With a trembling hand, she drew yet another rune, a rune Dagmar didn't recognize, not at first. "Banruud will deny him again. And in his denial, he will deny all Saylok. Salvation will come through my son, and only through him."

The child began to wail again, and with his cries, Desdemona began to slump into herself, the loss of blood stripping her of her strength. Dagmar wrapped his arms around her, overcome. His cheeks were wet, his sight blurred, and he pressed his lips into her hair, willing her to cease speaking. Her words were a blood curse, the most powerful kind, because the blood that spilled into the ground was her lifeblood, and her death would seal her prophecy. Her voice was a mere whisper, but her blade continued to carve lines into the sodden earth as she spoke again.

"We are abused. We are used. We are bartered and abandoned. But rarely are we loved. So be it. From this day forward, there will be no daughters in Saylok for *any of you* to love."

The ground rumbled as though pained by Desdemona's knife, and for a moment, Dagmar feared the earth would open and swallow them. But the tremors ceased almost as suddenly as they'd begun.

"I love you, Desdemona," Dagmar choked, wiping his tears in her hair. "I have always loved you. Do not speak this way."

"You left me, brother. And now I will leave you," she breathed, but the words caught and rattled in her chest, and the knife fell from her hand, her runes completed, her life finished. The babe cried again, a short, sad protest, and then he fell silent, his bow-shaped mouth rooting for his mother's breast.

But his mother was gone.

Dagmar felt the life lift from his sister and her limbs loosen. Her head fell back, exposing her throat, young, lovely, and streaked with crimson from her own hands. Dagmar shook her, demanding she wake as her babe latched onto a still-warm breast, taking what was left of her into himself. Dagmar was repulsed, horrified even, and he wept as the child drank, his little cheeks hollowing out, his tiny hands fisting the white flesh as he suckled his dead mother.

Dagmar wanted to pull the child away but knew the babe was innocent. Hungry. There was no evil in the act, and suckling was an innate response. Whatever sustenance her son received was the only gift Desdemona could give him. Dagmar looked away, ill and shaken, not wanting to release his sister because he would jostle the child. So he held her—held them—and studied the runes his sister had drawn into the bloody ground.

She'd drawn the sign of the woman and child, but the tail of a snake encircled them, its head and forked tongue rising up through a crown with six spires. Six spires for six clans of Saylok. She'd also drawn the rune of strength and power, but the ring around the second rune was not closed, and Dagmar wondered if that was intentional or if Desdemona had simply died before she could finish. He could close it, but the blood was not his, and he feared his interference might make things worse.

A closed circle meant finality. In a strength rune, a gap in the circle meant weakness. However small, however slight, but still . . . weakness. If the rune of strength was for her young son, Desdemona had inadvertently left an opening for a fatal flaw. With a flick of Desdemona's blade across his hand, a hand that still bled, Dagmar closed the gap.

"He will have no mother. No father. No clan. He will have only me, Allfather. And I don't know how I will provide. But as to any weakness he—Bayr—is cursed with, I will make up the difference," Dagmar prayed, and with an odd calm, he laid his sister against the earth she would return to and lifted the child from her chest. The babe had fallen asleep, releasing his mother's breast. He was warm and sticky, covered in blood and grime, but dark hair covered his head, and his limbs and trunk were well formed and pink, with small rolls of fat making him look like an oft-fed piglet. He was a healthy man-child, Dagmar thought. Perfect, even.

"You must come with me now, Bayr," he said to the child, calling him by the name his mother had chosen. She'd cursed Banruud, yet she'd still given his son the sound of his tribe. All male children of a tribe were given the first sound of their father's name. A female child was given the beginning sound of her mother's name. Dagmar wished briefly that his sister had given the child the sound of her own clan. The child's father had claim to him, but clearly Banruud had rejected both mother and son, and Dagmar vowed, anger swelling in his chest, that he would not let the man have him now.

Following his sister's lead, Dagmar tucked the child beneath his robes against the warm skin of his chest and began the long climb back to the temple, promising his sister he would return to her when her child was safe.

2

Dagmar almost turned back several times. He should keep the infant and leave the keepers. They would never allow him to raise the child in the enclave. There were a few women living on the temple grounds and more living in the servants' quarters in the palace, but no women lived within the walls of the temple itself. The keepers cared for themselves and the temple without female assistance, each brother assigned in rotation to the duties that daily life demanded. One could not pray, read, and write all day. The chores kept them grounded in the physical, which was easy to lose sight of in a meditative state.

There were soldiers on Temple Hill too, and a small contingent from the king's army were assigned to guard the temple from raiders and those who sought to trespass where they didn't belong. Temple Hill was like a small village run mostly by men, and Dagmar was quite certain he wouldn't find a nursemaid in the castle or living on the grounds.

Dagmar ran through all these details, mundane as they were, trying to imagine a child among the community on Temple Hill. The Highest Keeper, Ivo, would send him away. Dagmar hesitated again and turned in a circle, his eyes seeking the sky and the trees, looking for an answer to the situation he now found himself in. The infant against his chest began to squirm, but he didn't cry, and Dagmar patted his back instinctively, soothing him, soothing himself.

Dagmar couldn't leave. He had nowhere to go. He had no home in Dolphys. Not anymore. He shuddered to think what his father would do. He would start a war, that's what he would do. He would take the infant and ride into Berne, to the home of Chief Banruud. He would demand recompense for his dead daughter. The child would either be taken in by Banruud or raised by Dred of Dolphys, or whichever woman he hired to look after him while he pillaged and plundered the lands east of Saylok, across the waters.

Banruud had already rejected Desdemona and the child.

Dred was unfit.

And Desdemona had entrusted the child to Dagmar's care.

"Odin, Father of Saylok, have mercy on this child. He is of the lineage of your son, a direct descendant of the bear Berne and the wolf Dolphys." It was the prayer Dagmar had been uttering since leaving Desdemona, and he repeated it again as he resumed his climb and neared the gates of the temple.

"Keeper Dagmar, Master Ivo is looking for you." Jakub, a temple guard, was perched in the tower beside the gate, and he called down to Dagmar, his eyes filled with curiosity.

"What've you got there, Keeper Dagmar?" Jakub pressed.

Dagmar simply shook his head and didn't answer. The last thing he needed was word spreading through the temple guard and among the keepers that Dagmar had come home from prayer with an infant in his robes. Word would reach Master Ivo before he did.

Once, long ago, the Keepers of Saylok had offered human sacrifice along with their animal sacrifices. Every six years, six beasts and six men had been offered to the gods. The practice had ended with King Enos of Ebba. He'd been a traveler to the lands of the Christians and had adopted some of their ways. Jesus Christ had been added to the pantheon of the gods, and human sacrifice among the clans of Saylok had come to an end. Enos had not been baptized. He'd simply been intrigued, and he'd brought back a great gold cross and a book he called the Bible. Both were displayed in the temple beneath a mural of Enos's travels, a winged, golden-haired creature flying above his head, guiding his path.

Many things had changed in Enos's reign, but some things had remained the same. One thing that had not changed was the power of the Highest Keeper. His name was Ivo, a name he'd chosen himself, a name not associated with any tribe, for his duty, above all else, would be to remain impartial to the six clans, to guard the forbidden runes, and to provide for the spiritual welfare of all Saylok. He relinquished his old name, the name given him by his father, a man of the clan of Joran, and took on a new name, just as he took on a new life and a new role. Someday, if Dagmar became Highest Keeper, he too would choose a new name. But first he had to survive the day. Thoughts of becoming Highest Keeper seemed folly, considering what he was about to do.

Warmth spread across Dagmar's chest, and for a moment, he thought he was having a visitation, a holy moment of spiritual insight, and his heart leaped in gratitude. Maybe Odin would answer his prayers. Then the warmth became wet, and he realized the child clutched against his heart was urinating down his chest. Dagmar grimaced and kept moving. The soiling only served to underscore how real his problem was. There was an infant in his robes, and his sister's body lay in the woods. He grimaced again, and grief rose suddenly. His shock was ebbing, giving way to sorrow, and he stumbled and went down to a knee. The babe in his arms, now wet and plainly uncomfortable, emitted a wail.

"Dagmar?" A voice rose from the shadowy recesses near the inner sanctum where Dagmar knew he would find Master Ivo, the Highest Keeper.

"Yes, Master, it is Dagmar."

"Come here," Ivo commanded. There was an odd note in his voice, and Dagmar clenched his teeth and tightened his grip on the babe beneath his robes.

The sanctum was dark and cool, the rock that arched above and below the blood-red glass of the windows keeping the warmth of the day from permeating the space. Candles pierced the gloom, and Ivo sat in his chair above the altar like a king on his throne. There were seven chairs in total, Master Ivo's in the center. The three chairs on either side of him were empty, the six higher keepers representing the six clans having left their master to ruminate alone. It was not uncommon. They meditated together once a day and sat in their official positions only during ceremonies and worship services. But Master Ivo occupied the sanctum often, making it his personal space to conduct business and carry out the duties with which he was entrusted.

Dagmar's eyes struggled against the gloom, adjusting from the light of day to the darkness of the room, and for a moment he saw nothing but the flickering flames that topped the wax sticks on every surface.

"I've seen something that troubles me, Dagmar," Ivo said softly, and Dagmar's blood surged in his veins. He didn't slow but approached the Highest Keeper, halting just before the altar.

"What have you seen, Master?" he asked.

"The death of a woman."

"I too have seen her death, but not in a vision, Master. I saw it in truth," Dagmar said, and his voice cracked. Tears flooded his eyes and streamed down his cheeks, but he didn't acknowledge them.

Master Ivo did not look surprised, and his eyes did not leave Dagmar's face.

Dagmar told the Highest Keeper of his dreams, three nights in a row, and how he'd begun his sojourn with the intention of understanding what they meant. He told him how he'd made a sacrifice for wisdom, and how he'd seen his sister rise in a vision before him.

"I found her easily, Master. But it was too late to help her."

"She was dead when you arrived?" Ivo asked.

"No. But she was bleeding profusely."

"Why?"

"She had given birth to a child there in the woods. On that very spot. Something went wrong. There was far too much blood."

He didn't tell Master Ivo about the runes. Runes were forbidden to all but the Keepers of Saylok, and even then, only certain runes were allowed.

"What of the child?" Master Ivo queried.

Dagmar opened his robe, and with a belly full of fear and dread, withdrew the naked infant, holding him up toward the Highest Keeper with shaking hands. The babe had fallen asleep again, and the movement and loss of contact with Dagmar's skin caused his little arms to flail wildly.

Master Ivo hissed as though Dagmar had offered him a writhing snake.

"The child is healthy. Whole," said Dagmar. "And I am his uncle. I could not leave him to die in the woods."

The Highest Keeper stared in horror.

"Odin's uncle, Bestla's brother, taught Odin the songs of life. He taught him the eighteen charms. He didn't abdicate his responsibility because he was a god," Dagmar urged. "I cannot abdicate mine because I am a keeper."

"Who will feed the babe? You don't have teats, brother." Ivo's dripping disdain caught Dagmar off guard.

"One of the women in the King's Village will know what to do. If he must, he will drink milk from the goats, as we do," Dagmar murmured, trying to keep the fear from his voice. He wasn't afraid for himself. He wasn't afraid of Ivo's ire or displeasure. He was afraid Ivo would forbid him to keep the child at the temple. Then he would have to leave. They both would.

"Who is the child's father?"

Dagmar didn't hesitate. He'd been ready for this question, and he lied with great conviction.

"I don't know, Master."

Master Ivo grimaced in disdain, as if a woman who birthed a child without a man waiting to sever the umbilical cord with his teeth, a traditional act of ownership among the clans, did not deserve his compassion.

"She said the child's name was Bayr." Dagmar rushed to tell a truth to bury his lie. "She said he would be strong, that salvation would come to Saylok through him. And she asked me to take him. That is what I've done, Master. I beg you to let me raise him here, among us."

Master Ivo had grown pale and silent, his disdain slipping into contemplation.

"What did she mean . . . salvation?" the Highest Keeper whispered.

"I don't know, Master. It may only have been the dying wish of a mother for her son. But . . . it seemed more than that."

Silence grew and widened between them, filling the air with tension and, for Dagmar, torment. It wasn't until Ivo spoke again, several minutes later, that Dagmar's heart began to slow and his fear to diminish.

"I dreamed of her too, Dagmar," Ivo admitted. "Last night, the night before that, and many nights before that. I didn't know what it meant. But the woman . . . she reminded me of you. She *looked* like you. That is why I asked you to come to me. And here you are."

Dagmar's breath caught, and he bowed his head, desperate to keep his feelings to himself.

"Bring the child to me," Ivo commanded.

Dagmar obeyed, his legs trembling so violently he thought he would fall. He moved past the altar and up the steps to the dais where his master sat waiting. He had no idea what the man would do. His lips and eyes, blackened like those of all the Highest Keepers since Saylok was formed from the sea, moved with Dagmar's approach, his lips forming words Dagmar couldn't hear.

Master Ivo's long nails were sharp and curled, but he took the child between his palms with a gentleness that both surprised and relieved his uncle.

"His mother said he would be strong?" the Highest Keeper whispered.

"Yes, Master."

"I can see already that it is true. Look how he holds his head! That is unusual in a newborn child. He is watching me, Dagmar. His eyes are clear and fixed."

They were. The tiny babe was staring at Master Ivo with solemn wonder, his pink body clutched between the claws of the most powerful man in Saylok. More powerful than the king, for Master Ivo had the power to choose who would wear the crown. More powerful even than the gods and the three Norns that spun the fates of mankind, for in that moment, he held the child's life in his hands.

"What was your sister's name, Dagmar?"

"Desdemona."

"Desdemona," Master Ivo whispered, drawing the word out in a long hiss. "She who slays demons."

"Yes," Dagmar replied. "She was a great warrior in our clan."

"Women don't make great warriors," Ivo spat.

Dagmar didn't respond. He didn't agree. A mother was the fiercest warrior of all.

"If I told you to leave him in the Temple Wood, a gift for Odin and all the gods of Saylok, would you obey me?"

"No, Master," Dagmar replied, firm.

Ivo cursed Dagmar for his insolence, but his eyes didn't leave the child.

"We have not had a child at the temple since Bjorn, and he was ten years old," Ivo protested. Bjorn was now one of the higher keepers, a man well into his fiftieth year. "We have no way to know if this child will be a worthy supplicant."

"We have soldiers on the mount. Cooks and gardeners and laundresses too. We aren't all keepers or supplicants," Dagmar said carefully.

"This is true," Ivo allowed. A smile had begun playing on his lips as he gazed at the infant he held. Even soiled and stained, the babe was the picture of health and hope.

"What shall I tell the others?" the Highest Keeper muttered, and Dagmar's heart quickened at Ivo's obvious weakening toward the child.

"Tell them of your dreams, Master. No one will question your dreams."

"And *your* dreams, Dagmar?"

"I will say only what you tell me to say," Dagmar said humbly.

"So you will obey me in this?" Ivo's disdain was back. "But if I command that you give him to the gods, you refuse? You will take him and go? Mayhaps throw yourself off the cliffs of Shinway, eh?"

"Mayhaps. But his fate will be my fate, yes, Master," Dagmar confirmed.

The child bellowed suddenly, loudly, and Dagmar and Ivo both started. Ivo came close to dropping him, and his nail scored the child's skin, causing a thin weal of blood to rise along his tiny ribs.

"Bayr of Saylok," Ivo mused, his eyes on the blood. He laid the child on the altar before him and, running the soft pad of his finger over the oozing scratch, painted the child's forehead in the star of Saylok.

"Bayr of Saylok," Ivo intoned. "Bayr, nephew of Dagmar, child of Desdemona, son of the temple. Your life will be spared and guarded for a purpose I do not yet know, but I seal your mother's prophecy on your head, and will do my part to see that it is fulfilled."

Dagmar's strength left his legs, and he reached for the altar where the infant lay. Gratitude, guilt, and grief combined to send him to his knees. He had not told Ivo everything, and Ivo had just sealed Desdemona's words in blood on the infant's head.

"Take him. Make arrangements. Your duties will remain the same, Keeper Dagmar, with or without the child. Let us pray that he is amenable to life in the enclave. If he is not, he . . . and you . . . must go."

Bayr cried only at night when the temple was dark and silent, when the sound of his infant wails echoed through the corridors and made the keepers quartered in the same wing as Dagmar complain bitterly that the temple was no place for a motherless child. During the day, Bayr slept and blinked and cooed and kicked his small legs, but the nights were hard in the sterile room with the stone walls and the narrow bed.

Dagmar fashioned a cradle from a tinderbox, but the babe would not sleep or settle in the dark hours before dawn unless Dagmar was holding him, and Dagmar was too afraid to close his eyes for fear he would drop him while he slumbered. A week after Bayr's birth, Dagmar was so exhausted, he fell asleep spread out on his floor with the babe on his chest. They both slept so deeply, Dagmar relented, and from that day forward, the boy slept in his arms on a pile of straw and Dagmar's bed remained unused.

Having lost his own mother at an early age, Dagmar knew none of the soft ways of a woman. He had no breasts to offer sustenance and comfort, no songs or benign stories to entertain a child. His voice was rough and low, his hands large and clumsy, but his heart was broken and bleeding, and the baby boy, in all his helpless innocence, soothed something in him.

A woman from the King's Village, whose child had recently been weaned, agreed to come to the wall around the temple grounds thrice a day to nurse the boy, but it wasn't enough, and little Bayr was never full. Dagmar fashioned him a teat from sheep intestines and fed him goat's milk before bed and between feedings with the village woman, and the milk was reinforced with prayers. Dagmar pled for strength and stamina, that his arms would not fail him in the night, that the child would not wake his brothers, and that his own inadequacies would not result in tragedy.

Initially, the other keepers frowned in dismay and made life more difficult for Dagmar, but after the first sleepless weeks, they grew to accept the infant's presence among them, and more than one of the higher keepers had been caught smiling and waggling their fingers in the baby's face when they thought no one was watching. The Keepers of Saylok were all members of an exclusive brotherhood, but none of them would be fathers, and the small boy gave them a taste of something they would never have.

Dagmar fashioned a sling of sorts to free his hands, and wherever he went and whatever duties he carried out, Bayr accompanied him, secured in his pouch on Dagmar's torso. Dagmar practiced his runes with the babe strapped to his chest, began his day in chanting with the babe listening with wide eyes and cooing lips, and carried out his chores—including milking the blasted goats—all carrying the boy in the sling that he quickly outgrew.

For all his wide-eyed wonder and mellow adaption to temple life, within months, the boy was squirming to be let down, to scoot across the stone floors and the courtyard cobbles. Before long, he was pulling himself up, toppling into trouble, and crawling and grasping and tugging on everything he could get his fat little hands around. A keeper who was prone to complaining swore the child yanked a hunk of hair from his beard, and Master Ivo was astonished by the strength in the child's legs and arms, making the entire enclave gather to observe Bayr climbing the gnarled tree that had graced the inner court of the temple yard for hundreds of years.

"This is not usual for a child so young, is it, Keeper Dagmar? He is not yet six months old! Is it the milk from the goats or a gift from the gods?" Ivo marveled, but Dagmar could only watch in helpless wonder, bundling the boy back into the pack he'd moved to his back and adding yet another plea to his prayers, begging that Bayr would survive his first year and withstand the strength that his mother had blessed—or cursed—him with.

Bayr walked at eight months, and he didn't just walk. He ran and climbed and jumped and tumbled, a tiny child with the strength and coordination of one thrice his age, his stout legs and sturdy arms rarely still. By the time he was a year old, he could outrun the chickens, chasing them only to catch them and let them go. The angry rooster didn't care for the game and escaped by fluttering up to the top of the coop beyond the child's reach.

Bayr had watched him in frustration, wanting the colorful bird to come down, until one day, he grew tired of waiting. No sooner had Dagmar turned his head to the row of vegetables he was tending than the boy had scaled the enclosure to crawl along the ridgeline, his eyes on the irritated rooster. A year later, he rescued a terrified cat from atop the castle ramparts, scaling walls and running along rooftops with nary a misstep or an ounce of fear.

Dagmar trailed him in a constant state of terror and tied the boy to him in the night while he slept so the child wouldn't wake and wander away to traverse stone stairs or open windows or scale the walls that separated the temple grounds from the castle of the king nearby.

Dagmar carved runes of warning and protection on his chamber door and below his window. He hid runes on the beams that ran over their heads and in the stones beneath their feet, and his hands grew scabbed and sore from his constant bloodletting.

"The boy is favored by the gods," Ivo scolded when he noticed Dagmar's palms. "The Norns have shown me the strands of his fate, woven together in a long, colorful rope extending like a river beyond sight. He will not perish. Cease your blood runes, brother. You only weaken yourself. The boy will survive us all."

But Dagmar was not convinced.

"He hardly makes a sound. He doesn't babble like most children. He is so physically advanced—yet he doesn't speak at all. His strength far exceeds his understanding and maturity," Dagmar worried. "And strength without wisdom is dangerous."

"He is still very young," Ivo argued. "He will learn. He understands a great deal. You can see his mind working behind his eyes."

Dagmar could only nod helplessly, but he didn't stop carving his runes and making deals with the gods.

3

It didn't have a name, not in the traditional sense. It was simply called the King's Village. It rounded the base of the temple mount and extended out three miles in every direction. Atop the huge, wide mount rose the spires of the temple, and beside it, just as grand, just as soaring, was the castle of the king. It was not an accident that the temple was taller, nor was it unintentional that the two occupied the same hill, though it was more a plateau, the top shorn off by Odin himself and pounded flat by Thor's hammer. The Keepers of Saylok did not dictate to the king, nor did they involve themselves in the running of the kingdom. They were simply the overseers, the counterweight to royal power, charged with the selection of kings and the continuation of the crown. When one king died, the crown did not pass to his son or his daughter. It did not pass to his heirs or his clan at all. Instead, the crown moved from clan to clan—from Adyar to Berne, from Berne to Dolphys, from Dolphys to Ebba, Ebba to Joran, Joran to Leok, and from Leok back to Adyar again. The crown passed to the man of each clan who was chosen by the gods . . . and by the keepers.

The current ruler, King Ansel, was of Adyar, the Clan of the Eagle, and it was his daughter, Alannah, who had wed Banruud, the Chieftain of Berne. When King Ansel died, his family would leave Temple Hill and the castle of the king. They would go back to their clan, back to the lives they had led before occupying the castle, and a new king from a new clan would be chosen and crowned. It kept the power from being controlled by one family, one tribe, one man for too long. Saylok had been ruled thus for five hundred years. One king had reigned for seventy years, one for only seventy days. But the crown continued to move from one clan to the next without exception. The chieftains of the clans were most often chosen and crowned king. It was a natural choice, as the chieftains were powerful men, accustomed to running their lands and ruling their clans. Their people often supported the choice, and the Keepers of Saylok took these things into consideration.

Only five times in five hundred years had the keepers deviated from choosing a chieftain of a clan to be king. Once it had caused a near revolt, but the people of Saylok and the leaders of the clans—all but the chieftain who had been denied the crown—supported the keepers as the government was designed, and the choice of the keepers was upheld and supported. The Chieftain of Joran, who had been denied the crown, plotted to kill the man who had been chosen instead of him, and he succeeded in his murderous designs. The crown then passed immediately to the clan of Leok, the next land in the succession, to the aging Chieftain of Leok's eldest son, and the angry chieftain from Joran was beheaded.

The crown never remained with one clan, no matter how nefarious or unfair the circumstances of the king's death. There was a time when some clans plotted to kill the chieftains of other clans in order to hurry their own clans' ascent to the throne, but the Keepers of Saylok thwarted the attempts at power by choosing warriors or farmers from the clans and bypassing the chieftains altogether. Bribery was also attempted, though illegal, and four higher keepers had been blinded, stripped of their positions, and cast out, forced to leave the temple and beg for sustenance among the people whose trust they had betrayed.

The people of Saylok were unforgiving. They were already taxed to support the king and the temple and weren't interested in providing for corrupt keepers who had misused their power and failed in their sacred responsibilities.

Dagmar had little doubt that Banruud of Berne would be the next king. Ansel was growing old—he'd been a good king—and the Clan of the Bear was next in line. As chieftain, Banruud would appeal to the keepers, and his appeal would be soberly vetted before anyone else in Berne was considered. It was the right of any man in Berne to make an appeal to the keepers, but few did. The people were loyal to—and often afraid of—their chieftains. If their appeal was denied, and they had to return to their lands, ostracization or worse often occurred. If their chieftain became king, it was never wise to have been a challenger for his throne. Of course, the Keepers of Saylok had the power to select any man, even if he did not present himself as a contender for the throne, but that was so uncommon as to be almost unheard of. Dagmar knew of no instance when such a thing had happened.

Banruud was wealthy, powerful, and generally feared in Berne and throughout the clans. He would be the next king. It was only a matter of time.

Dagmar dreaded that day. Banruud of Berne, living on Temple Hill in the Palace of Saylok, so close to the son he'd never met, to the boy growing so sturdy and straight inside the temple walls. Word of his strength would spread. It already had in some quarters.

The villagers called Bayr "the Temple Boy." They'd heard tales of him from the laundress in the village who washed the temple linens, from the cook who worked in the palace kitchens, from the soldiers who guarded the temple walls and made wagers over the feats of strength and agility performed by the small boy. Dagmar had tried to shield the child. He'd tried to keep Bayr's strength a secret, but it had been impossible. By the time Bayr was three, he was skipping along behind the temple guards, mimicking their movements with both sword and shield. Now, at seven, he scampered up the hills with Dagmar struggling to keep up, he hefted boulders grown men would struggle to move, rocks he couldn't even get his arms around.

Master Ivo had proclaimed it—proclaimed *him*—a miracle, a child of Thor, strongest among the gods, and Dagmar had said nothing. He knew to whom Bayr belonged, and it was not the God of Thunder. Bayr's strength had been prophesied by his mother, and her blood sacrifice had borne fruit.

And that was not all.

In the seven years since Desdemona's death, not a single female child had been born in Saylok. Not in any clan. The first year, the people of the clans had rejoiced at the birth of so many strong sons and thanked the gods. The second year, they'd talked amongst themselves, amongst the members of other clans, wondering over the odd influx of boys. The third year, they'd begun to worry. The chieftains of all six clans had gone to the king, and the king had gone to the Highest Keeper. Ivo had gathered all the Keepers of Saylok together, and they'd spilled their blood in the earth. They'd drawn runes to coax the goddess Freya to give Saylok daughters. They'd fasted and prayed and sacrificed six male lambs under every harvest moon.

But no daughters were born. Not in the fourth year or the fifth. Not in the sixth. Not a single infant girl in seven years was born to a son of Saylok. And Dagmar had said nothing. He'd bled and carved with his brethren. He'd beseeched the gods, the Norse gods, the Celtic gods, the Christian god, but no daughters resulted from his pleas. In the beginning, his life filled with fatherhood, with the strain of raising an infant in an enclave of men who were as clueless as he, he'd had no time to worry over Desdemona's runes. But as time had passed, and the daughters of Saylok had failed to produce more daughters, when the years began to loom long and dry, Desdemona's bitter words had risen in his mind and tortured him every waking moment.

Guilt had gnawed at Dagmar's belly and grief had riddled his heart, but doubt and fear had kept him silent. Surely a rune could not hold so much power. Surely Desdemona was not the cause of such a scourge. It had to be something else. The girl children would return. Saylok would survive. Desdemona had said Bayr would be their salvation. But how? And *when*?

"What must I do, Odin? He is only a boy," Dagmar groaned aloud, his eyes closed in prayer. "And strong though he may be, he cannot shoulder such a weight." Dagmar went silent, listening, but the world around him was still, the forest deaf to his entreaty, and he scored his scarred palms and pressed them to the trunk of Desdemona's tree, hoping he would see her intent, that he would understand her final words, but he felt only the hum of life, the passing of time, and eventually he dropped his hands in futility.

Dagmar felt the boy before he heard him. It was always thus. Bayr moved silently, but Dagmar sensed his presence, saw him in his mind's eye, and hoped the boy had not overheard his prayer.

"Uh," Bayr grunted, announcing himself. He was trying to say uncle, but he could not connect one syllable to another without great difficulty, and he gave up almost as quickly as he made a sound. Bayr understood everything that was said to him. His mind was quick. But he couldn't speak without stammering so badly it took him several seconds to say a single word.

Incantations were easier. He joined the keepers in their morning verses, chanting the words he'd been hearing since the day of his birth, but when he was forced to speak on his own, he could hardly talk. It was an odd weakness in a boy so strong, stumbling over language when he stumbled over little else. It gave him cause for great humility and a heavy dose of insecurity. That insecurity kept him teachable—sweet, sensitive—and Dagmar was grateful for it, even though he worried for the boy's future.

Dagmar thought often about the small gap in the rune of strength Desdemona had drawn and wondered constantly if she'd known exactly what she was doing.

"Yes, Bayr?" Dagmar answered belatedly, turning away from the tree that shadowed his sister's resting place. He came often. It didn't surprise him that Bayr had known where to look for him.

"I-I-I-vo," Bayr stammered, and pointed toward the temple.

"He wants to see me?"

Bayr nodded, avoiding speech. Dagmar was convinced he and Bayr could have a conversation with gazes and shrugs and grimaces, and Bayr would greatly prefer it. He had an expressive face, his pale blue eyes and shaggy black hair giving him the wolfish appearance of his ancestors of Dolphys. Dagmar and Desdemona shared the same coloring. Bayr looked like them, but he had the size and strength of Berne, the Clan of the Bear, his father's clan, and if Banruud ever laid eyes on him, it wouldn't be hard to see the resemblance to his own tribe. But Banruud hadn't laid eyes on him. Very few had beyond the temple walls. Dred, Dagmar's father, had come looking for his daughter a month after her death, and Dagmar had shown him her grave at the base of the tree where she'd bled, never revealing there was a child who had survived her. Dred had gone, cursing the gods and his fortunes, cursing his dead daughter and his useless son, and Dagmar hadn't seen him since.

Without prompting, the boy prostrated himself beneath the tree, laying his face against the flat stone placed on the ground, directly above his buried mother's head, as though he pressed his forehead to hers. It was the way of their people, an acknowledgment of the dead. Dagmar had greeted her thus when he'd arrived to pray.

"M-m-mo-th-ther," Bayr stuttered, and was up again, turning toward the temple and slipping his hand into Dagmar's. His sweetness was at odds with his strength, and Dagmar welcomed it, squeezing Bayr's palm as he stared down into the boy's face. A savage protectiveness rose in his chest as he looked at his nephew, yet his fears for the boy were not of the typical variety. Bayr was more than capable of facing down physical threats. It was the political and spiritual kind Dagmar most feared.

"Have you been hunting . . . or wrestling?" he asked his nephew. There was an angry scratch on the boy's forearm, and Bayr eyed it, unconcerned, before meeting Dagmar's gaze.

"No wild pigs, wolves, or bears?" Dagmar pressed mildly.

The boy shook his head. The first time the boy had come face-to-face with a wild animal—a bear—was two years prior. They'd been in exactly that spot, and Bayr had been five years old. They'd been visiting Desdemona's grave when to their right a sudden cracking in the underbrush had interrupted their solitude. They'd risen to their feet in alarm, all sound becoming muffled by the fear that rent the air. Dagmar had heard his heart in his ears, his breath in his throat, but he'd been unable to hear the bear, even when it had charged forward, running toward him, running toward Bayr, who stood frozen at his side.

Then the silence had shattered, and Dagmar had reached for the boy, knowing he couldn't outrun the bear, couldn't do anything beyond wrapping Bayr in his arms, covering him as best he could, and praying to the gods for deliverance. But Bayr was no longer at his side. The child was moving, released from his own stupor, but he wasn't running away. He was running toward the bear as though he welcomed its arrival.

"Bayr!" Dagmar had shouted, but his voice was dwarfed by the guttural bellow that spilled out of the boy's throat, a sound so at odds with his size and the shape of his chest, of his *species*, that Dagmar had staggered back. The bear slowed but the boy did not, hurtling through the trees, his young arms and legs pumping.

Bayr had bellowed again, and the forest bowed, the leaves shook, and the bear veered. The boy followed, slamming into the side of the animal, his arms curled into his chest, his chin tucked, a human cannonball built of fearless fury and impossible faith. The bear tumbled almost comically—feet and fur and surprise—rising slowly, stunned, her mouth gaping in complaint, yawning a plea for mercy. Bayr had rolled alongside the bear, but came immediately to his feet, his arms extended, his legs wide, making himself bigger, fiercer, and he'd roared again.

The bear staggered away, crashing dizzily through the trees, two small cubs toddling behind her. The boy watched them go, his chest heaving, his hands clenched, and Dagmar had remembered how to use his limbs, how to breathe, how to speak. Then the boy was in his arms, clutched to his chest, his dark hair against Dagmar's lips.

"Never. Never. Never again, Bayr. You must never do that again."

"She is gone, Uncle. You are safe. She was afraid for her cubs, I think. Like you are, for me."

"Why did you do that? How?"

"She was going to hurt us." The boy was not stuttering. Not at all, and Dagmar stared into his guileless blue eyes, stunned once more.

"You must never do that again," Dagmar repeated.

Bayr frowned and bowed his head. His heartbeat was slowing. Dagmar could feel its cadence against his own chest, dancing with the beat of his own drumming pulse. Dagmar set the boy down, suddenly dizzy, suddenly weak. Bayr was much heavier than he looked.

"That sound . . . you sounded like an animal. How did you do that, Bayr?"

Bayr shrugged, his head still bowed.

"You ran toward the bear. Weren't you afraid?" Dagmar gasped. The boy's confidence scared him almost as much as his strength.

"I-I w-w-was a-afraid. B-b-but not of th-the b-b-bear." Bayr's stutter was back.

Dagmar knelt once more and stared into the boy's eyes, waiting. Listening.

"Af-fraid f-for y-y-you," Bayr whispered, patting Dagmar's cheeks.

"I am a man. I am your uncle. It is my duty to protect you."

Bayr shook his head, adamant, and thumped his chest, and Dagmar understood. The boy considered it his duty to protect Dagmar.

"Bayr. Listen to me. You must never put yourself between me and death if it puts your own life in danger. If the fates intend it, so be it. I am *your* guardian. You are not mine."

Bayr did not respond, but his jaw grew tight and his eyes sullen. He was not arguing, but he did not agree. The boy reminded Dagmar of himself when he'd told the Highest Keeper he would throw himself from the cliffs of Shinway if the keepers refused him. Dagmar supposed his own stubborn streak had come back to mock him.

"C-c-can't l-lose y-you," Bayr had stammered, and there were tears in his eyes.

"I am yours, Bayr. Always. My heart is yours. My spirit is yours, and even when I'm dead, I will refuse Valhalla, and I will follow at your heels, watching over you," Dagmar had promised.

Bayr had not believed him. Dagmar had seen it in his gaze. Or maybe he had simply wanted Dagmar among the living more than he wanted an angel at his heels. But he'd nodded agreeably, and forgetting the bear, had clasped Dagmar's hand like the child he was, forgiving his uncle for scolding him.

That had been the first of many feats by the young Bayr. Over the years, Dagmar had ceased scolding and forbidding. How could he chastise the boy for using his gifts? Bayr never looked for contention or confrontation, but he protected fiercely, as though it came instinctively, as though he was compelled to act, and Dagmar continued to cut his palms and say his prayers, drawing runes of patience and perspective into the earth that he might guide the boy—or survive the boy—he'd been entrusted with.

"What does Master Ivo want? Do you know, Bayr?" Dagmar asked as they came to the forest's edge and began the climb to the temple mount.

"D-dream."

"He's had another dream?" Dagmar translated.

The boy nodded once. "The k-k-king," Bayr said, forcing the word through frustrated lips.

Dagmar quickened his pace.

The earth began to rumble and groan, shifting and shuddering as Dagmar and Bayr loped up the path to the temple wall, and both were knocked off their feet, unable to walk on the angry earth. Dagmar sought to shelter the boy from falling rock even as Bayr found his balance and pulled Dagmar back to his feet.

All at once the shaking ceased, as though the world had decided it was not yet time to end, and screaming arose from beyond the wall, a terrified keening that made the hair rise on Dagmar's arms.

Without hesitation, Bayr ran toward the temple, and Dagmar rushed to follow. There was no guard on the west wall, but Bayr scaled it in mere seconds, unlatching the heavy door in the wall to let Dagmar through. Together they raced up the path that led through the gardens to the inner sanctum where Ivo spent most of his time. The quaking had weakened the walls of the temple and long cracks ran from the ceiling to the floor in several places, but the sanctum was still standing.

The screaming rose again, and Dagmar flung the door wide, fearful of what he would find.

A group of keepers was huddled around the stone table in the center of the room. The altar was split down the middle.

"The altar has fallen," Dagmar said, his throat closing in horror.

Terrified chatter echoed among the normally subdued brothers, and as Dagmar and Bayr raced forward, Dagmar saw the crumpled form of King Ansel pinned beneath the rock slab.

"Bayr, run for the guard," Dagmar demanded. The queen, her eyes crazed with fear, her face streaked with dust and tears, was huddled near the king's head, reassuring him that all would be well. His eyes were closed, his face still.

Bayr did not obey. Planting his legs in a deep squat, he gripped the slab, and with a roar not unlike the bellow from the long-ago day in the woods, he hoisted the stone from atop the king, tipping it away from his inert body. It crashed to the floor, making the room quake and groan once more. The queen screamed, and the keepers fell back, but the king was freed, and the walls held firm.

"Ansel!" the queen moaned, running her hands over the king's body. But the king's skin had grown ashen, and his chest, once broad and deep, appeared concave beneath the folds of his royal robes.

Ivo stooped and laid his head against the king's heart, the tips of his fingers against the king's lips.

"He is gone, my queen," he murmured, his voice steady, his eyes bleak.

$$\text{\small$\sim\!\!\mathcal{O}$}$$

Late in the night, when the king's body had been removed from the temple and Bayr had been sent to bed, Master Ivo summoned Dagmar back to the sanctum. Ivo didn't acknowledge him as he entered and walked soundlessly down the long aisle, but Dagmar knew his presence was noted. Ivo sat on his throne, his eyes on the broken altar, his hands with their long black nails curled around the armrests. Dagmar knelt at the Highest Keeper's feet, signaling his subservience and his willingness to be instructed, and then rose, his gaze following Ivo's to the stone table Bayr had heaved to the side.

"What happened, Master?" Dagmar's voice was hushed. Awestruck.

"The king has been taken," Ivo mused, his voice low and deliberate.

Dagmar stifled his sigh. He knew that much. He wanted to understand the things he had not been present for. He wanted to know why he'd been summoned from the forest earlier in the day.

"You sent Bayr to find me," Dagmar reminded him.

Ivo raised his eyes slowly, as though resurfacing from very deep thoughts.

44

"I sought to gather all the brothers. I have felt the king's passing for some time now. I feared he would be struck down. But his death was a merciful one. Sudden. It is the way any man would want to go, taken in an instant in the temple of the gods. Surely he will dine in Valhalla tonight."

"Why was he here?" Dagmar pressed. The king visited the temple infrequently. He had his own chapel in the palace and rarely entered the sanctum.

"The king and the queen came to seek my guidance. The king asked about his daughter. She is with child again, but all her children have died before taking their first breath. The queen asked that I summon the Norns and ask the fate of her child."

Dagmar was silent, waiting for Master Ivo to continue. He knew the Highest Keeper would tell him only what he wanted him to hear, and the less eager he appeared, the more Ivo would impart. Ivo made him wait, not speaking, yet not dismissing him either.

"I saw Lady Alannah holding a child," Ivo murmured finally. "She was overjoyed. I imparted this news to King Ansel and the queen."

Dagmar gasped. Banruud had another son. Desdemona had prophesied that Bayr would be his only child. Mayhaps her blood curse had come to an end.

"This is . . . this is . . . wonderful news," Dagmar stammered.

Ivo nodded slowly and closed his black-rimmed eyes as though he still saw the image behind his lids. "The vision gave the king joy in his last moments."

"We felt the ground shake as we climbed the hill," Dagmar said. He'd felt the earth quake in exactly the same way the day Desdemona died. It was something he and Ivo had never discussed.

"It was sudden, like a storm on the sea," Ivo ruminated. "The sanctum quaked, and I thought the temple would fall, that we would all be crushed. I urged the king to take shelter under the table, but the altar cracked, as though Thor smashed it with his hammer, and it fell, knocking us all to the ground."

"What does it mean?" Dagmar asked, unable to keep the wonder from his tone.

"There is no hiding from the gods when they call us home," Ivo said, and Dagmar winced, remembering the broken body of the king.

"We will be choosing a new king, Dagmar," Ivo said.

"Of course, Master." Ansel had been king all the years that Dagmar had been a keeper. He had never participated in the selection of a king, and his stomach twisted in apprehension.

"Bayr is Thor's choice. Thor broke the altar. He took the life of one king in order to reveal another," Ivo said, turning his black eyes on Dagmar.

Dagmar could only stare at the Highest Keeper, stunned.

"He is only seven years old, Master," he protested, his heart thundering in resistance.

"He has been chosen, Dagmar. He was chosen from the beginning."

"He has no clan," Dagmar stammered. "The people will revolt."

"His name is Bayr. He is of the clan of Berne. His mother knew it. You know it. And I know it as well, brother. I know he is the son of Banruud of Berne. The runes have shown me."

Dagmar shuddered, willing back the torrent behind his eyes. He should have known Ivo would discover the truth. Ivo knew everything.

"Chieftain Banruud will never claim him," Dagmar whispered, clinging to hope.

"It matters not. The Keeper of Berne will claim him," Ivo answered evenly. "And you will testify of his lineage if it becomes necessary."

"Please, Master. He is not ready."

"He is our salvation."

"He is a child."

"We have all witnessed his power."

"Power is not enough, Master. He must grow and learn."

"You will teach him. You will be his counselor on the throne until he is of age."

"Yes, I will teach him. I will give my life—I *have* given my life—for him. But he is a child," Dagmar protested, his chest aflame with fear for his nephew, for himself. He could not be counselor to a king.

"Your fate will be his fate," Ivo intoned. "Do you remember the day you brought the child, still covered in the blood and stain of his birth, into this sanctum?"

Dagmar nodded. The day was burned into his heart, seared into his consciousness, and never far from his thoughts.

"I knew then, Dagmar. I knew then that he would be king. He is Thor's son," Ivo stated, adamant. "We will call the clan chieftains together after the king is laid to rest. Then we will draw our runes and summon the gods. And we will choose a new king."

4

As the day of King Ansel's memorial drew near, the people of the clans began to move inland, making their pilgrimage to the center of Saylok to honor the late sovereign. The colors of the clans—Adyar gold, Berne red, Dolphys blue, Ebba orange, Joran brown, and Leok green—created a circular rainbow around the King's Village, the people camping in their finery, awaiting the royal processional. Mourners, their braids severed and their colors bright, lined the long road that climbed Temple Hill, the only entrance to the temple and the palace of the king that didn't require scaling cliffs or taking mountainous paths.

When the king of Saylok died, it was tradition that the men of the clans, in recognition of his passing, cut their hair. The long, tight braid they wore down their backs was removed—a braid that had been allowed to grow for the entire reign of the king—to signify the end of one era and the beginning of another. In Saylok, one could ascertain the longevity of a king by the length of his warriors' hair. One by one, the warriors of every clan laid their braids upon the king's casket as it trundled past. Ansel of Adyar had been King of Saylok for twenty years, and the braids of his warriors had grown long.

Women were not required to cut their hair when a king died, but many did, a sign of mourning and reverence, an indication of their personal devastation. The morning of the processional, the queen, her graying hair sticking up from her noble head in jagged tufts, walked behind the horse-drawn, open carriage where the body of her husband lay in a flag-draped coffin, the braids of his countrymen—a dozen different shades and lengths—spilling over the sides. People wept, and some women turned away, ashamed of their vanity in keeping their own hair.

The Keepers of Saylok never grew their hair at all. They kept their pates smooth, indicating their separation from the king and his subjects in every way. Master Ivo, his bare head gleaming, led the procession, his higher keepers behind him, the remaining keepers following in two straight lines, their flowing purple robes a reminder of their independence from any clan. Bayr did not walk with them. He was not a keeper—not yet even a supplicant—and his own thick braid had been lopped off at the base of his neck in accordance with the custom. When Dagmar had left with the other keepers, Bayr climbed the smallest turret on the north wall and ogled the colorful sea below him, the slow-moving parade, the mighty chieftains and the grim keepers, all descending the long road leading away from the temple and the palace of the king.

The chieftains, ordered according to their line to the throne, brought up the rear of the processional, Banruud of Berne first and Aidan of Adyar, the late king's son and the man now farthest from power, bringing up the rear.

"Saylok," Bayr whispered. He said the word with the same reverence Dagmar always did, and his chest grew tight with pride and wonder at the pageantry on display. But his pale eyes were continually drawn to the big man in blue, his brown hair swept off his handsome face, his flag held high.

"B-Ban-ruud of B-Berne," Bayr added, testing the name while no one could hear. The new king would be from Berne, and Bayr was intrigued. The chieftains rode chargers and carried the flags of their clans, and though the people gaped and admired the fierce and colorful chieftains just like the boy perched on the ramparts did, Bayr was too far away to hear the gossip that writhed and wriggled among the spectators. The gods of Saylok had taken the Chieftain of Adyar suddenly, violently, and the people were not convinced another chieftain was the response the gods—or the times—required.

It took all day to slowly circle the King's Village, and when the processional was finished, the chieftains and the king's guard escorted the coffin and the Lady Queen to Adyar, where King Ansel would be set out on the sea that rimmed his land, his funeral pyre aflame, his journey complete.

For six weeks the Keepers of Saylok would query the gods and summon past kings for wisdom and insight. The chieftains would be called to the temple for conference, each chieftain making his opinion known, and the keepers would sequester themselves once more.

When the six weeks were complete, Master Ivo and all the Keepers of Saylok would again walk in processional, rounding the village in their purple robes, the new king on horseback behind them. The people, clothed in their clan colors, would assemble once more, this time to see their new king.

Dagmar had been quiet and brief with his answers when Bayr asked him about the process of selecting a new king. Bayr had wanted to know every minuscule detail, every contingency, every possibility. He'd especially wanted to know more about Banruud of Berne.

Dagmar had pulled him close and explained what he could, but Bayr had seen the strain around his uncle's eyes, the tightness of his lips, the tension in his touch. He'd noticed the length of his uncle's prayers and the fresh wounds in his hands. Dagmar was drawing runes again, leaving Bayr behind when he walked in the woods. He said the trees sometimes spoke wisdom to him in whispers, and he couldn't hear them when Bayr came along. Bayr frowned in disagreement—he was very quiet—and had tried to follow at a distance, but Dagmar always knew he was there and sent him home.

Bayr's eyes lingered on the broad back of Chieftain Banruud, and he wondered what it would be like to be a king, to be the ruler of

Saylok. No one would be able to leave him behind or keep secrets from him. Dagmar would have to allow him to walk in the woods with him whenever he wished.

What would it be like to be king?

Bayr shuddered, abandoning the thought. He didn't want to tell others what to do, to have the six clans looking to him to lead, to command, to give fine speeches and sit on a throne. He didn't want to be king. Not even a little bit. He laughed to himself and rose, balancing on the ramparts like the ground wasn't a hundred feet below.

"L-long l-live B-Ba-Banruud of B-Berne, the ne-next K-King of Saylok," he shouted into the wind, grateful to the gods for making it so, grateful he was just a boy atop the parapets, hidden from view.

Banruud had been confident he would have the support of the chieftains, if only because they liked the precedent of a chieftain becoming king. But the chieftains had heard the hissing and the whispers in the crowds, and they saw fit to taunt Banruud with the rumors of the Temple Boy. The chieftains were bound only by their titles and their desire to see Saylok flourish, if only for their own wealth and power. None of them particularly liked him, and none would care if Banruud were denied the throne. They were gathered in Berne, in Banruud's keep, awaiting the word of the keepers, waiting to be called to the temple to cast their votes and crown a new king, and Banruud was slowly losing his mind. They were eating his meat and drinking his wine, sleeping in his beds and tupping his maids. Yet they persisted in the same conversation at every meal.

"Word is the Temple Boy has faced a bear and fought off a pack of wolves," Lothgar, Chieftain of Leok, muttered, his mouth greasy from the leg of lamb he held in his fist.

"He has killed a wild boar with his bare hands. My brother saw it," Erskin, the Chieftain of Ebba, added, eyeing Lothgar's greasy mouth with distaste. "He grabbed the beast by his tusks and spun him 'round. When he let go, the boar slammed into a tree and didn't get up again."

"He is naught but a boy, Erskin!" Banruud snarled at Ebba's chieftain.

"Yes. He is a boy. Seven years old. But he's said to be quite big for his age, and incredibly strong," Lothgar interjected, not raising his eyes from his food.

Banruud scoffed. "A boy of seven cannot be king. He has no clan."

"His name is Bayr. One would think he is of Berne," Dirth of Dolphys mused, raising one thick, black brow and lifting his eyes to Banruud in challenge. If the boy was of Berne, Banruud should claim him. And if he was of Berne, he could be king.

"My queen mother said the boy single-handedly raised the altar from my father's body. Three men could not make it budge," said Aidan, Chieftain of Adyar and son of the late king, with quiet authority.

Four sets of eyes locked on the young chieftain's face. Aidan had no chance of ever being king. A hundred years or more could pass before the crown returned to a son of Adyar, and Aidan would be in the ground. It gave his words more weight.

"The soldiers at Temple Hill say he has fought the mountain lion. He has climbed to the eagle's nest on the highest crags. He has ridden and tamed a wild horse. Do you know what that means?" Aidan asked, his tone nonchalant.

The men waited, knowing Aidan would tell them. As the youngest among them, Aidan enjoyed the attention more than he cared to admit.

"Adyar, the eagle. Ebba, the boar. Leok, the lion. Berne, the bear. Joran, the horse. Dolphys, the wolf. The boy has bested them all. The Highest Keeper believes he is destined to be king over the clans," Aidan elucidated.

"He is a child. He has no clan! He cannot be king," Banruud growled.

Aidan nodded slowly, clearly enjoying Banruud's rage. Aidan had always disliked him. He blamed Banruud for his sister's suffering. Even now, she lay in a chamber above them, preparing to birth yet another dead child. In seven years, she'd given birth to four infant boys, all of them stillborn, and with each labor, Banruud had wished only that she would die instead. She'd been a great disappointment to him.

Mayhaps this time it would be a daughter.

Banruud scoffed at his own thoughts, and the men around him interpreted the derisive sound as argument.

Aidan only laughed.

"Do not worry, Banruud, my brother. You will be king, just as you've planned."

The eyes of the chieftains locked on Aidan once more.

"The Temple Boy is an idiot," Aidan said, relenting.

"What do you mean?" Dirth of Dolphys asked, his voice soft, his gaze hard. Berne was next in line for the throne, but the clan of Dolphys would follow, and Dirth was almost as interested in the boy as Banruud.

"I mean he is blessed with unholy strength, but he can hardly speak a full sentence. He stutters when he speaks at all," Aidan finished, a smirk twisting his lips.

Banruud felt an easing in his chest, and Dirth threw his goblet against the wall in celebration. But Banruud of Berne could not completely drown out his fearful thoughts.

Adyar, the eagle. Ebba, the boar. Leok, the lion. Berne, the bear. Joran, the horse. Dolphys, the wolf. The boy has bested them all. The Highest Keeper believes he is destined to be king over the clans.

If Aidan was simply goading him into a rage, that was one thing. But if the Highest Keeper favored the boy, believed him to be called of the gods, then all was lost.

Erskin spoke again. "It is not unholy strength that will save Saylok. Even if the child were as powerful as Thor himself."

"We need women. Seven years, and not a single female born in all the clans," Lothgar grumbled, still eating. "Only women will save Saylok. Even if we have to take them."

And take them they had. Erskin of Ebba and Jaak of Joran had gone to the lands to the south, raiding villages and taking their women, spiriting them away aboard their ships to take back to their clans. Such raids were dangerous business, and the men of the Hinterlands didn't take the theft of their women lightly. And just like the women of Saylok, the women they stole gave birth to sons.

The last raid had ended badly for the Chieftain of Joran. He'd been killed in a battle on a distant shore, and his people were in the process of choosing a new chieftain. Banruud and Dirth, wanting to avoid the same fate, had decided to trade instead of raid, hoping to avoid war with the Eastlanders, and they'd brought home two dozen women—slaves mostly—but the Eastlanders had been quick to seize on their desperation. The women were sickly, plain, and expensive. Not good breeding stock. Three of them had died on the voyage back to Saylok.

Banruud had no daughters. He had no sons. He had a wife who had labored to give him both and had failed to give him either. Desdemona would have given him a son, but he'd wanted to curry the king's favor. Beautiful Desdemona of the black hair and wicked smile. Her father had come to him, raging at the squandered betrothal, blaming Banruud for her death. Banruud had wanted to kill Dred of Dolphys, but the Chieftain of Dolphys would have required recompense for the loss of one of his best warriors. Banruud had given Dred a bag of gold instead, and Desdemona's father had not been heard from since.

Banruud left his dining hall and the tables laden with food and wine and climbed the stairs to the room where his wife labored. The room stunk of sweat and smelling salts, and he grimaced as he approached her bed, a bed he hadn't slept in for ages. Agnes, the midwife, had kept

Alannah off her feet for much of her pregnancy, convinced that she could keep the babe alive if Alannah remained still. So far, the midwife had been right. The babe had continued to grow through nine long months. But in the last two days, Alannah had felt no movement in her womb. They feared the worst.

"How is she?" he asked Agnes, who hovered nearby. She'd been present for the birth of every one of his dead children. Mayhaps she was the cause. Mayhaps he should throw her from the window that stood open, airing out the sickroom. He could heave her heavy body into the moat that circled his keep. Only the knowledge that Agnes had helped birth dozens of live children throughout his clan stayed his hand.

"She is resting, my lord. Her pains are still far apart. She is not suffering. Mayhaps this time, Chief Banruud," the midwife said, smiling. Hopeful.

"Mayhaps," he agreed. It was what they said every time. And each time, they were disappointed.

∽

The farmer and his wife had waited until there was no one left in the hall, standing against the far wall near the large doors, watching as Chief Banruud repeated the blessing he bestowed on all the new infants of Berne. He'd smeared his blood in the shape of a star on the forehead of each child—all of them boys—and sent their parents away with a piece of gold. It was required in every clan, this presentation of a newborn child to the chieftain. Every child was welcomed and recorded in the book of Berne, just as it was in Ebba, Joran, Leok, Adyar, and Dolphys. Yet it had still taken them a year to realize the children being born in the clans were all sons.

In the beginning, they'd rejoiced. Sons were always preferable. Sons were the lifeblood. The protectors. The warriors. The farmers.

How foolish they'd all been.

"Bring the child forward," Banruud demanded of the couple, cross. He'd stayed up too late with the chieftains the night before. They'd commiserated too long, drank far too much of his best wine, and settled nothing. The day had been long, night would soon fall, and he was weary. Worried. And he had no patience for villagers who tarried when his day should be done. Usually his wife herded the villagers to him and escorted them away on blessing day, but Alannah was dying in her bed, dying with his child still in her womb, and Chief Banruud was stuck with her duties as well as his own.

He watched the farmer and his freckled wife approach, the babe clutched to the woman's chest. Their eyes were not on him, but on his guards still standing near the door, watching the final couple seek his blessing. When they stopped before his throne, the woman bobbed a stiff curtsy and the man bowed, but the woman did not offer up the child for his mark.

"We wish to speak to you without audience, Lord," the farmer whispered, his nervousness causing Banruud to finger the dirk on his belt.

"Why?" Banruud growled. The woman flinched, but the man simply lowered his voice and leaned into Banruud, showing more courage than was wise.

"This is the child of a slave—our servant girl—and . . . and the babe is . . . the babe is a girl child, Lord," the man mouthed, his voice so low, Banruud was certain he'd misunderstood. Glee and fear warred across the farmer's flat face.

"Leave us," Banruud said, raising his hand and his voice to his men. They obeyed immediately, the heavy door closing behind their hurried exit. The day had been tedious for them as well.

"Give the child to me," Banruud demanded. He kept his expression mild, his posture uninterested, but his heart boomed like a drum in his chest.

The farmer's wife obeyed, handing the sleeping child to her chieftain with excited trepidation.

"We call her Alba," the woman babbled.

Banruud pulled the blankets aside and unwound the rag wrapped and secured around the infant's nether regions.

He could not help the gasp that escaped his lips, but covered the babe swiftly, his eyes scanning the empty room around him as though an army stood at his gates ready to take his newfound treasure.

"The slave girl . . . her mother . . . tell me about her," Banruud insisted, cradling the child in his arms.

"She's from Eastlandia. Balfor brought her to Saylok in the last trade. She's only been with us four months. The babe would have been in her belly before she arrived, though she's hid it well. We didn't know she was expecting. She sleeps among the sheep. Takes care of them. No man wanted her, so we got her," the farmer said.

"Clearly some man did," Banruud snapped.

"No one wanted her because she is so plain," the woman explained.

Banruud laughed. The woman before him was homely and rail-thin, her cheeks windburned and ruddy, her graying hair frizzing from her enormous brow. She had little room to speak. Her cheeks flushed at his obvious derision, but she continued.

"She has no color in her skin or her hair, my lord. She is white like the snow . . . like a spirit. Even her eyes are pale."

"Her eyes are like ice, Chieftain Banruud. I can't stand to gaze at her long. She's fearful ugly. The Eastmen must have laughed when they sent her along," the farmer chimed in.

A memory niggled.

None of the women they'd acquired from Eastlandia had fought or resisted the trade. They'd been indentured since birth and had seemed resigned, even eager, to escape one master for another, especially if it meant they would be wives instead of slaves. None of the women they'd acquired in the trade had been mistreated, but they were all inspected.

If they were female and of childbearing years or younger, they were accepted. Banruud remembered a slight woman, not much bigger than a child, cloaked completely from head to toe, huddled at the back of the group of women the Eastmen had herded to the docks. Balfor, Banruud's overseer, had pulled the hood from her head, needing to ascertain the girl's age and general health. Her white hair had caused an uproar.

"This one's old. We asked for young women!" Balfor had protested.

"She's not old. She's just ugly." Another woman spoke up wearily. "We call her Ghost. Look at her skin. Nary a wrinkle or a blemish. Look at her form. Straight and slim. Look at her breasts, if you must. She's naught but seventeen. I've known her since the day she was born." The woman who spoke up for the girl wasn't much older than seventeen herself, but her tired eyes were rimmed and dark, her brown hair whipping about her face as if she were too spent to bind it back. Banruud had known then they were getting all the women no one else wanted. It didn't bode well for the continuation of his people.

Balfor had promptly ripped the ghost girl's gown from her neck to her navel, exposing her flesh to the cold air. She was so pale she looked like death, but her breasts were young and high and tipped in a pink so vivid, every man on the dock had turned to gape. She hadn't protested, but fixed her odd, stone-colored eyes on the horizon, awaiting her fate.

His overseer had grunted his acceptance and turned away. The woman had pulled her gown closed and lifted her muddy cloak over her cloud-like hair, and that had been the end of it. Banruud had not looked at her again, and he'd had no idea what had become of her once they'd docked in Berne.

"Why were you allowed to purchase her? The women brought back from the Eastlands were to be taken as wives," he pressed.

"Balfor gave her to me, Lord," the farmer rushed to explain. "He owed me money. And, like I said, no one else wanted the ghost girl.

The men were afraid of her. She's so strange. They thought bedding her might turn their cocks to ice."

"She's a hard worker, though. Good with the sheep. We haven't lost a one," the farmer's wife insisted, defensive.

Banruud cared nothing for hard work or sheep or frozen cocks. He was silent for a long moment, his thoughts churning. The gods were smiling on him this night.

"Who else knows about this child?" Banruud asked, his tone careful.

"Just us, Lord. We were afraid. We thought the babe might be cursed like the mother."

"Why?"

"Because the mother is so odd-looking. And . . . the babe *is* a girl, Chief Banruud. And she's not of Saylok. We thought she might be a changeling. Or a trick. What if she only appears to be a girl child but is really a monster?" the farmer reasoned.

The infant was fair, her thatch of hair almost as white as the ghost girl's. But her skin was warm and sun kissed, her lips and cheeks a deep pink. She was perfectly formed. Healthy. Beautiful. Not odd at all.

"And where is her mother now?" Banruud asked.

"With the sheep, Lord. She has work to do, and we told her the law required we bring the child to you. But she will be hungry soon," the farmer's wife answered.

"I will take her to the Keepers of Saylok," he said, his voice firm. "They will know what to do. They will know if this child is as she appears. You must tell no one until they have blessed her."

"But Lord," the woman protested, doubtful. "Her mother will need to feed the child. The babe will need her mother."

Banruud thought of Alannah, her breasts already full of milk, straining to give birth to yet another dead child. The babe would not need the ghost girl. But he would need to silence her.

"Go home and await my instructions."

The woman began to protest again, but the farmer was wise enough to quiet her with a tug on her hand. He'd seen Banruud's temper and knew his wife was in danger of offending her chieftain.

But Banruud was filled with light. His chest. His head. His future. All were bathed in a warm glow, and he smiled patiently at the couple who had given him the one thing that would grant him the power he desired.

Still holding the girl child, he loosened the coin pouch at his waist and presented it to the farmer and his wife.

"To compensate you for your loss. Speak nothing of the child until I send word from the keepers."

The farmer's eyes widened in appreciation, but his wife chewed her lip in obvious distress.

"Come, Linora," the farmer insisted, and bowed before Banruud, the gold disappearing into the satchel hanging from his shoulders. "It is for the best."

Banruud clutched the child to his chest and turned away, signaling he was through with them. He waited until they were gone, and when he heard the door of his great hall lumber to a close, he once again stared down into the child's face.

"You will be my salvation, Alba," he whispered. The name was perfect, as if the Norns had chosen it and whispered it into the slave girl's ears. Alba, the Bernian word for "white." White, for the color of her hair and the ghost girl who had unknowingly saved him. Alba, a name that began with the sound of Alannah's clan. For all Saylok would believe that Alannah of Adyar was this child's mother. He would announce it, and, once he had cleared up outstanding matters, no one would know the difference. He would declare himself her father. They would call him the curse breaker. Saylok would see it as a sign. Banruud of Berne had a daughter, and the Keepers of Saylok would make him king.

5

Alannah was asleep when Banruud slipped into her darkened room, the girl child in his arms. There was a fire in the grate though the day had not been cold. A maid moved around the room, gathering soiled linens, her movements sad and slow, and Banruud knew the fate of yet another son.

The maid turned, her face pale, and dropped the bloody bedclothes like she'd been caught in a crime.

"My lord! Agnes went to find you. The babe . . . your son . . . milady . . ." she babbled, unable to break the news he'd already ascertained.

"Go," he insisted, his tone level. Her eyes fell to the bundle in his arms, but she did as he asked, gathering the soiled linens once more, avoiding his eyes and the babe he held as she scurried from the chamber, but he knew what must be done.

Banruud laid the girl child in the cradle near the bed, a cradle built in hopes that a chieftain's child would someday grace it. Then he followed the maid from the room. She'd been hovering outside the door, as though she didn't quite know what to do, but when she heard him coming, her steps quickened toward the steep stone staircase at the back of his keep, the stairs the servants used to access the different floors without being seen by the lord and his lady or their guests.

"Run, little maid," he whispered, and she did exactly that, her arms full, wanting to be away from him, but in three swift steps he closed the distance between them. With a firm shove to her slim back, he hastened her escape, and sent her tumbling down the unforgiving stone steps.

She didn't even scream.

Banruud followed her down, taking each step with a measured tread. She lay in a broken heap at the bottom, the soiled sheets wrapped around her like a shroud, but she was not dead. She stared at him, her eyes wide, moaning in pain and fear. Her neck was broken, her left leg too, but he would relieve her suffering. He put his booted foot on her throat and pressed down with all his considerable weight, bidding her safe passage to the world beyond.

When it was done, he climbed the stone stairs with the same steady conviction with which he'd descended. If Agnes, the midwife, showed any inclination toward disbelief or disloyalty, he would silence her as well. He was counting on her devotion to her mistress and her belief in the gods to close her lips.

Banruud entered his wife's chamber once more, walked to the bed, and looked down at Alannah's slumbering form, her belly no longer bulging, her dead child wrapped tightly in a blanket, lying in the crook of her arm. Alannah insisted on holding them each time, and each time Banruud had to wrestle the small corpse away from her before it began to decay.

For a moment, he let himself feel the rage and loss he'd felt many times before. Four sons—five now—all buried in a straight row, four flat rocks above four tiny heads. And his wife lived on. He would have abandoned her—replaced her—long ago. But she was the daughter of his king, and he could not easily discard her.

But Odin had finally looked favorably upon him.

He unwrapped the dead child from the blanket Alannah had so carefully crafted and wrapped the live child in his place, tucking her against his wife's inert form. Taking the plain, rough blanket the girl child had been wrapped in, he bundled a loose hearthstone and his dead son inside, knotting the blanket firmly around both. He walked to the window and stared out into the gathering darkness. If anyone saw the bundle drop, it wouldn't matter. It would be gone before anyone could fish it out of the water, if they were even inclined to do so. He released it and watched as it fell, hit the moat with a barely audible plop, and disappeared almost immediately, the weight of the heavy stone pulling his son to a watery grave.

Satisfied that the worst was accomplished, he moved back to his sleeping wife and sat in a chair near the bed, waiting for her to wake, to find the gift he'd placed at her side. She'd been through two days of strenuous labor and the birth of yet another stillborn child, and she slept with the heaviness of post-hysteria. Agnes would have given her a tonic to take away her pain and suffering, if only for a time. She would have given her something to help her sleep, to forget. But he needed her to wake.

"Alannah," he whispered, shaking her roughly. "Wake."

She didn't even stir. He persisted, pinching her arms until she moaned and raised shaking hands to push him away.

"Alannah."

She moaned.

"Alannah."

Her eyes fluttered, and wan awareness lit her gaze. She closed her eyes again and turned her face away. She thought he was there to rebuke her. To mourn and rage. And she didn't want to face him.

He forced gentleness into his tone. "Alannah. We must celebrate."

Her chin wobbled, and her mouth turned down. Tears escaped from under her closed lids and trailed down her pallid cheeks.

"Look what you have given me, wife. Look at our beautiful daughter."

Her eyelids fluttered again, and blue eyes met his black gaze. She stared at him. Weary. Weak. Disoriented.

Good. Banruud needed her to be confused.

The babe at her side emitted a small cry.

Alannah looked down at the infant tucked against her ribs, wonder blooming across her devastated face.

"Look at your beautiful daughter," he said, laying the babe across her shoulder so she could see the flush of warm skin and feel the sweet breath on her cheeks.

"My baby?" she whimpered. "No. I . . . my baby . . . he died." Her face crumpled, and her hands fluttered to her eyes. She wiped at her tears, ignoring the wriggling baby lying against her.

"No, not this time. Your baby lives. Your daughter lives. You were in shock and Agnes gave you a tonic. It took away the pain. But it has made you forgetful." Banruud pulled her hands from her eyes, his fingers encircling her narrow wrists. He forced her arms around the child.

"Look at her, Alannah. Hold your daughter. She is hungry. She needs you."

He tugged at the front of her dressing gown, baring her engorged breasts. Her milk always came early, in anticipation of the babies who never survived. Her eyes, glazed and glassy, clung to the babe beside her.

"I don't remember her," she whimpered.

"I know. But you will. You will be so happy, just as I am."

Alannah's eyes left the child's face and found his. "You are happy?" she whispered.

"I am happier than I have ever been."

"She's mine? Ours?" she pled, begging for reassurance.

"Yes."

"A daughter?"

"A daughter."

Alannah touched the baby's cheek, astonishment infusing her tired face with hope. "I am dreaming," she wailed. "It cannot be true. My babies are dead."

"Yet she is alive."

The girl child began to fuss in earnest, and Alannah wept with her.

"Help me sit, Banruud," she cried, gathering the wailing infant in her arms. He did so, propping woman and child against the thick oak headboard of the enormous bed. Tentatively, with the instinct born of long suffering, Alannah guided the hungry babe to her breast. The baby latched on eagerly. Triumph surged in Banruud's belly as Alannah winced and then whimpered in relief.

"We will call her Alba," he insisted.

"Alba," Alannah repeated, her voice dreamlike as she gazed down at the nursing infant.

Banruud heard the screaming and the boots in the hall outside the chamber door, but no one entered or even knocked, and his wife, wrapped in a fog of euphoria and exhaustion, did not even register the commotion. Someone would be looking for him to tell him the news. Or mayhaps not. He had a steward and a housekeeper. They would handle the terrible accident that had befallen the maid. He felt a flash of remorse. He hated to kill a young woman of Berne when they were in such short supply. And tonight, he would kill more than one.

The door opened softly, suddenly, and Agnes stepped inside, the only person in the keep who would enter Lady Alannah's chamber thus. She saw Banruud first, sitting at his wife's bedside, and her countenance fell as her shoulders stiffened, bracing for his wrath. Then her gaze slid to Alannah.

The midwife gasped and stumbled back, her eyes clinging to the child suckling her lady's breast.

"Odin's eyes!" she hissed, making the sign of the star over her heart.

"She is so beautiful, Agnes. Come look at her," Alannah murmured, her voice still slurred and sleepy.

"W-what is this?" Agnes whispered, her hands fluttering around her throat, over her heart, and back again. For a moment, Banruud thought she would faint. She stumbled and steadied herself against the wall.

"The goddess Freya has given me a daughter, Agnes," Alannah said, her eyes still on the babe in her arms. "I have a child, just like you promised."

Banruud eyed the midwife, speculating. She had known Alannah since birth, had loved her and cared for her like a mother, and had come to Berne when Alannah became his wife. She'd been at Alannah's side through every pregnancy.

"You are a seer, Agnes," he purred. "And I am forever in your debt."

"But the child . . . I was coming to find you, Lord. I thought the child was . . ." Her voice drifted off. She couldn't say the words, not with Alannah holding the infant in her arms, an infant that was very much alive.

"Imagine my joy when I entered the room and saw my daughter," Banruud replied. "You said this time was different. You were right."

"A daughter?" she squeaked, and then caught herself. "Of course. A daughter. Praise the gods," she murmured, still clutching her chest. He almost laughed at her attempts to reconcile what she was seeing with what she knew. But the evidence was there before her. She must think herself mad or think them all bewitched.

"The gods have been generous this day," Banruud said, sincerity ringing in his voice. He would kill the fatted calf in their honor. But not before he announced the birth of his daughter to every chieftain now supping in his hall. And not before he made certain that the farmer and his wife and their ghost girl would never speak out against him.

Balfor sat at a table in the back of the hall, surrounded by Berne's warriors and content in his position as the chieftain's overseer. He'd grown a little too comfortable, Banruud thought to himself as he approached the table. His men stood immediately with a chorus of *m'lords*. Balfor was slower to rise.

"I would speak to you, Balfor," Banruud said quietly. "Alone."

When his men began to scramble to oblige his request, Banruud stopped them, and bade his overseer to follow him from the dining hall.

Thunder rumbled, and leaves scurried across the cobbles, but Banruud stepped out into the darkness and ducked beneath the eaves, his eyes on the grumbling skies, and waited for Balfor to join him. When he did, Banruud did not hesitate, but pounced, his voice low and hard.

"You gave the white woman, the one they call Ghost, to a farmer and his wife."

Balfor stiffened, and his eyes shot to the side. "I did, my chief. I owed him money."

Banruud nodded slowly. "And now you owe me money. She was not yours to give away. She belonged to the clan, not to you."

"She was feared."

"She was not yours."

Balfor nodded, agreeing with his chieftain, and waiting for his punishment. Banruud let the silence and reproach grow between them until Balfor was squirming with unease.

"The farmer—what is his name?" Banruud asked.

"Bertog," Balfor supplied.

"Bertog came to me today, into my hall. He waited until there was no one in attendance. He was afraid someone would see him. Apparently, the woman you gave him—the ghost girl—is diseased. She has infected his family."

Balfor cursed, deep and desperate, and Banruud continued.

"He wants recompense and he wants healing. I can offer him neither. I can only protect the rest of the clan from the sickness under his roof."

Balfor's eyes bulged and his breaths were quick and shallow. "What can I do, Chief?"

"You must burn down his house. Make sure they are inside, Balfor. The man, his wife, any servants they employ, any children they have, and the slave. And pray that no one else is stricken. He may already have infected my keep."

"Bertog's two sons are grown. They are warriors—raiders—and are in the Eastlands."

"Good. Then they will not have to know what has befallen their family."

"There are no servants," Balfor hastened to add. "Just the slave girl from the Eastlands."

Banruud nodded. "Good. Then go. Quickly. There is a storm coming, and the house must burn to the ground."

Balfor nodded once. He was not a squeamish man. In fact, Banruud knew he rather enjoyed watching people suffer. He would do what he was told without conscience.

"Tell no one, Balfor. We don't want the people to panic over a plague," Banruud warned. "We will watch and wait. And your debt to me will be paid."

"Yes, Chief Banruud."

"Find me when it is done."

Banruud, his eyes narrow but his thoughts wide, watched Balfor stride away. Then he turned back to the entrance, to the light and warmth of the dining hall, eager to announce his triumph.

He did not see the girl with the ghostly pallor and the moon-white hair huddling in the shadows only feet away. She'd come hoping to be reunited with her child. Weeping with fear, she sank back against the wall, her breasts aching with unexpressed milk, her mind reeling from what she'd overheard.

⁙

"Lady Alannah has given birth to a healthy child, and I am a father," Banruud roared, raising his glass to the room of warriors and chieftains gathered in his dining hall to sup. The room was silent for the length of a long, indrawn breath. And then pandemonium ensued, goblets raised and smashed as the men rose to their feet in wild-eyed wonder and celebration. They all knew Lady Alannah's troubles. They all knew Saylok's scourge.

"But I am not just a father," Banruud protested, leaping onto the table where the four chieftains sat. He'd left their company the night before, convinced his ambitions were in jeopardy, fearing the death of yet another child. What providence that they were gathered here, in his keep, for his announcement. Soon, word would travel to the Keepers of Saylok. Word would travel to every corner of the land, his name on every tongue.

The voices died down and all eyes looked on him, waiting. He smiled, showing his strong white teeth to the men who would soon call him king.

"Lady Alannah has given me . . . a girl child."

A shocked ripple wrapped the room in a euphoric bubble, and Banruud roared and beat his chest, once, twice, and then again. Some men fell to their knees, another wept, but then a cheer rose, and merriment erupted. His men sought to pull him from the table and carry him on their shoulders, but he laughingly denied them, his gaze on the chieftains who sat dumbfounded, disbelief coloring their bearded faces.

Aidan of Adyar stood abruptly, his chair clattering loudly against the stone floor, his eyes on his brother-in-law. "I want to see my sister. I want to see this girl child," he demanded.

"And you shall, brother. You all shall," Banruud promised, leaping down from the table. One by one, the chieftains rose, challenging him with their doubt and their undeniable hope.

"All of you. Come with me," Banruud commanded genially.

They followed him up the wide stairs and down the long hall to the chamber where Alba slept in Alannah's arms. His wife greeted them with smiling lips and tear-filled eyes. The chieftains greeted her with deep bows and congratulations. Then they stood in an awkward semicircle around the foot of the bed, their eyes on the girl child, watching as Alannah quickly revealed the child's sex, her tired face flushed with pride, before wrapping her up again and clutching her to her chest.

Lothgar of Leok was the first to fall to his knees, swearing fealty to the child. Brawny and golden-haired, he had a beard and broad nose that gave him the look of the lion on his crest. He cultivated the look, Banruud knew, as they all did. To be seen as the physical embodiments of Saylok's animal sons gave them standing among their people. Erskin was the only chieftain who sought to minimize his resemblance to the boar his clan was named for, but his small, powerful body and jutting jaw left little doubt of his ancestry. Aidan of Adyar was tall, beak-nosed, and sharp-eyed like his eagle forefather—too sharp-eyed for Banruud's liking—but Aidan's suspicion and disbelief wilted before the beautiful infant and his sister's triumph, and he too knelt in reverence. The chieftains of Ebba and Dolphys immediately sank to the floor beside him.

"The drought has ended," Dirth of Dolphys whispered. "We will have daughters in Saylok again. Praise Odin and praise our father, Saylok."

The chieftains from Ebba, Adyar, and Leok added their thanks and praised the slew of gods and goddesses, until every known deity had been cited and cited again. Then they bellowed and roared, snorted and shrieked, the sound of each clan echoing off the walls. The babe let out a startled cry, and the celebration ceased abruptly, comically. Chins fell and shouts were swallowed as the chieftains rose to their feet, laughing at the power of the girl child to silence grown men.

Then they turned and, one by one, bowed their heads to Banruud. A chieftain did not genuflect before any man but the king, but Banruud of Berne would be crowned the new ruler of Saylok, of that they were certain.

6

"Banruud of Berne has been blessed with a daughter."

A courier had brought the announcement to the entrance gate, and Edmund, a supplicant excluded from the proceedings until his ordination, had delivered the message to the sanctum door. The keepers were deep in discussion over the selection of a new king, and Dagmar, conflicted and quiet, had retreated as far from the conversation as he could. It was he who responded to the insistent knocking.

"A daughter has been born in Saylok!" young Edmund crowed as Dagmar cracked the door, and Edmund's excitement carried into the shrine.

The keepers, who had turned toward the interruption with mouths poised to rebuke, gasped in one accord. The gasp became a murmur, the murmur became a roar, and Master Ivo stood from his throne, raising his arms to calm the hiss of questions and concerns that filled the sanctum like a demon chorus. The higher keepers rose around him, the lower keepers rose before him, but all their rumblings ceased.

"What is this, Brother Dagmar?"

"Young Edmund has news, Master."

"Let him enter," Ivo demanded, and Dagmar opened the door to the supplicant. Edmund, bowing at the gaping keepers and trying not to smile under the weight of their undivided attention, made his way to the dais, Dagmar following reluctantly behind him.

"Speak, Edmund," Ivo commanded.

Edmund nodded, and with a deep breath, began again. "Banruud of Berne and Alannah of Adyar have been blessed with a daughter. A girl child."

Whispers and praise rose again.

"Silence!" Ivo snapped, and the rumbling ceased. "Is this all you've been told?" Ivo pressed, turning to the supplicant.

"Chieftain Banruud and his wife are coming here, to the temple . . . with their daughter. The chieftains have seen her, the girl child, and he has their support. They are coming too," Edmund added.

"But . . . they have not yet been summoned," Ivo protested.

Edmund gulped but did not answer. The keepers in the sanctum stayed silent as well.

"We will have to wait for Joran," Ivo mused. "The clan has no chieftain. We must have the support of all six of the chieftains before a king can be selected."

"I have news of Joran too, Master," Edmund offered, beaming with importance.

Master Ivo glowered at him, and Edmund spewed every detail.

"Joran has chosen a new chieftain. Josef, eldest son of Jurgen. He was selected two days ago, Master. He rode to Berne and saw the child and is riding toward Temple Hill with the other clan chieftains as we speak."

Master Ivo sank back into his throne, a bent, black crow beneath his dark robes. Like children, the other keepers mimicked his motion, falling back down onto their own seats as well.

"Should we alert the palace staff, Master?" Edmund asked.

"The rooms are readied. We've been expecting them," Ivo said wearily. "We just didn't expect . . . this."

The keepers around him nodded in stunned agreement, and for a moment no one spoke.

"You can go now, Edmund," Ivo grunted. "I'm sure there are others who will be eager to hear your news."

Edmund bowed, and Dagmar took his arm to escort him out.

Ivo's gaze swung to Dagmar, and he pointed a gnarled finger in rebuke. "You will stay, brother. You have avoided your duty long enough."

When the door to the sanctum closed once more, the mood in the room had changed dramatically.

"A girl child," Amos, Keeper of Adyar, marveled. "And from a daughter of Adyar, no less. Praise Odin. Praise Father Saylok."

His praises set off a chain of worshipful *amens*, voices rising and falling in wonder and disbelief.

"Surely . . . this changes things, Master," Dagmar offered quietly.

"Banruud should be king. It is a sign," Amos added.

"The gods have spoken, Master," another keeper concluded.

"Minutes ago, we were in agreement," Master Ivo protested.

"Minutes ago, we did not know that Banruud of Berne had a daughter—a daughter, think of it!" Amos insisted, garnering a few glares from his brothers. Keepers were not supposed to be biased toward any clan, and Amos was clearly overjoyed that a daughter of Adyar would be queen, that a daughter of Adyar had given birth to the first girl child in seven years.

"I saw the Lady Alannah with a child," Master Ivo murmured. "I saw her joy, but I did not see this."

"None of us envisioned such a thing," Keeper Bjorn said. "We have great cause to rejoice."

"We have great cause to be wary," Ivo warned. "We must seek the counsel of the gods."

"But . . . the gods have clearly spoken, Master," Amos ventured.

"Not to me, brother," Ivo barked. "Not to you, I would contend. Not to any of you. None of you have meditated on the matter. You are reacting without consulting the source. My feelings still remain. The boy should be king."

The room was quiet. No one raised his voice or his head. Every man was bowed in contemplation, but the resistance and restraint were palpable, a thumping heartbeat that continued to quicken and grow louder, until after an hour of silent prayer, Keeper Amos rose, and with a swift inhale, began shaking his bald head.

"I want to amend my vote. My misgivings over the boy, Bayr, being chosen as king were numerous, as you know." Master Ivo's eyebrows rose disdainfully. Amos had not voiced a solitary word of dissent, but he continued without pause. "I went along with the consensus because I have witnessed the boy's strength. It seemed as if Thor had indeed chosen him. But now . . . now the gods have spoken again. Freya has spoken, the goddess, and she has finally given Saylok a child in her image. I cannot disregard her preference."

Heads nodded and throats cleared.

Master Ivo sighed, closing his sooty lids and folding his clawed hands. "Then let us stand, one by one, and declare our thoughts. Briefly. Amos has spoken." He glowered at the keeper from Adyar as Amos made a move to speak again. "Bjorn?"

Bjorn rose and quietly added his voice to Amos's. One by one, the keepers, both high and low, cast their votes. Not all were in favor of Banruud of Berne, but the majority ruled in his behalf.

Dagmar huddled down into the bench, his hands folded, his head bowed, and he was the last to be called upon. He had not uttered a word throughout most of the weeklong proceeding. Instead, he had begged the heavens for intercession, for clarity, for reprieve. Now . . . it seemed as though his prayers had been answered. But Ivo would not be pleased.

"Dagmar? You are the boy's guardian. What say you?" Master Ivo prodded.

"Master . . . you should make this decision. I cannot," Dagmar murmured.

"That is not how this works, Dagmar," Amos snapped. He'd grown impatient with the sonorous opinions of his brothers—especially those who did not agree with him—when the choice was so obvious.

Dagmar touched the newest scab across his hand, wishing for his blade and his runes. With a heavy heart and a troubled soul, Dagmar stood and raised his eyes to Ivo's. The room grew silent again, as though the final word was about to be spoken.

"Bayr is only seven years old, Master. And he does not wish to be king," Dagmar said, his voice ringing like a death knell through the sanctum. No one breathed. "My father tried to make me into something I was not. And I hated him for it. I will not force the boy down a path he has no wish to take. If Thor wants Bayr to be king, Thor will have to provide another way."

An excited murmur rose and was immediately quashed by the Highest Keeper's dissent.

"The way is here! It is now, Keeper Dagmar. You are standing in Thor's way!" Master Ivo cried.

Amos stood to protest, but Ivo swatted him down with a black look and a slashing motion, silencing all but Dagmar.

Dagmar nodded, acknowledging Ivo's point, but he did not agree. "Thor has the power to move me out of the way, Master, if that is what he wishes. But I don't believe Bayr's time has come. He may be Saylok's salvation, but not yet. Not yet, Master."

Master Ivo folded his arms, his sleeves like wings, tucking himself away, burrowing down into his throne and closing his eyes. This time the keepers did not fall back to their seats alongside him. They all sensed his retreat and waited for him to dismiss them.

"I have heard you all. And you have heard me. Leave me now. We will hear the chieftains, and we will cast our votes again after they have made their case."

But when the chieftains arrived the following day, fresh from the glow of the miracle in Berne and flush with the wonder of a holy girl child, they stood, and to a man, lifted Banruud of Berne's name to the gods and to the Keepers of Saylok. Most of the keepers nodded in agreement, beaming with relief that the odd and inexplicable drought had ended and overjoyed that the path forward had been made so abundantly clear. Keepers who had sided with the wishes of the Highest Keeper found themselves wavering toward the brawny chieftain, his radiant queen, and the baby girl she held so lovingly in her arms.

Master Ivo was the only voice of dissent, and he had gone quiet, outnumbered and overruled. Dagmar felt only relief that his Bayr would not be called upon at such an age. Beneath the relief the fear remained, omnipresent and multifaceted, but it was fear that could be faced and defeated over time. Bayr would grow into a man under his father's reign—beneath his father's nose—but that was preferable to donning a crown he was not ready to wear.

In the following days, it was the girl child—little Alba—who softened the Highest Keeper's heart and loosened his lips. Her skin was golden—sun kissed—as though her mother had warmed her on a hot hearth and her skin, like bread, had browned in the heat. Her eyes were so brown they appeared black, with sooty lashes that brushed her golden cheeks, but her hair was as pale as corn silk, so light it appeared colorless under the flickering candles in the crowded sanctum, where the keepers and the royal family had assembled to give her a name and a blessing. She kicked her tiny limbs and wailed in protest as cold hands touched her naked flesh.

The altar stone had been replaced, and the Keepers of Saylok surrounded the infant offering, the tips of their fingers resting against her tiny chest. The keepers had pricked their fingers and joined their blood, drawing the star of Saylok on her brow, elevating her from a daughter of the clans to a daughter of the gods. Alannah, her mother, stood by, the only woman in the sanctum, watching the ceremony beside the king, Banruud, who had already been crowned by the keepers and would soon be coronated in front of the people.

"Alba, daughter of Banruud of Berne, King of Saylok, and daughter of Alannah of Adyar, Lady Queen of Saylok, we honor you and acknowledge you, a gift from the goddess Freya, a gift to the clans. May you usher in a new age, Princess, and lead all our daughters from the darkness of the womb to the light of new life," Ivo intoned as he blessed the baby, his voice reverent and low.

Dagmar raised his face so the moisture that wanted to seep from his eyes would not run down his cheeks and betray his tender heart. In the gloom of the domed ceiling above, the crisscrossing beams appeared to move, and his chest seized even as his eyes adjusted and registered the cause. It was not the beams that were moving, but the boy who crept along them.

Bayr stopped directly over the altar, a small, dark angel looking over the babe. Dagmar should have known Bayr would find a way inside. He'd climbed and clambered over the temple mount since he could walk. It was a good thing he was loath to speak; his stutter made him an excellent guardian of secrets. Dagmar would have to chastise him later, but now he lowered his eyes so the others wouldn't follow his gaze and make the same discovery. But the infant lying on the altar saw the boy who hovered above her, and her gaze was fixed on his face.

The palace was filled with celebration. The light and merriment spilled out the open doors and crept across the grass before coming to a halt at the rock wall that separated the temple grounds from the palace gardens. The chieftains had arrived with a caravan of warriors and wives, sons and siblings, and the sacred selection of the new king had become a rollicking reunion of six clans. In two days' time, King Banruud would mount his horse and present himself to the people. His queen, the chieftains, and the keepers would follow behind him in a parade for the newly anointed.

The keepers did not take part in the festivities in the palace. While Ivo stewed in the sanctum, the keepers celebrated quietly in the dining hall, and Bayr, under protest, was escorted to bed. Dagmar had little doubt that the boy would creep away to spy on the goings-on at the palace the moment Dagmar left his little room, a room tucked beneath the eastern eaves of the temple's rear wing. Dagmar still slept in the chamber where he'd once held the boy through long, desperate nights, but Bayr had outgrown his arms and the straw on the floor, and Dagmar had found him a little place to call his own.

The boy was irritable, though quietly so, and Dagmar sensed his impatience to have his uncle gone so he could scale the walls and watch the celebration next door.

"I saw you in the sanctum when the girl child was blessed," Dagmar murmured, sinking down onto the stool he'd fashioned for just this purpose.

Bayr's eyes snapped to his uncle's, gauging Dagmar's disappointment.

"Are y-you a-angry?" Bayr murmured. He didn't deny his presence in the sanctum or seek to excuse his behavior.

"Not angry. But if you don't do as I say, how can I trust you? You know the sanctum is holy. It is for sacred ceremonies. For keepers. Not for curious little boys with more skill than sense."

"T-today was s-special. N-not j-just for keepers."

Dagmar sighed heavily, acknowledging the truth of the boy's statement. The chieftains had been present; why not the boy who had almost been king?

For a moment they sat in silence, each pondering their private thoughts, until Dagmar, reaching a decision, took the boy's hand. Bayr's nails were dirty and broken, his palms stained deep in the crevices. It didn't matter how many times Dagmar instructed him on the importance of cleanliness, he was a boy, and he was always dirty. Dagmar rose and dipped a cloth in the water basin atop the small table in the corner. Sitting back on the stool, he washed Bayr's hands and used his blade to clean his nails. When he was finished, Dagmar set the cloth and the knife aside and ran his thumb across Bayr's knuckles, oddly close to tears. They were still dimpled with the softness of youth; Bayr was so young, so precious, and the gods had so much in store for him. It made Dagmar's heart quake.

"Master Ivo wanted you to be king, Bayr," Dagmar whispered, knowing he had to prepare his boy.

Bayr's hand jerked in his.

"M-me?" Bayr stuttered.

"Yes. You." Dagmar met the boy's gaze and held it, compelling him to understand. Bayr's face had grown pale, and his eyes were luminous in the paltry light. "You are not like other boys, Bayr. You know that, don't you?"

Bayr stared, the way he always did, intensely, demanding with his gaze that Dagmar explain.

"Surely you've noticed that you can do things others cannot?" Dagmar pressed.

"I-I'm s-s-strong," Bayr admitted.

"Yes. And fast. And agile. And very, very brave. You are but a boy, but you battle grown men in the castle yard with the skill of a seasoned warrior. The keepers and the palace guard are in awe of your prowess. Your reputation has spread throughout the clans."

"I-I am n-not b-brave. I a-am a-afraid," Bayr confessed, bowing his head.

It was Dagmar's turn to wait, urging the boy on with kind eyes.

"I d-don't w-want to b-be k-king, Uncle," Bayr whispered.

"I know. And I don't want you to be king. But, Bayr? There might come a time, when you are no longer a boy, when Saylok will need you to lead her. There might be a day when you will be called on to rule, and you must prepare yourself for that day."

"W-when I am grown, I w-won't b-be a-afraid," Bayr murmured, hopeful.

"You'll still be afraid. But you must do what is right, what you must, despite that fear."

"Are y-you a-afraid?"

"Yes. Every day," Dagmar said, laughing when Bayr frowned in disbelief. But his laughter quickly faded into memory. "When your mother brought you to me, Bayr, and asked me to take you, to raise you, I was terrified. I didn't want to be a father. I didn't know how to care for a child. But I did it anyway, because you needed me, because it was the right thing to do. And you have been my greatest joy." Dagmar's tears collected in his throat, and for several seconds he couldn't continue. Bayr's lips trembled, and he threw his thin blanket aside and crawled into his uncle's lap, wrapping his arms around him and tucking his head beneath his chin.

"When you were born," Dagmar whispered, fighting the emotion, "your mother told me you would have great strength. She also named you, and she said you would bring salvation to Saylok."

"Wh-what is s-sal-v-vation?" Bayr asked, pulling back to see his uncle's face.

"Hope. Rescue. Saving. You are a protector, Bayr. And I believe you've been given power to defend this land—every clan. You are not Bayr, the Temple Boy. You are not Bayr of Berne or Dolphys. You are Bayr of Saylok, and you must defend this land from her enemies within and without."

"I will p-pro-te-tect the princess."

Dagmar smiled, surprised. "Just her?"

"F-for now. Sh-she is p-precious."

"She is, indeed." Dagmar sighed, but there was more he had to impart, and it involved only pieces of the truth.

"When you were born, your mother was very angry. She didn't want to leave you, and she cursed all of Saylok with a blood rune."

Bayr's eyes gleamed and his mouth trembled. He knew blood runes were forbidden to all but the keepers, and even then, they were to be used only for wisdom, not for vengeance or power.

"Why w-was she a-angry?"

"She loved a man who did not love her."

"My father?"

"I think so, yes." Dagmar steeled his expression for the lie. "Though I do not know his name."

"I w-want you to b-be my f-father," Bayr whispered.

Dagmar kissed the boy's head. "I *am* your father. And you are my son. But I must tell you about your mother. And you must try to understand."

Bayr nodded, so serious, so intent.

"Desdemona—your mother—was very sad. And very . . ." Dagmar struggled to find the right word.

"A-alone?" Bayr supplied.

"Yes. Very alone. Men can be cruel, especially to their women. So your mother promised that there would be no women in Saylok for men to misuse."

"But not all m-men are b-bad."

"No. And not all women are innocent. But Desdemona was angry. She was dying. And she did a terrible thing. And now Saylok suffers— the innocent and the guilty alike—and I don't know how to fix what has been done."

"B-but there is a g-girl child." Bayr smiled hopefully.

"Yes. And it has given me great hope that your mother's rune has weakened, and that Saylok has shaken off the sickness in her soil."

"I w-will w-watch over her. Over A-Alba. I-if I take good care of h-her . . . may-ha-haps the gods w-will bless us w-with more."

"Mayhaps," Dagmar whispered. "It is all we can do. Now it is time for you to sleep. No creeping across the turrets and the walls, my son. I cannot bear to lose you, and I do not think our new king would approve of your spying."

The boy slipped from Dagmar's lap and crawled into his bed, burrowing down into the pillow and yawning convincingly. Dagmar stood and, with a brush of his hand over the boy's hair, turned to go, but not before extracting the promise that had inspired the entire conversation.

"The gods reward our faith in the face of fear, Bayr. On the other side of fear is triumph. You must promise me that when the time comes, when you are grown, even if you do not want to be king, even if you are afraid, you will do what must be done."

"I promise, Uncle," Bayr murmured, his tongue freed as he slipped into sleep. "I will do what must be done."

7

Word of the girl child had spread, and all of Saylok wanted to see her. Bayr abandoned his spot overlooking the temple entrance and the road leading down into the King's Village and wove his way through the throng, finding a perch here and there before abandoning each for something better, something closer, where he too might be able to see the baby girl.

He missed her.

The thought made him laugh. He'd stared down at her from the beams high above the altar, and she'd gazed back at him. She was only days old and so small he wouldn't dare touch her, even if it was allowed. She hadn't smiled at him even though he'd grinned down at her. He wasn't certain babies knew how to smile. If he saw her again he could teach her. He hoped one day to be closer than the beam above the altar.

He'd seen so few babies. There were other children in the village, but he spent so little time outside the temple walls among the people that the day felt like a holiday in more ways than one. A new king had been crowned, a girl child had been born, and Saylok's citizens had set their labors aside for a day of celebration. Dagmar had warned him to not stray too far from the temple and palace grounds, but Dagmar was walking in the king's processional and wouldn't know whether Bayr was as obedient as he'd promised to be.

He'd had a poor view for the king's descent from Temple Hill, but he'd climbed a tree with wide branches that hung over the thoroughfare, and as the king's procession turned the corner into the village square, he would have an unobstructed view of the entire parade, all the way to the very end, where the purple robes of the Keepers of Saylok rounded out the procession.

The chieftains, each carrying a standard emblazoned with their clan crest, rode at the front, a sign of support for and fealty to the new king of Saylok. Their hair was bound tightly in plaits that had no length, with ribbons extending down their backs, a symbol of hope that their braids would grow long under the new reign.

Bayr inched out onto the largest limb, his belly to the branch, so close that the gold flag of Leok would pass right below him. Banruud of Berne—of Saylok, for now he was king—rode behind the five chieftains on a horse so big and so black, the people pressed back, not wanting to spook the beast. The king, draped in red, was as intimidating as his horse, but though his progress was marked by the rippling wave of bowing onlookers, it was the girl child the people most wanted to see.

Behind the king, in a carriage not unlike the one that had transported King Ansel's coffin, Banruud's wife, Alannah, the new Lady Queen, sat holding the princess, though nothing was visible from Bayr's branch but a small bundle in a sea of red. Red was the color of Berne and now the color of the throne. Bayr didn't think the deep blood red suited the new queen or the tiny girl in her arms, and as Bayr watched the procession approach, he felt a tremor of foreboding run down his small back and settle in his hands. The Lady Queen, her face wreathed in smiles, waved to the crowd and tipped the babe toward the people to the left and then to the right so they could see her.

Below Bayr's perch, the people writhed and pushed, shouting out to their chieftains and raising the name of the new king, and, as was the nature of most crowds, tempers grew short and people were caught in the crush. A figure, cloaked from head to toe in drab brown, the cowl of her hood extending far beyond her bowed head, lost her balance in the swell. She was stooped in such a way that she appeared old, feeble, and the people ignored her as they moved and pushed around her, trying to get a better view of the oncoming parade.

Without a second thought, Bayr swung from his branch and dropped into the fray, shoving people aside in order to help the old woman to her feet before she was trampled. She felt frail to him beneath her cloak, but she rose with an agility that belied her age. She clutched at her hood, her hands covered in fingerless wool mittens, though the day was too warm for such attire. Bayr was shorter than she, and though she tried to shield her face, he had only to look up to see what she tried to keep hidden.

She was human—eyes, nose, mouth, smooth cheeks, and an unlined brow—but otherworldly, and Bayr was too young to know he shouldn't stare and too innocent to ignore her strangeness. She was not old, and her oddity was not in the formulation of her features, but in the complete absence of pigmentation from her eyes, skin, and hair. She was whiter than goat's milk. Whiter than the clouds that hovered over the peaks between Joran and Leok, whiter than the snow in winter, whiter even than the death that had settled on King Ansel's face in the sanctum.

The woman touched Bayr's shoulder, and her lips—the only color in her face—murmured her thanks. Bayr understood the word, but he could not place her accent. The clans all had their own variations of tone and speech that made a man from Adyar in the north sound slightly different from a man from Ebba in the south, but the woman didn't sound like she'd been raised in any of the clans.

Then he saw the tears on her face, the agony that twisted her otherwise regular features into grief's grimace.

"A-are y-you h-hurt?" he stammered.

"No," she said with a brief shake of her head, but her silver eyes had risen to the passing king. The crowd genuflected, clearing the view in rippling waves, and the woman began to tremble so violently, Bayr thought she might fall once more. The hair rose on his neck, and the people around them began to fidget and turn, sensing her distress. Unease rippled around her like a gathering storm, a disturbance in the air, felt but not seen.

The black horse carrying King Banruud suddenly shrieked and reared, and the crowd echoed the sound, collectively pulling back and cowering before the pawing hooves of the wild-eyed destrier. The king kept his seat, clinging to the flying mane, gripping the horse between powerful thighs, but he was not the only one in danger of being thrown. The once-docile white horse draped in red, pulling the carriage of the queen, suddenly rose on his hind legs, bucking and twisting in crazed contortions. The crowd gasped as the driver was tossed from his seat, hurtling into the screaming crowd.

The queen sat in the rear of the carriage, and though she was thrown to the floor, she managed to cling to her child and the side of the carriage. Beside Bayr, the white woman groaned, her agony becoming horror, and her distress was echoed throughout the crush. The white horse reared again, the carriage teetered wildly, and the crowd cried out once more. Bayr pushed his way through the flinching onlookers and rushed into the street, planting his legs and waiting for the white horse to thunder past him.

He heard Dagmar shout his name from somewhere in the distance, but his focus was centered on the careening carriage. He threw himself at the bolting horse, curling his hands into its mane and swinging himself onto the creature's back. Digging his small knees into the horse's withers, he gritted his teeth and bore down on the mane. The horse shrieked again, pawing the air in pain and desperation, his head folded back into Bayr's chest.

"Whoa," Bayr demanded. "Shh," he soothed, and the horse, quaking and chuffing, his eyes rolling back in his head, came to a complete halt. The crowd cheered, and the horse trembled, but he didn't lurch or bolt.

The parade came to a standstill, the keepers holding their formation in pious dismay, the crowd frozen in fear and fascination. The chieftains, still bearing the flags of the clans, looked on with incredulous grins, though their smirks faded when they saw the Lady Queen. Blood seeped from a gash at her hairline, but she rose under her own power, her wailing infant daughter clutched in her arms, and was helped from the carriage by the king's shamefaced guard. There would surely be a reckoning, though none of them were to blame. It was the white woman's fault, he was certain, though he could not say why.

Bayr thought he saw Dagmar racing toward him, but the king demanded his attention.

"What is your name, boy?" Banruud asked, lifting his voice for the sake of the crowd. He'd brought his own horse to heel and seemed cross that the carriage driver had not been able to do the same. His procession had suddenly become a fiasco, and he was no longer the center of attention.

Bayr tried to answer, but the word clung to his tongue. He tried again, stammering pitifully, and hung his head in embarrassment.

"His name is Bayr, Sire." Dagmar lifted his arms to pull Bayr from the back of the white mount, but Bayr clung to the horse's mane, afraid to release him for fear he would bolt again.

"Release the horse, Bayr. You're hurting him," Dagmar insisted, and Bayr, surprised, loosened his arms. The horse wilted, hanging his head in dizzy relief, and Dagmar pulled the boy from his shuddering back, clutching him to his side. The king watched with glittering eyes and frowning lips.

"Dagmar of Dolphys. It has been too long," Banruud boomed. "Or must I call you Keeper Dagmar?"

Dagmar bowed deeply.

"A dozen years, Sire. At least. Congratulations." He didn't remind the new king that he'd stood in the sanctum during the selection process, that he'd taken part in the coronation, and that he'd borne witness to the blessing of his daughter. He'd purposely hung back. Blended in. Averted his eyes. In his purple robes with his shaved head, standing among brothers similarly adorned, he was easy to overlook, and Banruud had clearly not noticed him until now.

The king reined his horse around and approached Bayr and his uncle, who watched his advance with shared trepidation.

"Bayr. It is a good name," the king said, nodding to Bayr. "You have shown great skill . . . and courage." The king's jaw was tight, and his nostrils flared like those of a beast catching the scent of his prey.

"The Temple Boy has saved the princess and the Lady Queen!" someone shouted, and *Temple Boy, Temple Boy, Temple Boy* rippled among the horde, reaching those who had not seen the events unfold.

The king unsheathed his sword and, playing to the crowd, laid the broad side of his blade on the boy's bowed head. Dagmar flinched, but Bayr remained still, silent, subservient.

"I dub thee a protector of the throne and a friend of the king, young Bayr."

The crowd roared again in a new wave of wonder. Bayr shrank back into Dagmar, embarrassed by the adulation, and King Banruud withdrew his blade. The king turned away and raised his sword, and with a blast of the trumpet, the procession continued without the queen, who, along with the princess, was being escorted back to the castle in a cart pulled by men and surrounded by an armed guard.

"I th-thought h-he was going to k-kill m-m-me," Bayr stammered, turning to his uncle with wide eyes.

Dagmar shuddered and said nothing, but his silence reinforced Bayr's conviction: the king did not like him.

"The p-p-pale w-woman s-scared the h-h-horses," Bayr whispered, badly shaken.

"What woman?" Dagmar replied.

Bayr shook his head and shrugged. It was too hard to explain, and he didn't want to get the woman in trouble. The king wouldn't like her either, Bayr was certain of it.

"I fear that we have placed a masked man on the throne," Ivo grumbled, after asking Dagmar to remain when everyone else had left the sanctum. It had been several weeks since the coronation, and Temple Hill had been a flurry of activity. A new king meant new policies, new rules, new discomforts. Banruud was preparing for war, with whom no one knew, and his warriors were in constant training, making worship and reflection on the adjacent grounds much more difficult. Banruud had very little interest in the keepers—or the temple—though he'd sought Ivo's company once to query the gods. He'd been having bad dreams.

"He has a fear of ghosts, of pale wraiths stealing his soul . . . and his daughter," Ivo revealed. "He has his men on the lookout for phantoms. I told him the gods have assigned the princess a protector in young Bayr. The king did not seem to like that response. He has demanded a sacrifice be made to Odin and runes hidden over every door."

"What do you mean, a masked man, Master?" Dagmar asked.

"Banruud is two men. One you see, and one you don't. If you loosened his braid, I suspect you might see another face, hiding beneath his hair."

Dagmar shivered at the image that rose behind his eyes. Ivo had a flair for the dramatic.

"I don't understand, Master. He was a good chieftain. Berne is wealthy. His people have not registered complaint. He is a powerful warrior and a worthy leader."

"This is all true. And yet . . . our duty has never been to embrace the obvious . . . or the easy. I fear we have done both."

"Master—" Dagmar protested, his guilt doubling the size of his chest.

Ivo waved his hand, silencing him. "Enough, Dagmar. You were not wrong. You love the boy. And you chose for him, not for me. Not for yourself. Not even for Saylok."

Dagmar's guilt grew another head. "Saylok needs a man on the throne, Master. Not a boy," he argued, weary. He had made the argument more times than he cared to.

"Better a boy than a beast." Ivo sighed, a petulant ruffling of feathers. "But it is done. And we must make the best of it."

"Do you truly think he is a beast?" Dagmar whispered.

"If Father Saylok had wanted only one man to choose the king, he would have appointed only one keeper. Our system has worked for centuries, and I trust it will continue to work, regardless of my distrust of—and distaste for—the new king," Ivo said, relenting.

"And the girl child?"

Ivo huffed, but his ruffled feathers settled as a rueful grin twisted his black lips. "She is a wonder. I have great hopes for little Alba."

"As do I, Master," Dagmar agreed. His hope had had him kneeling for hours in supplication.

"The king would do well to heed my advice," Ivo mused.

"Oh?"

"He should keep the boy close," Ivo said.

"I would rather he not."

"You speak selfishly, Dagmar. Bayr is a guardian."

"Bayr is Banruud's son," Dagmar whispered, trying not to hiss.

"And a threat to his power," Ivo said, nodding. "Banruud is jealous of the boy. But still . . . the king should heed my counsel, for the sake of the princess. The boy will not fail her. He will protect the girl child. I have seen it."

Dagmar's hands shook beneath the wide sleeves of his robe, and he folded them together. He did not want to know all that Ivo had seen.

Sometimes visions made a keeper blind to intuition. Dagmar's intuition screamed that Bayr should stay far away from Banruud.

"Was there something else you wished to tell me, Master?" he asked, desperate to leave the sanctum. The day had been long, and he hadn't seen Bayr since dawn.

"You have not seen any pale-faced wraiths . . . in your dreams or otherwise, have you, Dagmar?"

Dagmar didn't believe in ghosts. Surely the gods called all spirits home. Briefly he considered the woman Bayr had seen on coronation day, and then dismissed her with a mental shrug. It was not a crime to be pale-skinned, and she was a woman, not a wraith.

"No, Master," Dagmar said, sighing. "I have not."

"Hmm." Ivo rubbed his stained lips. "You must tell me if you do."

൭

Ghost was weary, and her breasts ached. She'd bound them tightly to keep them from filling with milk, but the liquid seeped out and soaked the rags she'd wrapped around her chest, chilling her beneath her cloak. She expressed the milk by hand when she could, needing to maintain her flow. Her baby would need milk if ever they were reunited. Unfortunately, her scent, ripe and loamy, drew the bugs.

It was spring, and the rains were frequent, soaking the Temple Wood and making her circumstances even more difficult. She'd been a shepherd and was accustomed to sleeping outdoors, to scavenging and hunting, but she was not accustomed to patrols. The king's guard traipsed through the forest and over the hillside as though they sought her. She'd discovered a crawl space in a small outcropping of rocks that provided a place to hide whenever they were close. She'd had to coax a family of field mice to find a new place to live, but mice and bugs were the least of her worries.

Everything she'd owned had been in Bertog's house in the land of Berne, and Bertog's house had been burned to the ground. She'd acquired a few things in the King's Village—a sharp knife, a cake of soap, a length of rope, and another dress—but people stared when she made her purchases, and that terrified her most of all. The shopkeepers would remember her face if someone asked about her.

She had an iron pot and a small box filled with gold coins that she'd dug up from the charred remains of Bertog's house. Bertog had been good with money. He collected favors the way his wife gathered eggs—gleefully, greedily, noting their size and their weight. Even the despicable Balfor had been in his debt. Bertog had kept his gold in a hole beneath his floor, but in the end, the gods—and Ghost—had owed him nothing. Ghost had seen Bertog count his gold. She'd seen him stash it too. When Balfor burned the house down, the box of coins—and the iron pot—had escaped unscathed.

Bertog and Linora had not been so lucky.

Ghost felt no sadness for them. They had been foolish to trust the chieftain. She'd been foolish to trust them. Now they were dead, and her child was gone.

Chief Banruud had stolen her daughter. He had claimed Alba as his own, he and his smiling, lying queen. And Ghost had no recourse. The knowledge filled her with helpless rage.

She had followed him from his keep, trailed his caravan like a beggar gathering scraps, walking in a sort of stupor from the valley of Berne to the rising plateau of the temple mount. It was beautiful, the soaring palace heights and the jagged temple spires, but she'd seen only the walls and the warriors and the distance from her child.

She had enough gold in Bertog's box to run away, enough to make her life bearable for a while if she was careful. She had hidden it in the cradle of the tree, where the heavy branches left the trunk and spread outward. But she had nowhere to go and she could not leave. If she managed to reach her child, to steal inside the palace walls, she and the child would not get far. She could not escape her cursed skin. She could not hide a babe in the woods. So she haunted the hills in hopes that for once in her life the gods would be merciful and return what was hers. Or at the very least, let her slay the king.

∽

Ghost saw that the Temple Boy, the one who'd calmed the horse, had been assigned to watch the sacrificial sheep. The old keeper who'd guarded them since she'd arrived had developed a hacking cough during the spring rains, and the boy had taken over his duties. He was a natural, keeping the herd together and happily circling the perimeter, watching for wolves and other dangers.

He'd sensed her.

Ghost had seen it in the furrow that marred his smooth brow. The sheep had sensed her too. She had that effect on animals. She always had. Often her affinity was of great benefit. Other times, like the day of the parade, she drove them mad. She hadn't meant to spook the horses in the processional. At least not the horse that pulled the carriage. She'd been so angry—so desperately sad—and her turmoil had set them off. The king had not been harmed, but the carriage had almost overturned. Ghost had run away, terrified by the danger she'd put her daughter in, and she'd hid among the trees until the sun had set and her tears had dried.

Since then, she'd watched the boy who'd been kind to her, the boy who now herded the temple sheep, hoping his access to the palace and the temple grounds would provide her an opportunity to creep inside. He was just a child, yet he moved like a man and cared for the sheep with quiet confidence. He was not like other boys, and she studied him with growing fascination.

He didn't sleep in the fields but herded the sheep inside the gates when the sun began to sink behind the palace spires. Each day he brought them out again, though often it was not until the sun was high in the sky. One day he brought a small book to read as the sheep grazed, and she wondered if he had lessons that kept him occupied in the morning hours.

Her chance came as chances do, suddenly and simply. A pregnant ewe, stubborn and stupid—there was always at least one—had wandered off and fallen into a thicket. She'd broken her leg, and she bleated piteously, calling to her young shepherd. Her cries echoed through the trees and over the hillside, and Ghost, lured from one of her hiding places, was tempted to cut her throat to end her misery. But Ghost hung back, not wanting to risk being seen, and watched as the boy made his way to the sheep. She wondered if he would have the skill and stomach to kill the wounded animal. It was an unpleasant task for one so young.

He sat back for a moment, hands on his thighs, head bowed in thought. Then, as though the sheep weighed no more than an unwieldy bag of grain, he scooped her up and slung her across his shoulders.

The sheep bellowed, and Ghost gaped, stunned at the boy's strength. The pregnant ewe had to outweigh him by five stone, if not more. It was almost comical, the braying beast with her spindly legs nearly brushing the ground, draped across a back that should not have been able to hoist such a burden. Yet the boy carried the sheep with a steady tread, singing an odd chant Ghost had often heard echoing from inside the temple walls. The ewe would have to be put down, but the boy clearly was unwilling to leave her.

Evidently, he was unwilling to leave any of them, and he began to gather the grazing herd, walking the perimeter, tightening the circle. He drove the flock up the hill toward the east gate, barking and pushing, urging them onward. And all the while he carried the injured sheep. Ghost hovered at the tree line, inching up the hill behind him, watching his progress with fascination.

It took him two hours, trotting to and fro to keep the herd moving in the right direction, before he finally rang the bell on the eastern

94

gate. The day was waning, he was drenched in sweat, but every sheep was accounted for. The dissonant clanging brought the watchman to the tower.

"Open the gate," the watchman bellowed, seeing the boy with his staggering burden. Nothing happened, and the watchman bellowed again, clearly perturbed.

"Hold on, boy. I'll raise it myself."

Ghost didn't stop to think or consider. She simply ran, flying up the rise from the little copse of trees a hundred yards from the east entrance. No one cried out from the wall, no horns bugled in alert. The Temple Boy, his view obscured by the animal draped across his shoulders, did not turn toward her. She would simply walk through the gate with the flock. If anyone saw her, she would appear to be helping him.

But no one saw her.

She brought up the rear, eyes down, trying not to pant and alert the boy. She swatted a woolly tail, willing the beasts to obey, to stay close, and to give her cover, and she strolled through the east gate as though she had every right to do so. No one stopped her—there wasn't another soul in sight—and when the last bleating animal trotted past her, she simply veered off into the shadows to await the darkness.

8

The queen had a beautiful voice. It carried across the mount on fairy wings, light and lilting, and Bayr sat atop the garden wall, listening, with his eyes on the stars. Baby Alba was whimpering—sometimes she cried in the night. Dagmar said Bayr had done the same when he was small, crying for no apparent reason, needing comfort and warmth and a gentle touch. The queen walked with the baby, patting her tiny back and singing songs that quieted the entire castle and drew lonely ears.

The night was temperate and the gardens fragrant, and ofttimes the queen wove her way around rosebushes, plucking petals as soft as her baby's cheeks, and Bayr would watch, wishing he could hold the child, wishing he could be held.

Dagmar had made him scrub in the cold iron tub. The weight and the woolly coat of the injured ewe had irritated his neck and rubbed him raw beneath his rough jerkin. The cold water had soothed the sting, but his heart was heavy, dragging his thoughts to lowly places, and he'd crept out of his bed and made his way up the wall. Now he sat, watching the queen and her infant daughter.

She was kind, the queen. It wasn't hard to see. She was soft where the king was hard, a light against his darkness, and the boy was quite bewitched by her.

"I see you there, Temple Boy," she called out, her voice a singsong croon. "If you can climb the garden wall, you can surely climb down and join us. I've been wanting to thank you for some time."

Bayr's pulse quickened and he considered slipping away, back to his room beneath the eaves. Instead he abandoned his poor hiding place and dropped down into the garden. He sidled to the queen's side, his eyes shifting between his feet and the infant in her arms.

"Your name is Bayr . . . Is that right?"

He nodded, grateful he needn't reply.

"You saved us . . . little Alba and me. In the procession. You were very brave and so skilled." The queen set her hand on his shoulder, anointing him with her thanks, and he shifted closer, drawn to her touch. The baby in her arms cooed and reached for his hair, tangling her tiny fist in the unbound black mass. Dagmar had not plaited it after his bath, and it had dried in unruly waves. Bayr laughed, stepping even closer, allowing her better access.

"Would you like to hold her?" the queen asked.

Bayr gasped and tried to withdraw, but the girl child squalled, refusing to relinquish his hair, and he froze midstep.

"I c-c-can't," he breathed, though he would have liked nothing more.

"If you can calm a crazed horse, you can hold a baby girl," the queen insisted gently.

Bayr lifted his eyes to the infant, and she smiled in delight, kicking her tiny legs.

"Sh-she s-smiled," he stammered, forgetting his fear.

"Yes. She smiles often. She is a happy child, most of the time. The nights make her restless . . . or maybe she just likes to come to the gardens. It is our favorite place."

Bayr held out his arms as though preparing to receive a bundle of sticks. Queen Alannah laughed and, with one hand beneath Alba's bottom and one hand beneath her right arm, brought the two children chest to chest. Instinctively, Bayr enfolded the babe, taking her weight against him and notching her downy head beneath his chin.

"See? You know what to do," the queen crowed. Bayr's cheeks flushed with pride and his eyes found the queen's before drifting down in bashful ebullience, but he didn't relinquish the baby.

"Would you like to walk with her?" the queen asked.

Bayr twitched in agreement and stepped forward with a tentative tread, moving as though he traversed a broken bridge suspended above a bottomless pit. The queen laughed again but inched along beside him.

"Master Ivo tells me you are blessed by the gods. He says you are Alba's protector. I feel very safe when you are near," she said quietly.

Bayr could only nod, his arms tightening on the princess in his arms.

The queen did not seem to mind that he did not converse, and they crawled along the petal-strewn paths, the queen softly singing, Bayr barely breathing.

The babe became boneless in his arms, her sweet breath tickling his throat, and before long, her hand fell from his hair.

"Alba feels safe with you too, young Bayr."

"I l-love h-her," he whispered. He hadn't meant to speak, but the queen didn't laugh at him. She only smiled, and her eyes shimmered down at him.

"I love her too. So very much," she said.

"I m-must g-g-go," Bayr said. He didn't want to. But Dagmar would check on him. He always did, and he would worry if Bayr was not in his bed.

"You will visit us again, won't you?" Queen Alannah asked.

He nodded, the joy in his chest stealing his breath. The queen kissed his cheek and slid her arms beneath the sleeping child. Bayr relinquished her with a whispered goodbye, and without another word loped toward the far wall. He scrambled up it, feeling the queen's gaze on his shoulders and the phantom weight of a sleeping princess in his arms. He thought he caught a shiver of white on the far side of the garden, but it must have been a trick of the moon, a glimmer of stars upon the garden stream, for when he looked all was still, all was dark, and nothing was there.

Ghost had fallen asleep in the palace gardens between the rosebushes and the southern wall. It had been cool and fragrant, and her belly was full. She'd raided the turnip patch and pocketed as many carrots as she could swiftly pull before ducking behind the greenery. The carrots were delicious, though the soil clung to their sunset flesh. Her hands had been even dirtier than the vegetables, but beggars—and thieves—could not be too fastidious or impatient. She had no plan, only purpose, and she'd waited for hours, hiding behind riotous blossoms, listening to the sounds of the castle yard, and resisting introspection. Avoiding despondency had made her drowsy.

Night had fallen while she slept, the darkness deepening from purple to black, from sunset to starlight. The soft cry of a child had pulled her from her dreams, and her body had reacted, sending milk to her glands and soaking the front of her dress. She had clutched her chest, remembering where she was, remembering her purpose, and she'd pushed the prickly vines aside, peering out from the shadows.

The rising moon cast the queen and the babe in a reverent glow, and Ghost tightened her hand around her knife, not realizing she held it by the blade and not the handle. The tickle of warmth beneath her sleeve, not the pain, was what alerted her to her mistake. Since her child had been taken, she'd been wracked by an agony so great, the sting of the knife did not register at all.

Her mouth moved around Alba's name, and she drank her in, remembering the tired cry and the flailing fists, the silk of her hair and the creamy scent of her warm, wrinkled skin. Being so close to her child, so close to salvation, drew the tears from her eyes, and she prayed to Freya to guide her steps and direct her blade.

She would kill the queen and retrieve her child. The gods had provided a way and delivered them both into her hands.

But the Temple Boy was watching too. The queen had called out to him, so Ghost had bided her time, listening, stretched behind the roses in her mud-colored cloak, waiting for her moment. They made a lovely picture, the three of them, traipsing through the garden, and Ghost had become lulled by the scene, entranced by the queen's song and quieted by the moon-drenched sky.

The Temple Boy—Bayr—had come and gone. He too had been caught in the queen's spell. He had held Ghost's child, his young face shining with adoration. Alba was so loved. So wanted. So revered. And the knowledge had filled Ghost with joy and hope.

Then the moon moved behind the clouds and the enchantment was broken. Hope became horror, joy became realization. The gods had not delivered the queen into her hands. They had shown her all the things she wasn't, all the things she couldn't give, and they had said, "Disappear, little ghost. Go away. Give us the babe. She belongs to us." And when the moon peeked out again to see if she'd heard, the beams of light revealed a hatch near the base of the south garden wall, wooden and welcoming, and slightly ajar.

"Disappear, little ghost. Go away," the gods whispered once more. They'd even provided a way out. The roses had brushed her skin, biting her with their thorns, forcing her out from among them and closing in like brambles behind her.

"Run away," they whispered. And she did.

It was much harder to get inside the walls than it was to get out. The garden hatch opened onto a flight of rough-hewn steps leading down to an earthen tunnel that eventually led her onto the heath far beyond the wall. The exit was so narrow a man would struggle to use it for escape, and it was concealed by grass and boulders and half covered by bushes that harbored all manner of creatures. The creatures urged her to flee as well.

Ghost raced across the moor, blood streaming from one hand, her knife clenched in the other, seeking the refuge of the forest, drawn to the tree where she had hidden her coins, to the place where the grass curled in ragged tufts, sprouting around shapes in the soil. A small stone was placed beneath the tree, too perfect and smooth to be coincidence, and she wondered if it marked a grave. Mayhaps it could mark her own. She had a knife. And she was brave. But she was not brave enough.

She collapsed beneath the boughs, hiding her face in her arms. She didn't want to live, but she was too tired to die. She was hot and cold, rage and resignation, but she'd made a choice. Alba could be a princess instead of a slave, a daughter of a queen instead of the offspring of a ghost. She would never look on her mother and see a monster or an aberration.

"I have nothing to give," she moaned, her face pressed to the earth. "I have nothing but love, and my love will not shelter. My love will not save, or clothe, or feed. My love will only harm."

She had hate—bitter and biting. She hated the king and she hated his queen. She hated the moon and the moor and the innocent door in the wall that should not have been so easy to find. She hated the burn in her heart and the faith she couldn't shake, even though life had never given her reason to hope. She hated the people of Saylok for bowing to a king who lied to them.

But her hate was no match for her love.

"I have nothing to give you," she moaned again, and this time she spoke to the child she'd borne, the child who'd grown in her body and reshaped her heart.

"So I will give you a queen. I will give you a beautiful queen who sings to you," she wept. "I will give you a father who rules a kingdom, and a boy to watch over you. I will give you a life without hiding, a world without fear, a home I cannot give you on my own. This is what

I will give you—the only thing I *can* give you. A life without me in it is the only thing I have to offer."

She ran her palm across the stone and closed her eyes, too tired to move, too weary to care that someone might find her when the sun rose. And then she slept, hoping she would never wake.

She lay facedown beneath Desdemona's tree, a rumpled brown cloak without form or features. At first Dagmar thought she was dead, an old soul who had sought solitude in the forest to meet her end. He knew immediately she was female. The white hair was loose and unplaited— the hair of a woman, not a warrior. He formed the star upon his brow and called out in warning, as much for her sake as his own, but she didn't move. No scent of death surrounded her, no blood stained her cloak, and when he rolled her to her side, he felt the warmth of life beneath his hands. Dirty streaks lined her cheeks, and the silvery brooms of her lashes made no headway in the grime. He realized she wasn't old at all, but she was clearly in trouble.

Her eyes fluttered open and he hissed, startled, and stumbled back.

She didn't scramble upright or scamper away, as he expected her to. Maybe she couldn't, but her eyes tracked him without interest or fear, as though she were resigned to whatever fate had in store. She gazed at him wearily for several seconds before closing them again, hiding her luminescent orbs under blue-veined lids.

"Are you wounded?" he asked.

She didn't respond, but she didn't appear to be in pain.

"If I help you sit, can you drink?"

She opened her eyes again, and he took her interest for assent.

He approached her once more and pulled his water flask from around his neck. Kneeling beside her, he slipped his arm beneath her shoulders, and propped her against him so she could drink. She didn't pull away or protest, and when he held the flask to her dry lips, she drank thankfully.

Was this the creature Ivo had spoken of? She was not a wraith, nor a specter, but she was frightening to behold. And she was thirsty.

"Who are you?" he asked. "Where have you come from?"

"Who are you?" she whispered, her voice as colorless as her skin.

"I am a Keeper of Saylok. I live in the temple."

"I am a ghost, and I live beneath this tree," she rasped, the words clear but oddly pronounced.

He frowned down at her, convinced Loki—or Master Ivo—was playing tricks on him. But the girl was not a vision or an apparition. Her flesh was real beneath his hands, and his water flask was completely empty.

"I am not the only one living beneath this tree. There is someone buried here. See this stone?" The girl touched Desdemona's marker. "It is a good place to die."

"My sister lies beneath this tree. That is her stone, and it was not a peaceful death," he contended.

She stared up at him, solemn, compassion in her gaze.

"Is that why you are here? To die?" he pressed. He did not want to think about Desdemona.

Her eyes closed again, and her slight form trembled against him. "It is what I wish."

"Why?"

She dropped her gaze and pulled the hood of her cloak over her head. Her pale nose, smudged with dirt and protruding from draped folds, was the only part of her face he could see.

"If you truly wanted to die, you wouldn't have drunk all my water," he said mildly.

"Mayhaps my body wants to live," she whispered. "But I do not."

"The will is a stubborn taskmaster," he agreed. "But if you aren't going to die, there are better places to live."

"Once I was bound to a tree like this. A great, beautiful tree," she murmured.

He wasn't sure he'd heard her correctly. Though her words were slightly slurred, she didn't appear to be sick or injured. Hungry, dirty, and tired. But not injured.

"You were bound to a tree?" he asked.

"Yes. The people wanted to give me to the gods. But the gods did not want me, and the animals did not hurt me. After three days the chieftain's wife untied me and put me back to work."

They did the same in Dolphys, in the Clan of the Wolf, though it was not a sacrifice to the gods but part of selecting a new chieftain. It was believed the wolves would not eat one of their own. Dagmar thought it ridiculous. Wolves, like men, were more prone to survival than loyalty.

"It was in Fiend. Do you know it?" she mumbled. She sounded so tired.

"Do you mean Fiend . . . in Eastlandia?" Dagmar gasped.

"Yes," she whispered. "Eastlandia."

"And . . . how did you find yourself here . . . in the Temple Wood?"

"I came to be a wife but remained a slave. And now, I am nothing."

"You are no longer a slave?"

"I have no master."

"I see," Dagmar breathed. He knew of the raiding in villages across the sea. He knew of the trading for women and children—mostly girls—to combat the years of female drought. This girl was clearly a victim of such practices.

"But why are you . . . here?" He had not heard of an influx of females in the King's Village. The clans who carried out the raids kept their bounty.

"Did you come from Berne?" he asked. "Did you come with the king?"

He saw the small tremor that she quickly suppressed. It was answer enough. His thoughts turned to Master Ivo's musings, to the king's dreams, and to the woman Bayr had seen at the parade. Of course, this was she. Dagmar's palms grew cold, and he reached for the knife at his waist.

"Did you see the king's procession?" he asked. The woman trembled again, and she drew her knees into her chest. "My boy told me about you. He believes you caused the horses to bolt. He doesn't know how . . . but he believes it all the same. He was frightened."

"I did not mean to. Horses are very sensitive to fear and . . . anger," she whispered.

"Sensitive to *your* fear and anger?" he asked, not breathing.

She offered a small affirmative jerk of her hooded head.

"Why were you afraid? Why were you . . . angry?"

"I lost a child . . . not so long ago. Seeing the . . . princess . . . was very difficult for me."

Dagmar pondered this for a moment, his eyes on Desdemona's stone. Odd how this tree attracted the desperate and discarded. Odd how he always seemed to find them. How they always seemed to find him. Still, he could not help this woman if he did not trust her.

"Will you give me your hand?" he asked. He hoped he would not have to force her.

She lifted her chin, her hood falling away from her questioning eyes. Slowly she withdrew her hand from the sleeves of her cloak and held it out to him. Her eyes were as bleak as the tale she'd spun, and a long gash bisected her palm. He would not need to cut her anew. She didn't flinch when she saw his knife or even ask his intentions. She simply watched as he reopened her wound.

Dagmar turned her bloodied palm and pressed it to the earth near Desdemona's runes. He had tried to dig them up, to burn them, to remove them with counteracting runes of his own. But they remained like hoofprints baked into stone, and he could not smooth them out. The grass grew in patches and whorls around the carvings, obscuring them from view, but to his eyes, they were as plain as the stone that marked his sister's resting place.

"Are you here to harm the girl child?" he asked.

The girl shook her head, vehement. "Never."

"Are you here to take her from Saylok?" he added, remembering Banruud's dreams.

Her gray eyes filled and shimmered like glass, and the denial from her lips was a broken shard. "No," she whispered.

With the tip of his finger, he drew a simple rune of truth upon her palm, mixing the blood and the soil and watching as both cleaved to the lifeline that ran from her wrist to her fingers.

She was not lying to him. He released the girl's hand and she let it fall, not bothering to wipe it clean or tend to her reopened wound.

Dagmar stood and extended a hand to help her rise.

"Come with me."

"I do not wish to lie with you," she muttered.

He flinched.

"My body is sore," she continued. "And I am tired. But I have a piece of gold I will give you if you will leave me alone."

If he'd wanted to lie with her, he could have stolen her gold and still taken her body, but he admired her resilience. He'd never lain with a woman, and he didn't intend to now, though his body had tightened with alarming interest. He sighed, disappointed in his flesh, and extended his hand again, insistent.

"I do not wish to lie with you either and would never ask it of you. I wish to help you. That is all," he said.

She gazed up at him, and he thought for a moment she would deny him again. Then her shoulders drooped, her chin fell, and Dagmar realized that she didn't have the energy to do as he demanded. Crouching, he swept her up in his arms and, praying for a measure of Bayr's strength, began the trek to the abandoned shepherd's cottage on the western slope of Temple Hill.

9

The man who called himself a keeper carried her until she found the will to walk. He was surprisingly strong, but after a while she felt his arms tremble and his breath grow labored, and she knew she could not continue to lie in his arms, wishing the end would come. The end was not going to come—not without her hastening it—and the man was not going to leave her alone.

His blue eyes were pale—his resemblance to the Temple Boy was marked—but the shadows on his jaw and on the dome of his head were black. She'd seen the hairless priests in their purple robes walking behind the king with measured gaits and clasped hands, but hairlessness was clearly easier for some than others. She was tempted to run her hand across the spiky growth to see if the bristles were soft or sharp.

"I will walk, Keeper," she whispered. "If I don't, we will both fall."

"It is not much farther," he murmured.

She arched her back like an angry child, and he immediately released her legs, letting her feet find purchase on the uneven ground. She tried to take a step and swayed. He wrapped an arm around her waist and continued forward, assisting her with every stride. When she was convinced she couldn't go a step farther, he lifted her again and walked the remaining distance with her in his arms.

The cottage was built into a cliff, more hovel than home, but to Ghost it meant shelter and the end of a journey, and her eyes clung to the small window and the closed door. Upon closer inspection, it looked sturdier than it first had, and herbs in clay pots lined the wall beneath the window.

"This is the shepherd's cottage," the keeper explained, setting her on her feet.

"I used to herd sheep," she volunteered weakly. "Is it yours?"

"It belongs to the brotherhood."

"But not to a particular . . . brother?" She was so weary, and she hoped she would not be faced with a houseful of curious faces and questions.

"There is no one here anymore. Keeper Lem, who watched the sheep, lived here when the sheep grazed in the western meadows. It was too far to move them back to the temple grounds each day. But Lem is ill and old, and his days with the sheep are done," the keeper said and pushed through the front door with complete confidence, helping Ghost across the threshold.

A straw mattress on a wooden frame was pushed against the wall, and Ghost stumbled toward it, too spent to do anything but wilt across it. She could hear the keeper moving around the small space and sometime later felt him roll her toward him. When she protested weakly, he reassured her with soft words.

"I am going to tend to your palm."

She didn't nod, but she didn't fight him either. The water was cold and the wet cloth soothing, and when he was finished rinsing the blood and dirt from her hands, he wrung out the cloth and washed her face. Ghost jerked and ducked her chin, willing him to stop.

"Shh. Surely you know I will not hurt you," he chided, wetting the cloth once more.

But he *was* hurting her. His kindness was like salt on raw skin. It would have been less painful if he'd struck her, and humiliating tears trickled down her cheeks and slipped between her lips. They were salty too, and the keeper sighed as he wiped them away.

"I will leave you here. There is water in the pail from a stream not too far from here and bread on the table. There's a bit of oil in the lamp and some kindling on the hearth. I've made you a small fire, but only for comfort. The day is warm."

She nodded but didn't open her eyes.

"I will come back tomorrow with supplies. We will talk then."

"Thank you," she mumbled, and listened for him to leave.

"What should I call you?" he asked.

"Ghost," she whispered, and let herself sink into oblivion.

She rose when dawn peeked through the crude window, lining the floor in thin strips of light. The keeper had not opened the makeshift wooden shutters, but the sun was a nosy stranger, and it found its way inside.

She filled the tin cup beside the pail three times before her thirst was quenched. She drank another cup after wolfing down the loaf of dry bread the keeper had left for her. The fire had gone out, but the sun was sufficient to warm the small room, and Ghost opened the shutters and acquainted herself with her surroundings.

She felt oddly restored, as if tears and tender ministrations had stitched some of her broken pieces back together. The stitches were loose, and her soul was still battered, but she no longer wished to cover herself in earth and cease breathing.

A wooden barrel, a table, two stools, three shelves, and a small pine chest were the only furnishings in the cottage, but there wasn't room for much more. A blackened pot and a matching kettle sat empty on the simple hearth. Two wooden spoons sat nearby, and a bowl and a plate matched the tin cup she'd used upon awakening. Another pail, two small lumps of soap, and an assortment of folded rags rested on a shelf. Two blankets, a needle and some thread, a small sack of meal, and a chamber pot completed the sparse living space.

She found a broom fashioned from sticks and straw propped against the chest and swept the space clean, chasing out the spiders and destroying their handiwork.

A woven rug had been tightly rolled and shoved beneath the bed, apparently to keep it from collecting dust while the owner was gone. She dragged it outside into the sunshine, beat it until her shoulders ached, and lugged it back inside. It made the room immediately cozy, and Ghost smiled down at it only to grimace at her poorly shod feet. The cottage looked much better, but she looked worse. The state of her shoes could not easily be improved, but her dress, her cloak, her hair, and her hands were in dire need of a scrubbing.

With one of the pails and a bit of soap, she went in search of the stream. To her delight, someone or something had created a small dam in the stream big enough to form a pool for bathing. Without hesitation, she shucked her clothes, gritted her teeth, and submerged herself in the cold, clear water, dragging her dress down with her.

An hour later, her hair and her skin dripping, her thin dress a little thinner from the thorough scrubbing against the rocks, she climbed from the stream, donned her still-soiled cloak, and spread her dress and underthings over sun-warmed stones to dry. Then she headed back to the cottage with a pail of water in hand.

She had company, but it wasn't the keeper. It was the boy—Bayr— and when he saw her, he nodded and hoisted the bundle at his feet. It was almost bigger than he was and knotted in such a way that he could sling it over his shoulder.

"F-f-for y-you," he said, patting the bundle. His voice was low and pleasing, but he struggled to release his words. He followed her inside and eased the bundle back down beside the table, opening it without delay.

He pulled a blanket, an assortment of vegetables and dried meats, six apples, a pound of cheese, and several different spices from his pack. A loaf of bread was next, followed by a purple robe, two pairs of stockings, a plain white undershift, a skein of wool, a darning needle, a mirror, a brush for her hair, and a large flask.

He didn't speak as he set each thing aside, though she sensed he had a thousand questions. She was too overwhelmed by the bounty to do more than stare at each item, her stomach growling and her tongue dry.

She cut off a hunk of the bread with her knife and handed it to him, not knowing what to do or say to put them both at ease. He seemed hesitant to take it, but she insisted, leaving her hand outstretched until he took it from her fingers. In trade, he handed her the horn slung across his chest.

She took a deep pull of the water and handed it back. She had water in a pail and didn't need his flask, but he shook his head.

"Keep. F-f-for t-tending sh-sh-sheep."

She frowned, not understanding, but kept the flask.

"W-who who who—" He stopped and took a deep breath. "Who a-are . . . you?"

"No one," she muttered.

He wrinkled his nose at her response. He patted his chest. "Bayr."

"I know who you are. You are the Temple Boy."

He sighed as though he did not like the name. She did not like her name either.

He leaned toward her, tentative, clearly worried he would scare her. Then he touched her hand. "Why s-s-so wh-white?" he murmured.

"I don't know. I was born this way. Why are you so strong?"

"B-b-blessed?" He said it like he wasn't certain, and she laughed, charmed.

"You are blessed. I am cursed. And neither of us got to choose which."

"G-g-ghost?" he asked. The keeper must have told him her name, though the boy seemed doubtful about it.

"That is what I'm called," she said.

He wrinkled his nose again. "N-not name?"

"I don't really have a name. So I suppose Ghost is as good as any."

He looked frustrated, as though he wanted to press the issue further, but the exercise took too much effort.

"The keeper . . . Who is he?" she asked instead.

"M-my u-uncle."

"What is his name?"

The boy stuck his finger in soot from the night's fire and wrote a word across the smooth stones of the hearth.

"I cannot read," she murmured, biting her lip. He clearly wanted to write the word because speaking was difficult, but she couldn't decipher it.

"D-d-dag-m-mar," he said, wincing. He used the broom to brush the word away. She wished he hadn't. She would have liked to study the shapes he'd made.

"Dagmar?"

A nod.

"S-stay?" he asked, pointing where he stood. She didn't know if he was asking her for permission to remain or if he was asking her if she was going to go.

When she shrugged, he picked up his now-empty bundle.

"Stay," he demanded, and smiled, heading for the door. His smile touched his eyes and revealed strong white teeth. He was a handsome boy, his dark hair pulled back from a face that would grow leaner and longer with age. He would look like the keeper, but his size and strength already hinted at harsher lines and heavier limbs.

"Stay," he said again, and seemed pleased with himself that he'd said the word twice without tripping. She didn't think he meant to address her as if she were a dog, and she nodded, agreeing.

He smiled at her response, and he opened the door and let himself out. She wouldn't be able to stay, but she didn't think she was strong enough yet to go. A day or two in the shepherd's cottage would do her good. Just a day or two, and then she would leave. She needed to retrieve her gold, and if possible, say goodbye to her daughter.

⁊

"You collect strays, Dagmar."

"Yes, Master. I seem to."

Ivo sighed, but his mouth curled under his beaklike nose. "But the gods send them to you for a purpose."

"Mayhaps they send them to us, Master," Dagmar said, his voice mild, his eyes steely.

Ivo's lips grew tight at Dagmar's insolence, but his gaze dimmed as though he saw something that existed in another place. For several moments he sat in perfect stillness, and Dagmar waited, his head bowed.

"Mayhaps you are right, Dagmar. There will be more," Ivo muttered.

"More, Master?"

"More strays, brother. Tell me about the latest one."

"She is a slave with no master. From Eastlandia. A woman."

"And why is she here?"

"She came with the king's caravan . . . or followed them, most likely. She had a babe once, a child. I got the impression the child died. She is lost, Master. And I truly believe she has nowhere to go."

"She is a woman. We are men. Keepers. She cannot live among us. You know this, Dagmar."

"Keeper Lem cannot watch the sheep any longer. He is getting old, and it is too much for him. Bayr had taken over his duties, but he has other needs and . . ."

"It is not the best use of his time," Ivo finished.

"Yes, Master."

"So Odin, in his wisdom, has sent us someone to watch the sheep. The gods always seem to provide."

"That is what I was going to suggest, Master. She need not ever enter the temple in order to care for the sheep, and she has been a shepherdess before."

"What is her name?"

"She calls herself Ghost, Master. Her skin is colorless . . . her hair and eyes too."

Ivo's brows shot up as his black lips turned down. "I envisioned a wraith, and the gods sent me a ghost!" he cackled. "Odin is a clever weaver of dreams, is he not?"

"I have shown her the shepherd's cottage on the western slope, Master. She is weak and tired . . . and filthy. But those things can be remedied."

"See that she has what she needs. Keeper Gilchrist will allot a stipend for her upkeep and supplies."

"Thank you, Master."

"Dagmar?"

"Yes, Master?"

"Is she beautiful?"

Dagmar frowned, startled.

"I don't know, Master. She is . . . frightening. And dirty. And sad. But . . . she could be beautiful if . . . someone . . . loved her." Heat rose to Dagmar's cheeks. He wasn't sure where his answer had come from, but Ivo studied him as though the answer had not surprised him in the least.

"Just as long as . . . you . . . don't love her, Keeper."

Dagmar flushed again. He had no intention of loving her.

10

Bayr came awake with the melody of his mother in his head. Or mayhaps it was not his mother at all, but the queen, who sang lullabies to Alba the way his mother never had. And this melody was discordant and shrill; the queen's voice was lovely and sweet. He lay in his bed, trying to imagine the woman who had wielded a shield and a sword as well as any man, yet had died giving life to him. Dagmar said she was beautiful and brave, and he tried to imagine how such a woman would look.

The sound came again, but this time Bayr sat up in his bed. It was not a song but a cry, and not a woman's cry or an infant's, but the wail of surprise and the muffled thump of attack. He leaped from his bed, climbing up to the window without thought of weapons or even shoes. Nothing moved in the gardens beneath the queen's tower, and no lights flickered from the windows. There was *always* light shining from the gable between the nursery and the queen's quarters. Something was wrong.

He flitted over rooftops and danced from the ramparts to the ground, scaling the wall between the temple and the palace in a matter of seconds. Another cry and a sudden shout, and he was sprinting to the tower where Alba slept. He'd climbed the tower walls before, when the world slept, simply to see if he could. A toehold here, a swinging clasp of a ledge there, up the side with fingers curled and toes clinging, his eyes on the stones above his head and the window he needed to reach.

The queen cried out, Alba wailed, and Bayr's fingers tightened even as his left foot slipped and regripped. Then he was up and through the window, hurtling himself toward men who would make a woman scream in the night. Once inside, he felt the first man before he saw him, and crouched to miss his slicing blade. Bayr swung his arm upward and slammed his small fist into the thundering heart of the sword-wielding assailant. The man gurgled and Bayr grasped, filling his hands with the man's clothes and hurtling him over his head out the open window he'd just entered.

The man had dropped his blade. Bayr felt the cool bite of the metal against his bare toes as he slunk forward, trying to see who else crept down the corridor toward him. The sword was too long, too awkward for the length of Bayr's arms, and he simply stepped over it. He needed his hands free.

Alba cried, and the queen called for help, and he rushed toward their voices. Through the door to the right were the queen's chambers. To the left, the nursery, an ornate wooden cradle the centerpiece of the room. He'd seen it in his explorations. He could see it now, gilded, a bed fit for a princess. That's why they were here, the men who crept in the darkness. He'd known they would come. She was too precious to leave alone. She was the jewel of Saylok, the treasure of the clans, and someone had come for her.

Two men rushed him at once, slinking black shapes in the unlit corridor. He brought their heads together, a satisfying thunk that broke their noses and made their legs wobble, lowering them to his height. He did not think or mourn or even cringe at the crunch of bone or the spray of their blood over his face. Fisting his hands in their braids, he swung them around, dragging them across the floor and propelling them out the window to follow the flight of their recently departed companion. And then there were three more, spilling out of the queen's chamber. One dragged the queen by her hair, a knife at her throat, another held Alba by her feet like a chicken being prepared for slaughter.

The men laughed when they saw him, a blood-spattered child without a sword. The man without a hostage strode toward him, his hand clawed to grasp Bayr by his hair. Bayr simply crouched and gripped the sword still lying at his feet. With a bellow and a thrust, he ran the man through, the tip of the blade pointing to the man next in line.

The queen reached for Alba, who still dangled from the meaty fist of the third man. He moved toward the stairs, and the queen screamed and fought to follow. The man dragging the queen released her and came at Bayr wielding the same blade he'd held to her throat. Bayr shoved the man he'd just impaled forward even as he extracted the bloodied sword. He hurled it like a javelin, and it pierced the oncoming man's shoulder, causing his blade to skitter across the floor. Then Bayr was past him, throwing himself on the back of Alba's abductor as the queen lunged for the child.

Grasping the man by his ears, he wrenched his head to the right. He watched the man's eyes, now facing him, flicker out. The man crumpled as Bayr released him, and the queen sobbed Alba's name.

"She is not harmed. Only frightened . . . and angry," the queen reassured herself, running her palms over the squalling infant whose little arms and legs were flailing in outrage. Bayr stepped around her, his eyes on the remaining attacker, who clutched at the sword piercing his shoulder and staggered back, his eyes round with pain and disbelief. He raised one bloody hand in surrender, and Bayr stood guard over the queen, not sure of how to proceed now that the man was no longer a threat. A light bloomed in the stairwell, and the pounding of boots on stone echoed up the shaft. The king's guard had arrived, but the saving was done.

"You are covered with blood, Bayr," the queen whimpered, but she reached for him, one arm clamped around the baby, one hand gripping his.

Bayr looked down at the ill-shaped nightshirt he'd gone to bed in, his limbs sticking out from the hem and the bell-shaped sleeves. His bare feet were splattered in gore, the pale fabric striped in crimson. His eyelids were sticky, and he knew his face must have fared even worse.

Then the vestibule was filled with torchlight and warriors, their swords drawn, ready for a battle that had already been won. King Banruud brought up the rear, his face terrible in the flickering light.

"Who did this?" Banruud demanded, his eyes on the dead and the dying. His warriors seemed equally stunned.

Bayr tried to explain but his tongue weighed more than the stone altar, and he could not make it move. He gurgled impotently and hung his head in humiliation.

"Bayr saved us," the queen said, and clutched little Alba, who had already stopped crying, her dark, wet eyes clinging to the circle of big men and gleaming swords.

"Three men, Banruud. And he is just a boy," one warrior observed, disbelief twisting his lips. He had come with the king from Berne and was not accustomed to Bayr's abilities.

"There were more," Queen Alannah insisted.

"Where?" Banruud barked.

Bayr pointed at the window and the man who still cowered beside it, bleeding and begging for mercy. The doubtful warrior walked to the opening and looked down.

"There are three men piled below, Sire," the warrior exclaimed. The king moved to his side, peering into the gardens below.

"What is your clan?" King Banruud turned to the wounded man. The would-be captor tried to shrink away, but the motion made him sway.

"I have no clan," the man groaned.

"Who sent you?" Banruud roared.

"We came for the child. There are people who will pay well for a girl." His companions were dead, and he soon would be. There was no one left to protect. Bayr knew the man's only hope was to die quickly.

"You had help," Banruud hissed, wrapping his hand around the hilt of the sword that still protruded from the man's shoulder. "You knew the lay of the castle."

"His name was Biel," the man panted. "It was his plan."

"Biel of Berne is one of ours, Sire," a guard confessed. Outrage shivered through the ranks, and the babe whimpered.

"Where is he?" the king ground out.

The wounded man pointed toward the window, clearly indicating the pile below. "There."

"And the boy?" Banruud hissed.

The man grimaced in confusion. "He is not ours."

"Did he assist you?" Banruud pressed, and the guards shifted in dismay.

The queen gasped, shaking her head, but Banruud silenced her with an upraised palm. Bayr twisted his nightclothes with nervous fingers but didn't attempt to defend himself.

"No," the man moaned, eyeing Bayr with fear. "He killed them all."

The king, gripping the hilt of the bloody sword, dragged it from the man's shoulder. The man screamed in pain and relief before his shout was silenced with another thrust. The king withdrew the blade once more, and the dead man paid homage to his boots.

Banruud turned, freeing his feet, and pointed his blade at Bayr's head. Bayr did not flinch; the weight in his mouth had moved to his limbs.

"You must not hurt him, Banruud," the queen implored, and the guards shifted in quiet agreement.

The king studied him, eyes flat, sword steady, ignoring the distress of his queen and his men. When he spoke, his voice brooked no argument.

"You will sleep here from now on, Temple Boy."

⁓

The keeper didn't come back for days, nor did the boy, Bayr, and each morning Ghost told herself she would leave the cottage beneath the cliff. There was a weariness in her limbs and in her head that made her shrink at the thought. Her mind would tiptoe across the green slopes and climb to the wall that circled the castle where her daughter breathed, where she lived and slept and gazed up into the face of a woman who was not her mother. And though Ghost was not within those walls, she was under the same sky, she breathed the same air and was warmed by the same sun, and she could not make herself leave.

It was a week before the keeper came again. She'd eaten all the supplies and had caught several fish from the cold stream. She hadn't retrieved her gold, but she didn't worry someone else would find it. The keeper wore a brown robe tied at his waist with a simple rope, the same clothes he'd worn when he'd carried her out of the woods. She supposed his purple robes were for ceremony or worship and wondered if the one he'd sent with the boy had once been his. It was worn on the edges—frayed like grass—but she could fashion something from it if she took the time. Mayhaps a dress that wasn't gray. Along with his simple robe he wore violet circles beneath his eyes, and the shadow on his jaw and across his pate seemed especially dark against his pale face.

"Are you unwell?" she asked quietly. The thought worried her.

"No. Only weary," he replied, equally subdued. "Forgive me for staying away so long. There was trouble, and I've been unable to get away."

In a few words, he told her of an attempt to take the princess and the queen.

"She was not harmed?"

"No . . . neither of them was hurt. Only frightened."

Ghost discovered her legs would not hold her, and she sat abruptly, making the stool beneath her tip precariously. The keeper steadied her with a gentle hand but lowered himself onto the other stool as if he too were feeling faint. He folded his hands between his knees, his wide shoulders hunched, his head bowed.

"The danger has passed?" she asked, hesitant.

"I don't know if the danger will ever pass," he answered, and grief rippled in his voice.

"What do you mean?"

He shook his head as though it was difficult to explain, and she waited, wishing he would talk to her a little more.

"She will always be a girl," he said at last. "She is of great value. Those that are of great value are also at great risk."

He did not have to explain further.

"Will the boy come again?" she asked, wanting to turn her thoughts from Alba's safety.

"I don't . . . I don't know." Again the odd grief. "He is . . . he is no longer . . . in my charge."

"Has he gone?" She didn't understand.

"No. He has been . . . he is now . . . in the employ . . . of the king."

Ghost frowned. "A servant?" she pressed.

"A guard. He is to remain with the princess at all times."

"But he is a child," Ghost whispered.

"He is . . . a warrior."

"Can you never see him again?"

He smiled ruefully. "Of course I will see him. It is not as terrible as I am making it seem."

"The king took your child," Ghost murmured, and her heart bled. He had taken her child too.

"No," the keeper whispered, but she didn't believe him. He stood and walked to the door, though he made no move to leave.

"I have brought you your gold." From the sack he withdrew the little box stained with soot. "I was praying. I visit that tree often. I looked up and saw your box cradled between the boughs."

"You could have kept it," she whispered, stunned.

"It was not mine." He met her gaze and then looked away, color staining his dusky skin. "You offered me gold to leave you alone. I knew it must belong to you."

Ghost could think of nothing to say. She considered opening the box and offering him a handful of coins but thought he might think she was telling him to go.

"Why did you choose that tree?" he asked.

"I don't know. It was easy to climb."

He laughed, the sudden eruption making her start.

"Now that you have your gold, you can go, if you wish. But . . . you can also stay if you like. Bayr can no longer tend the sheep. If you would like to live here in this cottage, the keepers could pay you to watch and move the herd."

"I could stay?"

"Yes," he agreed, though the thought seemed to trouble him. "You will be a woman alone . . . and not terribly safe."

"There is no such thing as safety. But I would welcome the work and the peace. However long both last."

"I moved the herd to the meadow down below. Brother Johan is watching them. There is an enclosure. You would not need to stay with them through the night. The herds of the king graze on the north and east sides of the hill. The meadows are larger, and the herds are far greater. The grazing here and on the south side, directly below the temple, will sustain them through the summer and fall. When the cold comes we will move them within the walls of Temple Hill. Many will be slaughtered, and you can remain here until spring . . . if you wish. I will come every week—or send someone in my stead—to give you a day of rest."

"I don't wish to be seen," she whispered. She felt his eyes, compassion in his gaze. He would think she was ashamed of her skin. Of her colorless face. He would think she didn't like the stares and the fear of those who lived within the Temple Hill walls. But that was not what she feared.

"You need never enter the temple mount if you do not wish. In the winter months, we will move the sheep inside the walls, as we always do, and you can remain here," Dagmar reassured her.

Ghost nodded, relieved. It was foolish to stay. The king might see her or hear of her presence and know his henchman had failed. People loved to discuss her strangeness. If he saw her, he would have her killed. But leaving Alba behind forever would be harder than death. Maybe, if she kept her distance, she could keep her life and keep an eye on her child.

PART TWO

The Temple Girls

11

For three years, Ghost moved the sheep through the seasons and slept in her cottage on the western slope when the sun dipped below the edge of Saylok. The keeper came as he promised he would. She rarely called him Dagmar. She called him Keeper, and he called her Ghost, and they spoke carefully of small things—the thickness of the sheep's wool, the heat, the rain, the village, the sky. They would watch the herd and discuss the grass, the gulls, and the joyful bounding of the lambs. But the lambs made them both sad, reflective, and silence would well up between them and around them, and the small things would become huge and heavy.

Then Ghost would make herself ask after his boy, even though she knew it pained him. His boy looked after her girl, and when the keeper spoke of them, she saw the days of Alba's life and the passing of time. Sometimes the keeper would drop details like shiny pearls, and she would pick each one up, stringing them into precious stories that she told herself when he had gone, and she was alone.

"He is tall for a boy of ten," the keeper would say, and Ghost would see a girl of three and wonder how much Alba had grown.

"He looks like a boy of fifteen, but his voice has not changed," Dagmar would report, and Ghost would wonder how well her daughter spoke.

"Bayr is afraid Alba will not learn to speak properly because he stutters. The king forbade him from speaking to her any more than necessary, but she is a little girl, and she doesn't understand when Bayr is silent. Alba is *never* silent," the keeper commented once, and for weeks Ghost tried to imagine what the child's voice must sound like. Sometimes she would forget herself and ask questions.

"Is she happy?" Ghost asked once.

"Yes. She is joyful like the little lambs," he had replied, and then the heavy things had settled back around them, forcing quiet and contemplation.

Days became weeks and weeks, months. Two more years passed, until one day Dagmar offered something Ghost would never have asked. Something she wanted more than all the gold in her box and all the precious pearls the keeper inadvertently left behind.

"When you move the sheep down to the temple meadow, I will see if Bayr and Alba can visit you. Alba would love the sheep," he murmured, his eyes on the woolly beasts. It was spring, and soon they would take the animals' coats and move the herd to the meadows below the walls. "Alba has a gift with animals. They follow her and bow at her feet. Even the rodents. She has only to sing and they come to her. Bayr is constantly chasing them from the castle."

"Would the queen allow them to come?" Ghost asked, guarding her hope.

"The queen trusts Bayr, mothers him, and she would allow it. Bayr will not let anything happen to Alba. He sleeps on the floor beside her bed. He knows her schedule, her tempers, her favorite things, her favorite colors, and the foods she won't eat, regardless of her mother's insistence. Alba smiles at the world and makes everyone believe they are being obeyed while doing exactly as she wishes. Bayr watches silently, learning how to communicate with winks and smirks and frowns and nods. Alba knows what Bayr is saying, though he hardly opens his mouth—at least not when the king or his men are around."

"And the queen?" Ghost thought about the queen almost as often as she thought about Alba.

"She is kind to him. Kind to us all." Dagmar's countenance darkened. "We pray for her."

Ghost tipped her head to the side. What would it be like to be loved enough to be prayed over, to have a temple of keepers advocating with the gods in your behalf?

"Why do you pray for her?" she asked, her voice curious but quiet.

"She is heavy with child. She has not fared well in the past. Alba is her only living offspring. All the rest, all sons, have died in her womb. She's lost two more babies since coming to live on the temple mount. She has spent time with Master Ivo, and we've drawn runes into her skin. She doesn't want to lose another child."

"Then you must pray often," she choked, and the keeper studied her, his gaze morose. "I would pray too, if I knew how," she added.

"Do you feel the sun on your shoulders?" Dagmar asked.

Ghost wore a scarf over her head, the front deeply cowled to keep the sun from her face. She loved its warmth on her cheeks, but her skin blistered easily and never deepened in color to protect itself. Dagmar's skin had grown brown through the warm season, though he spent less time out of doors than she. He should be pasty and pocked, like the moon, but he wasn't. She'd seen some of the other keepers, but only a few. Many stayed inside the temple walls, guarded by the king's forces on the ramparts and at the gates. The few she'd seen were almost as fair as she.

"Of course I feel the sun," she answered, lifting her eyes to his.

"Do you feel the hum in the air?" Dagmar pressed.

"Yes. I feel it."

"That's God—Odin or Father Saylok or the Christ God. If he has a name, I'm not sure we know it. But I feel him . . . or her . . . like a presence at my back, guarding me and guiding me, and pushing me onward. It is easy for me to imagine God's love. I have only to think about Bayr. About how deeply I love him, how much I would give to keep him from harm or pain, how my thoughts are never far from him, and how his happiness is my own."

Ghost understood that. If she understood nothing else, she understood that.

"Mayhaps we each have our own god, like our own mother, someone who gave birth to our soul and watches over us until our soul returns," she mused.

"Mayhaps," he said, gentle. "Did you know your mother?"

"No. She must have . . . been afraid of me. I was found in the woods, wrapped in a blanket, left to die. But I didn't. An old woman found me—she was almost blind and didn't realize I looked as I do. She was lonely, and her children were all grown. I stayed with her until I was five. When she died, her son made me a servant in his house. I've been in many houses since then. These last years are the first time I've ever lived alone."

Compassion shone from his face, but the keeper did not dwell on her past.

"I remember my mother. But only briefly. She died young," he murmured.

"Life is not kind to women," Ghost sighed.

"My sister said the same thing. But life is not especially kind to men either. Life is suffering, and we all suffer."

"Mayhaps God did not love your sister as much as his other children?" Ghost heard her bitterness and met his gaze with defiance.

"Or mayhaps he loved her more and could not be without her."

"You see good where there is none," Ghost whispered, moved.

"Even amid the suffering, the good is not hard to find," he said, his eyes soft on her colorless face.

"Will life be kind to Alba?" Ghost knew her wistfulness caught him off guard, and she looked away. She always tried not to ask after the girl, but she sometimes couldn't help herself. She thought the keeper took her interest as general, the interest anyone might have in a princess, in the only girl child, as so many in the village referred to her.

"If Bayr has any say in the matter, life will not dare harm her." Dagmar smiled. He rose and prepared to go. She was never ready for him to leave.

"How do I pray, Keeper?" she called after him.

"Just speak. Talk to the sky as though you talk to a friend."

Ghost frowned as she watched Dagmar lope away. Then she turned her eyes to the hills and the sheep, her thoughts heavy and her heart light. She would talk to her god the way she talked to Dagmar. After all, he was her only friend.

The boy had grown considerably. He was only twelve but looked like a man. He was not yet as tall as Dagmar, but his hands and feet were huge, his shoulders broad. From a distance, Ghost thought it was the keeper, come to visit. Bayr moved like his uncle, his back straight and his stride fluid, but his hair was not shorn and his clothes were different—a tunic of gray and hose a few shades darker. Still, it was the child he carried on his shoulders that had Ghost clutching her chest and leaning heavily on the staff she carried when she tended the herd. Ghost knew the infant she had pushed from her body—she visited the infant in her memories every day—but in five years, Alba had changed so much she was unrecognizable. The baby had disappeared. She'd taken on a new form and become someone else.

"We've . . . come . . . t-to . . . visit." Bayr's smile was open, his eyes full of light, and Ghost nodded, a jerking nod that must have made her look like an old woman having a fit. His duties at Alba's side had kept him from visiting her all these long years.

"Th-this is Alba," he said carefully, pulling the girl from his shoulders and setting her on the ground. She was slight for a girl of five, but taller than Ghost had expected. Alba clung to Bayr's hand and peered up at Ghost, her eyes as dark as her hair was light. The contrast was beautiful, and Ghost bowed so their faces were level and she could study her closer.

"Hello, Alba," she greeted the girl, finding her voice and steeling her heart. She would not weep and scare the children. She wanted them to come back.

"And Dagmar? Is he coming too?" she asked, needing something to say, needing his steady presence.

"No. The k-keepers are g-gathered in . . . s-supplication," Bayr spit out, and flushed at the difficulty the word represented. "The queen . . . is l-laboring."

"Mother is having a baby," Alba added, the words flowing from her mouth without hitch or hiccup. Clearly, spending time with the boy had not harmed her language skills.

"N-n-no one will m-m-miss us," Bayr murmured. "And the q-queen is suffering. Her pain is . . . our p-pain."

Ghost nodded once, understanding. Bayr did not want Alba to hear the queen's cries. She turned to the sheep, wanting to distract Bayr and Alba from their worries, and introduced many of the woolly beasts by name, telling the little girl and her looming protector about their antics and their moods, their personalities and their peculiarities, even pointing out the colors in their coats.

Alba liked the little lambs and made friends with them immediately, her hand outstretched, her voice soft.

"All th-the animals l-l-love h-her," Bayr said.

Ghost nodded, overcome with quiet joy as she watched the child who moved among the sheep as though she'd spent her whole life tending herds. Ghost had given her something of herself after all. One hour stretched into two, but instead of leaving, Bayr called to Alba and announced they would have lessons in the sunshine.

"Alba has lessons?" Ghost asked.

The boy nodded and gripped two handfuls of grass. He yanked it from the ground, bringing dark, damp soil up with the roots. He removed several more clumps, clearing a circular space, and then he tamped it down with his feet. Alba mimicked him, stomping and tangling herself around his legs, and he swooped her out of the way with a practiced swing.

"Let's draw," Alba cried, clapping.

"She is v-very smart," Bayr said. There was pride in his tone, and he glanced at Ghost with a glimmer of a smile. "Watch." He took her staff and, using the end, created a shape in the soft dirt.

Alba promptly named the figure, though Ghost wasn't certain she was correct. Bayr nodded and stomped the letter into oblivion. Ghost tried to capture the image in her mind's eye for later study. Bayr drew another shape, and Alba threw her hands in the air and shouted its name.

Bayr held a finger to his lips, quieting her, and pointed at the sheep. The little girl seemed to understand, and her next responses were considerably more subdued.

"Only five years old, and she knows more than I," Ghost murmured, smiling. "You have taught her well."

He shook his head and tossed it toward the palace that loomed in the distance. "Q-queen," he corrected. The queen had taught Alba to read.

"The queen is as intelligent as she is beautiful," Ghost whispered, and the knowledge made her glad, not envious.

A melodious chanting soared like a bird on the breeze, and Alba ceased her skipping and turned toward it, bringing her palm to her ear.

"Listen," she demanded. "The keepers are singing!"

The song was deep and resonant, mournful and mounting, and Ghost lifted her face to the sound. It was her favorite time of day, when the Keepers of Saylok sang their prayers. She missed it when she moved the herd too far away to hear. Increasingly, the song became heavy and the melody morose, a dirge instead of a delight. There was no praise in the tones, and the hair on Ghost's neck began to stand. The sheep, sensing her fear, began to bleat and trot in circles.

"W-we m-must go back," Bayr stuttered, hoisting Alba over his head and settling her back on his shoulders. With a farewell tip of his head, he was running back to the walls, his hands gripping Alba's ankles as she bounced above him, her pale hair floating out behind them like a stream of white light.

Bayr ran through the Temple Hill gates, Alba clinging to his head, her arms circling his brow like a crown of flesh. She was accustomed to riding on his shoulders; it was how he kept her close when he needed his arms and legs free, and she liked seeing the world from above him. She'd been riding on his shoulders all her young life. She didn't squeal in delight at his pace the way she usually did. She sensed the fear in the keepers' song, just as he did, and her grip was so tight his scalp grew numb above her hold.

The keepers were still in the sanctum, and the sound of their chanting rose from the rafters and spilled out of the bell tower like a death knell. The keepers were so loud, beseeching the gods with open throats. Or maybe it was Bayr's fear, his dread, thrumming between his ears and echoing their pleading. The queen was in trouble.

A voice yelled his name, but he ran through the gate, running toward uncertainty the way he'd run toward the bear in the woods, hoping that courage in the face of terror would send death fleeing.

Inside the palace, the servants were huddled at the base of the stairs, their faces lifted as though they waited for news to descend. They scattered before him, clearing the way, startled by his presence.

"Don't go up there, boy," a guard bellowed.

"Leave the princess here, Bayr," another voice begged, but he was sprinting up the wide stairway, his eyes fixed on the high window spilling light over the steps, his hands wrapped around Alba's skinny legs, holding her steady on his shoulders. He couldn't leave her behind, and he had to see the queen, had to reassure them both that all was well.

"Wait 'til the king has gone," the same guard bellowed, standing at the base of the stairs, but Bayr ignored him, and the guard didn't climb the stairs to stop him.

"Go!" he heard King Banruud roar from somewhere above him, and for a moment, Bayr faltered in his swift climb, thinking the king was speaking to him. Ice trickled from his head to his feet, and Alba's hands tightened in his hair. Seconds later, a maid rushed down the stairs past him and then another, tears streaking down their cheeks. One turned back to grasp Bayr's arm, urging him to retreat with them, but he twisted away from her and climbed the last few stairs to the wide foyer between Alba's nursery and the queen's chamber. The heavy wooden doors to the queen's room stood ajar, and he could see Queen Alannah in the enormous bed that faced the door, her eyes closed, her hands resting on the bright blue coverlet that matched the color of her eyes.

Relief filled his chest before he realized the queen was far too still, far too pale, and when Alba cried out for her she didn't lift her face or smile in response. The king stood over her, his hair spilling around his shoulders as though he'd run his hands through the length so often his braid had come loose. He turned his head, meeting Bayr's gaze through the open door, and his eyes flickered over Alba, perched on Bayr's shoulders. It was not sorrow Bayr saw in the king's face. Not loss. Not even shock or rage. It was frustration and cold calculation, as though the king were contemplating a battle from atop a hill, a battle he was losing. Bayr dared not take another step. He dared not open his mouth.

Alba was braver than he.

"Mama," she called, her sweet voice demanding her mother wake and acknowledge her. She wiggled her legs and yanked at Bayr's braid, demanding to be let down. Bayr took a step back, his hands tightening around her pummeling feet. He pulled her from his shoulders but kept her locked in his arms, her face pressed to his throat.

"No, Alba," he murmured. "No."

Banruud, his eyes still locked on Bayr and Alba, pulled the quilt from beneath the queen's folded hands and draped it over her lovely face and her tumble of golden hair. The coverlet became a shroud.

A wail rose and echoed like a howling wind, and for a moment, Bayr thought the sound emanated from Alba. But the girl grew still and the sound was all wrong. Bayr trembled, trying to place the source of the screaming, and the king turned, his eyes fixing on something—someone—Bayr could not see.

"She is gone, woman. Cease," the king snapped, but the wailing increased. "Her suffering is over," Banruud ground out. Then Bayr saw Agnes, the midwife, the woman who never strayed far from Alannah's side. She stumbled to the bedside and yanked the blanket from the queen, as though she couldn't bear to see her covered. Agnes's veil was gone, and gray strands fell about her face and stuck to her tear-soaked cheeks.

She screamed again, her grief terrible to watch. She pulled at her hair and ripped at her gown, and when she looked at the king, her eyes were crazed.

"You could not leave her alone," she shrieked. "You could not keep your filthy, evil hands from our queen. And she is gone. You have killed her."

"Silence!" Banruud hissed.

"Your belly is filled with snakes, your crown is paper, and your queen is dead. I was silent once. I will not be silent anymore!" Agnes raged. She lunged for the knife on the king's belt as if she wished to run him through.

Banruud, his eyes flashing and his teeth bared, pulled the dirk from the sheath at his waist. With a slash of the knife, he silenced the midwife's accusations. The scarlet spilled down her chest, too thick for wine, too red for tears. Her head fell forward, her nose touching her heaving bosom, as though her blood, the color of roses, smelled just as sweet. Then her legs buckled and her body bowed, and she lay prostrate at the king's feet.

Banruud wiped his blade across his tunic before sheathing it with a grimace of distaste. Her blood stained his right hand.

Bayr held Alba, his hand palming her head, keeping her eyes pressed to his chest. She thrashed and demanded release, beating him with small fists and feet. His eyes met the king's, horror clashing with spent rage, and Banruud's jaw jutted forward as his brows lowered over his black eyes.

"She forgot herself. Don't make the same mistake, Temple Boy," he warned.

Bayr turned and staggered down the stairs, through the corridors and the halls and out into the gardens where he'd fallen in love with the queen. Where she'd sung and walked beside him. And he soothed her motherless child.

12

"There are still no daughters, King Banruud." The statement was soft but it hissed like a snake through the assembled chieftains, and Banruud turned black eyes on his brother-in-law, the young Chieftain of Adyar, the only one who dared challenge him. They were all assembled in the king's hall, Banruud at the head of a table so long twenty of his warriors could sit around it. The chieftains were seated on one side, the high Keepers of Saylok on the other. Dagmar of Dolphys had taken a seat among the high keepers when David, the old keeper from Dolphys, had passed away, and he sat as far away from Banruud as he could, his eyes on the scars in the burnished oak surface. Banruud knew that Dagmar despised him, yet he never said a word. Banruud wished Aidan would hold his damn tongue as well, but he never did.

"My sister gave birth to a daughter five years ago, and yet the daughters of Saylok have not returned. Now she is dead," Aidan continued. "There will be no more daughters from Alannah." A wave of grief passed over his face and rippled through the assembly, and Banruud stifled a derisive snort. They all grieved for a queen who had not birthed a single, live child, thinking she was the mother of the princess. A dead slave girl was Alba's mother. Alannah had done nothing for Saylok. Neither had the keepers.

The queen's death had prompted a council of the clans. Master Ivo had wanted them to meet in the sanctum, but Banruud had insisted on assembling in the palace instead. In the sanctum, Banruud was not lord. In the sanctum, it was Master Ivo who sat on the throne. Banruud had no intention of standing before Ivo like a lowly supplicant, even in council. Past kings had lowered themselves before the Keepers of Saylok, but Banruud would not. If he had his way, Saylok would blame them for the dearth of girl children, and the keepers would become a thing of the past.

"It is true. Our women give birth to sons . . . or they die trying," Banruud said, turning his gaze on the Highest Keeper, redirecting Aidan's blame. "The only daughters are brought here from other lands or born of rape from raids by the Northmen, the Eastlanders, or the Hounds. There aren't nearly enough women to go around. And you, Master Ivo, cannot tell us why."

The Highest Keeper said nothing. His silence was almost as powerful as denial, and the chieftains turned their complaints to the row of quiet keepers just as Banruud had intended.

"Except for the princess, there have been no daughters born of Saylok in twelve years. We don't feel the lack yet . . . but our sons will. In another decade, there will be no women to wed," Benjie of Berne chimed in. He was the cousin of Banruud and had taken his place as chieftain when Banruud became king.

"We're spending our gold and our grain on females, and our weakness is becoming known to our enemies," Erskin of Ebba added.

"The villagers have started sacrificing female lambs, hoping to coax the gods into a trade, one female for another," Banruud accused. The sacrifices hadn't worked. The keepers had conducted similar sacrifices to no apparent avail.

"We can't continue to raid. We're stirring up other lands to come against us," Josef of Joran grunted. He was a farmer, not a warrior. Unlike some of the chieftains, who had been raiding for generations, he hated the necessity of the raids.

"Josef is right. We have staved off attacks from the Eastlanders on the shores of Dolphys. It will only get worse," Dirth agreed, nodding.

"The battle has already come to Ebba," Erskin growled. "The Hounds from the Hinterlands keep coming. If they defeat us, they will come for you next."

"Not all our enemies are raiders from foreign lands," Lothgar of Leok said. "There have been attacks from within too. Bands of the clan-less rove across the countryside, taking the girls and women from the farmers and killing their families when they resist. My warriors hunted some of them down. We put their heads on pikes on the border between Leok and Ebba. We have not had an attack since. But the people have started to disguise their daughters as boys to keep them safe . . . even from other clans."

"The problem is not with the women of Saylok. It is with the men," Master Ivo murmured. His voice was low and soft, but no one missed it.

Every eye narrowed on the Highest Keeper, and the chieftains fingered the hilts of their swords. The chieftains were virile and powerful, and none of them appreciated the quiet condemnation of the Highest Keeper.

"You gather women from other lands to make up for *their* lack . . . yet mayhaps you should bring men from other lands to make up for yours. To bed your women," Ivo cackled, unfazed by their displeasure. "Maybe the Hounds can help."

"If the keepers cannot tell us what plagues Saylok, then we must guard the few women we have," Banruud said. He waited until every chieftain nodded in agreement, their eyes on his, before he offered his "solution."

"Every clan will gather their daughters and bring them here, to the mount," Banruud insisted. Every brow instantly furrowed, but he continued, his voice coaxing and infinitely reasonable. He'd hadn't thought any of it through, but his heart pounded at the thought. One daughter had made him king. Many daughters would make him infinitely more powerful.

"The females will be kept safe, within these walls," he continued. "When they are of age, they will be promised to the sons of the chieftains first, then the warriors, then the craftsmen. If a man is not a value to his clan, he will have little chance at a wife. Mayhaps it will weed out the weak and the useless."

"All the daughters?" Aidan gasped. "You will have a revolt, Sire. Are you going to take Lothgar's daughters too?" Lothgar had already risen to his feet, his face twisted in protest.

"Every daughter in Saylok is already spoken for," Josef argued. "There is not a daughter in Saylok who has not been numbered and negotiated over. Would you void the betrothals drawn up at their births? Even the daughters of the slaves have been given standing."

"And the people will never agree to it." Aidan shook his head, adamant.

"You are a chieftain. Your job is to rule your people. Control them. Make them understand that it is for their own safety," Banruud shot back.

"We can keep our own women safe, Majesty," Lothgar growled.

"They are not your women, Lothgar. They are Saylok's salvation," Banruud roared.

"So clever of you, Majesty. If you control the women of Saylok . . . you control the men," the Highest Keeper mused, and the atmosphere in the room throbbed and thrummed.

"The mount cannot hold all the daughters of Saylok. Even with the drought, there are hundreds of daughters between the ages of twelve and twenty," Ivo added, his voice soft but his eyes sharp in his withered face.

Lothgar grunted and the chieftains began to nod. Banruud felt a swell of desperation in his chest.

"Then bring me one. One young daughter from every clan. If not for safety . . . then for symbolism. They can be raised in the temple by the keepers. Kept, like the sacred runes, safe and sound." Banruud had meant to mock, to shine further light on the ineptitude and uselessness of the keepers, but Master Ivo nodded as though he agreed.

"You mean to separate them from their families?" Chief Josef interrupted, troubled.

"A supplicant leaves his family when he comes to the temple, does he not, Master Ivo?" Banruud asked, though he knew the answer.

"He does," the Highest Keeper murmured, nodding.

"Well then." Banruud raised his palms with a shrug, as if his solution was a simple matter.

"Women cannot be supplicants, Majesty. And keepers are not nursemaids," Keeper Amos argued.

"But Master Ivo is the Highest Keeper. He can make it so. The Keepers of Saylok have the power to choose kings. Surely you have the power to do this. Women can be gods . . . Why not supplicants?" Banruud purred.

Amos bowed his head. Banruud turned his attention back to the Highest Keeper, sensing victory.

"Do you think you are above the gods, Ivo?" Banruud pressed.

Ivo regarded him silently.

"Why would the daughters be supplicants? You have no intention of them becoming keepers," Ivo stated.

"Do all supplicants become keepers?" Banruud inquired, innocence dripping from his words. "Your duty is to see to the continuance of the clans of Saylok. There will be no kings if there aren't women to birth them. There will be no keepers either, though I'm convinced you, Master Ivo, were hatched from an egg," Banruud said. No one dared laugh.

Ivo was silent so long the chieftains began to shift and squirm.

"Very well," Ivo whispered. "Bring the daughters here. Bring them to the temple."

"Very well," Banruud echoed.

"Six daughters of Saylok—one from each clan—will become supplicants," Ivo intoned, his voice dark, his eyes lit with unholy fire. "The king has decreed it. We have all witnessed it. Who am I to disagree?"

༒

"She is seven years old. Her mother was a concubine in King Kembah's court. They called her Bashti. King Kembah has more daughters than he knows what to do with. He is fond of his wives, but eager to make trades for his daughters. He gave us ten of them—all ages. Bashti was the youngest. I don't know what happened to her mother."

"Bashti of Berne," Chieftain Benjie grunted. "She will do."

"But she is not . . . of Berne, Lord," the warrior said.

"She is now."

"But the king wants a daughter of Berne," the warrior protested.

"Do you want to give your daughter to the temple, man?" Benjie asked, churlish.

"I have no daughters, Lord."

"No. Neither do I," Benjie snapped. "Do any of you want to give your daughters?"

The men who had daughters hung their heads. The men who did not stared at the little girl with the corkscrew curls and the dark eyes. She was as brown as tree bark and dressed like a little boy, though her hair and fine features made the attempts at disguise ineffective. She did not look like she hailed from the Clan of the Bear. No one would believe she was from Berne. Not the keepers, not the king. But she was a girl, and that was all that really mattered.

"Is she healthy?" Benjie pressed.

"My wife says she's never been sick . . . not even once. But she has a temper and doesn't like to keep still. The temple might not be the place for her."

141

"We will let the keepers worry about that." The Chieftain of Berne pricked the tip of his finger with his blade and smeared his blood on the little girl's brow. She didn't flinch but watched him with her hands clenched and her eyes wide.

"You are now Bashti of Berne. Daughter of the bear. Child of this clan. Supplicant to the Keepers of Saylok." Chieftain Benjie turned away and sheathed his knife, but not before muttering, "We're all doomed."

⁓

"The chieftain says we must have a daughter from Ebba. You will live in the temple. You will be safe," the woman said, trying to smile at her daughter, trying to convince her.

"I will work harder. I won't eat as much. I'll sleep with the animals," Elayne pled, clinging to her mother, frantic.

"Elayne, my sweet daughter. I am not sending you away. I am giving you to the gods."

"The gods do not need me. You and Father need me. My brothers need me," Elayne begged.

"I care only for your life. You are twelve years old. There have been no daughters in our village since you were born. You are one of the last. In a few years you will be pressed to marry and have children for the clan. You are so young, and I want so much more for you. If you go to the temple, you will be protected. Even . . . worshipped. At least for a while. Lord Erskin says the keepers will teach you. It will be a better life, Elayne, than the one we can give you," the woman cried. Her red hair and freckled cheeks were faded, as though strife had leached the color from every aspect of her existence. Someday Elayne would look just like her.

"Please don't do this," Elayne wept. "I don't want to go to the temple. I want to stay with you."

"You must do this for me, daughter. You must do this and give me hope for your life and your happiness."

"I could never be happy without you."

"And I will never be happy if I don't make you seize this chance."

"But what if . . . it is a bad place?"

"It cannot be worse than this," Elayne's mother whispered. "We are at war. To become a woman in the temple will be better than becoming a woman in Ebba."

⁕

"How old are you, girl?" the Chieftain of Leok asked. He'd demanded every girl child be brought before him. Thus far, not one family had obeyed the summons. The word had spread among the people that a daughter of Leok would be sent to live in the temple among the keepers, and none of them were willing to part with theirs. But one girl had come, seeking entry in his hall, asking for "Lord Lothgar."

She was small, but her sharp eyes belied her size. He repeated the question when she failed to answer him.

"I don't know how old I am," she answered, impudent. Her shoulders tightened and she stared down at her bare feet. They were black with filth.

"Where did you come from?" he pressed.

"I am of Leok."

"If you were born in Leok, I would have known."

"I am of Leok," she insisted, lifting her small chin.

"Why have you come?"

"I want to be sent to the temple."

"Who cares for you?"

"I care for myself."

"Where is your family?"

"I don't know."

"What is your name?"

"I do not know."

"What do you know?"

"I am of Leok," she insisted, her voice rising. "And I am a girl."

Lothgar barked in laughter and his brother, Lykan, cursed behind him. Lykan was always hovering in the shadows. The girl was small, but her tongue was sharp. She seemed to have a firm grasp on the situation, young as she was.

"You look like a daughter of Leok," the chieftain conceded. "Your hair is fair and your eyes are blue."

"She looks like your daughters, Lord. Like our mother too," Lykan mused. Lothgar turned his head to listen to his brother. "But she wasn't born in Leok. She is nine or ten at the most, and we would have heard. Mayhaps her parents were travelers between lands. Mayhaps she belongs to the rovers."

"I belong to no one," the girl said.

"Why do you want to go to the temple?"

"Because I belong to no one," she repeated. "In the temple I'll eat."

Lothgar nodded slowly and sighed. He had no one else to send. He could raid the homes of his people. Terrorize them. He didn't want to do that. He had known his task would be nigh on impossible without force. His daughters were all grown, but he would have slain any man who tried to separate him from them.

Yet here was this child. A girl child. A child washed up onto the shore, by all appearances. He had no idea where she had come from, but he found he didn't much care.

"You will have to have a name, daughter of Leok," he murmured. "What shall we call you?"

She was silent, and Lykan spoke up again.

"We should call her Liis. For our mother. Surely she sent her to us," he muttered.

Lothgar agreed, piercing his thumb and calling the girl forward for his blessing. The gods had spoken, and he would not refuse a gift so obvious.

"Liis of Leok it is."

⁀⊙

"Magda tries to hide her, Lord. She doesn't bathe with the other children. Magda calls her Dalys—a boy's name—but we all know."

"How old is the child?" Dirth of Dolphys inquired.

The woman squirmed and looked toward the kitchens, guilty. "Six. Maybe seven. She was brought over in a raid last year . . . with Magda and some of the others. Magda's been looking out for her ever since."

"You have a daughter. Why should we not send her?" Dirth asked, his eyes shrewd. He knew what the woman was about. Her husband was one of Dirth's oldest warriors, and she was a lady's maid to Dirth's wife. Clearly the woman had heard talk, and she didn't want her daughter to be sent to the temple.

"My daughter is spoken for, Lord. We need her."

"Magda is Dakin's woman. Mayhaps the little girl is also spoken for. Mayhaps he will protest."

"I am protesting first, Lord."

Dirth glowered at her impudence, but she gazed at him defiantly. The women of Dolphys were notoriously headstrong. But Magda was not of Dolphys. She was of Eastlandia, and if the child was not hers, she would have little room to argue.

He sighed and raised his face to the rafters, considering. "So be it. Bring little Dalys to me."

⁀⊙

Chieftain Josef had known immediately where he would turn for a daughter of Joran. She had come to his thoughts as the king had made his demands. He'd thought of her on the long ride home. His clan had chosen him as chieftain because his family had the largest holding of lands in the clan. He was fair, and he ruled as well as he could. Every clan had their fishermen, their farmers, and their warriors, and Josef was a farmer. Not a warrior. And if Jerom, the girl's grandfather, told him no, he didn't think he could enforce his wishes with a sword. He hoped Jerom would not say no.

Jerom's daughter had been ravaged in a raid from the Hounds of the Hinterlands. The clans of Saylok were not the only raiders on the sea. What they did to others was done to them. Jerom's family lived near the shore making their living off the water.

Jerom was a good fisherman, but he was not a warrior either. It would not have mattered if he had been. He and his sons were casting their nets when the Hounds had come ashore ten years ago. Jerom's wife and daughter had not been spared. His wife was killed, and his daughter had become pregnant from the attack. When she gave birth to a daughter nine months later and died in the process, Jerom and his two sons had been charged with the task of raising the girl child. The clan of Joran had celebrated the birth of a daughter even as they quietly acknowledged that she was not of Saylok.

When Master Ivo had insinuated it was the men of Saylok who were unable to father daughters, Josef had thought of the Hounds and Jerom's daughter. Of Jerom's granddaughter. They'd named her Juliah after her mother. Juliah of Joran. Juliah, daughter of a Hound.

It was not safe on the shores of Joran. Jerom knew this better than anyone. Chieftain Josef thought he might be able to convince Jerom to send young Juliah to the temple.

13

"I did not bring a daughter of Adyar," Aidan of Adyar said. "You already have one, Majesty."

The king raised a brow and folded his arms. The chieftains and their parties had begun arriving at sundown, and he'd greeted each one as darkness fell and the moon rose. No one had come inside. They'd pitched their tents on the grounds, the colors clearly indicating the separate camps. Servants had seen to their horses, but the crowd in the courtyard had grown as the arrivals continued. Aidan had arrived last, his retinue including the late king's queen. She had entered the castle with a low bow to Banruud and proceeded into the blazing foyer beyond with the confidence of one having lived within the palace walls for half her life.

Aidan hadn't yet climbed down from his horse, clearly preferring the height and dominance the animal gave him. Banruud had grown accustomed to Aidan. The young chieftain had all the fire in his family. Alannah hadn't had any, and her father, the previous king, had been as malleable as she. Still, Aidan of Adyar was no threat. He would never be king. He was a mouthy boy, intent on poking at the king simply because he thought he could. One day, when Aidan least expected it, that would end.

"My sister, Queen Alannah of Adyar, gave birth to a daughter," Aidan continued. "That daughter lives here, on the temple mount.

Princess Alba is of Adyar and can represent Adyar in the temple. She can represent our clan. Adyar has given enough, and we have no more daughters to spare."

"Yet you've come anyway, Adyar," Banruud said, scorn dripping from his words. "Why, brother?"

"I was curious. It seems the chieftains have obeyed their king."

"All but one," Banruud answered. Their eyes clashed, and Aidan's horse danced, sensing the nervous energy that swirled around him.

"I've brought you a woman," Aidan said, keeping his tone mild. "Just not . . . a young woman. My mother, Queen Esa, has come to see to the upbringing of her granddaughter. Now that Alannah is gone, you will need a woman to look after the princess. Unless . . . you intend to take another wife, Majesty? Mayhaps one of the clan daughters you've summoned?"

Aidan was purposely trying to inflame the other chieftains and Banruud ignored him, waving his hand toward his manservant, who trotted forward to assist the lord of Adyar, signifying his dismissal. Alba was guarded by the Temple Boy and tended by servants. The king rarely saw her. Still, Lady Esa could take Alannah's chamber if she wished. It made no difference to him. He was more interested in the girl children assembled to greet him.

"This is Elayne of Ebba," Chieftain Erskin announced, bowing slightly. He looked weary and planned to leave again at first light. The trouble in Ebba was worsening. Banruud had promised to join him soon, and the chieftains in every clan were sending warriors to his aid.

The girl curtsied deeply but didn't raise her red-rimmed eyes to the king. Her hair was a fiery tangle, her nose freckled, her lips full. She might grow to be a beauty or become plainer by the day. It was too soon to tell. She was lean and long and the biggest of the lot. In a few years, she would be old enough to wed. She'd clearly been born before the drought.

Banruud moved on to the next chieftain, his cousin from Berne. Benjie had always been easy to manipulate and control. Banruud doubted this time would be any different. A girl with glowing brown skin and coiled black curls watched him approach. She was dressed from head to toe in the deep red of Berne, but she was a stranger to the clan. The Bernians were typically pale-skinned.

"Who is this?" Banruud murmured. The girl did not shrink before him though he towered over her.

"This is Bashti of Berne," Banruud's cousin grunted. Benjie put his hand on the girl's back and urged her forward. She planted her feet and pressed back.

"Bashti of . . . Berne?" Banruud questioned.

"Bashti of Berne . . . daughter of Kembah, most likely."

"If she is a daughter of Kembah, she is not a daughter of Berne, Benjie. Plus, Kembah is a king," Banruud disagreed. "I doubt this girl is Kembah's. But if it suits you to pretend, cousin, I will not argue."

"Mayhaps when she is grown we can make an alliance," Benjie offered. He had clearly thought through his presentation on his journey from Berne.

"Mayhaps. If she has a womb she will grow into, it is enough." Banruud raised his voice, including the other chieftains in his query. "Have you all brought me foreign wombs to beget other wombs?"

No one answered. No one even breathed. But Banruud knew they had. They'd brought him the cast off and the captured. All except Erskin, who'd brought him the redheaded girl from besieged Ebba. Erskin said her mother had begged him to take her. He wondered if more would come, seeking sanctuary at the temple mount. Banruud's power would grow with their numbers.

The chieftains regarded him silently, their insolence and displeasure rolling from them in black waves.

"You said to find daughters. We found daughters, Majesty," Dirth of Dolphys ground out, his jaw tight, his blue eyes black with resentment.

"So you did," Banruud said. He only pretended displeasure. The assortment was exactly what he had expected. The children ranged from six to twelve years—five girls with bowed heads and thin backs, all of them older than Alba. Chieftain Josef had brought a girl named Juliah, her long dark hair braided tightly like that of a budding warrior. Josef said she'd been raised by men, and her hair bore witness to the fact. Lothgar had presented "Liis of Leok," her eyes as old and stony as the temple mount itself. Her golden hair, falling loose around tight shoulders and clenched hands, would draw the eye of kings. The girl called Dalys, sloe-eyed and sooty-locked, delivered by Dirth of Dolphys, clung to the chieftain's hand as though life in bloody Dolphys was better than life with a king.

"They will stay in the castle, under my watch," Banruud ordered, turning back toward his palace, indicating an end to all debate.

"You said they would be raised by the keepers," Lothgar protested. "In the temple."

"They will be raised with my daughter, in my house," Banruud shot back. "Princesses of Saylok, all."

"They are supplicants to the temple. It is what was agreed upon. They will live in the temple and be guarded by the keepers." Master Ivo stood in the courtyard, the light from the fat moon glancing off his face and hollowing out his black eyes and lips like caves in pale sand. He and his brethren had entered the gathering with no one noticing, their robes melding with the evening sky. His rasping voice raised the hair on Banruud's neck and the resentment in his chest. The Highest Keeper was a constant thorn in his side.

"It was what we agreed upon, Banruud," Aidan repeated, still astride his horse. Banruud's servant hovered helplessly.

"You have no say in the matter, Adyar," Banruud shot back. "You have come to the temple mount with your hands empty."

"I have promised this girl's mother she will live in the temple and be raised in the safety of the sanctum," Erskin of Ebba protested.

"I have made the same promise to Juliah's grandfather," Josef said, his eyes touching on the girl child with the warrior braid.

As if the gods chased her, Alba chose that moment to dash from the arched entry, coming to a teetering halt in front of the assembled chieftains and their retinues. The Temple Boy, her constant shadow, was only steps behind. A gasp rippled through the gathering. The chieftains had not seen the child since Banruud had taken the throne. He had kept her tucked away. Hidden. Even when the clans had come to the mount each year for the tournament, she and the queen had not taken part or made an appearance. Banruud had been afraid someone would take her—take them—from him. Men had tried. But mayhaps he needed to remind his chieftains that he had a girl child. A small, perfect girl child. And they had made him king because of it.

She was a breathtaking creature—light and dark together, as though the moon had made love to midnight and given birth to a human child. The chieftains fell to their knees, Aidan sliding from his charger without a word. Their foreheads touched the earth, and their braids, long again with the five years of his reign, coiled in the dirt beside their heads. Banruud felt a surge of power, and he swept Alba up in his arms. Her small body stiffened in surprise. He had not held her since she was an infant, since he had laid her in the arms of his queen. The chieftains did not bow to anyone . . . but they bowed to her. And because of her, they would continue to look to him.

"These clan daughters will be raised like princesses," Banruud repeated, pointing at the trembling girl children. "They will be raised beside my own daughter."

The five girls, standing by the kneeling chieftains, slowly sank to their knees as well. They were in the presence of the princess, the hope of Saylok, and Banruud held Alba even higher, reminding his audience what he had given them.

"No, Highness. They will be raised by keepers," Master Ivo insisted again. The Highest Keeper had not fallen to his knees. None of the keepers had. Resentment rose in Banruud's chest and built behind his lips. The Highest Keeper believed himself above all authority. He stood looking down his nose at the king as if he had Odin's ear. Someday, Banruud would strike him down. He would make them all kneel the way Agnes had knelt, her blood dripping from her slashed throat. Banruud had been certain the Temple Boy would run crying to the keepers after Banruud silenced her, but the idiot had held his twisted tongue. Banruud had given the midwife a burial she'd hardly deserved, laying her to rest at the feet of her beloved queen. No one had questioned him when he related her mad attempt to run him through.

"Daughters of Freya, goddess of fertility, goddess of childbirth, wife of Odin the Allfather, we welcome you," Ivo cried, gliding across the courtyard toward the massive Hearth of Kings that was as old as the temple itself. It only burned when a new king was chosen, and it had grown cold since Banruud was crowned. The higher keepers moved behind him, one representing each clan, as though they'd devised an entire ceremony beforehand.

"These daughters of the clans, these daughters of Freya, will be guarded, their lives revered, their virtue defended. They will be a symbol to Saylok just like her runes," the Highest Keeper boomed. In a show of sheer pageantry, he touched the sharp tip of his fingernail to his palm. The blood that welled became ink for the rune he painted upon the stone hearth. The rune became flame, whooshing up in a triumphant column.

"Saylok needs daughters. From this day forward, these daughters—your daughters—will keep the flame lit. As long as it burns, you will know that the daughters of Freya are tending it, that the Keepers of Saylok are tending them, and Saylok will live on."

The child in Banruud's arms was lit by the glow, and the jeweled crown upon his head cast a glittering rainbow across the faces of the keepers. Ivo was a magician, but Banruud was king, and his anger became an inferno.

"We will guard them well, just as we honor the princess," Master Ivo added, his tone placating but his gaze a challenge. The kneeling chiefs began to nod, looking from Banruud and his daughter to the Highest Keeper.

"Bayr of Saylok, a child raised here on the temple mount and blessed with exceeding strength, will be their protector as well, just as he has protected the princess," the Highest Keeper promised, extending his arms toward the boy as though he presented the chieftains with an incredible gift.

Word of the Temple Boy's slaying of the castle intruders had become a much-embellished legend throughout the land. To hear it told, the boy had defeated an army single-handedly with only his bare hands.

The Temple Boy was the size of a man, though he stuttered like a child and his cheeks were still smooth. He rarely spoke at all and did not attempt to voice his agreement now. He simply dropped to one knee and bowed his head as though being knighted to the cause. But it was answer enough, and the chieftains rose to their feet, nodding and clutching their braids as though they grasped the hilts of swords slung across their backs. Bayr met the gaze of each one and stood, clasping his own braid in a posture of promise.

"The Temple Boy will guard them," Aidan roared, releasing his braid and raising his fist to the sky. The chieftains of Ebba, Dolphys, Leok, and Joran copied his motion. Benjie was the only chieftain who hesitated, his eyes shifting from Banruud's face, to the men around him, to the boy who inspired such confidence in the clans. But Benjie's fist soon followed, striking the night sky with his own endorsement.

"From this day forward, we will call them the Daughters of Freya, and they will be a light to the clans," Lothgar boomed, repeating the words of the Highest Keeper like he'd composed them himself.

Alba was squirming to be released, and Banruud set her down, disgusted with his complete loss of control over the situation. The child ran to the Temple Boy, choosing him, completing the appearance of an anointing. Bayr took her hand and bowed to the chieftains again. Then he bowed to the Highest Keeper and finally to the king himself. And still he didn't utter a word. Banruud considered demanding an oath just to embarrass the boy and demonstrate his weakness in front of the chieftains. His stumbling speech would undermine their confidence in him. They were so quick to raise their fists and cling to a savior.

But Banruud could be magnanimous now. The Highest Keeper could have his flame, and the boy could guard it. The keepers were peasants in purple robes, the boy was a hulking idiot, and the chieftains were fools.

"So be it, Temple Boy. I entrust the Daughters of Freya to your care and to the care of the Keepers of Saylok," Banruud said, relenting. "Do not fail me. Do not fail them."

In the meantime, if something happened to one of their daughters, the chieftains and the people of Saylok would have someone to blame.

"What do we do, Master?" Dagmar worried, his eyes on the huddled daughters eating in the flickering candlelight of the temple kitchen. Dagmar had hoped the chieftains would not obey their king.

He should have known better.

The chieftains were afraid. Saylok was afraid. A girl child from each clan—adopted by each clan—was their way of fighting back against a faceless foe, of preserving life, of bartering with the gods. Bringing a daughter to the temple was like storing gold in the ground, sewing jewels into a cloak, or hoarding food against a weak harvest.

"They are supplicants, Dagmar. We will treat them as such," Ivo replied.

"They are not. They are little girls who have been ripped from their homes."

"Their sacrifice has been noted by Odin himself. We will give them a home here," Ivo soothed.

"It was you who taught me that the only sacrifice with any power is the one that is willingly made. These children are not willing."

Ivo sighed. "We ask nothing of them, Dagmar. Nothing. We will simply keep them safe."

"And their clothing? Their hair?" They were not warriors. They were not yet women. They were no longer even children.

"We are keepers. If they are to live among keepers, they must behave like keepers. They must look like keepers. We will cut their hair and dress them in supplicants' robes. It will offer them a measure of protection that their femininity does not."

"They are children," Dagmar mourned.

"You have raised a child, Dagmar. You have provided us all with invaluable experience."

Dagmar shook his head, fighting anguish. "My experience," he scoffed. "I cannot protect Bayr. I cannot protect these girls. You saw the king this night. Bayr is at his mercy. These girls are at his mercy. He will use them to increase his power. It is a sham, Master."

"Only to the king, Keeper. Not to me. Not to Saylok."

"Then . . . we will instruct them?" Dagmar whispered, his eyes still lingering on the lost little girls. "Even in the runes?"

Ivo was silent, contemplating, and then he sighed. "Not yet. Mayhaps not ever. We will see where the rune blood flows, if it flows at all. Not every supplicant becomes a keeper." His voice held a note of dark irony as he quoted the king. "But every supplicant is protected by the sanctuary of the temple, and no chieftain or king can withdraw a supplicant once they have been pledged."

"Only the Highest Keeper can release or refuse a supplicant," Dagmar whispered, realization dawning.

"Yes." Ivo nodded. "I didn't think it necessary to remind King Banruud or the six clan chieftains of that mandate."

"Oh, Master. You are wily."

"Prescient. I am prescient," Ivo sniffed, not liking Dagmar's description. "It is better to let Banruud think the idea was his own. When I resist, he is so much more eager."

Dagmar could only shake his head in wonder.

"Our goal is to make sure every daughter grows to become a woman. However long it takes," Ivo murmured.

"They are just little girls," Dagmar whispered. "Can we do this, Master?" Dagmar longed to sink to his knees and slash his palms to carve a rune of comfort into the stones of the kitchen floor, but he stayed still, trusting Ivo to do what must be done, though his heart bled instead of his hands.

"We can. We will. And when the king leaves for Ebba, you must retrieve the ghost woman from the fields and bring her here. She will help us."

∼◉∼

Ghost moved the sheep to the meadow below the palace the day the king left for Ebba with trumpets blaring and banners streaming. She uncovered her white hair and bowed her back, knowing it made her appear crone-like, and old women were generally ignored, though less and less so. She'd been heckled more in recent months than in all the years before that combined. Shepherding was a solitary profession, but there were bandits and rovers in the hills, and abductions of women—all women—in the King's Village had increased.

Dagmar had worried about her safety, a woman alone, but she'd managed thus far, surrounded by the sheep and tough terrain. She wore the purple cloak of a keeper, and from a distance, it had been enough to convince the curious that she was a bent old man, a Keeper of Saylok, tending the temple herd.

The summer day was warm, and the herd huddled in the shadow of the temple mount, grazing on the grass that had grown long in recent weeks. Ghost removed her cloak and sat inside a cluster of stones, her back to a boulder that provided a sliver of shade for her pale skin. She thought maybe Dagmar would visit today. Maybe Bayr and Alba too. From her perch, Ghost could see the spires rising on the other side of the wall, pricking the sky like clawed hands, demanding instead of beseeching, and she wished the spires would direct them to her.

The lambs born in the spring had grown and settled into the long summer days, and they were less likely to wander or draw the wolves. Ghost found herself growing drowsy in the late afternoon, lulled by the obedience of her flock and weary from hopeful waiting.

"It's a woman, all right."

The male voice came from her right, the exaggerated whisper more suspicious than a measured tone. Ghost kept her eyes closed, but alarm chased her heart.

"Younger than she looks, I'll wager," he added, still hissing like he believed himself undetected. The sheep shifted nervously, sensing strangers in their midst, and Ghost called them to her with urgent thoughts, willing them to draw together. They responded immediately, huddling together, closing in around her and the circle of stones where she rested. Reaching for the blade beneath her skirts, she stood slowly and faced the threat.

Ghost stood in the middle of the sheep, drawing them around her, a woolly moat between her and the three men who circled the animals, their eyes on her, a woman alone, ripe for the taking.

"Come 'ere, lass," one said, swinging his loop like she would simply come if he asked, as if she would wade through the bleating herd and let him lead her away at the end of his rope. One man held a long lash and the other a scythe, as though he'd seen her from the farmlands butted up to the foothills at the base of the temple mount and decided his harvest could wait.

"These are the sacrificial lambs of the Keepers of Saylok. You mustn't touch them," she warned, infusing her voice with as much courage as she could muster.

"She speaks!" the largest man crowed, snapping his lash in the air. The sheep moaned and trembled.

"Yeah. And her voice is all funny . . . like an Eastlander," his companion with the rope added. "That's good. Saylok's women are cursed. We can sell her for more if she's from somewhere else."

"These sheep belong to the keepers. The keepers are protected by the king himself."

"The king is gone. He and his warriors. We watched them ride out, woman. There's war in Ebba. Everyone knows that. We've nothin' to fear from him today."

Stones filled her pockets and a leather sling was looped over the rope at her waist. She considered which weapon would do her the most good, the sling or her blade, and decided the sling. She needn't get close for it to be effective. She was skilled with the leather strap. It worked on the wolves, but these were men, and they wanted her. Not the sheep.

The sheep hovered, pressing against her, feeling her need even as they trembled in distress. She should tell them to scatter, but she clung to them, to their simple warmth, to the mindless obedience they gave her, and though their bleating became an army of discordant trumpets, she did not release them from her compulsion.

The man with the scythe and the man with the whip began working their way toward her from opposite sides, shoving the sheep this way and that. The breach was met with trampling hooves, jostling bodies, and full-throated rebukes. The man with the scythe cursed and brought his weapon across the woolly back of the nearest sheep.

"Stop!" she shrieked, as the bleating became screams of pain. One sheep fell and the others reared, trampling the fallen animal, but the path was no clearer. If anything, the man had made things harder for himself. The sheep bellowed in terror, cowering and convulsing, and the man swung his scythe again. Blood sprayed in a wide arc and another sheep fell. Ghost scrambled atop the boulder where she'd been resting and, with a scream that tore through her belly and out her throat, commanded the sheep to flee.

Something caught at her left arm—the lash—sharp and stinging, but she pulled free, her attention on the sheep, urging them to scatter, scatter, scatter. The animals obeyed, bursting outward from the stones like ripples on a pond. But the rippling wasn't silent or soft. It was heavy, thundering, and the man with the scythe was knocked to the ground, his scythe falling from his blood-soaked hand. The other two men fell back, tripping and cursing, and Ghost threw herself from the boulder, sprinting toward the two sheep that had been struck down. One's throat had been cut, and he stared at her in gurgling despair. She soothed him once, a hand over his black head, and he was silent. The other sheep was struggling to rise, a deep slash turning his side into a crimson carpet. Ghost wrapped her arms around the beast, urging him to his feet, and succeeded only in bathing herself in his blood.

14

"Ghost!" Someone was calling her name.

The man who'd wielded the scythe had pulled himself to his knees. He'd taken a beating from the stampeding sheep, and he was wheezing for breath, clutching his chest. She scrambled for his scythe, and his eyes clung to hers, begging mercy.

"Ghost!"

Dagmar was calling her name.

She stood, scythe in her hand, and screamed out in warning, not certain where the other two men had gone, or if they'd gone at all.

Dagmar and Bayr were running toward her, Bayr picking up speed as he flew. Even at twelve, Bayr was more intimidating on his own two legs than an armed man on horseback. He held no weapons, but the fury on his face and the confidence with which he hurled himself down the hill was enough to send the two men running, their fallen companion abandoned. Bayr reached the scythe wielder first and, without questions or commentary, plucked the man from the ground, one hand at his nape, one hand clutching his belt, and hoisted him over his head as though to toss him down the hill behind his cohorts.

"Please," the man gasped. "Have mercy, Temple Boy."

"To sh-show you mercy now would be to sh-show no mercy to those you will p-prey upon next." Bayr stammered, but his arms did not buckle or bend, and he waited for Dagmar to reach his side. But Dagmar ran to Ghost instead. He took the scythe from her hand.

"I beg your pardon, Keeper. I'll not do it again," the man begged, his eyes wild, his arms flailing as Dagmar approached.

"Tell me the names of your friends," Dagmar demanded.

"Peck and Quinn of the King's Village. We saw the woman. We didn't know she was yours."

"But you knew she was not *yours*. You knew the sheep were not *yours*," Dagmar said. "Find your friends. Come to the temple and take your just punishment. If you do not, your sentence, when you are found, will be death."

Bayr set the man on his feet and released him without a word. The man toddled down the hill like a drunken sailor on board a shifting deck. Ghost felt the grass shift beneath her feet as well, and closed her eyes, awash in sudden dizziness.

The next moment she was being swept up, and she cried out, certain she was falling. Then Dagmar's arms tightened around her, and she realized she was being held.

"I w-will c-carry her, Uncle," Bayr offered.

"See to the sheep, Bayr." Dagmar sounded close to tears, and Ghost opened her eyes. Bayr had already turned back to obey his uncle.

"I will see to them," she insisted, but her words whistled past her lips oddly. She was panting, her fear distorting her voice. She tried again. "It was only fear that made me lightheaded. I am not harmed," she reassured him, concentrating on her speech. He had begun to move swiftly toward the temple walls at the top of the hill.

His arms tightened but he didn't slow. "You just can't feel it yet."

"Feel what?"

He snorted, as if she'd simply proven his point.

"You are carrying me again," she complained.

"I am. Thankfully we don't have as far to go this time."

"Put me down."

"No."

"You are a keeper, not a pack mule."

"And you are a shepherdess, not a soldier. That didn't stop you."

"I will go back to my cottage," she insisted.

"You will not. Not ever again."

His vehemence shocked her into silence, but only for a few minutes.

"Where are you taking me?" she asked.

"To the temple."

"I don't want to be seen, Keeper."

"Your hair is bound, and your face and clothes are covered in blood," he barked. "No one will see the color of your skin."

She closed her eyes and covered her face with hands that had begun to shake. She heard the gate swinging open, heard the call from the wall, the questions and alarm being flung at the keeper, but Dagmar didn't slow as he made his reassurances to the curious and concerned. The sound of his stride changed as dirt became cobbles and, beyond the cover of her hands, sunlight became gloom. Then the air cooled and the sounds slipped away, and Ghost peeked through her fingers in wary wonder. She had never been in such a place. The smell of incense clung to the beams and the floors, to the rock and the relics, and she begged again to be put down. Such a place required dignity.

Dagmar set her on her feet, but he did not release her. She could only stare at the soaring columns and the endless stone, the light filtering down from colored glass over arches and angles that stole her breath and raised the flesh on her arms. With the prickling came pain, and she realized some of the blood that soaked her sleeve belonged to her.

She gasped, and Dagmar's hand tightened at her waist.

"Come. Please," Dagmar said, urging her forward. He led her through one door and then another, winding his way to a room that contained vials and tinctures in long rows. A low wooden table laden with hooks and blades made her hesitate, but Dagmar led her to a long bench and bade her sit.

Shallow cuts crisscrossed her arms. The man with the whip had found his mark, but she'd hardly felt the tearing of her flesh. She hardly felt it now.

"They are just sheep, woman," Dagmar whispered, his eyes on her wounds. "You are not required to die for them."

"I am nowhere near death, Keeper."

"You were very near death today," he murmured. "Those men who attacked the herd are well acquainted with it. What happened today will happen again. I am surprised it has not happened before."

"It has."

His eyes snapped from the water he was drawing from a nearby pail.

"I have always frightened them away. I can be quite terrifying to look upon."

His pale gaze turned glacial.

"Are keepers healers?" she asked, eager to speak of something else.

"It is one of the ways we make ourselves useful." He washed the blood from her arms and then covered the oozing welts and lacerations with his hands like he believed his palms could close them.

"What are you doing?"

"I am asking the gods to close your wounds."

"Does that work?" Her doubt rang in her question, and he raised his eyes to hers, a slight smile on his lips.

"It doesn't ever hurt to ask. But the runes work better than anything. In some regards, they too are like prayers. The gods—or the fates—decide whether or not they are answered." He wetted his fingers in the blood that oozed from her deepest wound and began to paint shapes on her arm. It tickled, and she squirmed.

"Shh," he murmured. "Hold still." She did, her stomach fluttering oddly, her eyes on his bloody fingertip drawing pictures on her skin. He drew one at her wrist and another near her shoulder.

"Are those runes?" she asked, breathless.

He nodded once, whispered something in a language that she didn't understand, and then, dipping his fingers in a bowl of water, he wiped the drawings away.

"What did you say?" she pressed.

"I asked that all the poisons be kept from your wounds. It is a rune that works well on rodents and all creeping things."

"They weren't runes of healing?"

"Your body is very adept at healing itself if all invaders are kept out."

"Invaders?" she whispered.

"It is the invaders we cannot see that are the most deadly." He stepped away. "I will draw the runes again tomorrow when we change your bandages."

"Why did you not just leave the runes in place?"

"We draw the runes, ask the gods to acknowledge them, and then we erase them. They are sacred . . . and powerful. And we do not share them."

"If you leave them, I might learn them," she said, understanding dawning.

He nodded once. "It is the way we guard the power. Runes are forbidden to all but the Keepers of Saylok." He paused and then said with great emphasis, "But the keepers are not the only ones with power."

She met his eyes and frowned, not understanding.

"You do not speak to the sheep, but they listen to you," he said, his voice soft and his eyes steady.

Ghost scoffed. "It is not listening . . . it is obeying. Or . . . trusting. I have always been good with animals."

"You said they feel your emotion."

She cocked her head. He was intent on something, but she could not fathom what.

"Remember the horse the day of the coronation? You said he reacted to your emotions," he said.

164

"You remember that?"

"Yes. I've thought of it many times since while watching you with the sheep. That gift . . . or ability . . . is the same power that fuels the runes. It manifests itself in many ways and in many people. If you had been born in Saylok, you might have been a supplicant."

"What is a supplicant?"

"Supplicants are those with rune blood. They come from every clan, but they must have the support of their chieftain, and the Highest Keeper must grant them entry. Supplicants—most of them—eventually become keepers after their training."

"Does Bayr have rune blood? Is that why he is so strong?" she asked, the thought occurring like a flash of light.

"Yes. I believe he does."

"Will he become a keeper—or a supplicant—someday?"

"Not all who have rune blood become keepers. There are other paths . . . other worthy pursuits."

"All the runes must be drawn in blood?"

"Yes. It is the blood that gives the rune its power."

"So if someone does not have . . . rune blood . . . the rune itself will have no power?"

Dagmar nodded.

It was not something they had ever discussed. She wasn't sure why they were discussing it now, why he was being so forthcoming with things that were clearly so secret, so sacred. She wanted to know more.

"So why guard the runes if they are of no use to powerless people?"

"It is not the powerless people we must worry about. Because a man or woman has rune blood does not mean they have a pure heart. Power tends to corrupt."

"Does it corrupt . . . keepers?"

"Of course. Keepers are just men. But that is why we live here, without family or female companionship, without riches or reward, without the temptations that would make us susceptible to such corruption. It is a delicate balance. We don't use the runes for power or dominion. We do not use them for gain or glory. We seek wisdom, understanding, and patience."

For a moment they were silent, and then she raised her eyes to his, defiant.

"I would not have been a supplicant," she argued.

"No?"

"All the keepers are men. I am a woman."

"My sister . . . Bayr's mother, had rune blood. There are many women who do."

"Yet there are no females among you," she challenged him.

"Women are keepers of a different sort. Keepers of children. Keepers of the clans. Through the ages, women have been needed elsewhere. We men were more expendable. We are *still* more expendable. But there are Daughters in the temple now."

She searched his eyes and waited for him to explain.

"Today's visit was not happenstance. Master Ivo sent me to get you. It took me several days to do as he asked. I shudder to think what would have happened had I waited even one more day."

"He sent you to get me?" she gasped.

"He did. And when you have rested—mayhaps tomorrow—he will want to see you in the sanctum."

"I thought women were not allowed in the sanctum."

"It is not that. 'Allowed' is the wrong word. It is a place for runes and keepers. For the coronation of kings . . . and queens. Alba was blessed above the altar."

"She was?" Ghost breathed, trying to imagine it.

"Yes. We have had great hopes for the princess. We thought she was the dawn of a new day. We prayed other daughters would be born in her wake. But that has not happened."

Ghost could only hold his gaze, her heart echoing like an executioner's drum in her ears. "If it has not happened . . . how . . . why . . . are there Daughters in the temple?"

"They represent the clans." He sighed. "There is much to explain. But I will let Ivo do that."

"What will he ask of me?"

"He will ask you to help us care for them."

"You think because I am a w-woman, I know how to care for children? They are not lambs, Keeper," she stammered, horrified. She began to pace, wanting to escape, yet also wanting nothing more than to find a quiet corner and rest her now-pounding head.

"I think because you are a woman, you can instruct us. We need you."

"I do not know your ways. Your runes. Your customs. Your prayers," she argued.

"They are young girls, Ghost. Five of them. Six, if we include the princess. And we are lost . . . they are lost. There are things you will understand and anticipate that we . . . as men . . . cannot."

"You want me to live in the temple?" she wailed with disbelief.

"Yes." His voice had grown so soft, clearly in an effort to calm her, that she lowered her own to a whisper. Confessions were easier that way. Mayhaps he wouldn't hear.

"I cannot live here . . . I don't wish to be seen."

"You said that today. You said that when I first met you."

Ghost raised her eyes to his. "And nothing has changed." She felt the lie from the tips of her toes to the roots of her white hair. In truth, everything had changed. But that one thing had not. She did not wish to be seen, and she could never tell him why. To tell him would be to take the crown from her daughter's head.

"You have nothing to be ashamed of," he murmured. She laughed and his brows lowered, a hint of a scowl teasing his mouth.

"You say that as if you know me," she said.

"I do."

"You don't, Keeper. And yet . . . you want me to live here . . . among you."

"I know you, Ghost. We can only hide our true selves for so long, and you've had nothing and no one to hide behind. You can become one of us. A supplicant, just like the daughters who will represent the clans. If you must hide . . . you can hide among us. We shave our heads and blacken our eyes. We wear robes of the same hue. If you do not wish to be seen, what better way to disguise yourself?"

"Why do you blacken your eyes?"

"It is symbolic."

"Of what?"

"Of our own . . . lack of vision and understanding. Master Ivo blackens his lips as well."

"But . . . he is the Highest Keeper. He holds great power."

"Next to the gods and the Norns he is nothing. He is flesh. He is subject to fate and death and the gods' displeasure. So he blackens his lips to show his words are not God's words. He blackens his eyes to signify his sight is not omniscient."

"But you do not blacken your lips."

She felt odd speaking of his lips, and her eyes bounced from the swell of his mouth to his steady gaze before she fixed her attention on her shoes to avoid looking where she should not.

"Ivo is the only one who does both. And they are always black . . . though the keepers are the only ones who regularly see him. He doesn't leave the temple grounds unless the king summons him."

"Does the king summon him often?"

"The king wishes to make his authority and his dominance known. Especially over the keepers. Ivo finds it wiser to appease him on things that don't matter. The king would rather we didn't exist, I'm sure. We are a check on his power, and he certainly doesn't want our opinions. There is a tunnel—there are tunnels all over the temple mount—from the temple to the castle. From the sanctum to the throne room. The kings before Banruud made use of them often. Banruud has not used them yet. He summons us to him instead."

Ghost knew there were tunnels all over the temple mount. She'd found the one in the garden that night, years before, when she'd decided to leave her daughter in the arms of the queen. Now the queen was gone. And Alba needed a mother.

"I am not a keeper," she protested, but she had already made her decision, and she saw by the fleeting triumph that crossed his face that he knew what it was. Still, he insisted on extracting the word.

"Will you stay, Ghost? Will you help us?"

"I will stay."

"The ghost is unharmed?" Ivo asked, his voice muffled in his robes, his face flickering in and out of the darkness. Dagmar sank onto a bench before the altar, suddenly weak from the afternoon's excitement.

"Not completely. Her injuries will heal . . . but she was covered in blood." Dagmar choked on the memory. He cleared his throat and attempted a firmer tone. "They slaughtered two of the sheep, but the wool and flesh will not be wasted. Bayr has moved the herd inside the walls, but we will need to find someone else to tend them from now on."

"All is as it was meant to be. She is safe within our walls. You will bring her to see me on the morrow."

Dagmar's eyes clung to the dancing flames lining the sanctuary. It took two hours to light the candles each morning and another hour to extinguish them each night. "I have feared this day," he murmured.

"Be careful what you fear," Ivo replied, grave. "We draw the attention of the fates when our fear grows too loud. The fates are cruel, and they will reward you with what you fear most."

Dagmar could only nod, knowing Ivo spoke truth. He had feared so many things that had come to pass. But Ghost's death was not what he feared most. Her life—her presence in his life—scared him even more than her loss, for he knew how to mourn. He knew how to survive tragedy, to abide grief. But he wasn't sure he could withstand love.

15

On her first birthday, Bayr gave Alba a doll he'd made himself. He'd filled a small linen sack with grain and sewed the opening closed. Buttons for the eyes, nose, and mouth, and wool for the hair. The queen had helped him fashion a gown and a blanket from an old coverlet. Alba had loved it—it had been repaired many times—and named the doll Baby Bayr in his honor.

For her second birthday, he trapped two small mice and built them an enclosure so Alba would have pets. When the mice started reproducing, the queen had insisted he set Alba's "pets" free beyond the temple walls, but Alba still remembered them and was convinced she would find them again someday.

For her third birthday, Bayr whittled her a whistle, fashioned her a drum, and restrung an old lute so she could make music whenever she wished. For her fourth birthday, he painted a picture on each of her four walls, with the queen's approval. He wasn't a talented artist, but Alba had loved his misshapen animals and awkward landscapes. He'd drawn a picture of the two of them, Alba on his shoulders, climbing to the top of Shinway Peak.

On her fifth birthday, he'd found five blue robin's eggs, just about to hatch, and he brought her to watch their birth. Alba had been enchanted, and the mother robin had preened and whistled as though she knew she was in the presence of royalty. The robin had flown away to find food for her young, and Alba had wanted to fly too, so Bayr ran through the castle, holding her high above his head, letting her soar, her arms spread out like wings. Alba never grew weary of their games, and Bayr never grew weary of Alba. But now she was turning six, her mother was gone, and Bayr was at a loss.

He wasn't certain anyone in the palace knew what day it was. The king was not concerned with such things, and even if he had been, there was war in Ebba, and he had not returned. Bayr's own birthday often came and went without much fanfare, though Dagmar always remembered. Life was not a celebration on the temple mount. Life was hard, and survival was the most constant aim. But Bayr loved Alba, and her happiness was his chief concern. Lady Esa had moved into the queen's chambers, but she was easy to avoid and appease. She'd been there the day he'd lifted the altar from her husband's body, and he often found her staring at him with an awe and fear that embarrassed him. She was also easily tired and unaccustomed to Alba's energy. That day, when she retired early, Bayr loaded Alba on his shoulders, and without permission, he stole from the palace and loped through the queen's gardens toward the wall between the temple and the castle grounds.

"Are we going to find my mother?" Alba asked. She had asked him the same thing every day since the queen's death. She had not grasped the fact that her mother was gone forever. Each time, Bayr could only shake his head. He scaled the wall like he'd done a thousand times, and Alba tightened her arms without being asked.

Evening meditation had commenced, and the bells had tolled. Ivo would be in the sanctum, the keepers in their private quarters. Bayr knew where the girls would be too; he'd helped move the heaviest relics to other parts of the temple to clear out the long room where they now resided. He'd seen them traipsing behind Ghost in their purple robes like goslings behind a goose, and he knew their names and the way they spent their days. He guarded the temple the way he watched over Alba, though thus far, he'd done so from a distance.

He hoped Ghost would be among them. She slept in one of the beds in the long row, and Ghost knew him. She could speak for him. But when he and Alba slipped through the heavy door into the chamber of the girl children, Ghost was not present, and he hovered near the door with Alba on his shoulders, wishing he had practiced his words. Alba clapped excitedly, but he didn't set her down. He needed her weight to give him courage.

"It is h-her b-b-birthday," he said, in an effort to explain their sudden presence. The girls looked at him with varying expressions of fear and fascination. He was big and he was still a stranger, but they'd all seen him profess his protection in the courtyard the night they arrived. And he carried a princess on his shoulders.

"You are the Temple Boy," the girl from Joran stated. Her warrior's braid was gone. All their hair was gone, red, gold, and black length snipped away, leaving close-cropped caps behind, and Bayr wanted to hide his own braid in commiseration. They were dressed like suppliants, but their small bodies and big eyes betrayed them. The freckled one with the red hair, the girl who was closest to his own age, stood and took a step toward him and Alba.

"Happy birthday, Princess Alba," she murmured. "I am Elayne . . . of Ebba." She pointed to Juliah, the next oldest, and then to Liis. "This is Juliah from Joran and Liis from Leok." Liis did not smile at Alba or even acknowledge her presence, but Alba repeated her name anyway. Elayne continued. "Bashti is from Berne—she and Dalys are not much older than you, Highness. Dalys is from Dolphys . . . like you are, Temple Boy. Brother Dagmar too."

"He is Bayr," Alba protested softly, patting his cheek. "Not Temple Boy. His name is Bayr."

"Why have you brought her here?" Juliah asked, her eyes hard.

"It i-i-is h-her b-birthd-day," Bayr stammered again.

"You said that," Juliah snapped. Elayne flinched and Bayr stiffened. Slowly he brought Alba down from his shoulders. He'd wanted to give her six unique gifts. One for every year of her life. Then he'd realized there were five girls just over the castle wall. Five girls. Five friends. And Ghost. Ghost made six. And he'd brought Alba to see them, knowing it would please her more than anything else he could do. Now he stood before them, tongue-tied, helpless to explain that she was as alone as they, that she was motherless and sad, that she was everything good in the world. He touched Alba's pale hair, hoping she would not be hurt by the obvious hostility emanating from several of the girls.

Alba walked to Juliah and without hesitation, took the girl's hands and tipped her own head back with a smile.

"YOU-LEE-UH!" she sang the girl's name. "I am here to see you!" Alba laughed, the sound like sunshine through colored glass, and Juliah wilted.

They stayed an hour, Alba singing and hopping from bed to bed, making the girls smile in spite of themselves. Bayr hung back, watching, listening for prayers to end and the sun to set, and when the bells tolled again and the song of the keepers rang out to usher in the moon, he scooped Alba up and bowed to her new friends.

"Th-thank y-you," he stammered.

"Will you bring her back, Bayr?" the smallest girl, Dalys, asked. He nodded swiftly, and little Dalys wasn't the only one who smiled in response.

"I don't want to go, Bayr. Not yet. I want to stay here, in the temple."

He patted Alba's leg, dangling over his shoulder, but turned to go. It was time. With Alba's protestations in his ears and her small hands clasped around his neck, he whisked her away to her tower room, wishing they never had to go back.

They still slept in fitful huddles, small bodies beneath thin covers. Dalys cried in her sleep. Elayne cried *before* she slept. Juliah screamed and Bashti thrashed. Liis was so silent and still she hardly made a dent beneath the blanket. Ghost wasn't sure she slept at all.

The keepers had emptied a room of relics and replaced the ancient artifacts with a row of beds and a wooden chest at the base of each one for the girls to store their possessions. None of the girls had possessions enough to fill the space. The new supplicants were fitted for the purple robes of the keepers, and Ghost kept their hair short. It wasn't so different from shearing sheep; they weren't so different from the little lambs. The keepers weren't unkind, but they were awkward and afraid. None of them had been fathers. None of them were comfortable with women—of any age—and they avoided the girls with bowed heads and skittering eyes. They avoided Ghost. All except Dagmar and Master Ivo.

Master Ivo looked like a great, stooped vulture with talons and a beak of flesh. His black eyes and lips weren't as alarming as they might have been had Dagmar not explained their significance. Ghost found she trusted his ugliness. She'd learned long ago the physical form was simply a shell for all manner of evil. Master Ivo looked evil. But he wasn't. It was Ivo who insisted the girls be treated like little keepers—supplicants, he called them. They were instructed in reading and writing, and they were learning the songs and the incantations.

When Dagmar had brought her to the sanctum where the Highest Keeper spent most of his time, Ivo had studied her colorless skin and white hair with great interest, but it was her eyes he seemed most fascinated by. He had stood from his throne and drawn close, peering into them like a thieving magpie.

"They are like glass," he muttered. "A man will look at you and see himself. His beauty—or lack thereof—will stare him in the face."

Dagmar cleared his throat, and Master Ivo raised his unruly brows and flicked his hand toward him. "Go, Dagmar. I must commune with the ghost."

Dagmar sighed and hesitated, but Ghost did not watch him go. The Highest Keeper did not frighten her.

"So what do you see looking back at you, Master Ivo?" she asked, bold.

"I see my age . . . and my youth too. I see the sanctum . . . and my seat upon the dais. It is empty."

Of course it was empty. The Highest Keeper had vacated the dais when he moved to stand before her, but Ghost did not question him.

He asked her about her time in Eastlandia. Her birth. Her life. Her journey to Saylok. She was honest about everything. Everything except the king. Everything except Alba. She made no mention of either of them.

"You had a child." It was not a question.

"Yes."

"But no longer?"

She stared at him as though the question had an obvious answer. There was no child in her care. That much he knew already.

"The father was an Eastlander . . . like you? A servant?"

"No. He was as dark as I am light. He came from somewhere else. He was lost and alone. The shunned often find comfort in one another. We were both very young."

"You are still very young."

"I am old inside," she whispered, and he nodded as though he understood.

"Where is he now?"

"I don't know." Her eyes didn't waver. "He found his way. Comfort is not love, Master. Mayhaps it could have been, but time did not allow for such revelations."

"Time does tell us many things. Will you stay long enough for me to discover some of them, ghost girl?"

"I have nowhere else to go."

"There is always somewhere else to go."

"There is nowhere else I want to be."

He inclined his head, seemingly pleased. "Then we have an agreement. You will stay. And we will learn what time has in store."

It had been six months since the children had been brought to the temple, since she had been summoned, and they had all settled into a daily routine.

But they still slept fitfully.

Ghost shared their room, listening to their muffled sobs and feeling their longing to be somewhere else. They'd been afraid of her at first. Bashti was the first to thaw toward her, as if Ghost's strangeness lessened her own and she found comfort in it. Weeks after Ghost had come to the temple, the little girl crawled in bed beside her in the middle of the night, curling at her back. The next night, Dalys beat her to it. After that, Ghost suggested they push their beds closer together so they wouldn't feel alone while remaining in their own beds.

She'd cut her own hair short in solidarity with the girls. She would be a supplicant too. She donned the purple robe Dagmar had given her five years before and used the strands of her hair and a thin stick to craft a paintbrush for painting her face. Using the soot from the fireplace, she created a black paste that she used to rim her eyes and darken her white lashes. Her reflection terrified her; she looked like a monster with her silvery gaze emboldened by the thick black lines. She even rubbed a bit of the sooty paste into her brows. The effect changed her face. Instead of looking like a ghostly specter, she looked like a demon bride.

When Dagmar saw her shorn locks, he looked shocked. He reached toward her as though to smooth what remained, and then seemed to think better of it.

"I will miss it," he said softly. "It was glorious."

She'd wanted to cry then. Why hadn't he ever said so? She would have braided it around her head in a tight cap and kept it. Now it was gone, and she was left with a word. *Glorious.* He had thought her hair glorious. He said nothing about her blackened eyes and brows.

"Will this help us see?" Elayne asked, mimicking Ghost's actions. She looked more like a forest creature with her bright hair and glowing eyes, but the effect was still startling.

"I think it will help us to not be seen. We will look like the keepers. It is like a disguise. If we all look the same, we will be a group. A clan of our own," Ghost reassured her.

Alba did not sleep in the temple, though Bayr brought her to see the girls as often as he could. With the king squelching skirmishes in Ebba, those living on the temple mount exhaled and let the little princess have her way whenever possible.

There were rumors about what the king had done to the midwife, Agnes, after his wife's death. The palace staff and the royal guard whispered about it amongst themselves and grew even warier of Banruud. Ghost already knew to be wary of him and tried not to dwell on the day when he would come back.

The old queen was indulgent, and Dagmar had convinced her that the princess should attend lessons with the temple daughters. Whenever Alba visited, the girls greeted her with curtsies and bowed heads, but Alba embraced them with such enthusiasm and delight that they bloomed in her presence. *Ghost* bloomed in her presence. Each day was an awakening, a rebirth, and sometimes her joy was so intense, she thought her heart would break.

When it all became too much, Ghost would seek Dagmar and his quiet companionship. He was often stooped over scrolls, a quill in hand, turning one language into another, one man's writings into his own, but he would greet her with a smile and she would tuck herself nearby and let his presence calm the exquisite agony in her chest. Often, they never spoke at all, and Ghost would simply slip away when she could breathe again.

The Highest Keeper placed meaning in everything, from the contributions of a field mouse to the formation of the clouds in the sky, and Ghost became aware of things she had never thought about before. She was included in the education of the young supplicants, and she learned the prayers and practiced the incantations with an intensity that raised Ivo's brows and the corners of Dagmar's lips. Her fingers were always stained with ink and her eyes were often slightly dazed, deep in thought even when she performed her daily chores. She opened herself to the temple the way the temple had been opened to her, and her enthusiasm for learning was an example to the girls she'd been tasked to care for.

The clan daughters, as they were loosely called, were more similar than they were different—all young, all afraid, all female, all forsaken, with needs and desires and a sense of loss that permeated the temple walls. The keepers who had come to the temple as supplicants had all come of their own accord, knowing the life they chose. Even Ghost had chosen the temple over the sheep, and over leaving Saylok altogether. The clan daughters had been brought against their will, and they were unified in that reality. But each girl brought her own footprint to the temple grounds, and as time passed and fear abated, their differences became more obvious.

Juliah from Joran had been raised to battle, and she was constantly drawing Bayr into combat. She would jump from behind doors or spring from the rafters overhead, light as a cat, and try to catch him off guard. He bore her aggression well, the way he bore everything else. Dagmar had rubbed off on the boy; they were both unflappable and focused, introspective and observant, and instead of rebuffing her need for confrontation, he absorbed it, teaching her as he took her abuse, giving back enough that she sharpened her skill without breaking her bones.

The girl from Joran was not the only one who bubbled over in aggression, though where Juliah was action, Liis of Leok was a simmering pot. Her silence was a weapon, and she used it with considerable effect. So it came as a great surprise when one day, as the sun surrendered the day to the moon and the keepers were gathered in praise, Liis suddenly broke out in song with them, her voice piercing the air the way her silence usually deflated the room. She sang the song of supplication, the one most commonly raised in evening worship.

Mother of the earth be mine, father of the skies, divine.
All that was and all that is, all I am and all I wish.
Open my eyes to see, make me at one with thee,
Gods of my father and god of my soul.
Give me a home in hope, give me a place to go,
give me a faith that will never grow cold.

Her voice was crystalline and cutting, sitting above the tenor tones of the complacent keepers. It grew and climbed and carved a hole into the hearts of all who listened. The voices raised in habit became voices hushed in awe. Liis sang as though she cursed each word for making her ache, and the tears she wouldn't cry streamed from the eyes of the little girls who'd cried too much, from the eyes of the keepers who hadn't cried enough, and from Ghost herself, who only cried when she was alone.

If Liis made them weep, Bashti made them laugh. She had an uncanny gift for mimicry—her impression of Ivo had the girls covering their mouths and ducking their heads into their robes, so they wouldn't be caught howling with laughter inside the sanctum when they were supposed to be meditating. Bashti didn't like to meditate. She liked to imitate. It only took her a few minutes in someone's presence to lock in on their idiosyncrasies and speaking patterns. She mocked the king, the Highest Keeper, several of the brothers, and even Ghost, who took the ribbing with a delighted smile and a question: "I do that?"

Bashti could mimic the way Keeper Dieter teared up whenever he talked and the way Keeper Lowell spoke out of one side of his mouth. She even mocked the other girls and Princess Alba, though not mercilessly. The only person she was not allowed to impersonate was Bayr. She started to do so one afternoon, trying out an impression of the boy that was eerily apt and particularly brutal, stumbling with her words even as she puffed out her chest to indicate his strength.

Alba grew perfectly still, her eyes locked on Bashti's humor-filled face, and seconds later she was hurtling across the room, hands curled, arms extended, murder in her eyes.

"Never do that again," she said, clamping her hands over Bashti's gaping mouth. "Ever. Ever. You will not laugh at Bayr."

The room grew silent, and Bashti's eyes filled with tears. Bayr straightened from his position at the door and hurried to subdue his charge. The teasing hadn't bothered him—he'd been laughing along with the others. He wrapped his large hands around Alba's small wrists and pulled her hands from Bashti's mouth. He smiled at the girl and patted her head, as if to apologize for Alba. Then he took Alba by the hand and led her away. Alba had thrown a look of warning over her shoulder as she left the room.

"Never. Ever," she said again.

The next time Bayr brought Alba back for lessons, Ghost noticed that Alba embraced Bashti longer than usual, patting her back in apology, and she never spoke of the incident again. She never had to. For someone so small, Alba had a great deal of influence.

Dalys, the youngest of the five, was a year older than Princess Alba, but unlike Alba she'd had no formal lessons at all. Where Alba was confident, she was meek; where Alba excelled, she struggled. She shrank from any attempts to learn until Alba began to teach the girl herself, the way the queen had once taught her. Paints were hard to procure, so one of the keepers taught them how to make their own, and Alba helped Dalys create an alphabet that came alive in pictures drawn around letters, and letters combined into words. The words became a story that Dalys began to tell, and before long, Alba's gifts became Dalys's.

And Alba was truly gifted. She remembered everything as though she held pictures in her head, and she could describe—and re-create—the smallest thing with great detail. The keepers had grown very careful with their lessons when the princess was present.

Dagmar taught the daughters their first rune, an elementary drawing of a sun with seven beams radiating from it, six for the clans and one more that extended straight down, much longer than the others. He explained it was a conduit for happiness and understanding. The sun, in her golden generosity, did not want her children living in darkness. The girls used spittle to draw the rune instead of blood. Dagmar claimed it was the closest thing to it, and each girl placed their fingers in their mouths, wetting them before copying the simple depiction that faded on the dark stone almost as soon as it was created.

The simplistic nature of the rune had Liis glowering at Dagmar with distrust and Juliah proclaiming the sun rune childish.

"I wish to draw runes that can defeat my enemies," Juliah complained.

"Is not misery the greatest enemy of all?" Dagmar said softly. "This is the first rune because without light and belief, everything is darkness, and everything and everyone becomes the enemy."

That placated the girls, but Ghost hungered for more and considered her ignorance a darkness all its own.

Master Ivo rarely taught the girls their lessons but spent considerable time observing them and asking questions, though he never seemed intent on a particular answer. When the girls would seek a reason for his queries, he would simply say, "I seek only to know the gifts with which you were born. Knowing your gifts helps me know you. The Allfather does not sprinkle gifts and abilities like a farmer plants grain, tossing the seed from side to side, not caring where it lands so long as it is in the dirt. Odin is very particular about where he plants his seed."

The inference that the girls and their gifts were products of Odin's seed was not lost on Ghost. Mayhaps it was not lost on the girls either, though Elayne was the only one who seemed to grasp the double meaning. She flushed and studied the freckles on her pale hands, though

Ghost wasn't certain her discomfort came from the sensual context or the fact that Elayne was not particularly gifted.

She worked hard, and she was capable and efficient in her duties, but she had none of Juliah's warrior spirit or Liis's icy strength. Her voice sounded like a horse's whinny when she tried to sing, so she mostly mouthed the words. She wasn't particularly good at memorization either, and the prayers and chants and affirmations did not find root in her thoughts. She didn't read well, she had no aptitude for alchemy, and her drawings were infantile.

If she excelled in anything, it was kindness.

She nurtured the other girls, was endlessly patient, and was a leader among them simply because she was the oldest and looked out for the rest. But Ghost knew she fretted over her mediocrity.

They all fretted, though Ghost suspected their fears did not look the same.

When the temple was dark, and the lessons had ended, there was only worry over what would be and grief over what had been, and every night Ghost conjured Dagmar's sun rune, trying to drive out the darkness and cling to the light, willing his gods to watch over them all.

16

One night, after the girls were abed, Ghost went looking for Dagmar. She'd spent so much time alone in recent years that the constant company of children could be a strain. She craved a place to air her thoughts and someone who would listen without waiting to speak.

Dagmar was not stooped over scrolls or tucked into any of his favorite corners. She climbed the stairs to the rooms overlooking the castle yard, the rooms no one else seemed to want, and found his door ajar, light spilling out into the corridor, illuminating a stain on the pale threshold.

She said his name and remained in the hallway, not wanting to disturb him and desperately hoping he wanted to be disturbed.

She heard him stand, his stool scraping against the bare planks of the floor. Then he was looming in the entry, concern lining his brow, an oil lamp in his hand.

"Is something amiss?" he asked, alarmed.

She shook her head, adamant and a little embarrassed. He'd never seemed to mind when she'd sought him out before. But it was late and these were his private quarters.

"I didn't want to lie in the dark listening to children prattle."

He laughed, his face creasing in an entirely different way. "You need your own space."

"No." She shook her head. "Just . . . different company for a bit."

"I understand. Let's walk, shall we?"

She nodded, grateful, and he stepped back into his room to set the lamp aside. The light jumped and her eyes were drawn downward, back to the stain a foot from her toes.

"Is that a rune?" she blurted.

Dagmar started. "Yes . . . I . . . no one usually comes up here but me. I should have . . . covered it."

"Why did you draw a rune outside your door?" she asked, bemused. She studied it curiously, a memory niggling. "It is the same one you drew on my skin. The rune that discourages rodents and crawling things."

"You remember?" An odd note colored his question.

"I could not have drawn it myself. But I remember. Are you afraid of mice, Dagmar?" She laughed, charmed. Dagmar was always so wise and self-contained. The thought of him warding off creeping things with his precious blood endeared him to her.

"I am not afraid of mice," he said, color rising to his cheeks. "Warding off . . . rodents or infection . . . is not the only purpose of the rune."

"Oh? What is it you are trying to ward off?"

It was in the way his back stiffened and his eyes angled away, the way his thumb worried the scars on his palms, but Ghost suddenly knew what—who—he was guarding against.

"You don't want me to come in your room?" she squeaked, so surprised she had no room for hurt.

He didn't answer.

"I have never entered your room, Keeper. I have never touched your things or taken something that belonged to you. Why would you need to do such a thing?"

He held his tongue but not her gaze.

"Do you worry I will touch your skin while you sleep and turn you into a ghost . . . like me? Or maybe you think you must guard against the wiles of a woman?" She hated the welling in her throat and chest, the rising waters that would make her weak before him.

"Yes," he whispered. "That is what I guard against."

She turned away so he wouldn't know the pain he had caused.

"Goodnight then," she said, feeling awkward and more alone than she'd felt when she lived in the shepherd's cottage on the western slopes. Feeling more alone than she'd felt day after day among the herd.

"Ghost?" His voice was strained, and she knew he had not meant to wound. But she was wounded, and she bade him goodnight again, keeping her face averted.

She thought he sighed, but she was already moving, the moonlight winking through the window at the end of the long corridor. No one stuck his head out to see her flee. Dagmar slept alone in this wing, empty rooms on either side, each of them as barren and bleak as the next. She'd often wondered why Dagmar kept himself apart, until one day she'd asked him, and he'd told her he'd moved when Bayr was a babe, desperate to keep his cries from waking the other keepers. He'd never moved back, even when Bayr moved on.

Mayhaps she was not the only one he guarded himself from. But she was the only one who was crying over it.

She descended the winding stairs to the darkened halls that opened into the gallery outside the sanctum. The sconces were lit, and the art of ages past flickered in the dancing light, simulating movement, like the painted lived behind the pictures. She could feel Dagmar behind her, his regret and apology welling around him. She kept walking, circling the gallery with lengthening strides until he begged her to stop.

"Ghost. Cease. Please."

She obeyed, but she did not turn to face him.

"Surely, you must know how I feel," he murmured.

"You've made it abundantly clear."

His groan was almost inaudible. "I don't think I have."

"I am a nuisance. A diseased one."

"Not clear at all," he grunted. When he spoke again, his voice was so soft she had to strain to hear, but she kept her back to him.

"Master Ivo warned me not to love you. But warning against love is like shining a light upon it. From that day forward, I have guarded myself against you."

"Why would you need to be warned? Am I so dangerous?'" She swung on him, using outrage to cover her shame.

His shoulders slumped and his chin fell to his chest, weary. "Ghost. You are a woman. I am a man. Please, let us not pretend."

"No. By all means. Let's speak plainly. What do you mean?"

Dagmar's sky-soaked eyes were fixed beyond her head, clinging to the darkness, and frustration flared in her chest and curled her fingers into fists. He'd been kind. For so long, he'd been so kind. He'd been steady and safe and straightforward. She did not want to make him bend. She did not want to make him bolt, but she could no longer bear his distance.

"Please look at me, Dagmar."

His jaw tightened, and his eyes closed in denial.

"You make me want to be seen," she said, and his gaze shot to hers, searing, searching.

"I have *always* seen you, Ghost."

For a moment there was only silence between them, a weighty, question-filled silence that portended a deluge.

"Yes. You have. And I have . . . loved you . . . for it. No one warned me not to."

"I am a Keeper of Saylok. I cannot—will not—love you back."

"I am not asking you to . . . although . . . you are a fool if you think love can be forbidden."

"But it can be guarded against," he insisted sadly.

"The keepers leave home and family. They don't have wives. They don't have children. The temple exacts a very high price," she said.

"Yes. And love exacts a very high price. Very seldom can both be paid. We cling to one and shun the other, or we neglect one to better serve the other. Our love makes us vulnerable to using the power of the runes for our own purposes. We must never do anything that gives the runes power over us instead of us having power over the runes."

For the first time she understood why the Keepers of Saylok shut themselves away in the temple, away from the clans. To love was to be at the mercy of someone else. To love was to be controlled.

"I was certain when Bayr was born that they would make me leave the temple. I was compromised by my love for him. By my loyalty and devotion to him. I still am. I would abuse my power to save him. And yet . . . Ivo allowed us both to stay," Dagmar marveled.

"And he allowed me to stay."

"Yes." Dagmar seemed struck, as though the similarity had only just occurred to him. "And now you are one of us."

"A Keeper of Saylok," she said. The title made her want to laugh. She'd been a servant, then a shepherd, now she was a keeper. A keeper of secrets and unfulfilled longing.

"Will you always be a keeper, Dagmar?"

"It is all I ever wanted to be."

"Why? You are a man . . . you can go anywhere. Do anything."

He scoffed. "We are all bound by something. I chose to be bound to the temple instead of being bound to a clan."

"We are all bound by something," Ghost repeated. "But I am not one of you, Dagmar. I do not believe in your gods, and I am not here because I am afraid to love. I am not bound to your temple, and I am not bound to a clan."

"Then why are you here?" His voice was hesitant. He clearly feared her answer, feared she would tell him it was for him.

She was there because she was bound to a child. But she didn't say the words. She told him another truth.

"When I was a little girl . . . not much older than Alba . . . I remember wanting so badly to blend with the clouds—I thought that was where I belonged. I imagined I could walk into the sky and become mist, weightless. Part of something bigger than myself. The clouds would gather around the cliffs near the cottage where I lived. One day I ran as fast as I could and threw myself from the edge, hoping all that thick whiteness would absorb me. After all, I am a ghost." She smiled sadly. "I thought mayhaps I would become part of it. I would belong."

Dagmar's eyes clung to hers. "You threw yourself from the cliff?"

"Yes. And for a moment it was the most beautiful experience of my life. I was free. I didn't fall . . . at least . . . it didn't feel like falling. It felt like floating. There was only silence and softness. I was certain it had worked. And then I hit the water."

For several moments they were both silent.

"It was so cold. So sharp and stinging . . . I kicked and clawed my way to the surface. It was too hard to drown, and sadly . . . I knew how to swim."

"Why . . . sadly?" he asked, but she didn't answer. She didn't need to. She was certain he understood.

"I did it again. Every time the clouds wrapped themselves around those cliffs, I would throw myself from them."

"Why?" he pressed.

"Because the beauty of the fall was worth the pain of landing."

His eyes fell to her lips, and her pulse galloped.

"And falling was never fatal," she said.

"Mayhaps one day . . . it would have been," he breathed.

"We do not live to endure. We endure so someday we can . . . live. I have endured a great deal, but there have only been a few moments when I have truly lived."

With a deep inhale, she threw herself from the cliffs once more, knowing the impact would be painful, knowing the risk was worth it.

"I said once . . . long ago . . . that I did not want to lie with you. And you said you would never ask it of me," she blurted.

"I won't," he whispered but she rushed ahead.

"But I do want to lie with you. I ache with wanting. But it is an ache I can endure . . . an ache I *will* endure . . . happily . . . if I can only be near you. You are my dearest friend."

"Please," he moaned. "Please don't say these things. You will make things impossible between us."

"They are said," she murmured, closing her eyes so she wouldn't see his dismay. "But they are just words. And you have only to ignore them."

She heard movement and felt the warmth of proximity before his lips brushed her closed lids. Her fingertips rose to his rough cheeks, disbelief stealing her breath. She'd been brave when she believed him unaffected by her, brave when she believed he wouldn't bend. But now she was afraid; it was not only she who was truly alive in the moment.

Dagmar's breath was shallow, and his male scent filled her nose. She knew they would not speak of love again. He would not be this close, his breath on her brow, his pulse thrumming beneath her fingertips. Then his mouth brushed hers, a kiss no deeper than a raindrop, and she tightened her hands at his face, holding him to her. For a heartbeat they simply stood, mouths touching, and he began to say the words to the Prayer of the Supplicant.

"'I cannot see, my tongue is a traitor,'" he whispered, the whispered words tickling her lips.

"'My flesh is a foe, my heart a betrayer,'" she added and felt his intake of breath. He had not expected her to join him.

"'My eyes will I blacken, my lips will I close.'" His voice was so low she could only feel the shape of words on her mouth.

"'And let the runes lead me down paths I must go,'" she murmured, the words unintelligible with his mouth pressed to hers.

"'No man can follow. No man can lead. No man can save me, no man can free.'" They said the final lines together, whispering the words, their lips moving around the plea, touching and receiving, and then the prayer was finished, the kiss complete, and she stepped away from him, one step and then another, until the shadows swelled between them and she had the strength to turn away.

"Goodnight, Keeper. From now on, I will do my best to guard myself against you as well."

This time he did not protest but let her walk away.

"Goodnight, my Ghost." Regret rang in his words.

She knew he wished to better explain, but he needn't. His heart was already divided, and he worried that his love would be used against him, against the secrets he'd been entrusted with.

She understood.

She had secrets of her own. Secrets to guard. But he saw her the way she saw him, and in that, she rejoiced.

The Tournament of the King happened every year when the harvest was over and the cold had not yet come. The clan chieftains and their warriors would gather on the temple mount to compete in a slew of contests designed to measure strength and skill and to determine the fiercest clan. The tournament winners became the fodder of legends—usually started by the winners themselves—and for a week, the temple mount became an anthill. Great swaths of color snapped in the breeze—green, gold, red, orange, blue, and brown, and of course the purple of the Keepers and of Saylok itself.

The flags raised along the temple walls whipped and welcomed the citizens making the yearly pilgrimage to partake in the festivities. The temple doors were opened and the keepers on hand to bless and advise, to pray and pardon. During the festival, hundreds who received a hearing with the keepers were granted "new life" and absolution from their sins and sentences. In Saylok, the king made the laws and the chieftains enforced them, but the keepers could mete out mercy.

Justice was swift and severe in the clans, and very few of the accused or condemned actually made it to the temple mount to claim sanctuary or beg an audience with the keepers. The absolution granted was usually spiritual and rarely criminal, but during the Tournament of the King when the temple was opened, there was always at least one infamous outlaw who was granted pardon.

The king had decreed that the daughters of the clans, housed in the temple for over a year, would be on display at his side along with Princess Alba. The keepers had decided the daughters would wear the purple of the temple, but each would hold the flag of her clan to inspire and remind the people that all was well, even in a time of war. The king had even agreed to let Alba hold the gold flag of Adyar, the clan of her mother, so every clan would be represented.

Bayr had looked forward to the tournament with great anticipation. At previous tournaments, he had lurked on the edges or watched the contests from a perch on the parapets, longing to measure his skills against other men's.

But this year, he was fourteen years old—the age of manhood in Saylok—and he would be able to take part. With Alba and the temple daughters in the company of the king and his guard, Bayr planned to compete in every arena. He had no clan, but as long as he had a patron—in his case the Keepers of Saylok—and the entrance fees, he could enter as many contests as he was able. He had already pledged his winnings to the temple and to the Daughters of Freya. Master Ivo had assured Bayr he would be victorious and informed him that the brothers would be watching in "pious pose as he destroyed the competition." Dagmar had urged Bayr not to be boastful or to flaunt his abilities, but he too had given Bayr his blessing.

There had been some question whether the games would be held at all. Dirth of Dolphys had been killed in an attack on the east shores, and Dolphys—and much of Saylok—was in mourning. He had been the chieftain of his clan for three decades, groomed by his father to lead, but gifted by the gods to inspire. He'd been well loved, and Dagmar had grieved when he'd heard the news. Dirth of Dolphys had given him permission to become a supplicant to the temple when Dred, Dagmar's own father, had forbidden him to go. It had caused a rift between the two warriors that lasted many years.

"I don't know if my father ever forgave him. He certainly hasn't forgiven me," Dagmar mused.

"Who w-will b-be chieftain n-now?" Bayr asked. "D-does Dirth h-have a s-son?"

"He had two. And he outlived them both. To be a warrior in Saylok—especially in Dolphys—is to tempt the Norns. There are no warriors fiercer. It is often said in Dolphys that the Norns collect our braids." Dagmar ran a hand down Bayr's black plait, his eyes distant and troubled.

"Uncle," Bayr chided. Dagmar dropped his hand and released his breath, his eyes refocusing on his nephew.

"Bayr."

"The ch-chieftain?" Bayr pressed.

"I do not know whom Dolphys will choose, but some say the selection will occur after the tournament, while the clans are still gathered and Master Ivo can bestow his blessing. The warriors of Dolphys have requested his counsel and the recommendation of the king. There are a number of warriors from Dolphys who could take the place of Dirth of Dolphys, but no one will easily fill his shoes."

The clans were a warring people, but the tournament was not about bloodshed. Clansmen killing clansmen was not in the best interest of Saylok, and the events were more about skill than destruction. Six events took two weeks to complete. Some contests had so many entrants that bracketing was designed, each chieftain choosing how their warriors were stacked up against opposing clans. The bracketing was an art in itself. A chieftain didn't want his best warrior out in the first rounds of competition or too tired too soon. Some events required less time and fewer rounds—the footraces took place within the clans first so the fastest warriors moved ahead into the final contest. The clanless ran a race of their own, the fastest five advancing to compete again.

Bayr won the first race by several seconds, the next race by more, and even in the final race, against the fastest men in the clans, by a full body length. He was dominant in contests of strength—outlifting men twice his age and weight. He was not yet as tall as some warriors, nor as broad, but he was big. His power was impressive, but his speed took many by surprise. He did not have the experience of some of the best archers and was defeated by a bowman from Ebba who congratulated the boy when it was over, claiming Bayr's arm strength alone would have worn down the competition eventually.

"Accuracy is key, Temple Boy, but an archer without stamina is no good to his clan. He'll weaken on the wall. You don't weaken."

Bayr threw the axe with such force, even from thirty paces, that the handle vibrated like a lute string. He was viewed with awe by the shifting crowds and a begrudging respect from the warriors, who considered themselves the best Saylok had to offer. He wrestled the winners of past tournaments with a gleeful innocence, tossing one and then another from the circle with the joy of a child and the prowess of a seasoned competitor. He didn't study technique or prepare mentally for the bouts. He simply stepped into the circle and battled with all the fervor in his heart.

He was clapped on the back and roundly lauded, and he smiled and nodded and offered his hand, but he avoided conversation so completely that many assumed he'd been born with strength and not sense. Some even suggested he couldn't hear and forgot themselves in his presence, assuming he wouldn't—or couldn't—repeat what they complained about. He let them believe what they would, slipping away when the competition was done to guard the king's daughter and toss his winnings among the temple tithes.

At the end of the first week, flush from a triumph, Bayr was approached by a warrior he'd never met before. The man had not competed in the contests, nor had he sat among the chieftains who occupied positions of honor on the king's dais. But he looked like a man of consequence in Dolphys, the blue cloak all the indication one needed to determine his clan. A few warriors followed several steps back as though they were his guards or an entourage.

He was tall and muscled like a man in his prime, but his black braid was streaked with a wide strip of silver, indicating he might be a decade or two past it. Scars, both puckered and smooth, large and small, crisscrossed his powerful arms and bisected his sharp face. He looked as though he'd spent his entire life at war.

"Who are you?" the man asked, his brows, still black and thick, lowered over ice-blue eyes.

"Bayr . . . of . . . Saylok." Bayr breathed between each word the way he'd practiced with Alba, picturing the word before he released it. He did not want to stammer in front of this warrior. He looked like an older, wilder version of Dagmar, and Bayr was drawn to him.

"The Temple Boy?" the man asked, his eyes sharp.

Bayr nodded, not bothering to point out that he was no longer a boy.

"Who was your mother? What was her clan?" the man pressed, taking a step closer.

Bayr studied the man before him, not certain whether he should reveal such information to a stranger. No one had ever asked him about his mother. Usually, when he identified himself as Bayr of Saylok—the Temple Boy—everyone assumed he had no clan, that he had simply been born in the King's Village.

"Are you slow?" the man growled, impatient.

Bayr's hand shot out, unsheathing the man's knife even as he took the man's legs out from under him with a sweeping kick. The man landed hard on his hip but was up and reaching for his blade with impressive speed. His eyes widened when Bayr returned his knife as swiftly as he'd taken it.

"Only slow of speech," Bayr said, each word distinct.

The man threw back his head, his skunk tail of silver-and-black hair swinging with his mirth.

"I am Dred of Dolphys, Bayr of Saylok. You remind me a little of my son."

"Who . . . is . . . your . . . son?"

"Dagmar of Dolphys. He is a Keeper of Saylok." The man's voice was smug, but Bayr was too busy reeling from his revelation to register the surprising paternal pride, though he would remember it later.

"My mother . . . was Desdemona of D-Dolphys," Bayr said, so softly he hardly heard himself speak.

Dred of Dolphys became stone, hard and cold, and for a moment he simply stared at Bayr, showing neither motion nor emotion.

Bayr took a tentative step and then another. He was taller than Dred of Dolphys—he was taller than most men—but not a great deal taller. Bending down, his eyes holding the older man's gaze, he pressed his forehead to Dred's, and held it there for the space of two deep breaths before stepping away.

"Grandfather," Bayr said.

The man's eyes grew impossibly bright and his lips trembled. For a moment, Bayr thought Dred of Dolphys would weep. Then his jaw hardened, his eyes closed, and the emotion retreated as though it had never been.

Dred stepped forward and pulled Bayr's face to his own, their foreheads pressed together, their eyes—identical in shape and color—locked in acknowledgment.

"Bayr of Dolphys," Dred growled. "Grandson of Dred. Son of Desdemona."

"Nephew of D-Dagmar," Bayr murmured, determined to give his uncle his due, and he felt the tremor travel through his grandfather's body and tighten the hand still clasped around the back of his neck.

"He didn't tell me about you," Dred hissed.

"No," Bayr acknowledged.

"I should kill him for that."

"You would . . . have to k-kill me first."

Dred released him and stepped back with a sharp-toothed grin. "I would rather know you than kill you."

Bayr smirked and stuck out his hand, indicating they were in agreement.

Dred laughed, and his laughter became a shout, calling out to the men he commanded, telling them one of their own had been found.

Then heads were thrown back and howls of jubilant welcome echoed over the mount as the Clan of the Wolf welcomed a bear into their pack.

17

"Is she truly gone?" Dred of Dolphys asked, his voice low. He'd dragged Bayr to a feast in the tent of his clansmen, and Bayr, hungry for more than just meat and bread, had been unable to deny him.

Bayr set his goblet down, not certain he understood, not certain he was being spoken to. "What?"

"Desdemona. Dagmar said she was dead. He showed me her grave. Did he deceive me in that too?"

"She is d-dead," Bayr said softly. "I never knew h-her."

"And your father, does he know?"

Bayr frowned. "I d-do . . . not know who . . . my . . . father is."

"Dagmar did not tell you?"

"He d-does not know."

Dred's eyes blanked, and tension shifted and resettled over his features. "He does not know?" Dred asked, the words almost a whisper, and his hand moved unconsciously from his goblet to his sword.

"Dagmar is my father," Bayr insisted, unyielding. "I c-care not who sired me."

Dred nodded slowly, eyes glittering, lips pursed. But he said nothing more. Bayr was relieved. He had no desire to converse more than was necessary. His jaw was beginning to ache with the effort to control his stuttering tongue.

"Are you as strong as they say?" Dred asked, changing the subject and raising his voice to include his clansmen.

Bayr shrugged. He didn't know what people said. He certainly didn't care enough to ask.

"You are quick. And you are big. I watched you compete in the contests. But the tales . . . are they all true?" Dred pressed.

Another shrug.

"You must have a weakness."

Bayr thought of Alba with her pale hair and flashing smile. She was his weakness, if he had one, but he was sure that was not what Dred of Dolphys meant.

Bayr touched his lips.

"You've got a tangled tongue."

Bayr nodded.

"You need a wench to straighten it out for you . . . to show you how to use it."

Dred's suggestion triggered guffaws and groans. Bayr didn't think his grandfather was talking about speaking at all, and he flushed, wishing he'd not been so quick to confess his shortcoming.

"We brought back twenty harlots from King Kembah's harem in Bomboska. He won't miss them. He had ten times that many in his palace. We left the gold. We left the jewels. We just took a few women. He should be grateful. We could have taken his head."

As if on cue, a handful of women, their arms bare, their hair flowing free, and their bodies wrapped in brightly colored scarves and little else, entered his grandfather's tent.

Bayr gaped. Women from every clan came to the tournaments. But he'd never seen women like these before. One woman approached Dred and stopped beside him, but she trailed her finger down Bayr's braid, her face friendly and her gaze warm.

"She will show you how to use your mouth," Dred said, his eyes twinkling, his tone dry.

"You'll not stumble for your words when she's done with you, Temple Boy," a warrior with a gleaming pate and no braid said, smiling his reassurance.

"He won't be able to speak at all!" another warrior belched.

"There are many things my son didn't teach you, many things a man cannot learn in a temple. How many women have you known?" Dred asked.

Bayr shook his head. He'd known no women. Not the way his grandfather meant. His female interactions had consisted of the temple girls, Alba, Ghost, and a handful of villagers and women who worked in the palace. He'd never known women like these.

The woman tugged on his braid and blood surged in Bayr's loins. She released him and stepped back, expectant. When he stared at her blankly, she began to dance away, but extended her hand as if she wanted him to follow.

"She wants you to go with her, son. See how she beckons you?" Dred murmured.

Bayr stood, hypnotized by the curling fingers urging him forward, by the rhythmic sway of rounded hips and slim arms.

"Just don't let her get your knife. She knows how to use that too," he heard his grandfather warn, but his thoughts had already left the circle of men and the smell of roast pig and warm mead to trail after the woman who would teach him how to use his tongue.

Twenty minutes later, he knew a great deal more than he'd known when the night began, but he wasn't ready for all the lessons the harlot seemed to want to teach him.

"No," he panted, the urgency of her hands and her mouth making him tremble and quake, but he pulled back and gently pushed her away.

"Why?" she gasped.

He wouldn't explain it to her. Doing so would take more time and energy than he had, and if she grew weary of waiting for him to spit out the words and began to coax him with her soft body and insistent hands, he might not leave at all.

"Ch-children," he said instead, hoping she could deduce the rest.

"You don't want to put a baby in my belly?"

He shook his head.

"Is that not . . . the goal?"

He shook his head again and righted his clothing, keeping his eyes averted from her creamy flesh and splayed limbs. The warriors of Saylok rutted like mindless bulls, spreading their seed across the clans, convinced that it was their only hope. Bayr did not want to father a son he might never know, with a woman who was not his own, the way his father had sired him.

Dagmar had suggested that Bayr's seed might be the salvation his mother had spoken of, but one man's seed did not a civilization save, and he didn't have the arrogance or the desire to test his uncle's theory. Their father, Saylok, had sought to lay with a woman in every village, and his children were turned into beasts. Bayr did not want to follow in his stead.

When he fled back to the tent and begged for a jug of mead, stuttering through the request, his grandfather raised his eyes to the thirsty boy.

"Your tongue is still tangled," Dred remarked.

Bayr nodded, wiping his mouth. "I s-suppose I . . . need . . . more i-instruction." He smirked.

Dred howled with laughter, the sound like a hungry wolf on the hillside, and the men around him joined in, not even knowing why they wailed.

~~~

The melee was the final event of the tournament, and it was a contest open only to clansmen. Each chieftain chose ten warriors to compete, and all six clans were represented. Sixty warriors took the field in their clan colors, and only one clan could claim victory. The object was to be the last clan standing, even if it was only one warrior. There were no weapons, and no rules but one: take every man down. Once a man's body hit the ground, he was required to leave the melee until only one man—or one clan—remained.

Different techniques were employed by different clans, and the game was played year-round in Saylok to sharpen a clan's skills. A warrior seen as the biggest threat was often targeted first by a handful of warriors working together, but that could backfire as well. If a man fell in the process of toppling another, he too was eliminated. Every clan had known victory in the melee, but one year, before he was king, Banruud and the nine other warriors from Berne so soundly dominated the other clans that all ten of them were still standing when every other warrior from all the other clans had been taken down. Such a feat had never happened before or since.

The king didn't take part in the melee. His presence on the field was too dangerous to his person and too intimidating to the clans. And no one wanted to tangle with the king for fear that besting him on the field would result in quiet consequences off the field. As king, Banruud was required to be partial to none, but he was of Berne, and his preference was known. He sat, waiting for play to commence, Queen Esa, Alba, and the clan daughters on his left, the keepers behind them, and the clans creating a perimeter on every side. Bayr took a knee in front of the daughters, his hand on his blade, trying to keep his attention from straying from his duties as protector. As one of the clanless, he would not be participating in the melee.

"We've only nine, Majesty," Dred of Dolphys called out, striding forward. "We're a man short."

The crowd groaned. They'd been hopeful the melee was about to begin. The king raised his arms to quiet the commotion.

"Then choose another, Dred. Surely you have another warrior from the Clan of the Wolf willing to enter the melee."

"I claim him. I claim the Temple Boy." Dred raised his arm and pointed at Bayr.

The crowd crowed and the king laughed.

"He is not of Dolphys. He has no clan. He cannot fight with you. Choose another," the king replied. Bayr's heart began to race.

"I claim him," Dred insisted, planting his feet. "We have not yet chosen a chieftain. But I speak for my clan, as the oldest warrior on the field."

The crowd grew quiet, confusion rippling in silent waves. Dred of Dolphys was a seasoned contender, and he knew the rules of the melee. It was a contest among the clans. The clanless were not allowed.

"He is of Dolphys," Dred intoned.

"What are you babbling about, old man?" the king growled. His eyes were hard and his hands curled around his big knees.

"He is the son of my daughter, Desdemona, shield maiden in the Clan of the Wolf." Once there had been a contest for the women—a battle among the shield maidens—but the king had suspended it. The shortage of women in Saylok had made the clans cautious, and they did not want their women to be warriors. It was a risk they'd become unwilling to take.

The king grew eerily still and the crowd followed suit, the hush of a thousand held breaths. No one knew why the king had turned to stone, but none of them dared break the spell.

"He is fourteen years old, Dred of Dolphys. Why have you not claimed him before? This is highly suspect," Aidan murmured, the only man not cowed by the king. Yet even he recognized the king's shock and moderated his tone.

Dred replied, "I did not know he lived. His mother—my daughter—is dead. She has been dead since his birth fourteen years ago, Adyar."

"He is naught but the Temple Boy," the king ground out. The color had leached from his face and gathered in his dark eyes.

"That may be true, Highness, but he is also of Dolphys. And I claim him. We claim him. It is my right as acting chieftain unless . . . he has already been claimed by a clan or . . . a king." Dred's voice was mild and the onlookers nodded. It was the law of the clans. A man—or a woman—could be claimed, even if there was no familial connection. Adoption into a clan was common, especially in an age of raid and conquest. But a claim could be refused.

"Is this true, boy?" the king sneered, finding his composure. "Are you of Dolphys? If you accept this claim, you must live among your clan."

The crowd shifted, a nervous shuffling. A man—or a boy—was not required to live among his clan, but no one would argue with the king.

"Highness, it is a ploy," Lothgar interjected. "Dred knows he cannot win the melee with his pack of aging wolves. He thinks the Temple Boy is Odin's hound. He'll abandon him when the battle is over. Leave the boy be." The warriors already assembled for the melee, their blood pumping and feet stomping, grunted and agreed, pressing for a commencement of the contest.

"What'll it be, boy? Do you want to live in Dolphys?" the king pressed, venom dripping from his query.

"I a-am a s-servant of the t-t-t . . ." Bayr winced and tried again to spit out the final word. "T-temple." The warriors on the field laughed. Dred's face darkened as the king chortled with them.

"Do you withdraw your claim, Dred of Dolphys?" the king asked.

"I cannot withdraw my blood from his veins, or his from mine, Highness. But I'll not take the boy from his home . . . or his duties. We will play with nine. And we will win."

The warriors behind Dred reacted—clansman and opponents alike—with cries of denial and protest rising to chase away the awkward encounter, and Dred of Dolphys turned away, abandoning his claim.

Bayr wanted to turn away too, to run away into the setting sun, to flee the walls and wait among the trees for the warriors of Dolphys to head for home. He would join them and escape the confines of his confusion. He was not a keeper. He was not a warrior. He was a guard dog, The Temple Boy. He hated the king and would welcome the day when he never had to look on him again.

But he loved Dagmar. He loved Ivo. He loved pale Ghost and the temple girls. And he loved Alba. Little Alba. He would not leave her. Even to belong to a clan. Even for his grandfather. His grandfather. The thought made him want to wail like the wolf he descended from. His grandfather had claimed him and he'd been humiliated in front of the melee. In front of the king. Bayr had rejected his claim.

The melee ensued but Bayr did not watch. His eyes were fixed upon his feet, and when Alba began to droop on her little stool, Bayr stepped forward and, with great care, lifted her into his arms. Lady Esa rose as well, trailing him to the castle, calling to the handmaid who waited, and Bayr never discovered who prevailed. He had lost, and that was all he knew.

⌒◎

Bayr awoke to pain and a jolt to his chest. The king should not have been able to surprise him, but he had. Mayhaps it was that the king was not an intruder, not a threat to the princess. He was a threat to Bayr, but Bayr had never been as aware when it came to his own well-being.

The whites of the king's eyes reflected the light when all else was darkness, as though he was from the Clan of the Wolf and not the Clan of the Bear. Or mayhaps it was simply Bayr's fear that made him focus on the king's eyes and not the weight of his fists. The eyes would tell him whether he would survive the night.

It had happened once before, this awakening to terror and pain. The night of the temple ceremony a year before, the night when Bayr had pledged his protection to the clan daughters. That night the king was angry and mean with wine, but the beating hadn't lasted long, and Bayr had never understood what he'd done wrong.

He'd told Alba, when he couldn't hide his bruises, that he'd battled a dragon.

"What kind of dragon?"

He tapped his ear, and she had immediately begun to construct a story just as he'd known she would.

"Was it the dragon who lives in the cliffs of Shinway?"

He nodded.

"The one with all the colors of the clans in his wings?"

Another nod.

"Did he come to take me away?"

He nodded again.

"But you *stopped* him?"

He wasn't sure she was particularly happy about that.

"I would like to fly with a dragon, Bayr. Do you think next time you could let him take me? Maybe ask him if we could both go?"

He tried to smile.

"H-he is n-not a g-good d-dragon."

"Not like the dragon that lives beneath the temple?" It was another story that she'd conjured on her own when Master Ivo had promised that the Hearth of Kings would remain lit. She was certain the ever-burning torch was dragon breath, and she was comforted by its presence beneath the temple. Alba was comforted by odd things.

"No. H-he is n-not. And I c-can't t-talk to d-dragons," he said.

"True. I think I could. The mice and the birds and the pigs and the horses all listen to me. I'm sure the rainbow dragon would listen to me too. So wake me next time, please."

She was always telling him what to do. Such a bossy little thing. And so smart.

He had let her chatter, nodding as she imagined him bravely dancing around the room with a sword and leaping here and there, stabbing
at the winged creature while taking a beating with his powerful tail.

"Thank you for not letting him take me, Bayr," she said. "I really
don't want to live with a dragon."

Bayr had simply dropped a kiss on her soft hair and said goodnight.
He chanted a prayer in his head until dawn, the words tripping through
his mind though his tongue stayed silent. Alba already lived with a
dragon, and it was a dragon he could not defeat.

But the king was not drunk this night. Bayr came to his feet, not to
battle but to submit with dignity. He could not raise his fists to the king.

Banruud did not beat him with implements, but with his own fists,
as though flesh hitting flesh gave him greater power, as though causing
pain to one who did not resist created a dominance all its own.

"Your duty is here. You are a servant. You are the Temple Boy, not
a prince. Not a chieftain, not a god. And you will not forget it again,
will you?"

When Bayr did not answer, but bowed his head in silent submission, the king spit on his tightly coiled braid and slapped his face, begging for an excuse to claim an attack, to run the boy through, but Bayr
did not speak or even lift his arms to shield himself. He'd seen what
the king had done to Agnes. Bayr would not forget himself. If the king
was going to end his life, Bayr would not dishonor himself by giving
him reason.

Banruud resumed punching, and when Bayr failed to respond or
even fall beneath his fists, the king resorted to using his feet. Bayr braced
his legs and absorbed the blows. The king was going to kill him. The
king's rings were sharp, and in some places Bayr's skin had broken. His
eyes were swollen shut, his nose bent, his lips split. But there were no
defensive wounds on his hands or his forearms. The bruises bloomed
like thunderclouds across his torso and over his shoulders, seeping down
his back and covering his legs.

When Banruud used the butt of his sword against the side of his head, Bayr felt his consciousness ebb and his legs buckle. His slide to the floor was a merciful sinking.

"Will you not fight back, Temple Boy? Are you not the son of Desdemona of Dolphys? Are you not a warrior?"

Bayr did not answer. He hardly even groaned. The fog in his head and the damage to his mouth had put him beyond speech, even if he'd been able to convince his tongue to form coherent words.

This time, Alba was a year older and a decade wiser, and Bayr was too sore to stand. When Bayr tried to blame the dragon, she raised her eyes from his bruised flesh and shook her head.

"You are the strongest boy in the whole world. Why did you let him hurt you?"

He had no answer.

"We must draw the rune," Alba demanded. "The one that drives the crawling things away like Dagmar does."

"I don't r-remember it."

"I do. I love to draw."

"Yes y-you d-do . . ." His voice trailed off. It hurt his mouth to speak.

Alba dipped her finger in the blood dribbling from his split lip and drew a spider on his forearm, a spider with spindly legs, all of them folded across the body, giving the appearance of death. She hadn't missed anything. Her lines and her angles were perfect, and Bayr marveled at her abilities.

"That will help with festering, but the cuts aren't bad or deep. It's the bruises that we need to fix," she said, matter-of-fact.

"Th-they w-will heal."

"Yes . . . but you're hurting." The tremor that shimmered in her voice made him wince. She was afraid for him.

"T-tell me all the th-things that m-make you h-happy," he said, trying to distract her. It was a game they played.

"I am happy when you aren't hurting," she said, and her chin wobbled. She screwed up her nose and closed her eyes, as though trying to remember something that eluded her. She was so smart. So smart, and he was so proud of her.

"There is a rune for pain. I saw Dagmar draw it on Elayne's forehead when her head ached so terribly. I just need to remember it. He washed it away . . . but I think I can draw it."

"D-don't," he whispered. Playing with runes was dangerous. He well knew it.

"I drew it in my mind so I wouldn't forget." She dabbed again at his lip like an artist needing paint and, next to the spider, began to place the lines and shapes that became a rune of relief. He closed his eyes, trusting her, and felt the moment she was done. The pain ebbed as though it descended a ladder, each rung allowing a little more space between pressure and peace.

"Don't f-forget to w-wash the rune away," he whispered, the cessation of pain making him weak and weary. His swollen lids closed, and he didn't feel it when she did as he asked.

When he opened his eyes again, Dagmar's face loomed above him. He felt better. Alba's rune had eased his pain and left him drowsy. He should tell Dagmar to take more care. She would remember whatever she saw.

"I'm s-sorry. I w-was so t-tired," he muttered, and attempted to rise. The dawn had deepened into late morning, and he was still lying on

Alba's floor where he'd stumbled after the king had finished with him. A bolt of panic lanced his heart. "W-where is Alba?"

"She was afraid and came to find me. She said she put you to sleep. She is in the temple." Dagmar cupped his cheek, his eyes tragic. "What has happened to you, Bayr?"

Bayr looked into the face that had loved him all his life, and he could not speak. Shame filled his chest.

"Your face is swollen. Your eyes are black. Your lips are bloodied, and you sleep as though you're in need of healing."

"W-why does the k-king hate me, Uncle?"

"Did he do this?" Dagmar gasped.

Bayr closed his eyes and for a moment they each waited, willing the other to answer first.

"Tell me, Bayr. Tell me," Dagmar pled. "I can't protect you from what I don't understand."

"I d-don't under-s-stand either," Bayr whispered. He rolled to his side and, gritting his teeth, found his feet. "And it is m-my duty to p-protect."

"Oh, Bayr. Oh, my boy."

"I am n-not a b-boy, Uncle."

He could see that his uncle did not agree. Dagmar's eyes were bright and his jaw was clenched so tight a muscle jumped in pained protest. Bayr walked to the washbasin and picked up the pitcher, pouring water over his hands. They shook, and he quickly set the pitcher down. His throat was dust, but he would wait until his uncle was no longer watching to slake his thirst.

"I am n-not a boy," he repeated. But he felt like a boy. Like a helpless, hopeless boy, and he fought back tears.

"If that is true . . . then it is time for you to go," Dagmar whispered.

18

The temple mount was as dank and silent as a tomb. It was always thus after the tournament ended. The completion of the melee gave way to a night of drunken debauchery, every clan celebrating as though they were the victors. When the sun rose, the party ended, and all life lurched down the temple mount, abandoning drink and denial, leaving the keepers with the cleanup.

Dolphys had won the melee, one man short and with an aging warrior at the helm. Dagmar had watched from the crowd with his brothers, proud of his father even as he fought back old frustrations.

Dred of Dolphys had claimed Bayr in front of king and clan. Dagmar had always known the day would come. Dred had discovered the truth. Dagmar had no doubt the king knew the truth as well.

His stomach churned and his hands clenched. He'd been a fool. He should have sent the boy to Dolphys long ago.

The chieftains of all the clans, their top warriors, and the elder clansman of Dolphys had remained on the temple mount to counsel with the king. A new chieftain of Dolphys would be chosen in the days to come. The king had influence, but the choice was not his. The people of Dolphys would decide when the elder clansmen returned, but they would hear the recommendation of the king as well as the preference of the keepers.

The council would be over by now, and Dagmar sought his father in the circle of tents that remained. The grass was yellowed and bent where clansmen had pulled up stakes after the tournament. Finding the tent of Dred of Dolphys among those that remained was not difficult. When Dagmar lifted the flap and asked for entrance, Dred was deep in conversation with three men Dagmar immediately recognized. The faces had all aged in twenty years, but his father's company had not. They all rose in surprise. Dagmar greeted the men by name, and they touched their braids, recognizing him as a clansman before making the star of Saylok on their foreheads.

"Keeper Dagmar," they said, eyes shifting from Dred to his son.

"I would like to speak to my father," Dagmar requested. When Dred nodded, the warriors were quick to exit.

Dagmar kept his hands at his side and his eyes level, but his nerves were jangling. He had never been at peace in his father's presence, though his current state had more to do with Bayr than his own discomfort. Surprisingly, his father was the first to speak.

"I believe I will be chosen as chieftain," Dred said. "The king doesn't like me, but he has not objected."

"I know. Master Ivo asked my opinion on the matter," Dagmar replied, his voice mild. Dred had the approval of the keepers.

"And what was it, Dagmar of Dolphys, son of Dred, Keeper of Saylok? Did you tell the Highest Keeper how you loathe me? Did you tell him I wanted you to fight beside me and you chose to pray with him instead?" The words were rueful but they had no bite, as though Dred had come to terms with his son's choices long ago.

"The Highest Keeper knows how I feel," Dagmar said, admitting nothing. In truth, he'd told Ivo there was no better choice. Dred loved Dolphys and would lay down his life for her. Dolphys was to Dred what the temple was to Dagmar.

"I am not a young man anymore," Dred admitted.

"No. But it is a position you have long aspired to." Dagmar heard the tinge of bitterness in his words and cursed himself for the lapse in control.

Again, his father took no offense, and Dagmar felt a flicker of hope.

"That's true. But now that it is here . . . I find I do not wish it," Dred confessed.

"You can't refuse," Dagmar retorted, adamant. "As chieftain you will be able to better protect Bayr."

"How?" Dred huffed. "I will have no authority here."

"I want you to take Bayr to Dolphys."

Dred gaped, taken aback. "I thought you were the reason he refused my claim."

"He is a guardian of the clan daughters, of the princess, of the whole temple mount. He feels a great responsibility. You've seen what he is capable of . . . but he is still a boy."

"There is no such thing in Saylok. Daughters become mothers and sons become warriors as soon as they are able. Survival demands it and leaves no room for anything else."

"You've not changed much, Father." It was a lie. Dred had changed a great deal.

"Nor have you, Dagmar. We're both still of the same opinions, and your every move is meant to spite me," Dred shot back, his ire rising for the first time. He paced to the door of his tent and immediately returned, his hand on his blade and his eyes bright with an emotion Dagmar hadn't ever seen on his father's face.

"He is a fine boy," Dred said, his voice almost reverent.

"The finest," Dagmar whispered, and for a long moment he could not speak over the grief in his throat. "And he has been since the day he was born."

Dred ran his palm across his mouth, adjusting his composure, and Dagmar noted the wear on his skin and the strength of his sinews. His father was aging, but he was still a man to contend with.

"The king has not claimed him," Dred grunted. It was not a question.

"No. But he must know. Especially now that you have stated your claim. I think he suspected before, but he did not know for certain. He did not want to know, and he certainly did not . . . ask."

"What kind of man does not claim such a son?" Dred hissed, shaking his head.

"A jealous man. A man obsessed with his own power. But Bayr has more strength . . . more power . . . than Banruud will ever have. He has the power of the gods, and Banruud . . . fears him. He always has." Dagmar had never voiced the simple truth aloud, but it was the truth, and his trepidation grew.

"The clan of Dolphys is next in line for the throne. Now that Bayr has been claimed, he can become king," Dred whispered, realization forming.

Dagmar nodded. "Banruud suspects treachery around every corner because he is treacherous. He assigns guilt and betrayal because he is guilty of betrayal. If Bayr was a threat before, he is an even bigger threat now."

"Then Bayr is not safe here."

"The temple might not be safe if he leaves," Dagmar admitted. He regretted the words as soon as they were uttered.

"Would you sacrifice him for your precious temple?" Dred asked, bitterness dripping from every word.

Dagmar closed his eyes and pictured the day he'd climbed the temple mount, the newborn Bayr tucked in his robes, his sister lying dead in the forest, her rune carved into the earth.

"I would not," Dagmar whispered. "I would not sacrifice him for all the runes in the world and all the gods of Saylok, may they strike me down."

"Odin had many sons. He understands," Dred said, all trace of condemnation gone.

"He understands. But he does not condone. You must take Bayr away so that I will never be tempted to make such a choice. I have been entrusted with these robes, and I don't wish to defile them."

"And if he refuses to go?" Dred pressed.

"I will give him no choice."

"I gave you no choice . . . yet here we are."

Dagmar grimaced but his father laughed. The laughter eased the ache in Dagmar's heart, but the terror returned with his next words.

"Bayr has to go," he insisted. "Or Banruud will kill him. Ivo has seen it."

The laughter faded from Dred's face and his eyes grew flat.

"Banruud destroyed my daughter. He will not destroy her son."

"You will be Saylok's salvation," Dagmar said, almost pleading. He and Bayr were in the sanctum. Dred was somewhere waiting. Ivo too. The entire temple grieved, and Alba was inconsolable. Bayr was like a man condemned to the rack, and he could hardly meet Dagmar's gaze, his shoulders bowed, his hands clasped, his agony slicking his brow with sweat.

"W-what does that m-mean?" Bayr roared, his eyes gleaming with frustrated emotion. "S-salvation how?"

"I don't know, Bayr," Dagmar sighed. "I only know that the things your mother said have come to pass. I have to believe that all her words will come to pass, eventually."

"M-my mo-mother c-cursed this land."

"Or simply prophesied of what would be."

Bayr shot Dagmar a look so incredulous and scathing, his uncle flinched.

"She used r-runes," Bayr reminded him.

Dagmar nodded, chagrined. He had never stopped making excuses for Desdemona.

"I a-am not a w-woman." Bayr's point was clear. He could not birth children. He didn't have a womb. He couldn't repopulate Saylok with infant girls. Bayr was a man with the innocence of a boy, and his interactions with women had been extremely limited. His best friend was a wispy, golden-haired child, and when the two were together, it was she who spoke, she who directed their play, and she who dominated the relationship, for all her size and silliness.

"You are a man now, Bayr. You are powerful. Perhaps as powerful as the gods. You can't stay inside the temple walls forever, my son. You have to go to Dolphys. You have to find salvation. Whatever that may be."

Bayr looked stricken. "I c-can't l-lead."

"You will."

"I c-can't sp-speak."

"You can. When you must. But your strength, your example, that is what men will see. And they will believe in you as I do. As Alba does."

"But the g-girls. W-who w-will k-keep th-them, k-keep A-A-Alba . . ." Bayr stopped, unable to finish. Words were hard enough for Bayr. Great emotion made speaking almost impossible. He wanted to know who would keep Alba safe. He had always viewed it as his responsibility.

"Alba is the king's responsibility. She is safe here. They are all safe here. There is not a Keeper of Saylok who will not use all his power to protect them."

"Sh-she is s-salvation. N-n-not me," Bayr protested, shaking his head.

They had all believed it. Alba had ended the drought. Yet in the seven years since her birth, there had been no other female born. They'd all rejoiced, crowning her father king. And yet . . . a single rainstorm does not a dry spell end. The years had continued to pass without another girl child.

"Alba is special. But one woman cannot save a nation. We will need a thousand more."

"And o-one man . . . c-can?"

"The gods have made you mighty."

"And w-weak."

"Come with me. I want to show you something," Dagmar insisted. Bayr rose, differential as he always was, obedient as he'd always been . . . as obedient as any boy who had the power to do whatever he wished could be.

They walked side by side, and Dagmar marveled at Bayr's size even as he grieved again for the boy who was already a man, whether he was ready or not. The men of Dolphys were strong and broad-shouldered, but their muscles were more sinewy and lean, like those of the wolf they descended from. Bayr had the superior size of the bear, with a back that could carry the world. He was built more like the king.

The room Dagmar brought Bayr to was filled with scrolls and lined with books, books of ages past and books that were freshly inked, a daily record of Saylok and her people. It smelled of dust and diligence, and Dagmar patted the stool where he often perched, indicating Bayr should sit. On the lectern in front of him, he placed the story of a man he'd come to love.

"His name was Moses."

Bayr waited.

"I haven't told you his story."

"I'm n-not sure I c-can read it." Bayr stared down at the endless lines.

"It is in Latin. If you concentrate, you can make it out. I wanted to teach you so much more." Dagmar stopped and cleared his throat. There was no time left for Latin.

"The R-r-romans r-ruled the w-world," Bayr offered.

"Yes. But their empire has fallen. When King Enos brought back a Bible and a cross from the land of the Angles, he also brought back a priest."

"I r-remember. H-he w-was the first k-keeper."

"Yes. And the religion of the Christians met the gods of the north. His knowledge has been passed down from one generation to the next. I have taught you what I know in hopes that someday you might want to supplicate Master Ivo to become a keeper."

Bayr's mouth slackened in shock. "You w-want me to be a keeper?"

Dagmar responded to his surprise with a rueful smile. "I find I am more like Dred of Dolphys than I thought. But that is not your path."

"Why?"

"You are a warrior. Like your grandfather. And someday . . . perhaps you will lead Saylok. I feel it, as does Master Ivo."

"How?"

"I don't know. But I do know that this man, Moses, was called to free his people, just as you are."

"We are n-not enslaved."

"If nothing is done, we soon will be," Dagmar argued. "The wars in Ebba have spread to Dolphys. War took the life of the chieftain."

"I h-have no c-clan," Bayr protested.

"Dred has claimed you. You are of Dolphys now. But you were christened Bayr of Saylok. I was there the day Master Ivo painted a star upon your head. You must defend all the clans."

"I w-want only to d-defend the t-temple. And Alba," Bayr protested.

"There will be no temple if the lands around us are taken. Moses was like you, Bayr. God gave him his power, yet Moses resisted because he could not speak."

Bayr's eyes sharpened on his uncle's face.

"Look. What does it say?" Dagmar insisted.

"'But I am s-slow of speech, and of a s-slow t-tongue,'" Bayr translated, hitching his way through the sentence. His eyes shot from the difficult Latin to his uncle's face, his expression one of stunned disbelief.

"Yes," Dagmar whispered. "Don't you see? He is just like you."

"What did his . . . g-god say?" Bayr asked, abandoning the book to entreat his uncle.

"His god said, 'I have made thy mouth.'"

Bayr frowned, not understanding.

"He made his mouth weak for a purpose. Just as he made you the way *you* are for a purpose. He made your mouth weak to keep your heart strong."

Bayr shook his head, resistant to such a contradiction.

"Do not question it," Dagmar continued. "Do not fear it. You are perfect—you are marvelous and terrible—in your weakness."

"T-terrible?"

"Men will tremble before you. Yet when you speak, you tremble before god. That is how it should be."

Bayr did not argue, but he sat, his head bowed, his eyes on the page, trying to discern something more, something to give him courage. To help him walk away.

"The god of the Bible told Moses that he would be Moses's mouth. That he would tell him what to say," Dagmar whispered, pointing to the words. "You will know what to say. When the time comes, your words won't fail you."

Bayr covered his face with his hands.

"You are not just strong of body. You are strong of heart. You always have been. You have never wavered, never feared or faltered in the face of any obstacle. I watched you at five years old catapult yourself into a grown bear. You didn't even hesitate. Your strength is not just in your sinews and in your size. Your strength is in your faith and your courage. I've never seen you doubt."

"I c-can't sp-speak," he insisted.

"It is your weakness. But weakness can make a man wise. You will listen more. You will think before you speak. You will never believe yourself all-powerful and all-knowing. You will never say what you do not mean."

"I d-do not w-want to l-leave, Uncle."

"And I don't want you to go. But what we want is not always what is best for us. You must go, Bayr. And you must go now."

⌒❂

"You can't leave," Alba forbade him as they stood in the sanctum.

Bayr said nothing, only looking at his small charge with abject misery.

"Who will watch over me? Who will love me?"

"The keepers will w-watch over you. Dagmar w-will watch over y-you."

"It isn't the same. Dagmar doesn't play. He can't climb trees or carry me on his back. He doesn't laugh and listen to my stories. He is not . . . you."

Bayr took the girl in his arms and, with a ferocity he usually kept restrained, hugged her to him.

"Will you come back?" she asked, the tears streaking down her cheeks and wetting the front of his tunic.

He nodded once, not trusting himself to speak at all. His tortured tongue would choke on an answer.

"Do you promise?"

Again, a nod. His hand stroked the fall of hair that tumbled around her shoulders.

"Soon?" she wailed.

"N-n-not soon." Her tears came harder and his jaw ached from trying to keep his own emotions in check. Ivo had seen his return.

"You will be grown," the Highest Keeper had promised. "The princess will be grown. And she will need you. Then you will return. But only then."

"P-please, Alba. Don't c-cry," he begged.

"You must come back for my birthday. At least that!" she mourned.

He shook his head. She would have eight summers soon, but he would not be back for years, if he returned at all. He *had* to return. Alba needed him.

"I w-will come back," he vowed.

"Let me see your eyes," she demanded, pulling away and tilting her head as far back as she could so she could see his face, far above her own.

Her eyes were so wet and bleak, he didn't know how he would ever walk away. She stared at him, the candles of the sanctum making his shadow jump on the walls, a family of jealous gods surrounding them, taking her from him.

"Say my name," she insisted.

"Alba." He said it slowly so he wouldn't stutter.

"Promise me with words that we will be together again." She wanted to see if he spoke the truth.

"I w-will s-see you a-g-gain."

She sighed heavily, but he could see that she believed him. She'd been staring into his eyes for too long. All her life. And she always knew when he lied.

19

Dusk had gathered around the temple, and so had the chieftains. Dred had intended to keep his plans and his claim of Bayr to himself, but word had spread. Six warriors of Dolphys stood with him, braided and booted, their horses readied and their camp broken. For most people it was unwise to ride in the night, but the wolves had no difficulty traveling in the dark, and the warriors of Dolphys preferred it. Dred was eager to depart. Dagmar would tell the king when the boy was gone. A new guard would have to be appointed for the princess, and an increased presence would be demanded in and around the temple.

But the boy was resisting.

The hours had stretched on while Dred and his men waited, impatient to be on their way.

Aidan of Adyar planned to leave at first light, Benjie of Berne as well. They would travel north together before the Chieftain of Berne and his men split off for the east where the cliffs and the sea divided the two clans. Lothgar and Josef typically traveled much the same way, heading west together before their journeys diverged to Leok and Joran. Erskin would travel south at dawn as well, though he and his warriors seemed reluctant to return home. Erskin's lands had been hardest hit in recent years, and though the conflict had ebbed with the harvest, no one believed it was over. The tournament had been a respite Ebba's clansman could ill afford but desperately needed. Erskin had spent much of his time during the tournament warning of an onslaught and petitioning the other chieftains for support and supplies. Ebba was the southernmost part of Saylok, the tail of the star, and the peninsula with the calmest seas and the clearest coastline. They were the most exposed, and they'd paid dearly for it.

It was Erskin who saw Dred and his men waiting outside the temple. It was Erskin who divined his intentions.

"You made a claim for the Temple Boy, Dred. Is that why you tarry?" Erskin asked.

Dred considered not answering. His men shifted and their horses chuffed. It was obvious they were waiting for something, and Dred was patient enough for elaborate lies.

"Aye. He's accepted my claim. He'll be riding with us tonight."

Erskin did not argue. He simply turned on his heel and strode off to gather reinforcements. Erskin had been too long at war. He feared for the temple, for the heart of the clans, and he needed the king's favor. Dred knew then that they wouldn't be leaving without a fight of some sort.

Dred cursed and turned to face his clansmen.

"I am taking my grandson to Dolphys. He will be a credit to the clan. I ask you to stand with me in this."

"We should leave 'im, Dred," young Daniel grunted. "He doesn't want to go. We've been waiting for hours and there's going to be trouble. Mayhaps the Temple Boy should remain at the temple."

"And mayhaps I should have left you in Dolphys. But I didn't," Dred shot back, his eyes swinging to the lad. Daniel wasn't much older than Bayr, and he'd been dogging Dred's heels for the last year, the youngest warrior in the clan. Daniel was a nuisance—as were all untried warriors—but Dred had never spurned him. The boy grimaced in chagrin.

"I've never seen his like. The Temple Boy belongs in Dolphys," Dakin muttered, his hand gripping the hilt of his sword. Dakin's hair was as red as the blood in his veins and his thirst for a fight was ever-present.

He lived for the melee and was the reason they'd won. Dred had little doubt he'd enjoy a skirmish for the road. The rest of Dred's men grunted in agreement, but Dred hoped it would not come to that.

Dred threw back his head and howled, calling to his son, warning the temple and all its inhabitants. His clansmen joined the chorus, and Dred willed Dagmar and Bayr to appear before he had to draw his sword and storm the halls.

Within minutes, the purple-robed keepers descended the stone steps, surrounding the Highest Keeper, all in black. Dred sought Dagmar, trying to locate him in the identical robes of the brethren who stood with their faces hidden beneath their hoods, a row of slighter, smaller figures behind them—the daughters of the clans.

Dred howled again, urging Bayr to join him. But it was too late. The chieftains, led by Erskin and the king, were striding into the temple square, three dozen warriors following behind them.

"You cannot claim him, Dred," Erskin shouted as they drew near. His voice was bold but his gaze begged understanding. Dred would not extend it.

"I can and I have," Dred spat. "He is my daughter's son. He is my grandson. I have no other. I would not deny you, Erskin. Why do you seek to deny me?"

"He is the Temple Boy. He swore to guard the daughters of the clans," Lothgar of Leok bellowed, his gold beard trembling after the words. "We stood on these steps, gathered around this flame, and Bayr of Saylok promised to protect them the way he has protected the princess. He cannot break that vow. He must remain on the temple mount."

For a moment, Dred was silent, stunned at the development. He had not been present the day the daughters were brought to the temple. He had not seen the Highest Keeper light the torch and promise that it would continue burning in their honor. He had not seen Bayr swear to serve the daughters of the clans; Chieftain Dirth had been there that day. But Dred had heard the tale.

Bayr stepped out from among the robed keepers, his warrior's braid so long it touched the blue sash tied around his waist, an indication that he had been claimed. His shoulders were set and his hands clenched, and Dagmar was a step behind him. There was only one thing to do, and Dred didn't hesitate. He gave away all he had ever wanted for something he instantly wanted more.

"You cannot deny a clan their chieftain," Dred roared.

The men at his back grew still, and Bayr drew to a halt halfway down the steps. Dagmar froze beside him. Silence woke and reared her head, and shock galloped at her heels.

"What chieftain?" King Banruud growled.

The row of purple shifted, and the Highest Keeper emerged, his hands folded, his black lips curled, his eyes invisible beneath the drape of his robe. He halted behind Bayr, a small, black bird hovering over a beast. The king and the chieftains balked, and Dred heard the metallic whisper of swords being drawn. The warriors at the king's back were prepared to battle, but Dred kept his eyes on Banruud.

"Dolphys has yet to choose. The boy must go before the clan to make a claim."

"You will be chieftain, Dred of Dolphys," the king retorted. "We all sat at council when it was decided."

"One old man for another?" Dred asked. "That is not in the best interest of my clan." His clansmen shifted again, and Dred willed them to hold their tongues.

"You have the blessing of the keepers, the support of the chieftains, the nod of a king. Why do you insist on claiming the boy?" Aidan of Adyar asked, his voice thoughtful, his gaze shrewd.

"I am not the best choice. If given the opportunity, I have no doubt my clan will choose him." He pointed at Bayr, and all eyes followed his finger.

"Father," Dagmar said. It was only one word and not loudly spoken, but it was said with a reverence Dagmar had never bestowed upon his sire before. Dred's doubt dissolved, and his heart swelled.

"He is not yet grown," Erskin argued. "How can he lead a clan?"

"Have you killed a man, Bayr of Saylok?" Aidan asked, turning his eyes up the steps to where the keepers hovered around the Temple Boy.

Bayr nodded once. "Yes."

"Have you bedded a woman?" Lothgar boomed.

"Th-there w-was no b-bed," Bayr stammered.

Lothgar grinned and the men at Dred's back relaxed infinitesimally.

"Sounds like a man to me," Aidan said. "Looks like one too."

"He has protected the temple and the princess since the king was crowned. He has not failed or faltered. But he has a clan, and his clan has claimed him, and you cannot deny us our chieftain," Dred pressed, sensing victory.

He watched Dagmar wrap his hand around Bayr's arm, willing him to yield, to trust. And Bayr stayed silent though his eyes were wide and terrified, and his gaze pled for explanation.

"The clan has not made their selection. Your people have not spoken. You cannot speak for them, Dred of Dolphys."

"I can't. But the boy must come to Dolphys and be heard," Dred insisted.

Bayr's face grew as pale as the temple steps.

"This is a farce," the king argued, his tone glacial.

"It is not," the Highest Keeper intoned from the shadow of his hood. "Dred of Dolphys is a man of vision."

Erskin scoffed and Lothgar folded his powerful arms in disbelief. Dred was many things, but a visionary was not one of them, and they all well knew it.

"He forsakes his own claim to the chiefdom for another, better man," the Highest Keeper hissed. "Would you do the same? I can think of many warriors in Ebba and Leok who would lead their clans with great distinction."

"The clan will choose him." Dagmar's voice rose, strong and sure. "I am a keeper of Dolphys. In the temple, it is I who represent the clan. Bayr of Dolphys has my blessing."

"He cannot forsake Saylok for a single clan," Banruud protested.

"He is not a slave, not a supplicant, not the son of the king," the Highest Keeper said. "He has fulfilled a duty and will now fulfill another. When you were chosen as king, Sire, you did not break an oath to Berne. Someone took your place. Someone will take his place." The Highest Keeper's voice was so mild—and cutting—none could disagree.

"And if he is not chosen?" Lothgar interrupted.

"If I am n-not chosen . . . I w-will return," Bayr promised, and Dred wished for Thor's hammer to fall upon the boy's head. Damn his loyal heart. If he was not chosen, Dred would kill him.

But the boy's vow eased the tension in the chieftains, and Aidan of Adyar grasped his braid with one hand and his sword with the other. "He's been claimed. Let him go. If the Norns will it, he will return."

Lothgar of Leok mimicked the gesture, but Erskin of Ebba and Benjie of Berne did not. The king's face was a mask of indecision, his big legs planted, his arms folded, his shoulders set. Still, no one stepped forward to hinder the boy's progress as the keepers parted and Dagmar escorted Bayr to Dred's side.

Dred did not look into the eyes of his son or the boy who walked beside him. He feared what he would see there, feared his own reaction to the raw emotion rippling around them, to the parting that was about to take place.

"To Dolphys," Dred shouted, daring any man to disagree.

"To Dolphys," the warriors behind him bellowed, and as one they turned for their horses.

"To Dolphys," Dagmar ordered, his voice low and full of love.

And the boy obeyed.

"Please don't be afraid. I am . . . I am not supposed to be here . . . in the castle. But I knew you would be sad," Ghost whispered. She'd come through the tunnel that led from the sanctum to the king's throne room and then made her way to Alba's chamber, terrified that she'd be spotted, certain she would be found, yet unwilling to stay away. The grief on the temple mount was a thrumming heartbeat, but Alba would feel Bayr's loss most keenly. She had been raised beneath his wing, and the years ahead would be cold.

Alba sat up from the rumpled blankets of her bed. No one had braided her hair for the night or bade her change into bedclothes, and she still wore her day gown and leather slippers on her feet.

"Why would I be afraid?" Alba asked, wiping at tearstained cheeks.

"Sometimes the way I look frightens people. I have been told I am even more terrifying in the dark."

Alba studied her thoughtfully. "You look like the moon," she murmured.

"I do?"

The little girl nodded. "The moon isn't scary. The moon is the only light in the sky."

"What about the stars?"

"I can't see the stars tonight." Her voice turned dull as though she'd suddenly remembered all that had transpired. She lay back down on the pillows.

"Can I comb your hair and help you get ready for bed?"

The girl sighed and sat up again, pushing her unkempt hair from her eyes. "Very well. Grandmother tried to help me. But I was a beast."

"A beast?"

"Yes. I screamed and growled and scratched, and I made her go away."

Ghost was grateful the old queen had tried. "Why did you do that?"

"Everyone else goes away," Alba said. "Even when I am *not* a beast."

"I will not go," Ghost said soothingly as she picked up the brush on the gilded stand beneath the looking glass.

"The servants say my father is a beast too," Alba confessed.

Ghost stiffened but began brushing Alba's hair, disentangling one silvery lock from another.

"It's true," Alba continued in a whisper. "He is. He hurt Bayr. And Bayr had to go."

"He hurt Bayr?" Ghost asked. No one had told her this.

"Bayr would not fight. I saw him, and I was afraid. I ran away."

"Has he hurt you?" Ghost determined in that moment that if the girl said yes, she would take her from the palace, and somehow, someway, they would leave Saylok and never come back.

"Just my heart." It would have sounded pathetic coming from a grown woman, romantic and silly, but from this child it was a sharp blade in Ghost's chest, and it put her at a loss for words.

Alba seemed soothed by her presence and made no effort to fill the silence, though her head was bowed and her sadness palpable.

"Where I am from, your name means 'sunrise.' Did you know that?" Ghost asked her, desperate to brighten her thoughts.

The little girl shook her head.

"You were born just after dawn. The night had been so long and the pain so great . . . and then the sun peeked in through the window and welcomed you into the world."

"Did my mother tell you that story?" Alba asked.

Ghost could only nod.

"Did Bayr go to be with my mother?"

"No. Oh, no, Alba. He is not as far as that. He has gone to be with his clan."

"I want to go too. Where is my clan?"

"All of Saylok is your clan. The keepers are your clan. The temple girls. I am your clan."

"Princess Alba of Saylok," Alba murmured, and Ghost closed her eyes in silent supplication.

"Princess Alba of Saylok," she agreed, willing it to always be so.

"Do you promise you won't disappear?" Alba asked after a time, her voice slurred and sleepy.

"Yes. I promise."

"Do not let him see you, Moon Lady."

Ghost smiled at the name. "What did you call me?"

"Moon Lady," the little girl muttered, and she yawned widely. She crawled into Ghost's lap and laid her head upon her breast. "Don't let Banruud see you," she entreated. She called the king by his name as though she felt no affinity for him at all. She yawned again, and her body grew slack with approaching slumber. "He makes people disappear."

$\sim$

Ghost had expected an empty sanctum, and Dagmar's presence in the shadows made her start and clutch at her heart.

"Where did you go?" he whispered.

"The princess . . . I went to see the princess. She is so alone."

"Yes. She is. We . . . all are."

"But she is a child." Her voice was harsh, and Ghost flinched in remorse when he raised his bruised eyes to hers.

He nodded, and even in the wavering glow of the candles that circled the altar, she saw him swallow, his throat churning out words he didn't say. His face was wet and his shoulders hunched. She sat down beside him, a space between them, wanting to comfort him the way she'd comforted Alba and fearing his rejection.

"I climbed the bell tower so I could watch them go. The view toward Dolphys is clear for miles," he whispered.

"You're bleeding," she rebuked him.

"When I couldn't see him any longer, I drew a rune of sight to show him to me. When it weakened, I drew another. And then another." His hands were pocked with puncture marks. "I cannot do that again. I will drive myself mad trying to watch over him. I am a keeper, not a god. Seeing him will do me no good. It will do him no good. And it is a misuse of the runes."

"You will ruin your hands," she whispered.

He clenched his fists, hiding the wounds. She relented, reaching for him and drawing his hands into her lap. He clung to her hand as though he were drowning. Around the wounds, his palms were so rough and scarred it was a wonder he could feel her touch at all. He trembled and his eyes found hers.

"I have no defenses this night, Ghost. None. I cannot see purpose. I cannot see the dawn. Not even in the runes. I only see the darkness and my own despair. You should leave me." He rose from the bench, but he didn't step away and he didn't release her hand.

"Does my presence give you comfort?" she asked, rising beside him.

"Yes."

"Then I will stay."

He shuddered once and his hand convulsed around hers. She brought his left palm to her lips and pressed her mouth to the center. She thought of Alba, who had crawled into her lap and buried her face in her chest, and she wondered who had received the most from the exchange. No doubt, it was Ghost, and comforting Dagmar would be the same.

"Comfort is not love," she murmured, reassuring him, and she kissed his other palm.

"It is a form of it," he whispered. Then he pulled her into his arms and laid his cheek on her head. Ghost made herself breathe, resting her hands on his back, wanting to stroke the long lines but standing still within his embrace instead.

"Bayr grew so quickly," he mourned. "With abilities and strength like he has, it makes sense that he would quickly gain confidence. Confidence and independence go hand in hand. But I look back on the days when he was a newborn babe, when I had to hold him all night to keep him from crying, and I long for that time. There will never be a night like that again."

"No," she whispered, remembering the days after Alba's birth. "There never will be."

She felt the tremor of a building grief in his chest and could no longer keep silent.

"Why, Dagmar? Why did you let him go?" she asked, not understanding. "Why did you not keep him here, with us?"

He was suddenly striding for the altar, dragging her behind him like he had to escape, like he had to be free of the incense and the candles, the guilt and the grief. Beyond the altar was a wall that shifted and became a door, and when they stepped inside, he closed it again. The scrape of stone on stone was the only warning before darkness closed around them. Dagmar didn't slow, and he didn't explain. He just pulled her forward as though the lack of light was of no consequence. The passage smelled of earth and time and tenuous breath, and she didn't ask where they were going or how long it would take to arrive. She simply clung to his hand and reveled in the contact, trusting that they would reach the other end, yet hardly caring if they ever did.

They walked in silence for a dark eternity, hand in hand until the ground rose and the scent shifted, becoming grassy and open, the fragrance of air and space. Then Dagmar released her hand and unlatched another door, inviting the light of the moon to wash over them as they stepped out onto the hillside, the temple mount above them, the King's Village below.

"There are some secrets that can only be shared out of doors, beyond walls. I can't take the chance that they will linger to be heard again," he murmured, his voice so low Ghost had to lean into him to capture his words.

"Twenty years ago, when I was the same age as Bayr is now, I left Dolphys for the temple. I was so confident. So sure. I knew where I belonged. Now I am fleeing the temple because I know nothing. I am powerless. Unsure. And my heart is, at this moment, traveling back to Dolphys."

He paused, his eyes straying to the east, and Ghost knew he had not fled the temple to kiss her lips or lie with her in the grass. He had fled the walls because he wanted to follow after Bayr, and he needed Ghost to make him stay. The secrets he had to tell were not sweet professions of love or lust. He was a man weighed down by longing, but not longing for her.

"Bayr is the king's son. He is Banruud's son," he whispered, and his tears began to fall.

The breath fled from her lungs and her vision swam. She must have swayed in her surprise, because Dagmar pulled her down to the grass, enfolding her in his arms as though he feared she would run away and he would be left to carry his burden alone.

"Oh, Dagmar," she gasped.

He collapsed into her, his head in her lap, his arms encircling her waist, and she caressed the shadowy growth of hair that covered his head.

"Bayr does not know," he wept, and she wept with him.

"And the king?"

He shook his head, helpless, unsure. "My father claimed Bayr as Desdemona's son. The king is not a fool."

"You must tell me everything from the beginning," she begged, and after a brief hesitation, he relented, his words tripping like smooth stones, making hardly a ripple before they sank beneath the surface of the soft night.

"When my sister died . . . she drew two blood runes. Runes she should not have known. One of them required her life in exchange. But she was already dying. And she was angry, bitter. She cursed all the men of Saylok. She said there would be no girl children, no women for such men to love. She cursed Banruud by name."

"How?" she pressed.

"She said Bayr would be his only son, his only child. In the second rune, she said Bayr would be powerful, so powerful that he would save Saylok, yet his father would reject him."

"His only child," Ghost whispered. She wanted to tell him her story, but the words were too heavy and she'd buried them too deep to unearth them so suddenly.

"The runes are not all-powerful. Clearly. Banruud has another child. A daughter. He has Alba. Yet . . . the curse continues. The power of my sister's blood rune persists. I don't know how to break it or if it *can* be broken."

"Have you told Ivo . . . of the runes?"

"No," he breathed. "I can't."

"You must. He will know what to do." She bore down against the bile of her own hypocrisy.

"I can't," Dagmar insisted again, and she waited, her hand stroking his head, hoping he would share his reasons, that he would trust her. Mayhaps if he trusted her, she could trust him. If he could keep Desdemona's secrets, he could keep hers as well.

Then Dagmar sat up so he could look down into her face, and Ghost saw herself mirrored in the glassy fear of his gaze.

"If Ivo knows, he will be forced to act. As Highest Keeper he will do—he must do—whatever is necessary to destroy the power of Desdemona's rune," Dagmar insisted. "And I cannot take that risk."

"But . . . is that not . . . what you want?" Ghost asked.

"What if Bayr is the only one who can break the curse?" Dagmar asked, sorrow deepening his tone.

Ghost stared at him, not understanding, and his guilt and grief were terrible to behold.

"What do you mean?"

"Bayr's birth marked the beginning of the drought. What if his death marks the end?"

20

Bayr had lived his whole life on the temple mount. He'd never gone farther than the King's Village, never explored the lands beyond the Temple Wood or climbed higher than the temple spires.

He'd taught Alba to swim in the springs tucked back among the caves on the sheer north side of Temple Hill, showed her all the secret tunnels, the hidden passageways, the best caves, and the highest trees. But his world had been a mountain that rose in the heart of a land he'd never explored, and he was eager to see what lay beyond, on every side.

He'd never seen the pebbled beaches of Ebba or climbed the peaks of Shinway in Dolphys. He'd never seen the trees in Berne, trees so massive a bear could make a home in their branches. He'd never seen winter in Adyar, though he'd been told the icicles could impale a man if he walked beneath them. He'd never seen the lush farmlands of Joran or the whales off the shores of Leok. Liis claimed everything was big in Leok. The men, the boats, the beasts, the storms. Bayr wanted to see it all. Yet as he rode away from the temple mount on a horse that wasn't his, his grandfather beside him, a handful of grim-faced and grizzled warriors around him, he wanted nothing more than to return.

It was better that he struggled with speech, that words felt like bands around his tongue. If he'd been able to voice his feelings, they would have poured from his mouth the way the grief threatened to slip from his eyes. He wanted to cry for Dagmar because he knew Dagmar cried for him. He wanted to sob his frustration at the hateful king; Bayr had no doubt Banruud was the impetus for his expulsion. He wanted to wail for Alba, who was now completely at the king's mercy, now at the mercy of the tired, the busy, and the weak. No one would care for her as Bayr had. No one would love her as he did.

But Bayr could not weep among the warriors of Dolphys, so he prayed instead, beseeching Odin, Thor, and Freya to guard Alba from the ambitions of her father and the indifference of the keepers. Bayr had been seven years old when he had become her protector. Alba was seven now. Bayr's childhood had been as fleeting as hers would be. He prayed she would be wise. Shrewd. That she would see the world as it was and not as she wished it would be, if only to better shield herself from the forces around her. His last plea to Dagmar had been for Alba's protection, and Dagmar had given his word. His prayers and private thoughts were interrupted by the redheaded Dakin, who rode on his right side.

"You're black and blue. Someone put his hands on you, Temple Boy," Dakin said. Dakin's horse whinnied and shook his mane as though to say, "What a shame. What a shame."

Bayr said nothing, but Dred, who rode ahead of him, turned in his saddle and eyed him, waiting for a response. When he said nothing, Dred explained.

"It doesn't give the men much confidence in your strength or abilities. They are worried that the tales about you are just that. Tales," Dred said. Dakin grunted in agreement.

"I h-have n-never t-told t-tales," Bayr stammered.

"Others have," young Daniel piped up from behind them, and the men he had not yet been introduced to nodded and mumbled among themselves.

"At the tournament, I saw him lose to the bowman from Ebba," a warrior grunted. "He's good . . . but he's not the best archer. He can throw an axe with incredible force, but his aim is not without match. There are other warriors just as skilled."

"I saw him win the footrace," Daniel admitted. "But I doubt he could run for a great distance."

Bayr sighed. He could run for miles, but he said nothing. He didn't care whether Daniel believed it or not.

"He bested Lothgar of Leok in the circle. Lothgar has never lost before," Dred said, his eyes forward, his tone filled with warning.

"'Tis one thing to wrestle a man in the circle, to triumph in a contest of strength or even skill. It is another to face a village of swords or a man intent on killing you," Dakin answered.

"You said you'd never seen his like," Dred growled. "What is this game, Dakin?"

"I haven't. He is a boy who has the strength and size of a man—many men. He belongs in Dolphys. I welcome him. He will be a credit to the clan. But he should not be chieftain," Dakin said, blunt.

Bayr agreed but kept quiet.

"Would you have stood for me?" Dred asked, eyeing each one of his men. "Would I have had your support as chieftain?"

"Aye," Dakin answered, and the other men quickly added their *ayes*, gazes steady, nods firm.

"Then I ask you to speak for Bayr," Dred said. "To stand with him . . . for me."

"He is a stranger. The people will challenge him with tasks that will only succeed in getting him killed. We could all speak for him . . . and it wouldn't be enough." Dakin's voice was mild, kind even, and Dred's chin dropped to his chest and his shoulders slumped in brief dejection. Bayr wished he'd held firm and stayed on the temple mount.

"I will not speak for him, Dred . . . but I will not challenge him either," Dakin added softly.

"Nor will I." A warrior with deep-set eyes and cheekbones as sharp as the temple spires spoke up from the rear. "He can make his claim uncontested. I'll not stand in his way." Bayr had seen him on the field of the melee and again on the night of the feast. The man was almost as quiet as Bayr, but he seemed to hold Dred in high regard.

"Dakin. Dystel. My gratitude," Dred murmured gruffly, and Bayr made note of the second man's name.

"And the rest of you? What say you? Will you challenge him now that I have withdrawn my claim?" Dred asked the men who traveled in surly silence beside him.

"I'd never be chosen," Daniel said simply, shrugging. "It matters not to me if the Temple Boy wants to kill himself trying to become the Dolphys." The people of Saylok often referred to a chieftain by the name of his clan—the Adyar, the Leok, the Joran. The people of Dolphys were no different.

Dystel lashed out and pushed the boy so hard he almost fell from his mount. The others laughed, Daniel swore, and the warriors, all ranging in size and age, gave their consent.

"If Dakin and Dystel don't contest, none of us will either. They have the most claim, Dred." The man who spoke was completely bald like a keeper. He wore a wolf pelt for a hat, the teeth and snout sitting on his forehead as though his face was about to be eaten whole. The bushy tail had been cut into strips and plaited to give him a warrior's braid.

"So be it," Dred agreed, his eyes resting briefly on each man. "Then let us see what the people have to say."

They rode for almost two days, resting for brief stretches by rivers and streams. Water was plentiful in Dolphys, rocks too, but farmland was scarce. Dolphynians grew crops that didn't need much land—potatoes were a staple. Some farmed, some hunted; some fought, some fished. There were traders and trappers and miners and millers, and in the biggest valley, where the chieftain's keep and the holdings of the clan were concentrated, there was a little of everything.

To Bayr, life in Dolphys didn't appear much different from life in the King's Village, a life common in any of the other clans, though the land of Dolphys was formed of peaks and vales, rocks and crags, and Bayr imagined that if he climbed Shinway Peak, her highest point, he might be able to see all the way to the temple mount, ringed with clouds in the far distance.

When he asked his grandfather, Dred shrugged his shoulders and said, "I've never looked. You'd best not look back either, Bayr."

When they began to drop into the valley, tired and saddle sore, Dred held back and urged the other men to ride ahead and warn the village.

"You will tell them we're coming," he informed Dakin. "You will tell all in the fortress what has transpired. You will tell them I have brought my grandson back to Dolphys to make a bid for the chiefdom."

Dakin nodded, his eyes lingering on Bayr. "It is better not to wait, boy. You are weary. But they won't let you rest. May Thor lend you his strength and Odin's hounds guard your back."

Dakin tugged at his long red braid in a show of respect and spurred his horse forward. The other men followed, ready for their journey to be over, eager to spread the news.

Dred watched them go before he turned to Bayr. The lines across his brow and bracketing his grim mouth had grown more pronounced as he'd neared his home. Bayr had tried not to feel anything at all. The land was harsh, the men he traveled with even more so, and though the landscape had drawn his eye, it felt foreign and cold. *He* felt foreign and cold. The only warmth in him was the rage in his belly—disgust at his weakness, fury at his circumstance, frustration at the choices he'd not been given.

"Being the chieftain of a people you've never lived among won't be easy, but I promise you it will be easier than what is about to transpire.

You will have to impress them, Bayr. They've all heard of the Temple Boy. Dakin said you're a stranger, but you're not. You're a fireside tale. And that might make it even harder. They won't care that you are fourteen years old—barely a man. They'll expect greatness. They'll expect Thor. And you must give it to them."

Bayr gritted his teeth against the impotence that welled behind his eyes and raged to break free. He had not asked to be chieftain. He did not *want* to be chieftain. Yet he was going to try. He was going to kneel and grab his braid. He would make a vow. He would bleed and suffer and do what they asked. None of it was what he wanted. But he would do it, nonetheless.

"They'll not like your name," Dred continued. "It is of Berne, not Dolphys. I'll not take it from you. Your mother gave it to you. But they might try to change it. I'll let you decide if it's worth the battle."

Bayr scrubbed at his face, willing calm, fighting despair.

"Are you ready?" Dred asked.

Bayr shook his head. How could he answer such a question?

Dred reached over and touched his shoulder, encouraging him to raise his head, but he couldn't.

"This is not a world where a man or woman gets much choice in their happiness. We are born into war and each day is a battle." Dred paused and tightened his hand on Bayr's shoulder. "My son knew what he wanted. My daughter too. But I didn't listen. I was too afraid I couldn't give it to them." Dred's voice had grown thin with heavy regret, and he shook his head as though he had no idea how to continue. After a few moments, he took a deep breath and let it out in a long, shuddering sigh.

"What is it you want, Bayr? If you want to go . . . I'll go with you. Wherever it is. I've spent all my life wanting something I couldn't ever put a name to. I thought it was power, but I realize now . . . it was posterity. I thought I wanted to be chieftain. Then suddenly Odin opened his hand and there you were, right in front of me."

"I want to protect," Bayr answered without thought or hesitation. It had always been the single-minded purpose of his young life. "I w-want to protect Saylok and the temple. I w-want to protect the princess and the d-daughters of the clans. I want to protect D-Dagmar and the k-keepers."

"You want to protect those you love."

Bayr nodded, a short, hard jerk of his head. He wanted to protect those he loved and instead he'd been taken—sent—from them.

Dred was silent for a moment, studying him, and his eyes were soft in his hard face.

"If you stay here . . . you will grow to love Dolphys. She is harsh and hard to hold on to, but once she gets in your heart, she won't let go. And her people are the same. You will learn to love these people, and you will protect them too."

Bayr's anger began to evaporate in the midmorning sunlight, and he looked again on the valley of Dolphys and saw her with new eyes. He didn't want to lead. But mayhaps he could serve. Mayhaps it was the same thing.

"I know you didn't choose this, Bayr. But I will help you. I will be your right hand and your left. I'll watch your back and I'll guard your heart. I'll give you every last breath I can give. All of me. Everything I know. Everything I am. It is yours."

"Everything?" Bayr whispered, releasing his doubt and girding his faith.

"Everything," Dred promised.

"Do you h-have something I c-could eat?"

Dred's brow wrinkled in question.

Bayr smiled and reached over to tug at his grandfather's braid. "I c-can't do battle on an e-empty st-stomach."

❧

It was the last thing he would eat for some time. The people did not welcome him or his claim. Dred had done all the talking, and Bayr had simply done as he was asked. He threw his blades and demonstrated his skill in whatever way was required. They wanted him to submit to a duel with Dakin but were unwilling to endanger one warrior to legitimize the claim of another. The elders stewed, the old women spit, and everyone circled, pinching him and pulling his braid. No one seemed to know what to do with him.

"He is not a wolf. He is not one of us," declared an old man with tufts of snow-white hair escaping from his plait. Rings set with dozens of sharp teeth bristled from his fingers, and the people treated him with reverence and called him Dog. Bayr assumed he'd been a great warrior once. Everyone in Dolphys wore the pelts of wolves—gray, white, black and brown, big and small. Bayr wondered if he'd made a mistake riding into the village in only his tunic, hose, and boots. He had the coloring of a Dolphynian but not the attire.

"He is one of us," Dred roared. "He is my blood."

The people began shaking their heads, mumbling. Fearful.

"He must defeat Dolphys," the old warrior said, his tone final.

Dred didn't flinch, but the tremor that ran through the crowd circled and settled in the pit of Bayr's belly.

"So be it," Dred agreed.

Bayr wanted to ask what that meant but didn't trust his tongue.

The people shouted, and the circle around Bayr became two long lines that stretched in front of the chieftain's keep and down the thoroughfare. Grabbing clubs and rocks and whips, the people faced off as if to engage each other, yet they turned their eyes toward him.

"Take off your shirt, Bayr. And your shoes," Dred demanded, grim.

Bayr did as he was told. A fire was growing in his belly but his hands were ice. The bruises and welts inflicted by the king still colored his skin in blue and violet, and the people hissed and pointed.

"He has taken a recent beating," a few protested.

"He'll take more," Dred bellowed. "He'll take it, and he'll not fall."

Bayr looked at his grandfather in disbelief.

"You must run it, Bayr. Run between the lines."

Bayr gazed, flabbergasted, at the length of the parallel rows.

"They'll do their best to take you down. But I've seen you run. Keep moving."

Without giving himself a chance to think or the people a chance to prepare, Bayr leaped forward, dashing past the first third of the armed line without anyone realizing the gauntlet had begun.

A yapping and howling rose as though the people had morphed into wild dogs, and Bayr felt a lash dance at his heels and a blow glance off his right flank. He didn't look right. He didn't look left. He simply ran, flying for the space at the end of the rows, where torches beckoned and the pink horizon embraced a purple dusk.

He wasn't sure who wielded the club that bounced off his brow, but he finished the challenge with blood pouring from a gash at his hairline and a thundering in his chest. He'd never run so fast.

No celebration greeted his triumphant finish. He swiped at his eyes and turned back to the gathering, seeking reassurance and finding none.

"To the forest!" someone shouted, and Dakin and Dystel were suddenly beside him, their hands on Bayr's arms. They didn't seek to detain him, but to steer him, as though they knew Bayr could shake them free if he wished.

"If the wolves let you live, you will be their chieftain," Dakin said.

"Did I n-not d-defeat Dolphys?" Bayr asked, turning back toward the lines that had melded into a gathering mob.

"That was not Dolphys. That was a bloodletting designed to draw the wolves in. Dolphys is the wolf," Dystel replied.

Bayr could only shake his head, the blood streaming down his face obscuring his vision.

"Dred can't go with you. None of us can. You will be left alone in the woods. It is a trial few chieftains have endured, and only one has survived, but Dog has spoken, and now it is the only thing the people will accept."

Bayr didn't think being left alone sounded particularly daunting.

"No knife. No clothing. No weapons at all," Dystel added.

Bayr nodded, wishing only for a cloth to bind his head.

"They will secure you to a tree," Dakin said.

Bayr faltered, and Dakin's hand tightened in response. Dystel grasped his other arm and Bayr continued forward, the trees closing around them.

"You lifted an altar from the late king. My brother was there among the king's guard the day it happened," Dystel encouraged him. "But this final task is not a show of strength. You must not kill the wolves to save yourself. If you break your bonds it will be of no use. The wolves must choose you."

Bayr considered for a moment how it would feel to let the wolves have him. He was weary and bloody. He wished for Alba and her gift to woo the beasts. He wasn't convinced even Alba could soothe a pack of wolves if they were intent on blood. She thought she could talk to dragons, but she'd never met a dragon or a wolf, and a beast was still a beast.

"If the wolves don't come, you'll live. And the people will decide what that means," Dystel instructed.

"Pray that the wolves don't come," Dakin murmured.

"And if th-they do?" Bayr asked, his voice low.

"Do what you must to stay alive, Temple Boy. But if you kill the wolves, the people will take it as a sign."

They chained him in a clearing a half mile from the village square, the heavy links wrapped around his chest, his waist, and his thighs, pinning him against the massive trunk. The chains were secured to bolts as long as his palms and nailed to the tree to prevent his escape. He didn't resist them or beg for mercy. The throng that bore witness was a ragtag assortment of Dolphynian warriors, elders, and villagers, torches in hands, faces fearful and tones hushed. The mob had become a solemn assembly.

"Mayhaps your strength is great enough you can loosen the bands and climb the tree," an old woman added.

"Wolves don't climb trees," Dakin warned.

"Bears climb trees," Dystel added, the play on Bayr's name said with pointed gravity. "Are you a bear or a wolf?"

Bayr understood. The test was not to escape. The test was to endure. To withstand.

"Mayhaps he can break the chains," an elder said, hopeful. His hair was loose like a woman's, his warrior days past if they had ever occurred at all.

"'Twould be a feat none of us have seen. But killing the wolves will not make him chieftain. If you want to live, by all means, break the chains, Temple Boy," the old warrior, Dog, instructed. "We've heard of the things you can do. But if you want to lead, you have to tame the wolves."

Dakin gave him several mouthfuls of mead to help his courage and to wet his parched throat. Bayr feared the spirits would only pickle his loins for the wolves, but he was grateful for the small kindness all the same.

They left him there, secured to the tree, bidding him farewell and safe passage to Valhalla or the morning, whichever came first. If someone stood watch, Bayr did not feel him. If Dred was near, he didn't let it be known. Bayr suspected they kept his grandfather under guard. The night would be long for them both.

Bayr dozed briefly, exhaustion stealing his fear for a time. But as the moon rose and the stars deepened, he heard the rustling of unwelcome visitors and an expectant hush settle in the trees. A sudden howling raised his head and tested his bowels.

He wiped his brow against his shoulder, clearing his vision, and the action reopened the wound on his head. The scent would draw them in, and he cursed as one set of eyes and then another, and another, peered out at him from the undergrowth beyond the clearing.

He began to chant the prayers of his childhood, calling on Odin and his son, Saylok, the father of the clans. Calling on the Christ God, whom Dagmar had a special fondness for, calling on Thor, whose strength exceeded his own.

Mother of the earth be mine, father of the skies divine,
All that was and all that is, all I am and all I wish.

The blood rolled down his cheeks, dripped from his chin, and splashed on the pale skin of his bare feet. Planting his legs, he tested his bonds and felt an answering pop and rumble in the soil. The tree did not want to die either. The wolves crept closer and their snapping jaws echoed the sound of the protesting roots. His toes curled into the soil and his heartbeat filled his ears.

Did he have the strength to die when he could kill instead?

Could he wrench the tree from the ground or strip bolts from the bark? He could free himself and leave Dolphys behind. He could walk back to the temple, disgraced and demeaned. Shunned by the clan like King Banruud had predicted.

He could cower in the temple, hiding with Ghost, keeping his face averted and avoiding the king. Mayhaps, if he lived, the clan of Dolphys would let him stay, even if they rejected him as their chieftain.

Another droplet fell and then another, and he watched his blood trickle into the ground as the wolves crept closer.

Give me a home in hope, give me a place to go, give
me a faith that will never grow cold.

It was the blood and the soil and his homelessness that triggered the thought. Bayr had not been schooled in the runes, though Dagmar believed him to have rune blood, but he'd been raised in the temple, and he knew the most common runes—the sun rune and the rune for pain, and the rune that kept the creeping things away. With his toe he made a clumsy figure in the soil, his lines not nearly as straight, his picture half as good as Alba's had been. He extended the legs of the spider on either side, wrapping one spindly line as far as he could with the tip of his big toe, creating a perimeter around himself that butted into the base of the tree.

Then he bowed his head and let his blood weep into the body of the rune.

The wolves kept skulking, their bellies brushing the grass as they closed in around him. The growling became a whimpering, the snout of the largest wolf sniffing around the edges of the sloppy rune. The whimpering became a full-throated howl, and the pack began a mournful song full of desperate denial. They gathered around him, angry and anxious. But they did not cross the frail furrows of his rune.

All night they circled and shifted, snapping and sniffling against the simple shape in the soil, and Bayr stood silent, his head bobbing on his naked chest, making sure he fed the rune with his blood even as he waited for it to fail. He could have loosened the chains. He felt the weakness in the links, the warm thrumming of power in his arms and legs that promised salvation. He could have freed himself, but he didn't.

It was not until the pale light of morning began seeping into the trees that the wolves tucked their weary heads beneath their paws and succumbed to disappointed slumber. Bayr wanted to slip his cold, aching feet beneath the heat of their bodies—they were close enough for him to do so—but he feared waking them and losing his legs. Bayr could not feel his fingers or his arms, but the agony in his shoulders was a pulsing prison, and his legs knocked together in fatigue. The blood was dry on his face, his hair damp with morning dew. But when he heard the warriors of Dolphys coming through the trees, he ground out the rune with the heel of one foot and waited for the wolves to wake.

They bounded away as soon as they did, frightened by the approaching men, and hovered at the edge of the clearing.

Dred's eyes were rimmed in worry, and the lines of his face were deeper than the grooves worn into Bayr's wrists.

"He's alive," he cried, running toward the tree. The warriors on his heels rubbed their eyes and searched the trees.

"We heard wolves. All night, we heard wolves," an elder said in wonder.

Bayr simply waited for them to remove the chains.

"Look there," Dystel hissed, jutting his chin toward the pack that was clearly visible hunched beneath the thready morning mist.

"The gods have spoken," Dakin marveled.

"The wolves have spoken," Dog grunted, nodding. "Let there be no doubt."

"Take off the chains," Dred roared, wrapping his arms around Bayr as the bindings were removed. "You're alive," he moaned. "I feared the worst."

"At this moment I would rather be dead," Bayr whispered, and let his grandfather shoulder his weight as he was released. Someone pulled a jerkin over his head and helped him step into his hose.

"You need to walk into the village. You need to walk, Bayr. With your shoulders back and your head high. And they will bow," Dred urged.

"Goddamn you, Dred of Dolphys," Bayr muttered. "I never wanted them to bow."

"The gods have fixed your tongue," Dred marveled.

Bayr was too tired to test the theory.

"Long live the Dolphys!" someone shouted, and a dozen voices took up the cry.

"We have a new chieftain," Dred bellowed, and Bayr raised his head and straightened his back. With his arm slung around his grandfather's shoulders and his feet as bloodied and bare as the day he was born, he walked through the trees into the village he would now call home.

PART THREE

The Temple Keepers

21

"Saylok was the son of the god Odin—" Dagmar said, launching into the age-old tale. He'd promised the daughters a story, and Alba, whose turn it was to choose, always asked for this one.

"Not many knew he was the son of a god," Alba interrupted.

"That is true," Dagmar agreed. "Saylok cared little for the opinions of men. He also knew that, since he was the son of a god, many would seek to test his power or garner his favor, and he kept his identity secret. But though others may not have known his origins, Odin knew, and Loki, Saylok's brother, knew."

"Loki was very fond of mischief and loved to make trouble," Liis supplied, in case the other girls had forgotten, and Dagmar nodded, acknowledging that truth as he continued.

"Saylok loved to be out among the animals in the mountains and the fields, so Odin drew an island from the depths of the sea and named it for his son. He populated it with man and beast and gave it to Saylok, so he could live in peace and quiet, in a place where no one knew who he was."

"But Loki had other ideas," Dalys contributed.

"Indeed," Dagmar said. "Loki was jealous of his brother Saylok, and he enjoyed seeing him suffer. Loki also knew that there was only one thing Saylok loved more than the animals."

"Women. Saylok loved women." Alba inserted herself into the story once more, whispering the word *women* with awe. She was the youngest of the girls, and the farthest away from being a woman herself.

"Saylok loved women, yes, but he also wanted children. He wanted to father many children like his father, Odin," Dagmar said. "And in every village Saylok came to, he lay with a different woman hoping to beget a child. And before long, his wish came true. He begat many children."

"But Loki turned Saylok's children into creatures using the forbidden runes," Elayne contributed, her voice hushed with horror.

"Yes. When Saylok's six sons were born—one child in every village—they appeared perfectly normal. But days after their births, they began to sprout wings and claws and fur."

"One became a bear. One became an eagle, one became a boar, one became a horse, one became a lion, and one became a wolf," Alba murmured, her gaze thoughtful. She never tired of the tale.

"When Saylok realized what Loki had done, he built a temple and assigned keepers to guard the forbidden runes and petition the gods for each of his animal children, Adyar, Berne, Ebba, Dolphys, Joran, and Leok. Odin took pity on his son, and whenever the moon was full, he granted Saylok's animal children human form. As men, they fathered children who bore the same animal qualities, but with each generation, the animal characteristics fell away, leaving only size, speed, stealth, and strength in their stead. And that is how the clans of Saylok were born."

For several moments, the girls were silent, considering the tale as though they were hearing it for the first time instead of the hundredth. Their lessons were over, but Dagmar waited patiently, sensing turmoil beneath the quiet.

"Men cannot grow children," Liis said, her voice reflecting the same awe as Alba's had. "Even the sons of Odin. Even mighty Saylok. Even Bayr!" The mention of Bayr's name made Alba wince. Dagmar did not miss the fleeting expression on her young face.

"Yes. You will all be women, fully grown, someday. You will be the salvation of Saylok," Dagmar said, hoping fervently that it was true. Introspection among the girls continued for several more seconds, and then Bashti raised her eyes to the window, to the birdsong and sunlight, and asked if she might be excused.

Dagmar dismissed them, and the girls hurried out, anxious for the hour of leisure before evening chores. Alba remained behind.

"Do all men love women, Dagmar? Just like Saylok?" Alba asked when they were alone.

"Most men. Yes," Dagmar answered honestly.

"Do you love women, Dagmar?" The girls were supposed to call him Keeper Dagmar, but Alba never did, and Dagmar never corrected her.

"Yes. But I didn't . . . don't . . . love them more than I love the temple . . . or the gods."

"Is Bayr a god, Dagmar?"

Dagmar jerked, startled. Then he hesitated. It was not something he could easily answer.

"He has the strength of the gods," he admitted.

Alba was silent again, contemplative.

"My father says someday I will be a queen," she murmured, changing the subject.

"I have no doubt that is true."

"When I am gray and my breasts sway?"

Dagmar stared at her, aghast. He leaned his forehead low against his clasped fists, something he did often when she was around, apologizing to the gods he worshipped for her questions. He never scolded her, but he said silent prayers in her behalf, just in case she caused offense. Alba was too honest—and outspoken—for her own good.

"Not so long as that, Alba."

"But I can't be a queen if I am not yet a woman." In Alba's mind womanhood was most likely old and stooped, just like the women who worked in her father's palace and lived in the King's Village.

"You will be a woman before you are gray. And you will be a queen when your father decides to wed you to a king," Dagmar said.

Alba frowned, a deep groove forming between her dark brows, so at odds with her flaxen hair.

"I will choose a man of my own," she insisted.

Dagmar sighed, but his lips twitched.

"I hope you will do what is best for Saylok, Alba," he murmured. "We need you."

"Do what is best . . . like Bayr did?" she asked quietly. His name was a wound that never healed. He'd been gone for over three years, and Dagmar knew Alba missed him every day. Dagmar missed him every day. He knew Alba feared they would never see him again.

"Like Bayr did," Dagmar agreed. He thought she would leave then, joining the girls in the temple gardens to soak up the lingering rays, but she remained sitting.

"Did you always want to be a keeper, Dagmar?" she asked.

"Yes. Always."

"My father says you should have been a warrior for your clan, for Saylok. He said men like you should fight, not pray. Men like you should breed. That's what he said."

Dagmar choked again, and drew the star of Saylok on his forehead, reminding himself that he served the gods and Alba was still, mostly, a child. She made him laugh.

"We all have a purpose, and mine was never to wage war," he replied evenly.

"Or to breed?"

"Or to breed," he agreed, biting back the mirth bubbling behind his teeth.

"Bayr told me once that you threatened to kill yourself if Master Ivo refused to accept you at the temple. What if I refuse to be given away? I don't want to marry a king. Even for Saylok."

"Why?" he gasped. The girls talked incessantly of becoming mothers and queens, rulers of their own homes and their own lives, free of the confines of the temple grounds.

"I want Bayr." Alba's voice was firm and her eyes fierce.

Dagmar's heart ceased beating.

"When I am a woman, he will come back," Alba whispered. "Surely I can marry him. A god is better than a king."

"Oh, child. That will not happen," Dagmar moaned.

"Why?" The word was infused with anguish.

"Because . . ." Dagmar couldn't tell the girl Bayr was her half-brother. The words would never cross his lips. Such words could get him killed. And more importantly, he did not believe them. Desdemona had said Banruud would only have one child. Dagmar had come to believe that Alannah had taken a lover, and her indiscretion had fathered a daughter. No wife's infidelity had ever blessed her husband more. But Dagmar would never tell.

"Because Bayr is not a god . . . or a king. And you must marry a king, Alba. You must not marry a man of Saylok," Dagmar said instead.

"Why?" she pressed, insistent. Angry even.

"Because we must have more daughters, or eventually, the clans of Saylok will cease to exist."

⁀ꙮ

The people of Dolphys never called him Bayr. He missed the sound of his name—sometimes he whispered it to himself, feeling the word on his tongue, remembering the boy he'd been on the mount. They called him Chief or the Dolphys. He found it wasn't so different from being called the Temple Boy. His grandfather called him Chief too, his voice proud, his eyes bright. It served to remind Bayr who he was expected to be, and he didn't mind terribly. If his clansmen called him the Dolphys, or Chief, he didn't have to introduce himself. He worked hard, fought harder, and did his best to avoid a speech. When he wasn't fighting he was tilling the ground, or casting nets, or hunting in the hills. He had nothing else to give, and so he gave his strength and his stamina and his service wherever he could.

He lived in the chieftain's keep and slept in the vast chieftain's chamber, the fur and antlers of beasts he hadn't killed lining the walls. Dirth had left behind a wife, Dursula of Dolphys, who had resided in the chieftain's keep since becoming Dirth's bride at sixteen, more than thirty years before. In the clans, it was the new chieftain's duty to care for the old chieftain's family, and Bayr bade Dursula stay in the keep. She had outlived her husband and her sons, and her daughter was grown and gone. Bayr had no woman, no family in Dolphys but Dred, and he welcomed her presence. She ran the household—a household Bayr dwelled in but never called home—and tried to mother him, though he'd never been mothered before. Dred was fond of her and spent more time in the keep because of her, which also suited Bayr. Space and solitude invited loneliness, and loneliness invited thoughts of those he'd left behind.

Dred had been right about many things. Bayr loved Dolphys, he loved the people, and though he tried not to dwell on thoughts of his uncle, he saw Dagmar in his grandfather, in the stubborn set of his shoulders and the size of his hands. Sometimes he slipped and called Dred Dagmar, and Dred would laugh and shake his head, and that too would remind Bayr of the man who had raised him.

Alba's birthday had come and gone. One year. Two years. Three. Each year, Bayr sent a rider from Dolphys to the temple mount to deliver letters for everyone and gifts for Alba when her day drew near. Eight perfect feathers from a peacock, nine crystals from Shinway, ten silver bangles, eleven silk kerchiefs from a marooned ship of trade. She always replied with sweet thanks and a missive that brought her to life on the page. She was a far better writer than he, brimming with things to say, and he missed her desperately. Dagmar always sent letters back too, letters filled with tales of the temple and the girls that lived within her walls. After Alba turned eleven, he sent a letter that made Bayr so homesick and heart weary, he could hardly finish it.

My Bayr,

We all live for your letters. As for Alba's gifts, you have created an expectation that will be a problem in coming years, I fear. What will you do when you reach even greater numbers? I marvel at your ingenuity thus far. We are as well as can be expected. The daughters are growing and learning, and I find joy in them as I found joy in you.

Bashti longs for a life beyond the mount. She is a master at disguise and improvisation, and she has run away from the temple a dozen times. Her darker skin makes her more conspicuous, but like Ghost, whose skin is far more noticeable, she has learned to adapt and blend when need be. She claims when she is grown she will go back to Bomboska—she may be called Bashti of Berne, but she feels no allegiance to the clan. I fear Bomboska will not be what she imagines. No place ever is, and she is of Saylok now, whether she realizes it or not. I've come to believe that home is not a place. Home is inside of us. Home is the people we love. Home is what we strive for. Bashti is from Bomboska, but that is not who she is. In her heart Bashti knows this, for when she runs, she always returns.

Elayne of Ebba is a woman now, and her kindness and beauty are something to behold. Her only rebellion came when, two years ago, she refused to crop her hair. It is a glorious red, as you likely remember. She promised to braid it tightly around her head so it would not draw the eye. The other girls were quick to follow, and now all wear their hair in the same plaited wreaths. Even Ghost has quit shearing her locks, and it circles her head like a white crown. I fear the style does not accomplish what a shorn head would, but they have conformed in so much, Ivo has allowed it.

Since you left, Juliah of Joran has taken it upon herself to become their protector. She has demanded the daughters become proficient with a sword, and they spend time in instruction each day. Ivo has encouraged it with great enthusiasm. As you well know, all keepers, even the aged, must be able to protect the temple. We have never neglected the necessity of the warrior in ourselves and must not neglect it in these girl children. I see them with their heavy swords, and I think of you as a child, my Bayr, wielding your own, mimicking the movements of the keepers in their exercises, dueling with the king's guard, small yet full of grace and strength. I suspect you have grown since I saw you last.

Liis of Leok sings to us sparingly. She will join her voice with ours, and we all find ourselves singing as softly as we are able so that we can hear her, but she rarely sings alone. There is great power in her song. I think she fears it. She has rune blood, young Liis. But to be a keeper with rune blood is to carry the weight of worlds. We have not burdened her with knowledge that we can't expunge. If she is to be a keeper in truth, she will be committing her life to the temple, and that is a choice not made lightly. We will not force it upon her.

Alba has rune blood as well. You know this, as you warned me of the things she can do. She joins us in the temple for instruction—even instruction with a sword—but her father has suddenly become aware of her, and she has very little freedom. Mayhaps it is that she stands on the cusp of womanhood, and he knows her value. She is blessed with beauty and a placid wisdom that reminds me a little of Ghost. Mayhaps it is the time they spend together. I fear for her, Bayr, and I know you do as well. Know that, for now, she is well and whole, and in a time such as this, the restrictions on her freedom may be warranted.

There are still no daughters of Saylok. Daughters from other lands have come to the clans only to give birth to sons, and the drought continues. It has been eleven years since Alba was born, eighteen since your mother died, and I fear nothing will cure our ills.

We have more women at the temple now, from every clan. One by one, they began arriving at the gates of the temple mount with no place else to go, seeking asylum and sanctuary. Though most women are greedily guarded and accounted for in the clans, there are the few who have lost their protectors or been driven from their homes by raids or war. Some of them are grown—women of Saylok born before the scourge—some are children, brought here by trade or raid or by the marriage of their mothers.

We've become a school instead of a temple, a haven instead of a holy place. Ivo says we are Keepers of Saylok, and all who come to us are supplicants to be considered, though we haven't accepted a new brother since the daughters were entrusted into our care. If this continues, there will be more females than keepers in the temple. A few were only with us for a short while. Two women married members of the king's guard, and one girl's father came looking for her. She'd thought him dead and was overjoyed to see him. We do not demand that anyone stay, but if they do, they are taught the ways of the temple and the history of Saylok. We have not attempted to impart the wisdom of the runes or in any way share their power. It is not knowledge for the faint of heart or the shelter seeker. Those who are fully entrusted with the knowledge of the runes—true keepers—won't ever be able to leave the temple.

But I have digressed from my accounting of the daughters that you know. Dalys of Dolphys is still frail. The braid round her head is bigger than she is, and her eyes seem to be the only part of her that grows. She is older than Alba but much smaller. She makes lovely pictures and is quite content to dwell in her paintings where she is the master and creator. She cannot wield a sword, and we dare not spill her blood, even to power a rune. She becomes ill at the sight, and her illness doesn't pass. Ivo suspects she has rune blood, but we do not know. Do your people ask about her? I've wondered if the clans take courage from the temple and the torch that continually burns in honor of these daughters—of all the clan daughters— young and old. Do they represent hope or simply a world that is separate from their own struggles?

Saylok is suffering and splitting at her seams. I feel it. Ivo feels it, and it has aged him. I don't know if the king senses how volatile it has all become. Surely he must, as Ebba has been invaded twice and Erskin slain. The new chieftain, Elbor, was Banruud's personal choice. Dred was not in favor, as I'm certain he communicated to you. But the people of Ebba—what is left of them—supported Elbor's claim.

My father is proud of you. He reports that you have the love of the people and work tirelessly in their behalf. It is what I expected. I hope you will come to the mount when you are able. We miss you terribly. Do you remember when I promised I would refuse Valhalla and follow in your footsteps? I think of that often, as my heart is always where you are.

Be well, my boy.

Your Dagmar

The chieftains were often summoned to the temple mount, to the palace of the king, but each time Bayr had been afraid to leave his lands unattended and sent Dred and a handful of warriors in his stead. The attacks from the Northmen on Berne had bled down into Dolphys, and attacks from the Hinterlands on Ebba had done the same on their southern borders. Dred argued that Bayr had to present himself at the king's table and take part in the tournaments, but Bayr refused. He had little to say and no one had the patience for him to say it. They would not miss him at the council, but Dolphys would miss him on the battlefield. His very presence served as a deterrent.

Another year dawned and died, then two more, and Bayr stayed away from the Temple of Saylok. Instead he sent twelve colored stones from the Northlands, thirteen pouches of the sweetest tea from Bomboska, and fourteen pairs of new stockings along with a pair of beautifully crafted calfskin slippers from his own village.

When Alba's fifteenth birthday approached, Bayr sent fifteen vials of precious oil from the lavender fields that bordered Dolphys and Berne. The next year, he sent sixteen medallions, no bigger than his thumbnail, painted by an old deaf woman who had fled Ebba and taken refuge among the Dolphynians. Each medallion was decorated with a tiny, intricate scene that created an entire tale. He included a magnifying glass so Alba could discover them. But though Dagmar wrote him a lengthy letter to answer the one he'd sent, Alba did not. A simple piece of parchment rolled and bound with a bit of string was all he received from the girl. It read:

> *Bayr,*
>> *My sincerest gratitude for the lovely gift.*
>> *Alba*

He scoured Dagmar's letter for news of her, for the details he craved, but she was not mentioned. He fretted, but knew if something was amiss, Dagmar would have told him. The only indication he had of her at all was in his uncle's parting line:

> *You promised you would return. We patiently await that day.*

22

These Eastlanders did not want to talk. Bayr could not blame them. They were angry. Afraid. Their village had been ransacked by clans of Saylok before. Blood had been shed. Lives ruined. Bayr had hoped to negotiate with their lord, to make a trade. He and his men had waited on the beach for a sentry to arrive. But none had, and Bayr had known then that there would be a battle. They did not want to talk, and they did not want to trade. They poured from the trees with faces painted for war, and Bayr stood on the shore with the warriors of Dolphys and Berne, waiting to kill them.

Surely it was not what the gods had intended when they gave him such strength, to kill men who had just cause to come against the clans in battle. But he was Bayr of Dolphys, he'd been charged with the defense of his land, of his clan, and he had little choice in the matter. He would kill the men who ran toward him, teeth bared and swords drawn, because if he didn't, they would kill him, and they would kill men beside him. If he died, his clan would come against the Eastlanders again, provoked to vengeance, and the never-ending cycle of desperation and demand would repeat itself. His clansmen had not sought women from the Eastlanders to satisfy their lusts—not entirely. They took them because if they didn't, Saylok would perish.

The men he would kill this day did not deserve to die. But he would still kill them. He silently begged the Allfather for mercy and asked his mother to lift his shield and guide his sword. She had called down this plague upon them, and he prayed for the salvation she'd promised he would provide. Then he raised his arms, roared like the bear for which he was named, and charged forward, Alba's face in his mind's eye, her name on his lips.

∽

The blade scored Bayr's arm before he removed it from the woman's clenched fist, and Daniel lifted his hand to reproach her.

"No," Bayr grunted, restraining Daniel with an arm to his chest. The woman collapsed, sobbing, at his feet, and Bayr handed her blade to his protective friend.

He helped the woman rise, trying not to get his blood—blood that she'd spilled—on her dusty clothes. He kept his hands on her shoulders, just to make sure she wouldn't attack again. She was trembling with outrage.

"I w-won't harm you," he promised.

"You killed my husband!" she shrieked, her face wet with tears and red with fury.

"Your husband died in battle, woman!" Daniel roared in outrage. "He died with a sword in his hands! Don't make it worse for yourself."

"We have killed their men, Chief. What are they to do now?" Dakin murmured, his eyes on the women and children huddled in the church, the largest structure in the village.

Bayr was silent, fighting the urge to run, to flee back to the shore, to throw himself into the sea to wash off the blood and grime that still stained his skin. A warrior never washed before he demanded his winnings. It was proof that he had battled and that he'd been the victor. He would not have killed their men had they not attacked. But Dakin was right. He'd killed them all, and now these women looked at him with rage and fear.

"We will take them back to Dolphys with us. Half for us, half for Berne. There are two dozen women and at least twice that many children, half of them girls. They will thank us for providing for them now that their men are gone. 'Tis what we came for, after all," Daniel said, shrugging.

"We c-came to negotiate," Bayr muttered. He closed his eyes, trying to find wisdom and patience, but saw only the manic flashing of blades and the bodies falling around him.

"Tell them w-why we've come, Daniel. Tell them we did not c-come to slaughter but to seek. Tell them about Dolphys and Berne. About Saylok. About our n-need for women," Bayr ordered. Daniel's inability to keep his mouth closed made him a convincing storyteller.

"We will sound weak, Chief," Daniel argued under his breath.

"We have s-slain their men. They are at our mercy. If I must b-be weak to make them m-more willing, so be it," Bayr grunted. He was dripping blood on the stone floor; he needed to tend to his arm and impart his instructions among the warriors of Berne. Benjie never sailed with his warriors, and Bayr outranked them all. It was understood that he would give the orders and divvy the spoils between the two clans.

Daniel grinned as though he'd been let in on a grand scheme. His face and his braid were so blood-spattered, his white teeth glared in contrast.

"K-keep him honest," Bayr demanded of Dakin as he turned to leave. "Convince them. Don't c-coerce them. And make him w-wash his face first. We want wives, not c-captives."

"Aye, Dolphys," Dakin reassured. "I'll find you a woman like my Magda."

Bayr snorted and Dakin laughed, but it was not the first time his men or his grandfather had made such an offer or insinuation. His clan wanted him to take a bride.

"He is seeking an alliance," Ghost murmured, keeping her pace steady, trying not to let her terror show. The king had been gone for a month, usually a welcome event, but he was in the Northlands and King Gudrun wanted a bride.

"He has been seeking alliances for a decade," Alba said, tossing her hand like the matter was of no importance, but her brow furrowed in unease. "I am paraded in front of the chieftains, turned on the spit like a plucked chicken, dangled like a bundle of grapes over their gaping lips, yet Banruud never makes any promises."

"You're making me hungry," Ghost quipped, her voice as mild and dry as a summer day. Alba laughed, just as Ghost had intended. Her daughter did not laugh enough.

They walked the long road from the wide north gate down to the village below, a dozen members of the palace guard trailing behind them. They'd learned to converse with their voices pitched low, their heads bowed, their shoulders together, though Alba had long passed Ghost in height. She was tall and well formed, with steady eyes and a stubborn chin that Ghost recognized as her own.

It was not an official royal visit—Ghost never accompanied Alba on those. The princess waved to the children who came running as they neared the base of the mount, but she and Ghost turned and headed back up the hill without entering the village, though two of the warriors distributed drops of honey candy to the children, per Alba's instructions. It was one of Alba's duties to be seen and to make her presence felt. Banruud believed it kept the people content. The king had taken her on visits to the clan lands—every clan save Dolphys—for the same reason.

Ghost had lived on the mount for ten years. In the beginning she'd cowered in the shadows, terrified that one of the king's minions would see her pale face and tell the king of her presence. She wore the purple hooded robe of a keeper, the sleeves cut too long to better protect the skin of her hands. Her head was always covered, her face always shadowed, and little by little, year after year, she'd begun to believe the king had forgotten her. She'd grown bolder, become more visible, and now that there were other women on the mount—refugees and asylum seekers who had taken shelter among the keepers—it was assumed she was simply one of them, and since few people outside the temple saw her paleness, no one questioned it.

"I believe my father will use my presence as long as he is able," Alba reasoned, resuming their conversation. "I am of far more use to him as Princess Alba than Queen of the Hinterlands or part of King Kembah's court." She wrinkled her nose at the thought.

Ghost tended to agree, but conditions were worsening. In the last year, no daughters had come to the temple walls seeking sanctuary. Dagmar feared it was because the journey was too fraught with dangers . . . or worse, there were no daughters left to make it.

"But if an arrangement is made . . . and I wed . . . will you come with me, Ghost?" Alba asked softly.

Ghost halted, stunned, and raised her eyes to her daughter's troubled face.

"You want me to come with you?" she whispered.

"You have never left me," Alba said, and Ghost could not hold her gaze.

"I will follow you . . . wherever you go," Ghost reassured her, willing the tears not to rise and her lips not to tremble. For a moment, Alba clung to her arm as though she'd been afraid to ask, afraid to cause Ghost the discomfort of having to refuse her. Ghost would never refuse her.

"You would leave Dagmar?" Alba asked, awe tingeing her tone.

"He is not m-mine to abandon," Ghost stammered, heat climbing her chest and collecting in her cheeks. The day was warm, but suddenly she was sweltering.

"You love him. He loves you," Alba insisted.

"He doesn't," Ghost argued.

"Yes, Ghost. He does. It is as clear as the skies."

Ghost tilted her head up to assess the cloud cover, and Alba crowed.

"What do you know about these things?" Ghost grumbled, embarrassed.

"Only what I see," Alba replied. "You should make a rune to braid his fate to yours. Two souls together, throughout all eternity."

"Do you know such a rune, Alba?" Ghost giggled.

"No." Alba grinned, though it faded so quickly, Ghost wondered if she lied.

"Runes are chaos, Alba, not the cure," she warned. Alba was not a keeper, and her knowledge was a constant source of concern to Ivo. "Dagmar says no rune can take away a man's will or change his heart."

"And what about a rune to make a man return?" Alba whispered.

"Bayr?" Ghost asked. Alba never spoke of him anymore and changed the subject when Dagmar mentioned his name.

"Bayr," Alba murmured, wincing. "I don't want to change him, I just want to see him again. And I've given up hope that it will ever happen."

"The tournament is only weeks away."

"He will not come. He never does."

"Ivo says . . . he will." Ghost had not wanted to tell the girl what Ivo had seen, but she couldn't bear Alba's sadness a moment longer.

Alba's legs began to buckle and Ghost girded her up, sliding an arm around her waist. A guard called out to them, but Alba waved him off and resumed her climb, joy infusing her face.

"If Ivo has seen it . . . it must be," Alba whispered.

Ghost could only nod.

Dagmar had rejoiced at the prediction, and Ivo had patted his cheek with a gnarled hand and demanded preparations be made. But when Dagmar left the sanctum, Ivo had wilted into his throne. He often claimed the decades and the demons had whittled his flesh.

"Death rides on his heels," he had muttered, raising his black-rimmed gaze to Ghost. "The son returns, but night will follow."

The winds did not cooperate, gusting up from the gulf and rushing toward the Northlands instead of blowing west toward home. Instead of two days back to Dolphys, it became an interminable week in a village where they were not wanted, waiting for the winds to change. The good news was, by the time they set sail for Dolphys, a few more women had mellowed on the men from Dolphys and Berne and changed their minds about coming with them. Twelve women and twenty children, half of them daughters, would be adopted into each clan.

They arrived home, victorious and relieved, only to find that a tiny village called Sheba, sitting at the border where wolf met bear, had been terrorized in the dead of night by a raiding party the previous week. Bayr, Dred, and six warriors climbed from the bellies of their boats to the long backs of their horses and headed for Sheba without rest or reprieve, a clean change of clothes and a few days' rations in their saddlebags.

The people of Sheba had fought back, though two men had died and three were injured in its defense. Four women were dragged from their beds only to struggle free when the raiders had to fight off the whole village. Many of the marauders had escaped into the night, but more had died for their mistake. The dead were clothed in the garb of the clanless, simple tunics and hose with no colors to call attention—or blame—to a clan, but a few of Sheba's farmers were unconvinced.

"The tracks we followed the morning after led north at the neck. Toward Berne," one claimed.

Bayr raised his head, meeting the man's gaze, waiting for him to continue making his argument.

"Two of the attackers called each other by name—both names of the bear. We captured one, and he admitted his brother was a warrior of Berne, a warrior in the raiding party set to return with you, Lord. He also claimed there were Northmen camped on Berne's beaches."

"Where is he now? I'll make him talk," Dred growled.

"He is hanging from the village gates," another man piped up.

Justice was swift in the clans, especially when the whole village bore witness to your crimes. Dred snorted and Bayr nodded, turning toward Berne, unconvinced.

"It was Berne, Chief," one farmer said, his countenance grim. "These men were from Berne, I have no doubt."

"Do they not know of the Dolphys?" Daniel interjected, gaping. "Do they not know what will happen to them if they attack his clan? The Bernians think they can defeat the Dolphys?"

Bayr silenced Daniel's effusion with a wave of his hand, but the farmers nodded, as though they'd considered that.

"They waited until you were gone, Lord. They knew you were in Eastlandia. While you were fighting there, they attacked here," one farmer reasoned.

"Their warriors beg to raid with us because they know the strength of our chief. Then, while our backs are turned, their brothers steal from us," Dystel murmured, disgust clinging to every quiet word.

"The same kind of raids are happening in Joran too, though from Ebba. Elbor has lost control of his lands," Dred said, nodding. "Bands of young men are becoming violent in the villages. Farms are being burned. Instead of worrying about the Hounds of the Hinterlands, Josef of Joran is erecting fortifications on the border with Ebba."

"Benjie is weak," Dystel spat. "He has not traded or raided in years. He sits in his keep and lives off his people. His warriors have been seen in Adyar too, small war parties that pick off the outer settlements looking for women and children."

"Show me w-where those tracks led," Bayr said quietly.

$\sim\!\mathfrak{I}$

Bayr and his men followed where the farmers led, winding down into Berne, their mounts draped in Dolphys blue to avoid being accused of the same deception they were attempting to prove. The path they'd taken from Sheba eventually intersected a well-traveled dirt road that forked in three directions. Trees crowded the thoroughfare, creating a canopy that appeared to extend for miles.

"We didn't go beyond this point, Lord," a farmer said, patting his old dappled mare. It was a good thing; the horse looked ready to collapse.

"They could have gone in any direction, Chief. Or all three. And a week has passed," Daniel grumbled.

Bayr sat in his saddle, his gaze trained on the hard-packed earth, puzzling over what should be done. With the thumb of his right hand, he absently traced the shape of the skull—the rune for wisdom—into his palm. He never used blood and never believed Odin answered his prayers, but the exercise calmed him and directed his thoughts.

"I hear bells," Dred murmured, staring this way and that. "Is it just the madness of an old man?"

Dred had the keenest senses of all the warriors of Dolphys, young and old, and Bayr raised his head, listening. It was faint, but he heard them too. He waited and the sound grew, becoming a cacophony of clanks and jingles coming from the north fork. The way was obscured by the curvature of the road and the boughs of the trees, but before long, a traveler came into view.

A portly peddler approached, his wares hanging from his clothes and the sides of his mule, his clatter scaring the birds and spooking the horses. He didn't seem alarmed by the sullen warriors in his path and drew to a stop with a rattle and a clink.

"Hellooooo," he called. "Fine day, men of Dolphys. Fine day. I am Bozl of Berne, hailing from the village of Garbo. I have wonders from the north and marvels from the east. Can I interest you in a bauble for your ladies or a button for your coat?"

"We have no ladies," Daniel complained.

"You have c-come all the way from Garbo?" Bayr asked, his eyes narrowing on the plump little man.

"I have, sir. I have. Do you know Garbo? It sits right on the sea, and I have gathered all the best treasures from the ships that come to trade. Would you like to see?"

"Are there no customers closer to home?" Dred pressed.

The peddler hesitated. "Of course. But let me show you what I have."

"Have y-you heard tales of Northmen on Bernian shores?" Bayr asked.

"Aye, Lord. I have," he said with a nod, his cheeks quivering with the movement. He looked frightened. "I've seen them myself. 'Tis why I left."

They clung to the west border of Berne, where the clan lands met the lands that circled the temple mount fifty miles in every direction, lands that the people simply called Saylok, where herds and farms were run by clanless tenants of the king. To ride on clan lands without permission from the chieftain could be dangerous, and Bayr had never been so far north into Berne. He had no idea what he'd find nor the approach he should take to see for himself if the Northmen had stayed.

Anyone would be able to hear Bozl and his mule coming a mile away, so Bayr purchased the peddler's entire inventory and saddled the dappled mare and the flabbergasted farmers with enough baubles and buttons to adorn all Saylok. Then he demanded the peddler take them to Garbo. Bozl, stripped of his wares but a good deal richer, had agreed, but by the following day, as they dipped down toward the coast of Berne, he became increasingly nervous.

"We've gone far enough, Lord," he argued. "The Northmen are vicious. They won't be so easy to kill as a few hungry Bernians. They are all as big as you, Dolphys."

Bayr had no wish to fight, only to see with his own eyes what Bozl described. Instead of entering the valley of Berne, they skirted the edges, dipping into Adyar before coming out on the highlands that jutted up between the two clans. The heights gave them a view of the sea in front of them, the northern coast of Berne on the right, and the coast of Adyar on their left. They crawled on their bellies up to the overlook, and with spyglasses extended, studied the fishing village below. Long docks extended from shore to sea, but many of the boats clustered there did not have the sails common in Saylok.

"He's right. They are the long ships of the Northmen. I count ten in total," Dakin said, grim.

"Why have w-we not heard of this?" Bayr hissed.

"They did not just raid. They stayed," Bozl explained.

"And no one challenged them?" Dred asked.

"Those that did died," Bozl rushed to explain. "Those that didn't want to die or submit moved inland. They left their homes, their boats, their shops, everything . . . as did I."

"And the Northmen . . . have they m-moved inland?" Bayr asked, still holding the spyglass to his eye.

"Not yet, Lord. There are not many of them. But we fear there will be more."

"And what of Aidan of Adyar? Surely he knows there are Northmen living on the other side of the highlands," Bayr asked, incredulous.

"You did not know, Chief," the peddler said with a shrug, and Bayr could only nod, conceding the point.

"Chief Benjie offered them gold to leave. But they don't want gold. They want land," Bozl said. "Some say they want Saylok."

"We have to tell the king," Bayr said.

"He knows, Lord," Bozl countered.

The warriors turned on the unhappy peddler as one, their jaws slack, their gazes blank. Outrage followed on fleet feet, and Dred ground his teeth so hard, Bayr heard a crack.

"King Banruud offered them a Daughter of Freya," Bozl claimed, morose. "The king of the Northlands wants to see our temple. He is fascinated by the daughters . . . and the keepers."

Bayr felt a wave of fury so hot, he could not be still. Bozl rose beside him, as though he thought Bayr did not believe him.

"But they will not leave," Bozl wailed. "Some say that men and women—families—from the Northlands will heal the scourge. But so far, we've only seen warriors. Not women. Not families."

"The king . . . where is he now?" Bayr asked. If he was near, Bayr would kill him. Then he would kill Benjie of Berne and drive the Northmen out himself.

"There is talk that King Banruud went to the Northlands and met with their king," Bozl offered. "But I don't know if he has returned."

"What do we do, Chief?" Dred ground out. He turned his gaze on his grandson as if he should know. And suddenly Bayr did. It was the only thing he *could* do.

"I am going to the temple mount."

Dred frowned in surprise. "To see the king?"

Bayr nodded. To see the king . . . and the keepers. It was time. Benjie would be of no assistance. Benjie had bigger problems than the Clan of the Wolf. If something wasn't done about the Northmen, Berne would fall. And if Berne fell, Adyar and Dolphys would follow. He could not send Dred to be his voice, not again. If the king would not act, then Bayr would have to appeal to the chieftains still in power in their own lands.

"Tell no one I am g-gone. I just returned, and I put the clan at r-risk every time I leave."

"I will not let you go alone, Chief," Dred said, his mouth hard.

"Nor will I," Dakin grunted. "You need a man on each flank."

"I need m-men in Dolphys," Bayr commanded.

"I will follow you if you deny me," Dred shot back.

"You are a s-stubborn old man," Bayr sighed. "But we cannot both go. If you are in Dolphys, the p-people will believe I am not far. It is how we've always been."

"And the tournament?" Dred pressed.

Bayr could hardly believe they were talking of such things with invaders on Saylok's shores. He could hardly believe the tournament would even take place. Still, Bozl's account indicated that the situation had not worsened in the month since he'd fled. It was a small comfort, but still . . . comfort.

"Go to the tournament. I w-will await you there. Bring the men you must have. But leave most behind. The people will want to m-make the journey for the festivities; do not d-dissuade them. They are safer on the m-mount than in their own beds these days."

"I fear that is not true, Chief. Not with Banruud as king," Dred worried.

"I will go with the Dolphys," Dakin insisted again, speaking of Bayr as though he were a precious urn.

"Dakin, you will stay with Dred," Bayr said, tolerating no argument.

Dakin glowered in protest.

"You will c-carry on as though I am just a glade away," Bayr ordered before turning to the peddler. "Bozl, you may travel as f-far as you wish with my men. You are welcome in my clan and in my village."

Bozl nodded, suddenly tearful, and he climbed back on his mule like he couldn't wait to leave.

"If I d-do not return," Bayr said, eyeing his men one at a time, "do not make Daniel your chieftain."

His warriors brayed in raucous relief—even Daniel—their tension easing as they turned toward home.

"Long live the Dolphys," Dred shouted, his hand on his braid, and the warriors around him took up the call, howling as they left him. But Bayr's eyes were already trained toward the temple mount, rising up in his mind's eye. In a mere two days' time, he would see his family, and his heart left his chest and fled on ahead, unable to wait.

23

Dagmar was facing north in the bell tower when he saw him coming, a rider that could have been anyone, a dark speck on a green landscape littered with plow fields and homesteads, still a good distance beyond the cluster of cottages that huddled against the base of the temple mount. The day had threatened rain, but the clouds had continued to swell and gather without releasing a drop.

He should have come from the east, but Dagmar did not question it. Even without a rune to improve his vision, he knew it was Bayr. He wanted to run down the long road, sprint through the village, and hurtle over the fields to reach him, but he made himself wait, watching as the speck became a tittle, and the tittle became a jot. When the jot widened and lengthened, becoming a minuscule silhouette, he could no longer hold back his tears. He rang the bells in jubilant welcome, bouncing from the heavy rope like a drunken fool, crying and laughing. He stumbled down the tower steps and ran to the north gate, swiping at his blurry eyes, frantic that when he joined the sentry on the gate overlook, he would not be able to find Bayr again.

But he did, and his emotion grew with the approach of his boy, now a man, who rode his horse like the chieftain of a clan, back straight, one hand on his thigh, one hand wrapped in his stallion's hair.

Dagmar found he could not call out, could not even speak, and the sentry at the gate—a man who had never known the Temple Boy—called down in greeting and inquiry.

"I am Bayr, Chieftain of Dolphys, here to see King Banruud," he said, and though he paused every third or fourth word, he did not stumble.

"Open the bloody gate!" Dagmar bellowed, clambering down to the winchmen who controlled the grates.

"The king is not here, Chieftain. But Keeper Dagmar has vouched for you and has bidden me open the gate," the sentry replied good-naturedly, and, with a bellow slightly more subdued than Dagmar's had been, granted Bayr entry.

Then he was coming through the gate, his eyes trained on Dagmar, who had placed himself directly in his path. Dagmar wouldn't remember who took Bayr's horse or how they traveled from the vast courtyard to the temple steps. He would only recall the joy of Bayr's return, the feel of his heart pounding in his chest, the way Bayr swept him up, laughing and saying his name.

"I see Dolphys in you—the clan is in your blood—but you are still Bayr, though you are more boar than cub," Dagmar choked, laughing through his tears.

"I am no bear. I am a wolf, Uncle. Though I do run a bit b-bigger than most of them." Bayr's grin was blinding, and Dagmar found he could not release him, though his girth—hardened and honed—felt strange in his arms. Bayr embraced him in return, kissing his bristled pate with all the affection of the child he'd once been.

"I s-see gray in your whiskers, Uncle," he growled, and Dagmar laughed again.

"Your stutter is much improved! And I am not yet gray because I am not yet old."

"He has always been old," Ivo cackled from the shadows of the temple steps, and Dagmar made himself let go, though he followed at

Bayr's heels, unable to abide any distance between them. Bayr strode forward and enveloped the Highest Keeper in an embrace that should have reduced him to dust, but Ivo curled his arms around the chieftain and uttered not even a peep of protest.

"We've been waiting, Bayr of Saylok," he murmured, as Bayr released him.

Dagmar knew Ivo had a great deal more to say, but the Highest Keeper urged Bayr into the temple to see the others who were gathering to greet him. Ghost and the clan daughters hurried down the stone steps on the east side of the grand entry, having heard the commotion from the upper floors. From the west staircase, a stream of keepers began to pour, voices raised in welcome, hands clasped in excitement at Bayr's return.

When Ghost reached out a hand to Bayr in greeting, her smile as careful and quiet as it had always been, Bayr bowed above it, kissing her pale white knuckles. Her smile became sunlight breaking above the eastern hills.

"You are s-still beautiful, Ghost," Bayr said softly, and the final pieces of Dagmar's composure crashed to the floor. Of course Bayr would think her so. That he would tell her without artifice or awkwardness was a reminder of the sensitive boy they'd known and the confident man he'd become. "Thank you for l-looking after him," Bayr added, casting a brief glance at Dagmar so there would be no question to whom he referred.

"Your uncle looks after all of us," she replied, and pink suffused her alabaster cheeks. Watching them thus, the two people he loved most in the world, was a joy so searing and sweet, Dagmar had to look away to find his breath.

"You are all . . . w-women," Bayr stammered, raising his eyes from Ghost to the five females who had stopped a few paces behind her. Elayne, Juliah, Liis, Bashti, and Dalys, uncertain how they should greet their old friend, laughed and bowed in the way of the keepers, their years in the temple never more apparent than at that moment. Bayr gripped his braid as though he greeted the king, and his fealty and reverence were not lost on Dagmar.

In response, Juliah grasped the heavy coil that circled her head.

"Mine is not a warrior's braid, but a warrior's crown," she said, a smirk twisting her soft lips.

"The Warrior Queen?" Bayr asked, and her smile widened.

"There has been no coronation, but I accept your title," she said, lifting her chin like royalty, and her eyes caught on something just over Bayr's shoulder.

"Bayr?" The voice came from behind him, and for a moment Bayr froze, as though he knew exactly who spoke. He seemed to brace himself before turning, but the shudder that wracked him was visible to all who observed.

"Alba?"

She was framed by the light of the gray afternoon. The heavy temple door had been pushed wide upon Bayr's entry and never closed. Alba stood on the threshold, perfectly still. In that moment, Dagmar saw the woman and not the child. She was no longer the girl he'd watched grow, day after day, year after year. He saw her the way Bayr would see her, and his heart stuttered and stopped.

She was tall for a woman, taller than many of the keepers, and straight and strong in her carriage and character. She wore her hair loose around her shoulders, the pale gold waves like the long grass in late summer against her deep-blue gown. The light at her back shadowed her features, but Dagmar knew her eyes were as dark as the soil of Saylok, and they were fixed on Bayr's face. A heartbeat later, she was hurtling through the entrance hall, her skirts clutched in her hands to free her flying feet, her hair streaming behind her. Then she was in his arms, caught up against him, her feet no longer touching the floor, as though she'd leaped past the last few steps.

All was silent around them, a small crowd of stunned observers, watching a reunion that was as wrenching as it was wonderful. Bayr and Alba did not speak, didn't chatter and preen excitedly the way long-lost friends often do upon finding one another again. They simply stood, locked in a desperate embrace, clinging to each other in quiet commiseration. Dagmar could see Bayr's face, the closed eyes and the clenched jaw of a man overcome. Alba had begun to weep, her shoulders quaking, her face buried in Bayr's neck. Bayr simply turned, still clutching her to his chest, her feet still dangling, and strode into the sanctum. He closed the double doors behind him with a shove of his boot.

Among the keepers and the daughters, there was not a dry eye. Ghost, who rarely wept and never admitted it when she did, turned and quickly climbed the stairs, fleeing the loss of her self-control. Dagmar wiped at his own face, wondering whom he should comfort, whom he should go after, or whether he could flee himself. Bayr and Alba weren't children anymore. Bayr could not sleep at the foot of her bed or carry her on his shoulders. It would not be wise to let them spend time alone. But he could not find it in himself to deny them. To intervene in a welcome home so long awaited would be cruel, and he turned to Ivo, seeking guidance.

"The king is gone, and it's just as well," Ivo intoned, always perceptive. "For tonight we will feast in the temple, and Bayr can await Banruud's return among us."

Bayr didn't release Alba, but held her locked in his arms, letting her tears dry and his own settle. The sanctum was a shadowed tomb, the dome spilling light on the altar in straight lines. The colored glass that depicted the story of the clans created a rainbow pattern across the stone floors. The sconces had not been lit for evening, but candles flickered and pooled on every surface. It had looked exactly the same the day they said goodbye, and for a dizzying moment, Bayr tightened his arms around the woman, remembering the child.

But the child was gone.

Alba wasn't the same.

He wasn't the same.

He set her on her feet and carefully released her, taking a step back, then another, suddenly shy. This was not his Alba. This was a woman grown, and he didn't know what to say. He'd brought her into the sanctum so the keepers wouldn't see him weep. He'd wanted to guard the moment, to shield it from view, to keep it for himself. He hadn't wanted to share it . . . or her . . . with another soul.

She wiped at her cheeks with the base of her palm, a gesture he instantly remembered, and his sudden discomfort eased slightly. But when she raised her eyes to his, he forgot himself again, his disorientation rearing its spinning head.

She was so beautiful.

The softness of her child's face had sharpened into hollowed cheekbones and a slim neck. Dark eyes, pale hair, warm skin, rose-petal lips. All of it, Alba. Yet not Alba at all.

☙

"When you left you were a hill. Now you are a mountain," Alba teased, though she feared her nervous swallowing betrayed her.

Bayr was huge, muscled and towering, and she didn't like the marked contrast between them, a contrast that she'd never noticed before, oddly. He'd been her Bayr, her best friend, her confidant, her protector, the person she loved most in the world. And now he was so obviously a man, a man like her father, hulking and fierce, with no twinkle in his eyes or softness 'round his lips.

He laughed, his white teeth flashing between lips that weren't harsh or hard at all.

"There's my funny little Alba," he said. "I thought she might be gone."

"I am here. I never left," she murmured, her heart quickening at his familiar grin.

"You've grown too. You were once a flower. Now you're a sapling," he said, each word a well-placed rumble. "I can hardly lift you. What will I do when you want to fly?"

"A sapling? I am an oak," she said with mock outrage. "Another year or two and I will be as tall as you."

He laughed again, the sound so filled with fondness that her tears welled again, and without hesitation, she stepped back into his arms.

He welcomed her return to his embrace, his arms tightening around her, and she stood, breathing him in, her nose pressed to his chest. To tell him she had missed him would be false. She had ached and mourned and cried and counted the days. She'd banished him from her thoughts and her heart only to beg the gods for his well-being. Last year, she'd even given up hope. Another year, another gift, and still no Bayr. Now that he was here, she wanted only to hold him for a moment, to feel only the joy of his return.

"Are you s-standing on your t-toes?" he laughed, his stutter peeking through to remind her of the boy he'd been. They put her at ease, those small hitches. He was still Bayr.

"Yes. I am." She laughed with him, the sound choked by emotion she could not contain. The top of her head didn't even reach the top of his shoulder, and she was taller than most women, or so Dagmar claimed.

"Seventeen years old," he whispered. "Tomorrow is your birthday. W-what would you like, little Alba? Seventeen roses? Seventeen sugared plums? Seventeen d-diamonds to wear in your crown?"

"I want seventeen days," she countered quietly, stepping back in the circle of his arms so she could see his face. As soon as the words left her mouth, she realized there was nothing she wanted more. "Seventeen years would be even better."

His eyes changed, softened, and he touched her nose with the tip of his finger.

"I can't give you that, Alba."

"Twelve days?"

He shook his head.

"Ten?"

Another no.

"Nine, then. And that's as low as I'll go. I'm Princess of Saylok, and you must do as I say."

He laughed again, a booming sound that made her chest swell with so much happiness, she thought she might burst into tiny particles of light.

"I can give you a week. Maybe less."

"A week?" she whispered. "You are leaving so soon?"

"Yes. I will only stay until the k-king returns."

Her happiness seeped from her chest, ran down her weak legs, and pooled beneath her feet, leaving her as empty as she'd been yesterday and the day before.

"I promise you s-seventeen perfect hours. All yours. The b-best hours in all of existence," Bayr whispered. "We will fly and s-swim and swing and eat all our bellies can hold."

"Fly?" she asked.

"And swim."

"And we won't waste time with sleep?"

"Not a wink." He grinned, and she realized suddenly how weary he must be. How far he had come. Yet he stood before her, and she would not waste her time dreading his absence. She took a deep breath and released it. Grabbing his hand, she pulled him to the bench nearest the rainbow colors and sat down, unwilling to wait to embark upon her perfect hours.

"Tell me where you've been," she demanded, breathless. She wanted to know everything. Every moment of his every day for the last ten years.

"Everywhere. Though in these last y-years, I've rarely left Dolphys. Until now," he replied, sinking down beside her. She didn't release his hand, but kept it wrapped in both of hers.

"Everywhere? I want words, Bayr. Details," she cried.

He smiled again and groaned. Then he tapped his ear.

Her heart leaped at the old game, and she let him maneuver around her request, the way he used to do.

"Have you been to Eastlandia?" she asked, settling into the rhythm of their old ways. Yes or no questions so he didn't have to speak.

He nodded.

"Is it bigger than Saylok?"

With his free hand he plucked a candle from its holder and, tipping it to the side, drew a shape with the melted wax on the stone floor in front of them. He drew another shape, a star, about the distance of a handspan away from the first.

"Saylok," Alba said, pointing to the star.

He nodded.

"Eastlandia," she guessed. "Is it really that big compared to Saylok?"

Again the nod.

"Where else?"

Little by little, he drew the shapes of the countries, the world beyond Saylok, and Alba studied his map in fascination.

"For all Dagmar's knowledge, he has not been to these places either, and the maps he created are not to scale," she murmured.

"I know only what I've been told and what I've g-gleaned from the people we brought back. Size is hard to measure w-when you are only a man and not a great, soaring bird."

"But you are a chieftain," she said, a smile teasing her lips.

He nodded, reverting to their game, but his eyes were troubled.

"Isn't it what you wished for?" she asked quietly. Most men would. He shook his head once, a single, firm denial.

"No? Why?" she pressed.

"I have only ever w-wished for one thing."

"Tell me."

"To be here. Near you. That is all." His face was so raw with honesty, with truth, that Alba could not look away. The people around her were careful with their secrets. The temple girls. Dagmar, Ghost, Ivo. Her father. Everyone lied or misled or simply stayed silent. Some did it out of love. Some out of fear. Some for power, some for protection. But not Bayr. He had never been like that.

She didn't ask him why he couldn't stay. Dagmar had explained, time and time again. And Alba understood what it was to want what you could not have, to not control your fate or your fortunes. She bowed her head, her hand tightening around his, and when she found her voice again, she moved on.

"Tell me about Dolphys," she whispered, and he relented, his voice low and careful, forming his words far better than he used to, and she listened, intent upon each one. One question spurred another, and Alba found herself speaking more than she cared to, though Bayr listened with the same rapt attention she had shown him. When the colored light disappeared, darkness chasing the day away, Ivo opened the sanctum door, his long staff clutched between his knotted hands. He didn't move as well as he once had, and didn't see as well either, though he peered at them with all-knowing eyes.

"Ten years is too great a span to travel in one afternoon," he rasped. "Come join us for supper, and we will continue the journey."

Together they rose, her hand tucked in the crook of Bayr's arm, and followed Ivo from the sanctum. Alba did not allow herself to count the hours that had passed.

24

Twenty-nine. He'd been back for twenty-nine hours. Alba had bidden him goodnight just as she had the night before, and her guards, who had waited outside the temple all day, escorted her from the temple to the palace, where she was greeted by her aging maid. She dismissed the old woman without making use of her services, telling her she would manage on her own, and climbed the many steps to her room in the tower. Now, hours later, she waited, hoping Bayr would keep his word. He had promised not to sleep.

Finally, not able to wait a minute more, she threw off the light bedcovers and pulled on her shoes. With the blade she kept beneath her pillow, she nicked her hand, just enough to make it bleed. With the tip of her finger she drew a tiny half-moon on her palm, its tip and tail touching two sides of a triangle, its back brushing the third. She smeared a final drop across its surface, smudging the image, like clouds hiding a night sky. Then, before her rune could dry, she left her room. She glided past the guard who stood at the base of the stairs leading to the tower. He didn't even blink in her direction. She scurried past a maid in the corridor and a porter dousing candles near the door to the gardens. Neither turned their heads. She slipped out into the darkness, breathing a faint sigh of relief. The blood often dried too quickly, and there had been times in the past when she'd been spotted before making it to her destination.

She found the door to the tunnel in the queen's garden that burrowed beneath the wall and out onto the hillside. She and Bayr had discovered the door long ago, when she wasn't quite so tall. She'd used it more times than she could count. She winced at the moldering smell of the tunnel, but didn't slow, though she had to stoop the slightest bit. She should have drawn a rune for light, but she'd been in too great a hurry.

In minutes the air became sweet, the darkness not so absolute, and Alba realized the hatch at the other end had been propped open. Bayr was waiting for her, stretched out beside the opening, his long legs crossed as though he had enjoyed the wait, his enormous arms folded over his heart. He was asleep. But he was there, just like he'd said he would be.

She perched beside him, not making a sound. She wouldn't wake him. Not yet. It was enough in that moment to sit beside him and celebrate his return. She tried to study the stars, to appreciate the escape from the heat of the day. It had been unseasonably warm, and though the harvest was ending, the days felt more like summer than autumn. But she'd seen the stars plenty of times, and Bayr was a whole new universe. She could not pull her gaze from his face, from the straight line of his nose, the swell of lips softened by sleep, the peaked line of his dark hair that he wore braided, like all warriors of Saylok. The constancy of her stare must have tickled his senses, because he opened his eyes minutes later.

"You owe me an hour," she whispered as his lids fluttered, awareness hardening his jaw and the hue of his ice-blue eyes. He gazed up at her as though he wasn't certain whether he was dreaming.

"No matter. I haven't begun counting yet," she murmured. Seventeen hours could last a long time if they never began.

His eyebrow quirked, a question without a sound. It made her laugh, the way he communicated, and her heart quickened in fondness even as it thundered in sudden desperation. He was going to leave again. She couldn't bear it. She felt it like a threatening storm. Her father had plans for her, plans that would separate them forever, and the seconds rushed toward a final parting.

He unfolded his hands from his chest and pressed a thumb to the groove between her brows. She leaned into the pressure, her eyes closing and her breath gusting through parted lips.

"You are sad."

"No. I've simply begun counting."

"What can I do?" he whispered.

"We are going to swim and fly," she said, pulling air and denial into her lungs. She rose to her feet with a swish of her skirts and extended her hand to Bayr. He scoffed at her attempt to pull him to his feet and bounded up with the ease of a cat.

"Will you w-walk or will you ride, Princess?" he asked, bowing, a smirk on his lips. For a moment she was seven again, perched on his shoulders as he loped across the fields and climbed the hills. She'd ridden more than she'd walked in those days.

"Those days have long since passed, Bayr," she said quietly. He straightened, his smirk fading.

"So they have, Alba. So they have."

They descended westward for two hours, talking softly, eyes on their surroundings, thoughts on each other, winding their way through meadows and wooded groves, until they reached the waterfalls tucked into the final slope of the temple mount. There, all the water from storm and stream converged, pooled, and then tumbled again. The highest fall split into two separate cascades, one emptying into the river below, one spilling over into an inlet, cold and deep and tucked back from the main body of the river. It was the place where Bayr had learned—and subsequently taught Alba—to swim. A grassy overhang, thirty feet above the inlet, marked the point where the trail zigzagged down to a pebbled beach below.

"It hasn't changed," Bayr marveled, peering over the ledge into the water, the tumbling falls misting the air and cooling their skin. Alba yanked at the ties of her gown, loosening them even as she stepped out of her shoes. While Bayr's back was to her, she pulled her outer sheath over her head, leaving only a thin shift that wouldn't weigh her down.

Laughing, she sprinted to the edge of the overhang, her arms and legs pumping, her hair streaming, and Bayr roared, demanding she stop. She didn't.

She sprang into the abyss and disappeared beyond his sight.

Moments later he followed, jumping into the space where she'd disappeared.

She came up laughing, he came up sputtering. Furious. And she ducked beneath the water again, disappearing before he could grab her by the hair and drag her from the water. Rocks rimmed the crystalline water like a crown and he swam toward them, his arms windmilling in angry strokes.

"Wh-why d-did you d-do th-that?" he bellowed, his tongue tripping over his outrage. He climbed onto the rocks, great sheets of water slewing from his shoulders, and shivered violently. She'd abandoned her gown and her shoes, but he was fully clothed, his sword across his back, boots on his feet, a dirk strapped to each leg.

"Why didn't you remove your boots? I've jumped before, and you know I can swim. You taught me!"

"S-sometimes you can't see what's beneath the surface. I c-can't protect y-you from d-dangers I can't see."

"And who protected me when you were gone? I can protect myself," she shot back. There was no accusation in her voice, but Bayr still flinched.

"You should have w-warned me," he muttered, turning toward her. "My h-heart is still up there with your gown."

She pulled herself up onto a smooth, flat rock that rose at the water's edge and flopped onto it the way she'd done as a child, turning her face up to the sky and wringing out her hair. But she wasn't a child, and the thin, wet shift she wore was translucent. The darkness provided a little cover, but she heard his gasp, and warmth pooled in her belly the same way the water from her shift pooled on the rocks. He yanked his boots from his feet and wrung the wet from his clothes. The cove was quiet, save the lapping of the water and the muted crashing of the falls. It was a steep climb back to the top, back to her gown. Bayr turned toward the trail, clearly not wanting her to traipse to the top wet, half-naked, and missing her shoes.

"I don't want to leave yet," she protested.

"I will go alone."

"I don't want *you* to leave yet."

"What if a hungry g-goat happens along and eats your g-gown?"

She snickered, and Bayr relaxed. He never could stay angry with her, though she knew she had often deserved a good dose of his wrath.

"I will come right back . . . on the path, not the cliffs," he added, his tone pointed. He scrambled up the steep trail and was back moments later, her gown and shoes in hand, hardly winded. Alba pulled the dress over her head and tightened the stays without meeting his eyes, suddenly awkward and woebegone, feeling like the child he still seemed to think she was.

When she sank down onto a dry rock, he sat down beside her, his eyes forward, his hands folded.

"I'm sorry I scared you," she muttered. "I thought . . . I thought you would think me brave. I thought you would . . . laugh."

"It was always my d-duty to protect you. It was my s-sole purpose in life. It is a hard habit to break."

"I do not know my purpose," she whispered.

He waited, the way he always had, knowing she would eventually fill the silence the way she always did. But she didn't.

"You were b-blessed on the altar of the temple, and the keepers p-painted a star in blood on your brow. You are Alba of Saylok. You are a princess," he said slowly, prompting her.

"And that is my whole purpose in life? My whole reason to exist?"

He sighed once more, as though he'd known he should just remain silent.

"What makes you happy?" he tried again. It was a game they'd played, once upon a time. When either of them was brokenhearted, they'd listed the things that made it better.

"Sleep, song, safety, the juice of an apple, the sound of the keepers chanting in morning prayer, Ghost. Dagmar. The daughters of the temple." She stopped, suddenly so bereft she could not continue.

"Yet . . . you are unhappy," he said. "Not just . . . now. But . . . every day." It wasn't a question. He was summarizing what he saw.

She nodded, swallowing back the tears in her throat, comforted by his simple understanding.

She said, "Though I struggle to find happiness in the small and simple things, I cannot escape the misery of the big things."

"W-what are the big things?"

"There's one very big thing sitting next to me." She wanted to make him laugh.

He didn't.

"I make you miserable?"

"Yes." She raised her brown eyes to his, exhaling on the truth, and saw her own pain echoed there. "Being with you . . . is like holding water in my hands," she murmured, and he furrowed his brow, still waiting.

"I want you to stay here . . . with me . . . and I know you can't. I know you won't. I'm dying for a drink, and it's like holding water in my hands," she repeated, enunciating each word. "I'll never get enough to quench my thirst."

He didn't argue or try to convince her that she felt otherwise. He just stared, his gaze soft on her face, and gave her his hands, palms up, as if offering to hold the water for her.

She studied them, so big and calloused, and tried not to cry. If she could drink water from his hands, she might not be so thirsty after all. The thought sent a quiver from her heart to her lower belly and reinforced her resolve.

"There is something else I want for my birthday," she blurted, hurtling from yet another cliff, hoping he would follow.

"Oh?"

"Yes. When Ivo predicted your return, I promised myself I would ask you for this . . . one . . . thing. But . . . I want time more than I want anything else. So if I have to choose between time and . . . the second gift . . . I still choose time."

"Tell me," he said, gentle.

"I want seventeen . . . kisses," she confessed, keeping her voice as steady as she could. Then she added, "From . . . you." Trust Bayr to find seventeen of the homeliest village boys to line up with their lips pursed, ready to deliver her birthday gift.

Bayr's chin fell to his chest, his long, dark braid falling over his massive shoulder. She counted his breaths, deep and slow—three of them—before he raised his head again.

"I am not a boy, little Alba," he murmured.

"And I am no longer little Alba, Bayr."

"You will a-always be little Alba," he protested, but Alba saw the lie in his eyes the way she always had. And she saw the truth too. He *knew* she wasn't little Alba. She'd felt his eyes clinging to her face and her body when he believed she wasn't aware. She'd heard the hitch in his breath when she brushed against him. It echoed the hitch in her own.

Bayr's eyes fell to her mouth, and his chin hit his chest once more.

"I d-don't know what to do," he whispered. "I w-would give you anything. Anything. But n-not that. It is not . . . you are not . . . mine." His hands tightened around hers in apology.

"I have always been yours. And you have always been mine. Haven't you?" she asked, trying to fight the humiliation creeping up her neck, ignoring the sting of rejection that made her long to run away. But if she ran, she would never get what she wanted. And she desperately wanted Bayr.

He sighed, the sound agonized. "Yes. Always."

"If you don't know what to do . . . I could teach you," she said, hesitant, hope thrumming in her veins.

He laughed, a humorless chuff, and withdrew his hands to run them over his face.

"And wh-who taught you?" he asked.

"Ghost taught me."

His head shot up in horror.

"I haven't had any actual experience, but I know what to do," she assured him. "Ghost was very specific . . . about many things. And I've thought about it a great deal. I'm sure I can guide you."

He groaned, a sound so full of disbelief and pain, she grasped his hands once more.

"You love me," she said. She didn't know many things, but she knew that.

"Yes," he admitted.

"And I love you. I have loved you all my life."

"Loving and k-kissing are two different things."

"Yes . . . but *we* are different now. We are grown," she insisted.

"I am grown. You are . . . you are . . ."

Alba leaned forward suddenly and pressed her puckered lips to his protesting mouth, silencing him.

Her lips burned, her blood was ice, and her hands shook, but she didn't close her eyes. She didn't look away as she withdrew. She waited, trying not to pant or plead, trying to act as grown as she claimed to be.

"That was one. I want sixteen more," she demanded softly.

"That is w-what Ghost t-taught you?" he whispered, and something in his tone made her think he was trying not to laugh, but his eyes were intent on hers, his mouth unsmiling.

"Not everything she taught me," she replied, defensive.

"No?"

"No."

"I see." His gaze lowered to her mouth. "Well, then. Perhaps you . . . should . . . show me . . . after all."

She curled her long legs beneath her and rose up onto her knees. Even sitting, he was much taller than she was, and she'd had to lurch to kiss him the first time. She didn't want to lunge at him like a snake. She inched closer on her knees until their faces were aligned. She could feel his breath on her mouth and smell the musk of his skin. He smelled faintly of incense, as though the roots of his childhood had flowered in his pores. Once the Temple Boy, always the Temple Boy. It was a scent she dreamed about, a scent she'd always associated with him, and she breathed deeply and closed her eyes, savoring his nearness. Then, closing her eyes, she puckered her lips once more and carefully placed them on his. It was lovely, feeling the smooth, soft skin of his mouth pressed against hers, and she left them there for several seconds before retreating once more. Her mouth tingled and her pulse pounded, but she thought she'd done a little better that time. She opened her eyes to find him staring at her, completely still.

"Lesson number one. Close your eyes while kissing," she said.

"And lesson number two?" he asked, very serious.

"Ghost says you don't have to hold still when you kiss. You can move your lips back and forth, softly, almost like you are nodding your head. I'll show you."

"Yes. P-please show me."

She leaned forward and took his face in her hands to steady herself. Then, with her eyes open so she could gauge how her lesson was being received, she brushed her lips over his—back and forth, back and forth—painting his unpursed mouth with her own. Realizing that he wasn't puckering like she did, she relaxed her mouth to instruct him, but his hands were suddenly in her hair, holding her in place. He copied her small strokes—back and forth, back and forth—but he kept his lips soft, smoothing out the tight rosebud Ghost had taught her to make. He nipped at her top lip, pulling it gently between his own, before moving to her lower lip and repeating the caress.

Her eyes fluttered closed, and she forgot what lesson number three was, until he pulled away ever so slightly to allow her breath.

"I must be a very good teacher," she murmured.

His breath fluttered across her lips as though he exhaled on a smile, but his hands tightened in her hair when she tried to pull back to see if he laughed at her.

"You are. Very good. But I owe you at least a dozen more," he murmured, not stumbling over a solitary word.

She wrapped her arms around his neck—she'd just remembered lesson number three—and slanted her mouth over his, feeling like a seasoned courtesan with so many kisses already under her belt. Somehow he knew to wrap his arms around her as well. Then he was kissing her with a confidence not present for their previous kisses, meeting her seeking lips with welcome abandon.

She felt the heat of his tongue slide against the entrance to her mouth and remembered lesson number four. She'd thought lesson number four would be something she wouldn't enjoy, yet she found herself opening to him like a flower to the sun.

He tasted her with a tentative tongue, as though walking in the dark, brushing the walls of her mouth with a careful touch, allowing her to lead him in his blind explorations. He discovered without invading, coaxed without controlling, and she answered with a whimper and a whisper, his name a prayer in her head.

He kissed her until her mouth was sore and her lips swollen, until his breath filled her lungs and his large hands, molding and remolding her back, were the only thing that kept her from melting like hot wax against his chest. Then his mouth trailed across her cheek and settled in the curve of her neck. For a moment he kissed her neck the way he'd kissed her lips, insistent yet reverent, and then he raised his head, saying her name like he needed her to beg him to cease. She never would.

"Alba," he whispered, fire in the word, and she tried to open her heavy lids—once, twice—before gazing at him in a love-drunk haze.

"More," she pled, catching his mouth with hers all over again. He capitulated for several seconds, his tongue dancing with hers in a desperate embrace, before he rose to his feet—back bowed so he could keep kissing her—and severed the connection with a frustrated groan. The sound was more animal than man, a rumble that resonated in his chest. He retreated several steps, turning away from her, his long braid trailing down his broad back. She watched as his inhalations slowed and became undetectable to her eyes. He turned and walked back to her, not meeting her gaze. Then he reached down and clasped her around the waist, setting her on her feet before turning away once more.

"We need to get back," he said, firm. No stuttering. No room for argument. But Alba still tried.

"I'm not sure that was a dozen more. I think it may have been four or five very long kisses . . . so we might have to have more lessons before you . . . go," she babbled, breathless.

"I do not need lessons, Alba."

She was silent for several long seconds.

"I know," she murmured. "You are a very good kisser. How silly of me to think you didn't know how. I have been waiting for you. I thought . . . maybe . . . you had been waiting for me."

He spun on her, his face filled with such frustration that she stumbled back. Bayr had never looked at her thus, not even when she had scared him to death, when she had covered his eyes and made him run blind, when he had to trail her around the market, holding baskets filled with fripperies and lace, hour after hour. Not when she'd demanded he swing her over his head again and again so she could see how it felt to fly.

He was instantly in front of her, panting through the lips she had just kissed. A man his size should not be able to move so fast. But no one moved as fast as Bayr. No one was as strong. Or brave. Or true. There was no one like him. And he was hers. In her heart, he had belonged to her, and she had known one day, when she was grown, she would be able to claim him. The way Dolphys had claimed him.

She reached up and touched his face.

"I have been waiting so long, Bayr. Don't you understand? I love you. I know you don't see me as I see you. You don't see us as I see us. I was a child that you cared for. I was your charge. Your responsibility. Your princess."

"My Alba," he groaned.

"Yes. But you were everything to me. Always. I've had my heart set on you all my life. Ask Dagmar. He tried to convince me otherwise. But I wouldn't listen. He said it could never happen, that I must leave Saylok and marry a king of another land. He thinks the men of Saylok are cursed—including my father—and that I must leave to help her. Like you have. I would gladly leave this place. But not without you."

His eyes shone, and his hands shook, and for a moment she thought he would kiss her again.

"Your father w-will never allow it," he whispered. "If he knew I had laid a hand on you, if he knew I had kissed you . . ." His eyes darkened, and his throat worked like he couldn't believe he'd done such a thing. "If he knew, he would cut off my braid and have my eyes b-burned from my head. Master Ivo saw this. He saw us. He warned me to wait . . . but I couldn't stay away. Not forever."

"You promised me you would come back."

"I shouldn't have."

"You are the strongest man in all of Saylok. If anyone can stand up to my father, it is you."

"I am one man. I cannot d-defeat the world by myself. Even for you."

"Then promise me this—"

"No more kisses," he interrupted.

She tried to smile but could not. Nor would she make such a vow. "My mother was sixteen when she married Banruud. Ghost was fourteen when she first . . . knew . . . a man. You know I am of age, Bayr. Of the few women Saylok has, all have long been married at my age."

"The king will want to w-wait until he makes the most advantageous match."

"My mother was the daughter of the king. She married a chieftain. You are suitable in every way."

"Not to Banruud," he retorted. He was so adamant in his arguments, and with every word her agony grew.

"But . . . would you want me?"

"My life is not about w-what I w-want, Alba. It never has been."

"But . . . if nothing stood in our way . . . would you want me?" she asked softly, her hands pressed to her chest to shore up her heart. "Would you run away with me?"

"If nothing stood in our path, we wouldn't need to run away."

"That is not what I asked," she wailed softly, hardly able to continue.

"Yes. Yes. Yes," he hissed. "Yes!" He curled his hands into the tight weave of his braid and glared down at her. And then she realized he wasn't angry with her. He wasn't even arguing with her. He was arguing with his helplessness, and he was impotent with fury at the position she'd put him in. He would have gone on pretending, loving her in the way that was allowed. And she'd shattered all pretense.

All at once, he seemed to wilt, as though she'd drawn a rune upon his skin and pulled his heart from his chest. He fell to his knees, his head bowed at her feet, and wrapped his big hands around her ankles, shackling himself to her.

"My b-body is yours. My heart is yours. My s-soul, my thoughts, my d-dreams, my life. Yours. I will do whatever you ask. Whatever you wish." He raised his eyes to hers, his gaze as tormented as his voice. "But know this, your father will not allow it. And when he d-discovers that I love you, we will both suffer. I can b-bear my own suffering, but I can't bear yours."

She sank down in front of him, and his hands slid from her ankles to her hips, pulling her into his lap as her lips found his all over again.

"You can't prevent me from suffering," she moaned into his mouth. "I ache with it. I am nothing but pain. But there is no Alba without Bayr," she whispered. "Not now. Not then. Not ever again."

And for a time, sheltered by the shadows and soothed by the thundering falls, she made him believe it.

25

The king did not return. Not the next day or the next. The grounds began filling with the tents and wagons of tradesmen preparing to sell their wares at the games, and the next night, the mount was flooded with clans and chaos as the Tournament of the King commenced without the king. The temple opened her doors to travelers making their yearly pilgrimages to worship within her walls, and the keepers heard the complaints and the confessions of the condemned. Three chieftains arrived—Aidan of Adyar, Lothgar of Leok, and Josef of Joran—and Bayr engaged each of them in private conversation. News of the Northmen on Berne's shores had traveled, yet each chieftain had received reassurances from the king that measures were being taken to reach an agreement that did not result in war. According to Dred, the same reassurances had not been delivered to Dolphys. Elbor arrived at dusk on the second day, and he surrounded himself with soldiers, doing his utmost to avoid the other chieftains. Benjie of Berne was notably absent.

Alba greeted the crowds with upraised arms and a welcoming smile. When she declared the tournament open to "all of Saylok's people, to her clans and her colors," no fear or discomfort tinged her voice or chased her words, and Bayr watched her with awe and pride. The people called her Princess Alba like they knew her and threw flowers at her feet like they loved her. At the commencement of each contest she wished the entrants "the wisdom of Odin, the strength of Thor, and the favor of Father Saylok," and they battled as though they had all three.

It was not until the fourth day of the tournament and well into the afternoon that a lone horn sounded from the watchtower and a cry went up.

"The king has returned! Ready the mount for His Majesty, King Banruud of Saylok."

From the King's Village to the top of Temple Hill, one trumpeter signaled another, each wailing a note that rose at the end like a question, the sound growing louder and louder as it climbed the long road to the mount. Along the ramparts, another chorus of horns sounded, verifying the message had been received.

The grounds were thick with clansmen and villagers, but every contest was halted as people ran to the gates and spilled down the hill. No clan wanted to be accused of not honoring the return of His Majesty, and the road was flooded with clansmen mere minutes after the horns were sounded.

Aidan, Lothgar, Josef, Elbor, and Bayr stood on the palace steps, their most-trusted warriors behind them. The keepers, as was tradition upon a monarch's return, stood on the temple steps, filling the space with rows of purple, the five daughters among them, the wreaths of their hair the only thing that set them apart.

The king's guard began to clear the enormous courtyard between the temple and the palace, forcing the curious and the clustered to move out onto the grass and the grounds to give the king and his retinue wide berth. To return during the tournament created a chaos the king's men clearly weren't accustomed to, and more than one villager was shoved to the ground in an attempt to clear the square. From outside the walls of the mount, a rumble began to swell and spill through the gates, a wave of shock and speculation that tumbled from one mouth to the next.

The horns bellowed again, indicating the king was nearing the gate, and Alba appeared at the top of the palace steps in full regalia. She had opened the tournament wearing only a long white dress and a simple gold circlet on her brow. Clearly Banruud expected a more formal greeting. Her crown was a smaller replica of her father's, with six spires, each with a jewel that matched the color of the clan embedded at the base and the tip. Emeralds for Adyar, rubies for Berne, sapphires for Dolphys, orange tourmalines for Ebba, brown topaz for Joran, and golden citrines for Leok. The glossy black of her royal mantle, trimmed in white rabbit's fur, should have been too much for her pale hair, but it accentuated it, highlighting the contrast of dark eyes and light locks. The chieftains and their warriors moved to the sides, creating an aisle for her to descend between them, but she stopped in their midst, Bayr on her left and her uncle, Aidan of Adyar, on her right.

Alba didn't look at Bayr, but tension radiated from her straight back and her slim frame. Her face was perfectly composed, her hands at her sides; no fidgeting, no nervous chatter, no shifting or craning of her neck. Her crown had to be heavy, but she stood with her eyes forward, waiting for the king and his entourage to enter through the gates and give her leave to greet them.

They had slept very little since Bayr had arrived; at night they stole beyond the walls where the darkness gave them cover, where they could swim and fly and talk and touch without watchful eyes or wagging tongues. They hadn't admitted they were hiding their relationship, but they both knew they were.

He had promised her he would make his case to the king when he returned, that he would bow before him and pledge all his strength to Saylok for her hand. He turned his head the slightest degree so he could train his eyes downward on her shining crown and the hair that spilled over her black robe. He had touched that hair. He had wrapped his hands in it as he kissed her mouth.

When he kissed her, she was not so composed, nor was she still or silent. He had kissed her so often that her lips were red and sore, and the soft skin of her neck burned from his rough cheeks. He was a man undone by love, unstrung by devotion, and though he would not give her his seed, he did not deny her in any other way. He had filled his hands with the length of her hair and buried his face in the sweetness of her body. He'd kissed the soft skin of her breasts and held her hips in his hands as she pled for relief beneath his mouth. When she touched him in return, her eyes wide, her fingers roving, he had moaned her name and begged her to save him. And she had, sending him to his knees over and over again, bled of all strength but completely reborn.

In the days since he'd arrived on the mount, he'd thought only of her.

Not his clan, not his duty, not his purpose. Just her.

He hadn't worried about the Northmen or the longboats in the harbor of Garbo. He hadn't dwelled on the raid on Sheba or the battle in Eastlandia. When Dred and a handful of his warriors had arrived for the tournament, armed and watchful, Bayr had seen to his responsibilities with the same quiet efficiency they were accustomed to, but his heart and his head were far away. For the first time in his life, he was consumed by his own desires, and everything else became a distant landscape. He'd spent the daylight with the keepers or his men, stealing sleep in patches, a bit at dawn, a bit at dusk, but he spent the nights with Alba.

Now, standing at her side, close enough to reach out and touch the smooth line of her jaw and the length of her throat, he could only mourn that the nights were over. He would do anything to have her. He would give away all his power to keep her. But deep in his chest, where honesty lived and hope languished, he knew it wouldn't be enough.

Through the fog of his infatuation, he noticed that the villagers that had been cleared from the central courtyard had begun to turn and point, to clutch each other and cower. All at once, he was doused in the painful present and shaken from his love-drunk haze. His fear for Alba—for all Saylok—stretched and shuddered, coming fully awake inside his chest.

"He's brought the Northmen to the temple mount," Aidan growled.

Lothgar cursed, a stream of foul words that grew into a roar that was muffled by the distress of the crowd.

"It is King Gudrun," Alba said, her voice low and dull, as though she too had been cruelly awakened from a beautiful dream.

King Gudrun wore his eyes rimmed in black like the keepers, but his hair hung in dirty coils down his back. The top was gathered into a knot pierced by animal bones to keep it from falling in his eyes. His men wore variations of the same thing. All had leather hose and tunics studded with metal, swords strapped across their bodies, and blades bound to their boots with long leather straps. The horses they rode were heavy bodied—thick backs and legs, giant hooves and heads. They had to be to carry such big men, and the Northmen were big. Bozl had not exaggerated when he said they were as big as Bayr.

"My people. My daughter. My chieftains. My keepers," Banruud boomed, his arms raised to call the crowd to attention. "In the spirit of peace and negotiation, I have brought King Gudrun of the Northlands to see our temple and to take part in our tournament. We welcome him and his men among us the way I was welcomed among his people. We are in need of strong alliances. May this be the first of many such visits."

The people murmured nervously; no one jeered, but there was no jubilance in their greeting, no cheers or waving of their colors.

Alba began to descend the final palace steps, her sense of duty demanding she bid the visitors welcome, but Bayr moved forward with her, unwilling to let her approach a foreign—and reputedly vicious—king by herself. Aidan was of the same mind, for he too remained at her side. Josef and Lothgar trailed them as they walked out into the courtyard to present the Princess of Saylok to the King of the Northlands. Elbor, not wanting to be left behind, hurried to join them, though he cowered behind Lothgar. Benjie of Berne was mounted just behind the king, a few of his men around him. Bayr should have known he would be wherever Banruud was.

As Alba neared, King Banruud dismounted with the ease of a much smaller, much younger man. His hair was shot with silver, but he was otherwise unchanged. His eyes, when they met Bayr's, were as flat and unforgiving as they'd always been.

"Father, I thank Odin for your safe return," Alba greeted Banruud, stepping away from the chieftains and pressing the invisible star on her forehead to the back of his outstretched hand. Turning to the North King she curtsied, low and lovely, and rose up gracefully. "King Gudrun, we welcome you."

There was an appreciative murmur among Gudrun's men, and the North King slid unceremoniously from his horse and grasped Alba's fingers as though to press a kiss on her knuckles. At the last moment, he turned her hand so her palm was facing up. With exaggerated pleasure, he licked upward from the tips of her fingers to the pulse at her wrist, and his men roared in rowdy approval.

Bayr growled, a deep guttural rumbling that caused Gudrun to raise his eyes and withdraw his tongue.

"Is that not how it's done in Saylok?" the North King asked Bayr, sardonic. "Or is she yours, Chieftain?"

"May I present my daughter, Princess Alba of Saylok," the king interrupted, but his eyes censured Bayr, his expression hard, his mouth tight. "The Temple Boy has fallen back into his old ways. He returns to the mount after a decade and immediately considers himself the princess's protector."

"Temple Boy?" Gudrun repeated, his eyebrows raised in query.

"I am Bayr. Chieftain of Dolphys," Bayr said, carefully. Slowly. He did not acknowledge Banruud but kept his gaze on Gudrun.

"Ah. I have heard of you, Dolphys. You are known for your strength. I should like to test it," Gudrun hissed.

"These are my chieftains—Dolphys, Adyar, Joran, Leok, and Ebba. You've met Berne," the king said, tossing his hand toward the men who trailed his daughter. Bayr was not the only one who bristled at the introduction. The clan chieftains were subordinate to the king, but the implication that they were "his" did not sit well.

Banruud offered his arm to Alba, who took it without hesitation, though her fingers barely touched his sleeve and her posture did not relax. Banruud nodded toward the keepers standing in silent observance on the temple steps. Ivo had moved out in front of them, a stooped crow bent around his staff.

"Gudrun, may I present the daughters of the clans," Banruud boomed, striding toward the robed assembly. Gudrun followed eagerly. Gudrun's men dismounted, eyes suspicious, hands on their weapons, and trailed after their king.

"I see only old men," Gudrun mocked. The daughters had melded back behind the rows of keepers, who stood with their hands folded and their heads down, creating a wall of faceless purple around them.

"We want to see the daughters, Master Ivo," Banruud ordered, coming to a halt before the Highest Keeper.

"They are not yours to command or display, Majesty," Ivo replied, his tone mild, like he spoke to an insistent child.

Banruud moved so close to the Highest Keeper he appeared to be speaking to a lover, whispering assurances in his ear, but the Highest Keeper raised his eyes to Gudrun, who stood over the king's shoulder, and spoke to him directly, ignoring King Banruud.

"What is your purpose here, Northman?" Ivo queried, his tone so cold the crowd shivered.

"I want to see your temple, Priest."

"I am not a priest. I do not save souls or speak for the gods. I am a Keeper of Saylok."

"And what treasures do you keep, old one?" Gudrun grinned, and his men laughed around him.

"Let us see the daughters," Elbor shouted, showing his support for the wishes of the king. "They belong to the people. Not the keepers."

A few people cried out in agreement. Others protested, frightened by King Banruud's company, unnerved by the Northmen inside the walls of their precious mount.

Benjie, still seated on his horse with a handful of Gudrun's men and Banruud's guard, raised his voice in agreement.

"You worship the gods, but you obey the king, Highest Keeper," he said.

Lothgar grunted his agreement and Josef stepped forward, demanding a viewing as well.

"Daughters of the clans, come forward," Banruud bellowed, his hand on his sword. The keepers shifted, a pathway opening among them, and the five daughters, their eyes fixed above Banruud's head, their robes hiding them from neck to toe, stepped down from the steps.

The crowd strained to get a better view, and Gudrun smirked as they stopped in a straight line before him, not shrinking, but not acknowledging him in any way.

The North King touched the fiery coils of Elayne's hair. She swallowed, her pale throat working to stifle her fear, but she did not pull away.

"Elayne of Ebba," Banruud said.

"Elayne of Ebba," Gudrun repeated, his eyes shrewd. He moved on.

"Liis of Leok," Banruud intoned. Gudrun studied Liis, his brows raising at her golden beauty and piercing blue eyes. He moved his face within an inch of hers, willing her to meet his gaze, but she was stoic, even as he blew a stream of warm air against her pink lips. He laughed as though her stillness impressed him and moved onto Juliah as the king said her name.

Juliah was not ice, she was fire, and when he paused in front of her, she glowered at him disdainfully, her top lip lifted in the smallest of sneers.

"Juliah does not like me," he murmured. "Though I might enjoy changing her mind."

"Dalys of Dolphys," King Banruud intoned.

Dalys had begun to shrink, her slim shoulders bunching around her ears, but Gudrun ran the tip of his finger along the silky underside of her jaw and demanded she lift her face.

When she did, his lips curled.

"Your chieftain is so big." He shot a look toward Bayr. "But you are a runt. I want a woman," he said, dismissing her without another word. The crowd rumbled and the Highest Keeper hissed, but Gudrun wasn't finished. He moved to Bashti, who met his gaze with all the disdain he'd just shown Dalys. She was not a big woman either, but she demanded attention. Gudrun gave it to her.

He pressed his thumb to the swell of her full lips as though he intended to check her teeth. When she snarled and snapped at him, he laughed and lifted his eyes to Banruud, releasing her before he lost a finger.

"You have six clans, Banruud . . . but only five daughters," he mused.

"The princess is of Adyar." Aidan spoke up. "She represents our clan among the daughters of the temple." Aidan had remained by Bayr's side though his eyes had clung to Elayne of Ebba throughout the North King's inspection. His voice was controlled but his hand gripped the hilt of his sword, and Bayr wondered if he was not the only chieftain who nursed secret affections.

Gudrun turned and considered Alba once more. Like the daughters, she was unflinching beneath his scrutiny. Bayr was not. His stomach was filled with hot coals, the heat wafting from his mouth and his eyes, steaming from his ears and causing his palms to tremble and his legs to shake.

It would take so little to make him draw his sword and ease his agony. He would slay the North King first. Banruud would follow.

Bayr felt Ivo's gaze, cold and creeping, like icy fingers across his blazing skin and knew the Highest Keeper divined his fury. Ivo simply shook his head.

"I think you lie, Chieftain. Who is that?" Gudrun pointed, his eyes sharp. "Do you seek to hide the white daughter from me?"

Ghost stood among the keepers, Dagmar beside her, but the hood of her robe had fallen back a few inches, and her thick, white braid was a stark contrast against the vivid hue of her robe.

If Bayr had not been so aware of Alba, he would have missed the moment Banruud recoiled, drawing Alba back with a vicious jerk. His eyes were wide with horror.

"I want to see her, Keeper," Gudrun insisted, curling his fingers at Ghost, beckoning her forward. Ghost had already ducked her head, shrinking back into her robe, an ivory slice of cheek the only visible part of her face. Dagmar was rigid beside her.

"She is not a daughter of the temple, King Gudrun," Ivo replied, but his eyes were glued to Banruud.

"No?" Gudrun sneered. He began mounting the stairs, shoving keepers aside. The crowd cried out, frightened by his aggression. Gudrun stopped in front of Ghost and pulled her hood from the wreath of her silvery-white hair. Her chin snapped up, her eyes gleamed, and Gudrun cursed and stumbled back, almost falling when his foot glanced off a step. The crowd gasped, the collective inhale like a crack of angry thunder.

"She is not a daughter, Majesty," Ivo repeated, though it was not clear to which king he referred. "She is a keeper." He paused, his gaze still clinging to King Banruud. "We call her . . . Ghost."

"I want to see the temple," Gudrun demanded, his voice ringing imperiously, but he had retreated several more steps. Ghost did not re-cover her hair or drop her gaze, but Dagmar had taken her hand in his, and without a word, the robed keepers moved back around her protectively.

"And you shall see it, King Gudrun," Banruud promised, finding his voice, though it rattled oddly. "It is open to all during the tournament. But we've traveled far and you are hungry. We will dine first and enjoy the games. The temple can wait."

Clutching Alba's arm, Banruud turned away, dismissing the Highest Keeper and drawing Gudrun and his men forward with a flick of his hand. Gudrun followed him reluctantly, turning back more than once to study the temple, her daughters, and her rows of huddled keepers.

Bayr and the other chieftains fell into step behind him, grim-faced and silent. Even Elbor seemed shaken. The king had some explaining to do, and Bayr, signaling to Dred and Dakin to accompany him, was not willing to let Alba out of his sight.

26

Ghost didn't feel herself fall. She must have locked her legs or forgotten to breathe, but one moment she was staring into the pale green eyes of an unkempt king, and the next she was in Dagmar's arms being carried into the shadowed recesses of the temple, the daughters hovering around her, Ivo's staff clicking against the stones from somewhere behind them.

King Banruud had seen her. He'd seen her and he knew. The memory flooded back, the snippet of time she'd lost, the details etched in black and underscored by the sharp gasp from the horrified crowd.

She'd grown complacent. She should have kept her head down. She'd been facing the setting sun, the pinks and golds of Saylok's skies warming the temple stones and her pale cheeks. She'd forgotten herself in her fear for the clan daughters—in her fear for her *own* daughter— and she'd stood among the keepers instead of staying safely inside the temple walls.

He'd seen her, and he knew.

"Are you unwell, Ghost?" Elayne asked as a gentle hand passed over Ghost's brow. Her kohl-rimmed eyes met Ghost's, and Ghost shook her head in shame.

"I'm a fool, Elayne. I was afraid, and I forgot to draw sufficient breath. I'm fine. See to the others. You were all so brave . . . and I am so proud."

"Go, Elayne," Dagmar urged kindly. "I'll look after Ghost."

"Our life together is marked by moments when I find myself in your arms, and I never get to enjoy it," she whispered at Dagmar as he eased her down onto a cold bench in the sanctum. Ivo had instructed she be brought there.

He grinned back, his eyes wrinkling at the corners, his concern easing infinitesimally, but his mirth died without having fully lived.

"What are we going to do?" she whispered, and he shook his head, helpless. He rose from her side and stepped away, turning as Ivo entered the sanctum, his black robes melding with the shadows that jumped from stone to stone.

He did not sit upon the dais but stopped in front of Ghost, his hands wrapped on the knob of his staff, his chin resting on his hands. She tried to rise, but her head swam and she closed her eyes, gathering her courage and finding her balance.

"Why does Banruud fear you, Ghost?" he whispered, his voice curling under her closed lids and skittering beneath the folds of her robe to settle on her cold skin.

"He does not fear me," she choked, but the truth of her past clawed at her throat and a scream was building on her tongue.

"He will give the princess to the North King to stop their advance into Saylok, and young Bayr can do nothing to stop it," Ivo said, his voice so soft it should have been lost in the temple dome, but it hovered instead, inflicting guilt and pain.

"I will go with her," Ghost panted. The scream grew another tail that beat against the back of her teeth.

"You are a keeper—you will not," Dagmar shot back, incredulous. "You've been entrusted with the knowledge of the runes. And that knowledge stays here, in the temple."

"I gave my word to the princess," she ground out, her jaw locked.

"You gave your word to me," Ivo hissed. "To Dagmar. To Saylok."

"I care nothing for Saylok," she bellowed. "I care nothing for the bloody runes. What good are the runes if they can't protect us? If they cannot right these wrongs?"

Ivo swayed as though he too had lost the strength to stand, and he turned away from her and walked up the long aisle to the dais, his head bowed, his shoulders stooped, and Ghost rose and followed him, Dagmar beside her, unable to resist the pull of his displeasure.

"He is going to her," Ivo accused, sinking down into his chair. "Even now. And you say nothing." Ivo raised his black gaze to Dagmar. "Have you not seen the way they look at each other?"

Dagmar halted as though he'd been struck, and the scream in Ghost's mouth slipped out as a moan.

"These secrets have been kept too long, and this one will destroy them, Dagmar. And still . . . you . . . say . . . nothing."

Tears had begun to course their way down Ghost's cheeks, the pressure building beyond her ability to contain it.

Dagmar replied, "They do not understand that the connection they feel is a connection of the blood, of the heart, but it can never be a connection of the body."

"It is . . . not . . . a connection of the blood," Ghost wept, the words so faint she wasn't sure she'd even said them. But she had. She'd said the words aloud. Dagmar turned shattered eyes to hers, and Ivo beckoned her forward, curling his fingers toward his palm.

"Tell me!" Ivo hissed.

"Alba is not Banruud's daughter. She was not Alannah's daughter. She is not a daughter of Saylok at all. She is the daughter of a slave." Her words had wings, and she felt the fluttering in her chest as she released them, letting them go free. Her silent scream rose up into the dome and dissipated without ever having been uttered, and Ghost began to shake.

"Banruud took her from her mother only days after she was born. And you made him king," she mourned. It was not an accusation, but an explanation. "You made him king. You made her a princess. And I could not take that away from her."

"But . . . in my vision . . . I saw . . . her mother's . . . joy," Ivo stammered. "Alannah gave birth to a child. I saw it."

"And I saw . . . her mother's pain," Dagmar whispered, understanding dawning. "You are the slave girl, Ghost. *You* are Alba's mother."

"I am Alba's mother," she breathed. "I am Alba's mother." She wanted to shout so the whole temple mount would quake, but the truth was too precious, too sacred for sound, and when she said the words again—"I am Alba's mother"—they were hardly more than a whisper.

"Tell me everything," Ivo demanded, harsh and exacting, and Ghost submitted, spilling the story with the relief of the long damned.

"My masters . . . a farmer and his wife . . . brought the babe to the Chieftain of Berne. They told me it was custom—law—and that they would return with the child and a piece of gold. I waited for hours. I worried. I needed to feed her. I went to the chieftain's keep and watched them come out. They didn't have my daughter. They said . . . they said the chieftain wanted to bring her to the Keepers of Saylok to determine whether she was a changeling . . . a monster . . . or a blessing."

Dagmar blanched and cursed beneath his breath, but Ghost continued, needing to confide, desperate to release what she'd kept secret for so long.

"I watched her—I am called Ghost for my skin and my hair. But I have become one. I have learned how to blend in, to disappear, to be invisible. I waited and I watched. I planned. And then one day, I got my opportunity. But I couldn't do it. As much as I hated the king for what he'd done, what he'd taken from me. I could not hate the queen, a woman who so obviously loved and cared for my daughter. She held her so gently. She was so patient . . . and kind. And she was able to give her a life . . . that I could never give her." Ghost raised her eyes to Dagmar and then to the Highest Keeper, pleading for them to understand. "My daughter was a princess. And I was a ghost. I could not take her from the people who loved her so perfectly. There would have been nowhere I could go, no place to take her where I wouldn't have been hunted down. In this world, in this temple . . . she had a protector."

"Bayr," Dagmar whispered.

"Yes. And all of you."

"That is why you are here. That is why Banruud dreamed of pale wraiths who came to take his child. Today the king . . . has seen his ghost," Ivo said, sinking back into his chair, his staff clattering to the floor.

"He thought I was dead. He sent men to kill me then. He will send them to kill me again."

"What have you done?" Ivo moaned, and Ghost's grief swelled into fury at his condemnation.

"I have watched my daughter grow. I have seen her raised as a Princess of Saylok. She is loved. She is protected. She is safe." The final words rang false, and Ghost closed her eyes on her fear.

"She isn't safe, Ghost. You aren't safe! Banruud saw you, and Alba is about to become Queen of the Northlands," Dagmar moaned.

"Better Queen of the Northlands than the daughter of a ghost," she shot back, wounded, and Dagmar touched her hand as though he'd forgotten Ivo observed. But Ivo was already speaking, his voice a weary wail.

"We made Banruud king. We made him king. And the curse upon the clans continues. We have failed the people. Bayr was our salvation. And I knew it. I did not listen to the gods. Now it is too late."

"You m-made Banruud king," Ghost stammered. "You gave him his power. Can you not . . . take it away?"

"How?" Ivo asked, raising his clawed hands to the heavens. "We are a temple of aging keepers and hunted women. We have no power to remove Banruud. Should we seek to remove him by the sword? We have lost the faith of the people and the support of the chieftains. You heard the crowd today. The keepers have failed them. The Northmen are at our door, the king conspires to sell our daughters, and the temple—even Saylok—hangs in the balance."

"Surely . . . surely the runes . . ." Ghost pled, desperate against Ivo's despondence. Dagmar stood silent and grim beside her.

"The runes are only as powerful—and as righteous—as the blood of the men and women who wield them. And we have tried every rune, beseeched every god, and bled into the soil of every clan," Ivo said. "The keepers have failed. I have failed. And Saylok will fall."

The feast was raucous and rowdy, the North King taunting the chieftains and refilling his goblet with abandon. Banruud made no effort to subdue him, though he dismissed Alba before the first course was finished. Bayr watched her go, his teeth clenched in helpless fury. He was not alone in his frustration, for when the meal was done and Gudrun lay stretched out in front of the hearth on the black bearskin of the king's clan, Lothgar rose, Aidan beside him, and demanded an audience with their king.

Banruud, his blade drawn to pick at his teeth, sat back as though he considered refusing the big Chieftain of Leok. When Bayr joined Aidan and Lothgar, and Chief Josef followed, the king sighed and sheathed his knife.

"So be it."

"Benjie and Elbor should be p-present as well," Bayr demanded.

"By all means," Banruud mocked. "It will be your first council, Temple Boy. We welcome you."

Banruud snapped his fingers and instructed half his guard—a guard mostly made up of the clanless, well paid and wanting in every area except savagery—to accompany him. He bade the other half remain behind with the sleeping North King and his unruly cadre.

The chieftains, rattled by the king's sentry, signaled for their own men to follow, and every man eyed the others with open distrust, clan colors and weapons on full display. Aidan pounced as soon as the council chamber door was closed and the chieftains were seated.

"You bring the Northmen to the mount, you parade the daughters of the temple in front of their bloody king, and you have not consulted about it with any of us."

Banruud studied the hostile room with slow nonchalance before answering the Chieftain of Adyar.

"I am the king. I do not take instruction from Adyar, or Leok, or Dolphys, or Joran. I will hear your complaints. But I will do as I wish, just as other kings have done before me. Just as other kings will do when I am gone."

"Do you take instruction from Berne?" Bayr interjected.

The king lifted one dark eyebrow, and Benjie huffed, but the other chieftains waited for Bayr to continue.

"We have s-suffered attacks from Berne. Benjie d-denies it. But our villages have been attacked. We repel attacks on our shores only to be attacked on our f-flanks by his clan." Bayr had rehearsed the lines so he would not stumble overmuch, but he had to pause several times and speak more slowly than the king had patience for.

"Benjie cannot be blamed for rogue bands of marauders." Banruud sighed.

"He can."

The king sneered at Bayr's response.

"Benjie encourages it. He is . . . em-emboldened . . . by his . . . relationship to you, S-sire, and has no r-respect for other c-clans or other chieftains."

"Do you stutter because you are frightened, Temple Boy?"

Dakin and Dred hissed, hands gripping their blades, drawing close to Bayr's chair. The king's guard drew their swords, a rippling of steel that stiffened the backs of every man at the king's table.

"He is the Dolphys. Not the Temple Boy, Banruud," Dred growled.

"And I am the king, Dred. And you will address me as such, or you will lose your tongue."

Bayr turned slightly and lifted a hand, settling it on his grandfather's arm, and Dred glowered at the king and did not retreat. Dakin remained at Dred's side, his eyes level and his body tight, and Bayr tried again.

"I care n-not what you call me, Majesty. But you will not be k-king of Saylok if the c-clans destroy each other."

"You threaten me?"

"If the clans fall, the k-kingdom falls."

"And who will be king when I am not, hmm? You? The next king will be from Dolphys, and you believe the keepers will choose you. Is that why you've finally taken your place at the council table, Temple Boy? You wish to kill me and let the keepers make you king?"

The room became tomb-like with the accusation, and Bayr did not seek to break the silence. To protest was to give credence to the king's claim.

"You are naught but a hulking ox. An ox has great strength, but we do not make an ox our king," Benjie mocked.

Bayr did not react, but he could feel his grandfather's rage behind him.

"I have no w-wish to be king," Bayr stated firmly.

"A king must command his people, and you can barely speak. The tribes of our enemies would breach the temple mount before you could call out the order for attack," Elbor snickered.

"Better a hulking ox than a blathering idiot," Josef of Joran murmured, shooting a withering look at Chief Elbor. Elbor's chin began to tremble in affront.

"Better a good man than a glib man," Aidan of Adyar purred.

"Better a tangled tongue than a forked one," Dred growled.

Every man in the room had his hand on his sword, and for a moment no one breathed, wondering who would be the first to lunge. The king stood slowly, his eyes filled with challenge.

"What do you want me to do?" Banruud turned his palms out slowly, as if to show how empty they were, how void of blame. "I am a king, not a keeper. I am but a man. I am not a master of runes. We support the temple on the mount, the people worship the keepers, and yet they cannot answer our prayers. My daughter is the last girl child to be born to a son of Saylok. In twenty-four years, she is the only one." Banruud paused, letting the reminder sink in around him.

"Yet you come to *me* as though I can heal *your* seed," he hissed. "Why do you not ask the keepers what they have done to end the scourge? Do they not guard the holy runes? Do they not commune with the fates? Do they not have Odin's ear?"

Banruud waited again, and when no one disagreed, he continued.

"Five daughters have grown to womanhood in the temple walls, yet they have not been returned to you, to their clans," Banruud cried, fervor ringing in his voice. "Their wombs are empty. What hope have they given you, Chieftains of Saylok? What hope have they given your people? Our sons turn on each other. And you come to me with your hands extended, asking me to cure this ill. Why do you not ask the keepers?"

Elbor began to nod, the color in his ruddy jowls becoming deeper as he pounded his fists on the table. The men at his back, all draped in Ebba orange, began to grunt in raucous agreement, the sound like a herd of starving pigs.

The chuff and growl of the warriors of Berne, the Clan of the Bear, became a competing swell, and Bayr resisted the urge to cover his ears. Lothgar of Leok, his mane of gold hair faded to white in the ten years since Bayr had seen him last, threw back his head and roared just to compete, the sound reverberating like that of the lion he claimed to descend from.

"There is no order," Bayr said, his voice firm, each word succinct, and the cacophony ceased.

"It is not the keepers who rape and pillage. It is not the keepers who send their warriors to plunder the lands of their neighbors," Dred hissed.

"We take what we must to survive," Benjie shouted.

"You are lazy, Benjie. Your land is overrun with young men who follow your lead. Our women are few, but it is not the women who plow the fields or trap or fish or fight the Northmen. It has never been the women. So what is your excuse?" Dred was accustomed to speaking his mind in council, but he was not the chieftain, and Benjie seemed intent on reminding him of it. When Benjie lunged at him, a dagger clutched in his hand, Bayr shot to his feet, stepping in front of his grandfather. Before anyone could assist or resist, he'd grabbed Benjie by the throat and the crotch and bodily threw him across the round table the way he'd once thrown Ghost's attackers down the hill. Benjie cleared Lothgar's head by several feet and landed at the feet of his sons in a jumble of limbs, his blade skittering across the floor.

Shock rippled from the table to the warriors who lined the walls. Bayr wasn't certain if it was awe at the feat or fear at what it would incite.

Lothgar roared again, but this time in laughter, and his sons helped the Chieftain of Berne to his feet. Benjie looked as though he'd suffered a blow to his head, and he swayed and clutched at his shoulder, his attack forgotten.

"The Chieftain of Dolphys is not wrong," Aidan contended as Lothgar's merriment subsided. "We too have been beset by raiders from Berne. The fish have not stopped filling our nets. There is bounty in the land, and our men continue to be fierce in battle. But there are too many of them without families or female companionship. And some grow aimless . . . and vicious." His eyes shot to the king's guard.

Josef of Joran, his farmer's face as weathered as the palms of Dagmar's hands, raised weary eyes to the king. "We are under constant threat from Ebba. Some of the Ebbans who seek refuge have nothing but the clothes on their backs. But they are willing to work. Others who come want only to take what does not belong to them. We have had to put warriors on the border, and now all who seek entry are turned away. We simply cannot absorb all of Ebba. Elbor sends his poor, and he sits like a pig on the spit, an apple in his fat snout."

Elbor rose, his lower jaw jutted out, his small eyes mean. "We have been suffering attacks from the Hinterlands for more than a decade," he shot back.

"As have we," Josef replied wearily. "It has always been thus among the clans on the southwestern shores. We battle the Hinterlands, Dolphys battles the Eastlanders, Berne and Adyar battle the Northmen, Leok battles the storms. But we have never come against each other, clan on clan."

"You t-tax your people into the ground, Elbor, while you do l-little to protect them," Bayr argued.

"I collect coin for the keepers. And what do they do for us?" Elbor bellowed, echoing the accusations of the king.

It was a lie. Bayr was well acquainted with the minimalism inside the temple walls. The keepers lived on very little, herding their own sheep, milking their own goats, and tending their own gardens. Whatever coin came from the clans by way of the king was a pittance. Alms were collected during the tournament, and every farthing went to the preservation of the temple itself. There were no wealthy keepers.

"You collect coin for yourself and for the king. As do we all." The tithes the king demanded were a strain every season. Bayr collected them himself. What he kept for Dolphys, for the maintenance of a fighting force and the governance of the people, was far less than the king required for his own coffers.

"Careful, Temple Boy," the king whispered, the words like a snake slithering between their chairs.

"This is all true," Lothgar interrupted, oblivious to the tension that coiled around him. "Yet . . . I have wondered why the keepers can do nothing to end the scourge among our women."

"As have I," Josef admitted.

"Aye," Elbor agreed, eager to turn the subject away from his own failures.

"Something must be done," Benjie agreed, and his acquiescence had the king sitting back in his chair, his fingers steepled and his eyes narrowed as though deeply pondering the question. Bayr had seen the look before. It was the same expression Banruud wore when he'd studied the body of poor Agnes, lying at his feet.

"Something has been done," the king said, eyeing his chieftains as though he held redemption in his hands. "I have reached an agreement with the North King. The princess will be a queen."

Bayr's head rose slowly, but he didn't question. He'd learned the art of waiting for men to talk. And talk they always did, even King Banruud.

"She will leave with King Gudrun for the Northlands in two days. In return, the North King has agreed to pull his warriors from Berne. An announcement will be made after the melee tomorrow. Your precious daughters of the temple will be left to age beside your useless keepers," the king said mockingly.

Silence wrapped the room in guilty relief, and the chieftains began to nod like it was the only feasible course of action. Benjie stood as though it were settled, and Elbor lumbered to his feet as well, clearly eager to escape further condemnation.

"She should not be sold," Bayr said, focusing on saying the words precisely, breathing between each one, speaking slowly even though his heart raced.

"She is not being sold. She is going to be a queen, and she will help her country in the process," Benjie argued.

"She should be queen of Saylok. She is the only one . . . of her kind," Bayr insisted.

Banruud crossed his legs and steepled his hands, giving the appearance of deep thought, but Bayr saw the smirk that played around his lips, half hidden by his prayerful pose.

"And how would she be queen of Saylok? Did you think . . . you might have her? Did you suppose you could marry the princess . . . and when I die . . . you and she could reign in my stead?" Banruud's voice was hushed with mock surprise, and Elbor grunted.

"That will never be, Temple Boy. Alba's future does not include you," Banruud said, his tone flat.

Bayr was silent. He didn't want to reign. But he did want Alba.

"You are a bloody cur, Banruud," Aidan of Adyar growled. He stood abruptly, his chair scraping stone, an echo of his disgust. He left the council table without another word, striding for the doors with his men trailing after him. Lothgar was slower to follow, but his aging lion's face was set in resignation. He did not argue the king's decision or seek to offer an alternative solution. He followed Aidan from the room.

The king waved his hands, dismissing those who still lingered. Bayr did not move. The room emptied around him until the two men sat, alone but for a handful of the king's guard, who hovered near the doors, and Dred and Dakin, who stood in silent support of their chieftain.

"Don't do this . . . to Alba. To Saylok. The people . . . look . . . to her. She is their . . . only hope," Bayr pled, his voice low, his heart shattered.

"It is done," Banruud ground out, enunciating each word with a thump of his fist upon the table. "Leave me."

Bayr didn't rise, but his eyes closed in brief prayer. "P-p-please," he stuttered, unable to keep the desperation from the word, and in his desperation, he became a stumbling child again.

"P-p-please," Banruud mimicked, exaggerating the sounds so he spit with every syllable. "You dare question me? You love my daughter, and you think I don't know? She is your sister, you fool. You cannot wed your sister."

Bayr jerked as though he'd been lanced.

The king laughed and threw his feet up on the table, his teeth flashing and his hands folded over his flat stomach. His casual pose contradicted his black glower.

"Surely you knew. Surely your beloved keeper, Dagmar, told you who you are? I thought you slow but not entirely ignorant."

Bayr stood in horrified disbelief.

"You are my son, Bayr. You are Alba's brother." He lifted his hands, palms up, as though bestowing a gift, and then he shrugged, letting them fall.

"I am not," Bayr asserted, his tongue so heavy he could not stammer. The heaviness spread, numbing his lips and his neck, his shoulders and his chest, closing his veins and hardening his blood.

"Oh, but you are. You are of the Clan of the Bear. Named for me, your father. Desdemona was a passionate wench . . . and so dramatic. Even in death, I'm sure."

Dred howled in fury, and Dakin threw himself in front of him, wrapping his arms around the incensed warrior, saving him from taking vengeance upon the man who could have him put to death. The king's guard leaped forward, protecting the king and dragging Dakin and a thrashing Dred from the chamber.

"You will leave the mount, Temple Boy," Banruud ordered. "And take the old man. If you want to live—if you want him to live—you won't return."

Bayr could not feel his legs. He could not feel his hands or his heartbeat. He felt nothing at all. No sensation. No sadness. No breath. No being.

The king's guard circled around him, swords drawn but giving him wide berth. No one dared engage him. They'd all heard the tales. They'd all seen proof of his power. Yet he stood, arms at his sides, like he'd been carved from stone. Then, slowly, his hands steady, he drew a small blade from the belt at his waist. A member of the king's guard yelled out in warning, but Bayr ignored him. He ignored them all.

Grasping his braid in his left hand, he drew his knife through the thick plait with a slash of his right. With a flick of his wrist, he tossed his severed braid at the king's feet. Then he turned and walked from the room, his blade still in his fist, the king's guard clinging to their swords, uncertain what had just occurred.

27

Bayr's hair fell in his eyes and curled around his sweat-slicked face, and he swept it from his skin, impatient. He would take it all off, like the keepers, so nothing remained to remind him. Darkness had fallen as he'd cut through the Temple Wood, racing his horror and his hate. He'd been traveling for miles, unwilling to stop, for in stopping he would have to face himself.

He'd walked from the palace out into the courtyard, across the temple grounds and out the east gate of the mount. He'd kept on walking, his eyes forward, his soul stripped, his mind emptied. He'd never wanted to die before. Not in his loneliest hours or on his worst days. But in this moment he wanted nothing more. If his men had seen him—if anyone had noticed at all—they'd not tried to stop him. He'd been walking for hours, his sword slapping at his thighs.

He followed the stream that trickled down from the temple mount and sliced through the Temple Wood. It continued toward Dolphys, eventually feeding into the Mogda River that spilled into the sea. Eventually he knelt beside it, his thirst penetrating the fog in his head and the hole in his chest.

Dagmar had known. Dred had known. Bayr was certain of it. Had they all known? Had they all watched him with pitying eyes, keeping their secrets as he stuttered through his life, blind and trusting? Had they sent him from the mount to save him or to be rid of him?

He'd never understood Banruud's hatred. He didn't understand it now. Had he not wanted sons? Queen Alannah had died trying to give him one while Bayr grew beneath his nose. He had not wanted Bayr, that much was certain.

But Alba wanted him. Alba loved him. Alba needed him.

Her name, surfacing through the tangle of his thoughts, had him groaning aloud and collapsing into the grass beside the stream, covering his face in his hands and fisting his hands in his hair.

She would be sent to the Northlands. She would be sacrificed on the altar of Saylok, and no one would speak for her. No one could. The clans would celebrate her sacrifice, throwing flowers at her feet, but they would wave her off, bride of Gudrun and daughter of Saylok, soon to be queen of the North.

He would go with her. He would kill the North King and bring her back.

And death would follow them home.

Bayr bellowed in hopeless fury. It would start a war. His love for Alba would start a war, and Bayr would be an army of one. He would not have the support of the clans or the blessing of the king. If Dolphys stood with him, her citizens would fall beneath the sword, and their deaths would be on his head. If the keepers came to his defense they would be hewn down like the grain in the fields, the runes lost, the daughters scattered.

There would be no Saylok when the battle ended. There would be no temple and no clans. And Alba would still be his sister.

The warriors of Dolphys came to the temple not long after sundown, in search of their chieftain. Dagmar had slipped away to pray, and Ivo could only listen to the men with an ever-increasing sense of doom, the keepers gathered around him, Ghost and the Daughters of Freya wan and watchful as the warriors relayed their account of the king's council.

"He knows, Master Ivo. The Dolphys knows the truth, and I fear it has broken him," Dred confessed, his face streaked with worry and wear. The Dolphynians around him shifted in distress, and Ivo did not have to ask of what truth Dred spoke. Their faces held traces of their own shock and disbelief, as if they too had been seared by the knowledge and the mistreatment of their chieftain.

"The king has banished him," Dakin said, grim. "But he is the Dolphys, and our allegiance is to him first. We will not let this stand."

"We need to find him, Master Ivo," Dred begged.

The keepers nodded in agreement, gazes solemn, and Ivo relented, withdrawing his dagger from his robe. He drew a seeker rune, mumbling Bayr's name as he traced the lines of his palms in blood and cupped them over his eyes, waiting for the web of worlds to find the lost. Within seconds, he located Bayr in the darkness, his head bowed, his back bent as though he were being crushed by the universe around him. Ivo clutched his chest and clawed at his throat, afraid of being pulled too deep.

Dred cursed in trepidation and someone cried out, startled by Ivo's violent reaction. The Highest Keeper straightened his hands and steadied himself before covering his eyes once more, this time watching from farther off until his blood dried and his vision cleared.

"There are trees all around him and water nearby. But it is dark, and I cannot see beyond that." Ivo paused, gathering his thoughts. He'd felt Bayr's confusion and anguish, and he did his best to interpret it. "He is not broken, Dred of Dolphys. But his suffering is great. He is . . . undecided . . . about how to go on."

Dred nodded, despondent, and Dakin took his arm as if to gird him up. They would all need girding before the night was through. Ivo could feel the icy breath of the Norns kissing his neck and flowing in his veins.

"What should we do, Highest Keeper?" Dakin asked.

"Wait for him at the base of the mount near the Temple Wood," Ivo answered. "He will not go far. His heart is here. His . . . fate . . . is here too."

☙

Dagmar picked his way down the east slope, taking the path he'd taken a thousand times before, fording the stream on slippery stones, his blade in his belt, his eyes on the Temple Wood where once, a lifetime ago, he'd lost his sister and gained a son. The sun had set and the keepers had bidden it farewell with their evening prayers, chanting as one voice, their song spilling over the temple mount, causing the games to cease and the people to halt, their hands tracing the star of Saylok on their brows. It had always been his favorite part of the tournament, walking among the people, welcoming them into the sanctum, drawing runes of life and love upon their palms as he heard their troubles and calmed their fears.

Oddly, he was not afraid. He knew he should be. Saylok was crumbling around them. But Ivo was wrong. He had not failed. Dagmar had failed. He had failed to confess his darkest fears. He had kept a secret that may have condemned a people. And he would keep it again.

He stumbled in the gathering dusk and caught himself, abrading his hand on the stony ground. In a heartbeat he was back in Dolphys, climbing the peaks of Shinway, scampering after his sister and a fat gray rabbit. Desdemona's palms had bled too. Dagmar made a fist around his weeping hand and continued walking. It was just as well. He would need blood for his rune.

It had been a while since he'd prayed beneath Desdemona's tree. When Bayr had left the mount a decade before, he'd been unable to face it. It hurt to stand beneath the boughs and remember the child, the boy born to a mother who would mark him, a father who would forsake him, and a world that did not welcome him. For all his strength and humility, for all his goodness and grace, Bayr had never once asked for anything. In that too, Dagmar had failed. Dagmar had kept secrets to protect him, and in keeping secrets, he'd allowed a bitter rune, powered by bitter blood, to shape their lives.

If only he'd known. If only he'd understood. He felt a flash of anger and hurt, mouthing Ghost's name as his thoughts churned around her beloved face.

"She should have told me," he whispered aloud, and his own voice mocked him. Ghost had been protecting her child. Just like he had been protecting Bayr. Dagmar had never believed Banruud was Alba's father, yet he'd never said a word to Ivo. To Ghost. To Bayr. Desdemona had cursed Saylok's men, and Dagmar had cursed them all by keeping her secret.

Dagmar knelt beneath her tree and pressed his forehead to her stone, just like he'd taught Bayr to do so long ago. The night above the trees was void of color. Black branches, white stars, gray sky. With the tips of his fingers Dagmar found the whorls in the earth marking his sister's rune.

"I need to understand," he whispered. "I need to see." His belly filled with dread, and he swallowed a moan. He did not want to draw the rune. He did not want to see what the Eye might show him. He'd drawn runes for wisdom and runes for sight, but he'd never drawn the Eye again. Not since the day he'd stood in the cave, a child of eleven, silently pleading with the gods for the power of the keepers. It was one thing to see the present, to sharpen the eye, to travel across a distance knowing what one sought. It was something else entirely to be flung into the future and the past, into time and space, to receive what the Eye would reveal without knowing where the journey would lead . . . or end.

He didn't carve the rune into the earth but used his blood to trace it upon Desdemona's stone, hoping her death would guide his query, hoping her life would mark the path. His trepidation grew as he formed each line, but he did not stop. He was desperate, and he did not know what else to do.

Just like before, he was plucked into the sky like a root pulled from the earth, from darkness and warmth to cold light. And sound ceased.

He was a bird. He was a moonbeam. He was air and space. He was nothing at all. He sped over the treetops, chasing yesterday . . . or tomorrow . . . he wasn't certain. The landscape flashed and re-formed, and he knew where he was.

Dolphys. He was in Dolphys. He'd returned to where it all began.

Sound returned, growing like the chatter of an approaching flock of gulls. A child laughed and then another. Daughters. There were daughters. Everywhere there were daughters. Fair and dark, short and tall. Infants and mothers whirling in a May Day dance. His consciousness was swept up in their game, darting between their clasped hands as they whirled around and around.

"The Dolphys," a little girl shrieked, clapping with glee. "It is the Dolphys. He's coming." The daughters ran, racing toward the setting sun. Dagmar tried to shade his eyes, to see within the silhouette of the warrior who walked toward him, but his hand had no shape or substance, and he could not block the light.

"Bayr?" he whispered, overjoyed. There were daughters, and Bayr was alive and well in Dolphys, still the chieftain of his people. Dagmar wished to be near him and suddenly he was.

But the man they called the Dolphys was not Bayr. His hair was full of fire, and he swooped the smallest girl into his arms, laughing up at her as he made her fly.

Dagmar flew with her, but when she fell back into her chieftain's arms, Dagmar continued upward, tumbling back across the distance to the center of Saylok, but he did not flutter back to the earth. He stayed in the skies, hovering above the temple mount, watching as night became day and day became night.

The temple crumbled and rose again, stone by stone, season after season, and from his vantage, Dagmar could not discern whether he witnessed what was or what would be.

Suddenly, he sat on the hillside watching the sheep, Ghost at his side. The sun warmed her white cheeks and turned her hair to drifted snow, untouched and unadorned. Dagmar's heart swelled and his eyes filled. He had spent seventeen years sitting beside her, in some way or another, and he'd never admitted he loved her.

Banruud would destroy her like he'd destroyed Desdemona.

Dagmar leaned forward, desperate to save her, and he kissed her mouth. It was sweet and pink, the only mouth he'd ever wanted to kiss, the only woman he'd ever longed to touch. Ghost caressed his face and opened her rain-colored eyes.

"I've been waiting so long," she said, but the voice he heard was not hers, and the kiss was no longer theirs.

"I've been waiting so long," Alba cried, and the sound of water rushed around him and through him, tumbling over falls that never ended. The falls became unbound tresses streaming past naked limbs and moonlit stone. Bayr and Alba lay intertwined, unaware of the world around them.

"There is no Alba without Bayr. There never has been. There never will be," Alba said. Bayr moved over her, a supplicant and a savior, kissing her with fervent lips and careful hands.

"Alba," Bayr sighed, and Dagmar wanted to look away, to close his eyes on the fated lovers, but he had no head to turn or lids to lower, and his spirit shuddered with the need to escape.

"There is no Alba without Bayr," Ghost pled, the sound echoing like a song. *No Alba without Bayr, no Alba without Bayr, no Alba without Bayr.*

No Bayr without Alba.

Then Alba was weeping, bent over Bayr's motionless form. Bayr was drenched in blood, Desdemona's rune encircling him in endless ripples. Dagmar's grief became a gong that split the sky and sent him back from whence he came, back to the woods where Desdemona found her final rest.

He saw himself, body stretched out just as Bayr's had been, his eyes fixed on the branches above him. It was not Alba who knelt beside him, but Ghost, her hands on his cheeks, her breath on his mouth.

"Dagmar," she mourned. "Dagmar, where have you gone?"

In an instant, he was no longer watching. He was within. He was aware. His limbs prickled and his heart leaped, and he drew breath. Once. Twice. And again. He felt the soil, cool and moist beneath him, and reveled in the warmth of the woman above him.

"Dagmar, come back to me," Ghost pled. And he obeyed, blinking eyes that were his to command once more. He stared up into her frightened face and lifted his hand to touch her luminous skin.

"What happened to you?" she moaned. "What did you do? I've been trying to wake you."

He could only shake his head and trace the swell of her parted lips, remembering the kiss from his vision. She covered his hand with hers, her fear becoming confusion at the intimacy of his touch.

"Dagmar?"

"Once . . . I found you . . . beneath this tree," he whispered with a voice that began in his chest and rattled through his throat.

"Yes. You did." She tried to smile, but it wobbled around her worried lips.

"When I saw you that day, I thought you were dead," he rasped, remembering. Reliving.

"I *was* dead," she whispered. "And you brought me back to life."

He closed his eyes, aching for the girl she'd been and for the fool he'd become. Oh, to do it all again! But it was not to be. They were not to be.

"You were lying exactly where Desdemona died." He opened his eyes and found her again. "I couldn't bring *her* back. She wanted revenge. She wanted her blood curse more than she wanted to live," he said.

"Yes. She did. And I wanted my daughter more than I wanted to die. We both chose, your sister and I," Ghost murmured, and grief and regret lined her face. "In the end, we both chose. We all . . . chose."

For a moment they were silent, studying each other, hiding nothing.

"I'm so sorry," he whispered. "Banruud took your child, he took Alba, and we made him king. I . . . made him king. I did not stop him. And now I must. Now I must, or he will destroy her, and he will destroy Bayr."

There is no Alba without Bayr.

The words became a beating drum. Time was growing short, and Dagmar still had so much to say.

"I love you, Ghost," he confessed, despairing.

Her lips trembled, and her gray eyes became mirrors, reflecting his feelings, suddenly so simple. So clear.

"I have loved you from that very first day when you told me you lived beneath this tree. You were so young and sad, and yet you made me laugh," he said.

Her cheeks flushed, and she looked seventeen again, the same age she'd been then, the same age Alba was now.

There is no Alba without Bayr.

"Since that day, I have loved you . . . and I have feared you," he admitted, rushing to confess all.

"As I have feared you. There is no love without fear. They walk hand in hand," she said with a small smile. "That is why it hurts so much."

He could not speak, so great was his agony, so complete was her understanding. She took a deep breath and closed her eyes, as if she petitioned Odin for courage. Dagmar pulled her face to his, awkward and afraid, yet bolder than he had ever been. When her lips touched his, the fear fell away, leaving only wonder, only want. He deepened the kiss, drowning in his own submission, savoring the wet intimacy of her mouth against his.

She moaned, the sound both tortured and triumphant. Love rushed into longing, and desire grew into a deluge. They sought no shelter but let the torrent take them away, the kiss a skiff in the storm. Their lips clung and clashed, a frantic coupling fraught with both pleasure and pain. When Ghost gasped for air, he buried his face in her throat, suckling her skin like a hungry child.

"I fear you are saying goodbye," she cried.

Dagmar's heart broke even as his body wailed, railing against the injustice of denial and the inequity of time.

"You have to take the clan daughters and go, Ghost. You have to leave the temple mount," he pled, forcing her eyes to his and his mouth from her skin. "You have to leave now."

She cradled his face, dazed, desperate, and he pressed his lips to hers once more, hungry for a final taste, for a precious moment more.

"I will not leave you," she panted, adamant. "I will not leave Alba."

"She must go with you. Take her and the clan daughters and go to Dolphys."

"The king will come after us."

"Bayr and I will stop him," he promised. "The keepers will stop him."

"Bayr is gone, Dagmar," she moaned. "He knows the king is his father. That is why I came to find you."

Alba had fallen asleep. She'd been sent from the feast, from the presence of the Northmen and the antics of Gudrun. The chieftains were a bristling pack of dogs, eyeing each other with distrust, snarling at the king, yet united in their horror at the presence of the Northmen on the temple mount.

She'd kept her eyes averted from Bayr from the moment her father returned. To look at him would be to give herself away. To look at him would break her control and dash her hopes. His tension quivered beneath her skin and stole her breath.

She was exhausted, and she'd removed her gown and crawled beneath the coverlet, closing her eyes to sleep until she could see him again. When she awoke, her chamber was cloaked in shadow and the sky beyond her windows was dark. She sat up abruptly, then stumbled from the bed to draw back the curtains whispering softly in the night air. She didn't know what time it was, but the moon was high and the hour was late.

Bayr would be waiting on the moor beside the hidden door. He would be waiting and worrying. She pulled her dress over her thin sheath and shoved her feet into the leather slippers she'd abandoned hours before. The coiled sections of her hair were coming undone, and she pulled out her pins and ran hurried fingers through her tresses, leaving them loose around her shoulders.

She cleaned her teeth, dabbed herself in rose oil, and pricked her finger, squeezing out just enough blood to pinken her pale lips and cheeks and draw her rune. Then she pulled a deep-blue cloak around her shoulders and left her bedroom. She flew down the tower stairs and into the body of the palace, past guards and lounging Northmen stretched out in the great room as though they intended to stay indefinitely. She wasn't worried about them staying. She was worried about them leaving and taking her with them as Gudrun's bride.

He wasn't waiting. The hillside behind the temple was hushed and haunted with the revelry from earlier in the day. The tournament brought all manner of tents and temporary shelters, but most of the visitors stayed on the mount itself and spilled down into the village on the north side of Temple Hill. The south side was pocked with ravines and rocks, the rolling meadows that stepped off into forests and foliage not as desirable for making camp. All week, she and Bayr had avoided company by trekking to the falls or hiding away in the old shepherd's hovel Ghost had long abandoned. They'd walked in the woods and lain in the long grass, and Alba had been so careful to keep the rune around them, terrified that someone would see, that someone would tell, and that Bayr would pay the price.

She sat in the grassy gully where the tunnel opened up onto the slope and bit down on her dread, willing herself to wait. The chieftains had called the king into council. She'd heard the talk among the guard and the castle staff as she'd tiptoed beneath their noses.

Time trickled on, the moon lifted and lowered, and still he did not come. She was cold and the damp of the grass had seeped into her clothes and frozen the tips of her fingers and toes. Fall was coming, but she knew Bayr was not.

Panic swelled in her stomach once more. *Where was he?* Had he come and gone before she'd arrived, assuming she'd been unable to meet? Had he made his bid for her hand like they'd planned? Had he made his pledge and petitioned the king?

Memory flickered behind her eyes, her father pummeling Bayr with his fists and feet as Bayr refused to protect himself at all. She flinched and gritted her teeth against the recollection, but she did not seek to suppress it. She never had. Her memories were clear and stark, crystalline against the dark backdrop of long loneliness. She remembered everything.

She could still feel her mother, the comfort of her presence and the depth of her devotion, but her earliest memories were of Bayr. He permeated every one of her beginnings, every hope and every happiness. Bayr was the enduring contrast to her father's shadow, always hovering at the edges of her childhood, the source of constant apprehension.

She longed to be free of her father, and Bayr had escaped him, only to fall subject once again.

Because of her.

Alba moaned aloud, her fear breaking free. *What had she set in motion?* Bayr was no longer a boy but her father was still the king, and to stand against him as chieftain, to defy him, was to pit his entire clan against the kingdom. Bayr was not weak—not by any measure—but neither was he loud or rash. He would not speak unless he absolutely had to, and he would sacrifice himself before he would commit his people to war, but Alba would not sacrifice him.

28

Hours later, Ivo could only hope the warriors from Dolphys had heeded his counsel and left the mount as the residents of the temple were dragged from their beds by the king's guard and driven into the center of the sanctum at knifepoint. Keepers, daughters, and refugees huddled together as the temple was ransacked—the tables overturned, the beds toppled, and the cupboards emptied. The doors were barred against any outside intrusion, but the night was deep, the dawn hours away, and the rest of the mount slept on, unaware of the raid inside holy walls. Alba was missing, and the king was convinced that the keepers and the Temple Boy were to blame.

No one was allowed in or out. The king paced from room to room, checking the progress of his men, demanding they start again when their efforts yielded nothing. When they came up empty-handed, he returned to the sanctum, his men trailing behind him, their tension echoing his.

"You have no authority here, Banruud," Ivo said, but they both knew no one would stop him. The chieftains of Berne and Ebba were under his thumb, Bayr was gone, and the others slept. If the princess was truly missing, they too would demand a search. The temple guard, once formed to protect the temple, were now just an extension of the king's army. They would not interfere with his wishes.

"Where is she, Ivo?" Banruud snapped, towering over the weary Highest Keeper.

Ivo stared at the king balefully. "Where is who, Majesty?"

"My daughter," Banruud ground out.

"But Majesty . . . you have no daughter," Ivo murmured. "Only a son. And he has been sent away."

Banruud's countenance darkened and his gaze swung to the women and girls gathered at the rear of the room. He walked among them, his lamp held high, looking from face to face, until he turned back to the keepers, searching them the same way.

"Remove your robes!" he demanded. The keepers gaped and shrank from him. "All of you, remove your robes," he insisted again, yanking their hoods from their heads, their gleaming pates vulnerable in the orange glow of the temple torches.

Ivo watched his brothers obey, opening their robes without argument and dropping them on the sanctum floor. They all stood in their simple bedshirts, the tails falling above knobby ankles and bare feet. They'd had no time to grab anything but their outer robes to be donned as they were herded through the corridors. Dagmar was not among them. Nor was Ghost. And Ivo took heart in their absence.

"Separate them!" the king demanded, instructing his men, and they immediately began spreading the disrobed keepers from one end of the sanctum to another. When he commanded the same be done among the daughters, pushing them apart, Ivo dragged his sharp nail across the papery skin of his arm, creating a thin bead of blood to form his rune. The end was near.

As Banruud searched, his anger grew, and he turned back to the Highest Keeper once more, his boots echoing across the stone floors like a spike being nailed home.

"Where is she?" Banruud snapped, his face pressed up to Ivo's, spittle flying in the Highest Keeper's face.

"Who, King Banruud? Who is it you seek?" Ivo asked, his voice barely audible and perfectly mild. His folded arms were hidden beneath the long sleeves of his robe, and he began to carve shapes into his skin with his talon-like nails, even as his eyes remained steady.

"The white woman. The wraith. Where is she?" Banruud hissed.

"Ah. The white woman. You have sought her for some time. Mayhaps she has taken your daughter. Or . . . mayhaps . . . you . . . have taken . . . hers."

Banruud's nostrils flared and something flickered in his eyes, and Ivo saw his mistake. He'd confirmed the one thing the king feared most. He knew what the king had done, and that would not stand. He'd never been able to hold his tongue, and his task was unfinished.

The king's hand shot out, plunging and retreating, a slippery eel with sharp teeth. Ivo stilled, his runes wet on his arm, his blood pooling at his feet. His robes, black and voluminous, hid the life that seeped from his skin and the eel that silently slid away.

The king stepped back and watched him crumple, folding into himself without a word of protest.

"We're done here," the king called to his guard. "Keep men at the doors. No one goes in and no one goes out until the princess is found."

Dagmar climbed the eastern slope from the Temple Wood, Ghost's hand clutched in his. He was still shaken from the rune, still disoriented and despairing, but his mind was oddly quiet, his path clear. Desdemona's bones had risen from the soil in the Temple Wood and were clattering up the hill behind him. Her spirit was all around him.

"I must tell Alba who she is," Ghost said, her voice pitched like the breeze, soft and nearly soundless. "Before it is too late."

Dagmar tightened his hand and said nothing. It was already too late.

They entered the tunnel that burrowed under the mount and opened into the sanctum, and hurried through the darkness, hand in hand. Ghost's fingers were cold and her breaths were harsh, though he knew it was not from exertion but from fear.

Dagmar expected the silence of a sleeping temple on the other side of the shifting stone wall, but when they slipped into the sanctum, they were met with blazing sconces and a crowded room. Every keeper was present, every daughter, every refugee; and every eye lifted as he stepped out onto the dais behind the altar, Ghost beside him.

The entire room was kneeling in supplication, but they did not ring the altar or pray beside the stone benches. They faced the far corner, away from the dais, as though they waited for Odin to come through the doors. Keeper Amos arose amid the kneeling throng and walked toward the dais, and Dagmar noticed his feet were bare and dipped in blood. When Amos spoke, his voice echoed with blame.

"The king has killed the Highest Keeper. His men stand at every door," he cried.

"Master Ivo is dead," Juliah said, coming to her feet. The other daughters began to stand around her. Their hair was unbound, streaming around them. They'd clearly been roused from their beds. In the orange glow of the flickering sconces, they were far fiercer than the keepers who huddled around them. They wept, but they did not cower.

Ghost cried out beside him, and she fled the dais for the circle of kneeling mourners, stepping over and between them until she halted, her hands clutching her robes, her eyes on the ground. When she fell to her knees, Dagmar raised his gaze to the dome and begged the Allfather to keep him standing, to keep his heart beating for just a little longer.

Ivo's black robes were soaked in blood, making them shine in the torchlight. In death he was not powerful; he was not the Highest Keeper. He was an old man, an abandoned shell, his skin spotted with age, his features flaccid, the black stain from his lips smeared across his papery cheeks. Dagmar crouched beside him and lifted him from the floor, unable to bear the indignity of his death, unwilling to look on him that way. Ivo's body was frail and insubstantial, like an armful of autumn leaves, and Dagmar carried him to the altar. Ghost rushed to help him straighten his limbs and smooth his robes as they presented him to the gods.

"There are runes on his arm," she gasped, pushing back his sleeve. "He has carved them here, above his wrist."

Dagmar could only stare.

"I don't know these runes," Ghost murmured, raising her grief-stricken gaze to his.

Dagmar knew them. One was the soul rune, used to connect one spirit to another. Ivo had been reaching out to someone in the final minutes of his life. The other rune—man, woman, and child separated by a serpent—was Desdemona's.

"The second rune is unfinished," Ghost whispered.

"Someone tell me what happened here," Dagmar demanded, bearing down on the fear that threatened to engulf him. Amos, always the most outspoken among the keepers, proceeded to describe the events that had unfolded.

By the time Amos had finished his account, Dagmar had sunk into a chair on the dais and the daughters and the keepers had gathered around him, clearly as stricken and lost as he. But Ghost remained beside the altar, her white head bowed, holding Ivo's gnarled hand. The hem of her purple robe was black with Ivo's blood; a long crimson streak stretched from the altar where she stood to the rear of the temple where he'd lain, marking her path.

"Who will come to our aid?" Dalys asked, her voice small.

"We will save ourselves," Bashti hissed.

"But . . . even Bayr has forsaken us," Keeper Bjorn complained, and Ghost raised her head, her eyes meeting Dagmar's across the altar.

"The gods have forsaken us," Amos intoned. "We have failed to lift the scourge."

"The king must die," Juliah growled.

"We must get a message to the chieftains. We must tell the people what he has done," Elayne pressed.

"None of them will care," Keeper Dieter argued.

"Aidan of Adyar will care," Elayne shot back. "Lothgar and Josef will care."

"No one will stand against Banruud," Keeper Lowell said. "There are Northmen on our mount. The clans are afraid, and the king has offered a solution."

"What solution is that?" Dagmar interrupted, harsh.

"He has announced the marriage of Princess Alba to the North King. Gudrun has promised to leave the mount and to withdraw from Berne," Amos supplied, a hint of admiration tingeing his words. "It is the only solution."

Ghost shuddered and released Ivo's hand.

"Why would Gudrun agree to such a thing?" Dagmar asked.

The keepers gaped, not understanding, and Amos was the first to recover. "The princess is beautiful. She is a great prize, a valuable treasure. She is the hope of Saylok," he stammered, outraged.

"The hope of Saylok," Dagmar repeated softly. For so long, they had pinned their hopes on one small girl child. They had placed responsibility on an orphaned temple boy.

And they had all waited to be saved.

"What assurances does the king have that Gudrun will leave?" Dagmar asked.

The keepers had no answer, and their aging faces grew grim. Ghost turned from the altar, her gaze clinging to Dagmar's face. He silently begged her for forgiveness.

"Gudrun wants the temple," Juliah muttered.

"And the mount," Bashti added.

"He wants Saylok," Liis said.

"And if no one will stop Banruud . . . who will stop Gudrun?" Bjorn asked, and his cry echoed in every chest.

"We will stop him," Dagmar whispered, and though he knew it to be true, there was no victory in his voice. He bowed his head and closed his eyes. "Ivo has already begun."

☙

Alba waited until the sky began to blush in the east before she gave up on Bayr. She considered pricking her finger once more, drawing the rune to hide her as she returned, but knew her blood would likely dry before she reached the garden door, so she waited.

What she needed was a rune for courage, a rune to give her peace, and a rune to make her father a different man, but she had no such weapons in her arsenal. She knew runes to heal and runes to hide. She knew runes to hear words that were far away and runes that brought the distance into focus. She could quiet the birds and calm the beasts, little tricks that gave her a sense of freedom and a whisper of influence. But they gave her no power. She could not call down a curse or strike down the North King. She could not command armies or control men's thoughts. She could not even control her own. Whatever abilities she possessed, whatever magic fed her runes, it was not enough to alter her existence in any way. It was not enough to protect Bayr.

Arriving at the hatch, she brushed herself free of the detritus of a night spent on the hillside and a trek through the tunnel, and drew her rune before stepping out into her mother's garden. Skirting the sharp rosebushes, she hurried down the long rows of late-blooming flowers and carefully shaped shrubbery, feeling scattered and scared. She'd waited on the hillside longer than she should have. The castle was awake, the cattle lowing from the barn, the chickens squabbling from the yard behind the kitchens. She would wash and change her clothes and set about finding Bayr. She ducked through the arched terraces and hurried through the rear entrance to the gardens to find the palace in a state of uproar. Porters rushed through the hallways, maids scurried, the kitchen was filled with clatter and chaos, and the guard was in a frenzy.

They were looking for her.

The crowded corridors and the king's men assembled in the wide foyer at the base of the stairs would be almost impossible to navigate. The rune made her blend in; it did not make men blind. The guards were reporting back to Balfor, her father's longtime henchman, rattling off the results of their search as she crept among them, hugging the edges of the room, her eyes on the tower stairs.

"She was not in the temple, Captain."

"We've combed the village."

"Every room in the palace has been searched."

"No one has seen her."

"She is not in the square."

She formulated excuses as she neared the landing, praying her maid was not waiting in her room. *Almost there.* She began to rush past Balfor, who blocked her path, while holding her breath and clutching her skirts, but at the last moment, he shifted to the left and brushed against the back of her hand where her drying rune was drawn. He felt the contact and swiveled his head.

"Princess," he gasped, surprise lifting his brows.

She continued past him, willing him to let her go, but he clutched her arm, detaining her with a shout.

"Alert the king," Balfor boomed. "The princess is here."

A sentry scrambled to obey him, but the guards around them gaped, momentarily speechless at her sudden appearance. Seconds later they were dispersing to report she'd been located, clearly relieved that the crisis had passed.

"Where have you been, Princess?" Balfor hissed. "The whole mount was looking for you. The temple was searched—the keepers are not happy with you—and the palace turned upside down. Yet here you are, looking deliciously rumpled."

"Let go of me, Balfor," she demanded, jerking her arm from his grasp. Balfor had always regarded her in a way that made her skin prickle and her hands sweat. He'd come from Berne with the king seventeen years before, and he'd never strayed far from his side. The way he said *Princess Alba* always sounded like a slur, and Alba avoided him whenever possible.

"Gudrun and the Northmen will leave after the melee. You will be going with them," he whispered. "Your trunks are being prepared. We thought you'd slipped away with the Temple Boy." He grinned, revealing his blackened and missing teeth. "We have a patrol out looking for him. He's to be hung if he's found. Mayhaps your return will convince the king to show mercy. But Gudrun does not want a soiled queen. Are you soiled, Princess?"

"Balfor." Her father was striding toward her. "Leave us."

Balfor slunk away, instructing the remaining sentries to "stand guard at every entrance and be vigilant." Alba turned on her father, her chest hot with terror, her throat closing around the flame.

"I was not with Bayr," she insisted, her voice pitched low for privacy, striving for calm. "What is the meaning of this?"

Her father stopped in front of her and tipped her chin up in consideration, gazing down at her with flat eyes. His hair was messed, long silvery pieces falling from his braid, and there was blood splattered over his clothes. "I have been preparing you for this day—don't act as though it is a surprise. You will be a queen before the sun sets, and Saylok will sing your praises for delivering them out of the hands of the Northmen."

"Where is Bayr?" she asked, pulling her chin from his grasp. "What have you done?"

"You have a long journey ahead, Daughter. You should prepare yourself. Your people will want to see you off. You will join me and King

Gudrun at the melee. A wedding feast will follow. And then we will bid you both farewell." Banruud stepped away from her, turning his back as though the matter was settled.

"I am not leaving, and I will not marry the North King. If you force me, I will gouge out Gudrun's eyes and cut his throat in his sleep. And then I will make a rune, fed with my lifeblood, and I will curse you as you've cursed me. I will turn your limbs as black as your heart, and you will die as alone and miserable as you've lived."

Banruud swung back around, insolence curling his lips. He tugged a length of rope from his black vest and tossed it at her feet. "The Temple Boy left this for you. I thought, given your long friendship, you might want it."

It was Bayr's braid. A streak of long, pale blond was woven through it from tip to tail; she'd wound a lock of her hair into its length only days before. Her fear became blind terror, and she fell to her knees, desperate to deny what she was seeing.

"He cut his braid. Do you know what that means, Alba? Do you know what it means when a warrior cuts his braid in front of his king?" Banruud asked.

She rose, clutching the plait to her chest, the heavy rope of Bayr's hair spilling from her fists, anguish spilling from her eyes.

"It is treason. A braid is severed when a king dies or when a warrior refuses to fight for him." Her father closed the distance between them and wrapped his hand around her neck. Then he pulled her to him, pressing his lips to her brow.

"He will not fight for me. He will not fight for Saylok. He will not even fight for you, Daughter." His words burned her skin. "So why . . . are you fighting . . . for him?"

"What have you done?" she whispered.

"I have done nothing. The dog has gone back to Dolphys. You will be a queen. And you—and I—will never see him again."

29

From two hidden doors in the sanctum wall, two tunnels forked. One led down to the hillside overlooking the Temple Wood, and one snaked beneath the palace and ended in the throne room, where kings of Saylok's past had reigned with the authority granted them by the keepers. During Banruud's rule, the passage had been neglected, and in recent years, Ivo had sealed the iron door with an intricate rune. Banruud had not sought their counsel from the beginning, and the keepers had feared for their safety.

Their fears had proved well founded.

There was no key to open the door to the throne room. Rune blood was required, and Ghost raised her lamp to press her scored palm into the dust of a decade. The door groaned open with an inward swing, and Ghost moved into the narrow channel, trying not to brush the crawling walls. Dagmar had begged her to leave, to take the daughters and the refugees out onto the hillside, but Ghost had not lived in the shadow of the temple for seventeen years to turn her back on her daughter now. They'd all heard the shouting when she was found.

"Go to Dolphys. Follow the stream," Dagmar had insisted. "You will be safe there. I will come for you when the trouble has passed," he promised. But she'd seen his face in the wood and felt the goodbye in his long-awaited kiss.

The final day of the tournament and a sudden betrothal demanded a great deal of the palace staff, but the throne room was empty and silent, the banners of the clans and the tapestries of bygone eras muting the clamor in the corridors beyond. Ghost drew a rune to hide herself and closed the wall behind the throne to obscure the secret passageway, praying it would open for her again. Then she slipped out into the hallway.

The palace was a flurry of frantic activity—guards and gardeners, counselors and cooks, men and maids all tripping around each other to carry out the king's orders. Ghost was not detained or even glanced at. The guards outside Alba's chamber stared, puzzled, when Ghost depressed the latch on the door and walked inside, but when they stuck their heads into the room to verify the princess was where she belonged, they closed the door again, having never noticed Ghost at all. Ghost pulled her hood from her hair and rubbed at the rune on her palm, wiping it away.

Alba stood in front of the window, looking out over the queen's garden, her golden tresses curled and braided in elaborate swirls and waves. Flowers wreathed her head, and her gown was the pale pink of early-morning skies. Her beauty battered Ghost's chest, and when Ghost said her name, gentle, beseeching, the word sounded like a prayer.

Alba turned at her greeting. Her brown eyes were shadowed, and her skin was pale, but her chin carried the stubborn set of a settled mind. She clutched a long black braid in her hands, and Ghost knew Banruud had done his worst.

"You must come with me, Alba," Ghost said.

"And where will we go?" Alba whispered, her lips curving sadly.

"We will go to Dolphys. You and me, and every woman in the temple. We will all go. We will be safe there. Dagmar has seen it." Ghost repeated Dagmar's assertion, though she didn't believe it herself. She needed to convince Alba; she would worry about everything else later.

"And will Dolphys be safe if I am there?" Alba asked. "Or will I drag hell to her doorstep?"

"I fear hell awaits you at Gudrun's side," Ghost answered, dread tightening her stomach and emotion welling in her eyes. She had not expected Alba to argue. She should have known better.

"I cannot leave you," Ghost pled.

"And you cannot come with me," Alba agreed, nodding. "I know. I was foolish—selfish—to ask. You are a keeper."

"I am a mother first," Ghost said, and her tears began to fall, coursing her cheeks. She swiped at her face, impatient. She had a lifetime of pent-up rain and precious little time to weep.

Alba stepped toward her, not understanding. "You're a mother?" she asked, her voice raised in soft surprise.

Ghost fought the urge to lie, to recant, to draw a rune to make the words disappear. But there was no rune to alter the truth and no time to make it more palatable.

"Your name means 'sunrise' . . . Did I ever t-tell you that?" Ghost stammered, not answering directly, needing to help Alba understand.

"Yes. You did. Once . . . long ago," Alba murmured, tilting her head to the side. She touched Ghost's cheek with compassion, wiping her tears away, and Ghost clasped her hand for courage.

"There was so much pain . . . so much fear . . . and then the sun rose, pink and gold and soft . . . and I held you in my arms. I have never known such joy . . . such perfect, inexpressible joy . . . and I have loved you the very best I could since that day." Ghost stumbled over the words, stifling her sobs.

"You held . . . *me*?" Alba whispered, her hand falling away.

Ghost covered her mouth with a trembling hand, desperately trying to quiet her grief, but her confession continued to tumble forth.

"I carried you inside me. I felt you grow. I felt you move. And I watched you come into the world," Ghost gasped, her throat raw with suppressed emotion.

"You are my mother?" Alba asked, the words barely audible.

"I am your mother," Ghost repeated, each word a plea for mercy.

Alba's legs folded as though they'd lost all feeling, leaving her a crumpled pink flower in the middle of the floor. She braced her hands on the floor, her hair a veil around her, and Ghost knelt at her side, afraid to touch her, afraid to say more. For a moment, there was only silence, suspended breath, and disbelief.

"And Banruud?" Alba asked, her voice strangled and small. "Is Banruud my father?"

"Banruud took you away from me when you were only days old."

"He took me away?" Alba whispered, dumbfounded. "He took me away," she repeated, more firmly.

"He said you were his . . . and everyone believed him."

"He . . . is . . . the . . . reason . . . you . . . hide." Alba lifted her stunned gaze.

"Is he not the reason we all hide?" Ghost murmured, quietly weeping.

Alba's face crumpled, and she shook her head as though she couldn't grasp what she was being told.

"Banruud is Bayr's father, Alba. Not yours. He has no right to give you to the North King. He has no claim to you at all," Ghost said. Time was growing short. Dagmar would be frantic.

"Bayr's father?" Alba gasped, horrified. "He is Bayr's father?"

Ghost could only nod in commiseration. "Banruud told him. He told Bayr you were his sister . . . and Bayr severed his braid."

"Oh, Bayr. Oh, my sweet Bayr," Alba moaned, pressing Bayr's braid to her lips, talking to Bayr as though he could hear. "What has he done to you? Where have you gone?"

"We will find him together. But you must come with me now, Alba. You must come with me to Dolphys," Ghost begged, rising to her feet and tugging on Alba's arm.

Alba seemed too shocked to think for herself, and she rose wood-
enly, letting Ghost settle her cloak on her shoulders and draw a rune
upon her palm. Ghost had no plan but to flee, but hiding the princess
was a start.

"No," Alba said suddenly, pulling her hand away. "No." She shook
her head, fierce. Adamant.

"We have to go, Alba. There is no time," Ghost pled. "They will be
coming for you."

"I can't. Don't you see? If I go, people will die. I have a duty to stay."

"You are not the Princess of Saylok," Ghost argued, aghast. "You
are my daughter, and I cannot leave you behind."

For a heartbeat, Alba wilted, her chin falling to her chest, but when
Ghost sought to take her hand once more, she resisted.

"Alba . . . please," Ghost urged, but Alba slowly shook her head
again.

"It was not my father who made me Alba of Saylok. It was you. It
was the keepers. Bayr told me I was blessed on the altar of the temple,
and a star was painted in blood on my brow."

"Oh, daughter," Ghost wept. "I can't save you. Not this time. You
have to save yourself."

"Bayr never tried to save himself," Alba said, adamant. "Not even
once. I will not start a war others have to fight."

⚲

No warriors from Dolphys took the field for the melee. The clans met in
the wide castle yard lined with flags of every color. Adyar, Berne, Ebba,
Joran, and Leok assembled their strongest men, grim-faced and with
teeth gritted, the tension between warriors indicative of the broader
plight of Saylok. They squared off in strategic huddles, their chieftains
standing at the edge of the field, the king and his guests from the north
filling the seats on a makeshift dais. Alba sat beside the North King,

her gaze fixed straight ahead, her hands folded in her lap. Her back ached and her head pounded, but she had no hope for rest or relief. She breathed, in and out, and did her best to empty her head. If she did not think, she would not feel.

"I see only five clans. Where are the warriors from Dolphys?" King Gudrun asked, his tone suspicious. "Why are they not here?"

"The Dolphynian wolves have gone home with their tails between their legs," King Banruud said. "There will only be five clans in the melee this year."

Gudrun grunted and eyed his men. He seemed pleased by the news.

"Would you like to participate?" Banruud asked the North King, his brow lifted in challenge.

Gudrun spit and looked at Alba. "I will save my strength for better things."

The horns sounded and Banruud lifted his hand, indicating the melee should proceed. The field became a swarm of stampeding men, hurling each other to the ground as the crowd roared and the Northmen watched silently.

The warriors from Dolphys weren't the only ones not in attendance. The Daughters of Freya and the keepers of the temple did not make their customary lines behind the king and the chieftains. They were being kept away. The king's guard ringed the temple; the people assumed it was to protect them from the Northmen. Alba knew better. Ghost had told her Ivo was dead. Banruud had killed him. Hopefully Ghost and the Daughters were at this very moment headed toward Dolphys. They didn't need to leave the temple by its doors to leave the mount. But mayhaps they would wait for darkness.

Mayhaps they would wait for her.

Alba bowed her head, willing her weakness away.

The crowd screamed, and the Chieftain of Berne stood and pounded his chest. A moment later it was Lothgar who thundered. Alba raised her head. Lothgar's son stood over the flattened figure of an

Ebban warrior, his hands clenched and his mouth gaping on his roar. With fewer men on the field, the melee didn't last as long as usual, and when an Adyar contender was bested by a man from Joran, only to be tossed to the ground himself, the Clan of the Lion found themselves the victors.

Barrels of the king's wine were rolled out in royal congratulations, and the warriors raised the cups in a show of goodwill and gracious loss. The drinking always began early on the last day of the tournament, especially when one celebration spilled directly into another.

Alba was escorted into the great hall on the arm of King Banruud. The final feast of the tournament had been transformed into a marriage celebration fit for a false princess. The late queen's garden had been stripped of every last bloom to decorate the tables and adorn the room.

"To King Gudrun and Princess Alba," Banruud cried, lifting his glass. Alba lifted her own, but she did not drink. She was afraid if she began, her will would weaken. Gudrun drained his goblet, but when his glass was refilled he abstained.

"To the late queen," Aidan of Adyar added, making a toast of his own. "Alannah is here in spirit, if not in body. Your mother would be proud, Alba," he said, meeting her gaze. She looked away. Ghost was her mother. Ghost, who promised to find her, who swore that when the danger was past, she would travel to the Northlands and never leave her side. But Alba feared the danger would not pass.

Aidan had always been her champion, and she had always called him uncle. But he was not her uncle, and he was not her champion. Not now. He had not stood against the Northmen, he had not stood against her father, and he had not stood up for her.

Round after round of spirits and spiced ale, roasted pig and duck, and platters of lamb and tender veal were passed down the long tables. Baskets of bread of every kind, stuffed with fruit or cheese or dipped in butter and sugar and spice followed. The chieftains and their warriors ate and drank with the gusto oft displayed toward good food after competition. The feast after the melee had always been Alba's favorite part of the Tournament of the King, with the endless food, countless flowers, and more excitement than her life typically provided, but tonight her stomach would not settle and her throat refused to swallow.

When Banruud stood and announced that the wedding processional would begin, the room was stuffed and slightly drunk, making it a jovial wedding party that left the hall and crossed the courtyard to the temple steps. The king's guard had stepped back to make themselves more discreet, and the massive temple doors were pushed wide and welcoming as though a joyful event were about to take place. Inside, the keepers were robed and silent behind Dagmar, who stood behind the altar in the black robes of the Highest Keeper. Confusion trickled through the clansmen as they whispered and wondered about the whereabouts of Master Ivo, but Banruud kept the processional moving forward, his men lining the aisle and manning the doors.

The daughters sat on the front row, across from the altar, but if Ghost was present she remained hidden. King Gudrun leered at them, but he seemed more fascinated by the sanctum itself, and his eyes lingered on the tangled runes carved into the altar—lines and blots and intersecting shapes that had no meaning to anyone but the keepers who had passed the knowledge down, keeper to keeper, through the ages. The runes were intertwined to obscure their true form and function, and Alba had grown dizzy trying to unravel them in years past. There were such runes, camouflaged and cloaked, in every corner of the temple. To bleed on the walls would be to unleash hell on the world.

The ceremony was a ruse, designed to appease the people; the princess could not be sent to the Northlands without becoming a bride. There would be vows, but vows were meaningless without belief, without intention, and Gudrun was not a son of Saylok. The service meant nothing to him.

Gudrun would not kneel at the altar. Nor would he allow the keepers to touch him. His men stood around him, their swords drawn and their eyes jumping. The bones in their braids clicked with every swivel of their heads.

Dagmar did not draw the star of Saylok on their brows as was customary in the rituals of the clans. He intoned the tale of Odin and his sons, of Father Saylok and his animal children. When he asked Gudrun to take Alba's hand, Gudrun took her arm instead.

"Be done with it, Priest," Gudrun hissed.

Dagmar pronounced them man and wife, tracing the star above their heads, his voice gentle, his expression bleak.

Alba of Saylok became Queen of the Northlands, and Gudrun dragged her toward the temple doors. The bells began to toll, a deafening clangor that rattled her teeth and reminded her of the day Queen Alannah died. But there was no keeper song to mourn the passing, and no Bayr to shield her eyes or shoulder her cries.

⁌

Bayr stood in the sanctum among the keepers and the king's guard, his vision cloudy and his arms weak. He was not himself. His body was frail and small, the bones of his hands brittle like a bird's, the skin on his arms like parchment beneath the sharp tip of his nail. Mayhaps he dreamed or mayhaps he had died; but neither felt true.

"Where is she, Ivo?" Banruud hissed, bearing down on him, and Bayr lifted his chin to meet the king's gaze. Odd, to be so short when he was accustomed to being so tall. King Banruud sounded hollow, like he spoke from inside a tomb.

"Where is who, Majesty?" Ivo's voice rattled from Bayr's chest and whispered past his lips.

"Where is my daughter?" Banruud asked. His image undulated as though Bayr gazed on him through a pool of water.

"You don't have a daughter, Majesty. Only a son . . . and you've sent him away," Ivo replied, and Banruud spun away, his countenance black, shouting orders and searching for Alba.

Alba. Where was Alba? Bayr turned Ivo's head and found the huddled daughters of the clans, their hair streaming and their feet bare. Ghost was not among them. Dagmar was absent as well. Bayr felt Ivo's relief swell in his own chest. But where was Alba? Where had she gone? *You don't have a daughter. Only a son.*

"Where is she?" Banruud was back in front of Ivo, his face flushed, his eyes gleaming.

"Who, King Banruud? Who is it you seek?" Ivo answered, his voice gentle inside Bayr's head.

"The white woman. The wraith. Where is she?"

"Ah. The ghost. You have sought her for some time. Mayhaps she has taken your daughter. Or . . . mayhaps . . . you . . . have taken . . . hers."

Pain skewered Bayr's belly, hot and cold, sharp and dull, and Ivo fell to the stones of the sanctum, his runes unfinished, his breath burning in his chest.

"Bayr," Ivo warned. "There is no daughter without the son, no son without the daughter."

Bayr opened his eyes, and Ivo melded into changing leaves and gnarled branches. The dome dissolved into a drawn and quartered sky, peering through the boughs. The sanctum stones softened to earth and grass, and Ivo's pain became the anguish of waking and the agony of remembering.

The stream gurgled beside him, and the night chirruped and hummed. He'd fallen asleep with his face in his hands, his elbows on his knees, and his back against a tree, miles deep in the Temple Wood.

His hair fell over his brow, and he flinched, thinking a spider skittered across his face. He was unaccustomed to the caress of unkempt hair. He ran cold hands over the short, curling strands, seeking to dislodge his unsettled thoughts and displace anything that had nested while he slept. Weary, he rose to his feet, his limbs stiff and his hands cold. He leaned into the tree, waiting for his body to warm and his senses to waken. His arm stung, and he held it out to the moonlight, studying the welts seared into his skin a few inches above his wrist.

In one rune, two lines met and knotted, only to separate and continue on, forming a cross. The other rune was a cluster of angry lines and interwoven symbols, partially surrounded by a snake consuming its own tail. The Highest Keeper had marked him, finding him in his sleep and carving the rune into his skin.

There is no daughter without the son.

The moon shifted, a horse whinnied, and the soft tread of moving feet murmured through the trees. Bayr froze. As he waited, eyes trained toward the approaching sound, one man morphed into another and another, a battalion of shadows traipsing through the Temple Wood. One passed so close to the tree Bayr was pressed against, a gusty exhale would have stirred the man's tangled hair. The bones in his ears and dangling from his clothes clicked softly, obscuring Bayr's thundering heartbeat. Northmen. Dozens of them, moving toward the mount under the cover of darkness. Walking among them were a handful of warriors from Berne, some of whom Bayr recognized, their braids tight and long, setting them apart from the raiders of the Northlands.

Bayr waited until the last man disappeared and the forest exhaled, the night sounds resuming as the danger departed. Then he fell into step behind them.

30

The Northmen stopped just behind the edge of the Temple Wood at the east side of the King's Village, where the cluster of cottages ended and the forest began. Dawn broke as they rested and took turns keeping watch. Bayr could not get close enough to determine exact numbers, but it had to be over a hundred. A hundred warriors armed with axe and shield, guided to the mount by Bernian warriors. Gudrun and his men, already within the walls, would make fifty more.

The mount was overflowing with the old and the young from every clan. Most were not warriors. Most would not know how to wield a sword. One hundred and fifty hardened Northmen would be enough to hew them all down. But the clan chieftains and many of their warriors— at least as many as the Northmen—would still be within the temple walls. To attack the mount when Saylok's warriors were all assembled made little sense on the surface. Yet an army of Northmen stood just beyond the tree line, studying the mount from the Temple Wood.

As the bells marked the noon hour, the villagers left their homes and climbed the hill for the final day of the tournament. The gates were wide open and welcoming. Banners fluttered from the wall, and even across the distance, Bayr heard the peal of the trumpets indicating the commencement of the melee. A feast would follow, and the villagers wouldn't return until after dark. Everyone all in one place, drunk on wine and merriment, lulled by the engagement of their princess, convinced that war had been avoided.

The rune on his arm began to throb.

Bayr crept along the edges of their encampment. The Northmen were waiting for something. They didn't climb the hill or send sentries or scouts up the mount. No fires were burned, no laughter heard, no chatter exchanged. They waited, speaking in low-pitched tones when they spoke at all, and they watched, sharpening their weapons and sleeping in shifts. They awaited King Gudrun, he had little doubt, but whether they were simply protection or they planned an assault, he couldn't be sure. He needed to warn the mount and alert his men.

He'd left them all behind.

He'd left Alba behind.

He'd stumbled from the mount in a horrified stupor, disemboweled and dismembered, a dead man walking.

He could cut back through the forest and climb the mount from the south side, but that would force him to abandon his watch. He feared the Northmen would storm the front while he was scaling the back. There were too many to defeat by himself—Bayr was strong, not indestructible—but if they swarmed the gates with him still behind them, he could make a wide swath from the rear, shaving their numbers and slowing their attack.

The afternoon deepened, and the bells began to ring once more, sonorous and slow and completely unexpected. Bong, bong, bong, bong, bong. They didn't mark the hour or sound an alarm. The melee was long over, and the final feast well underway. Yet the bells continued to reverberate. Bayr frowned at the clangor, reminded of the terrible tolling the day Queen Alannah died.

And then he knew.

The bells were being rung not for a funeral but for a wedding.

As if they'd been waiting for their cue, the Northmen began to enter the village in small groups, moving past animal enclosures and slipping inside empty huts. If anyone remained inside, Bayr had no doubt they were quickly dispensed with. The army in the Temple Wood grew more and more sparse as the Northmen moved into place, until Bayr was the only one who remained.

Then the trumpets began to sound, playing the taps of a royal procession, and Bayr began to run.

The flowers from the feast tables had been gathered and tossed on the cobbles in the courtyard, and the clanspeople raised their voices and their colors in false jubilation as Alba walked at Gudrun's side down the temple steps. The wine flowed again, and Alba was prepared for her departure. Her blush gown was removed and her traveling dress donned. Her long hair was woven into a plait to keep it from tangling in the wind and collecting dust during her journey to Berne, where the longboats of the Northmen waited to take them across the water.

Shadows had gathered alongside the waving well-wishers, though sunset was still a ways off. Few had abandoned their libations since the melee had ended hours before, and the merriment would continue until the people collapsed in drunken piles. It was always thus when the tournament ended. The Hearth of Kings, representing the presence of the Daughters of Freya, sent smoke rings into the sky, though Alba prayed they had made their escape. The king's men surrounded the temple once more, and the doors were closed to the visitors of the mount. No one seemed to notice. No one seemed to care.

A handful of aging mistresses and doddering manservants would go with her, a retinue to attend her in her new life. Many of them were crying as though they'd been sentenced to death. King Banruud stood on the palace steps, bidding his guests goodbye, a weary guard on either side. The courtyard was in a state of drunken dishabille, and the Northmen seemed eager to be on their way.

The chieftains of the northern clans—Berne, Adyar, and Leok—would ride with Alba until they reached the port, ensuring the agreement was kept. Each chief had a cluster of his own clansmen mounted and ready, but many of the warriors had taken part in the melee and nursed black eyes and sore bodies. None of them appeared especially fit to travel, and many swayed in their saddles.

Aidan rode on Alba's right, Lothgar on her left, and Benjie led the way, his shoulders draped in the skin of the bear but his back slumped as though he were already half asleep. King Gudrun rode near the front, a group of his warriors leading the way with another bringing up the rear. Their numbers seemed diminished, and Alba wondered dispassionately if some of them had gone on ahead to make camp. It was only hours until dark, and they would not travel far.

Alba did not look back as they passed through the gates, the horns trumpeting in final farewell. She would lose her courage if she turned her head, and she kept her gaze fixed forward, blind, deaf, and dumb.

She ignored Aidan when he came to an abrupt stop beside her.

"Halt!" he bellowed, his voice ringing with tension, but the party continued down the road without him, and a Northman grunted and urged him along. The trumpeters ceased their heraldry, their duties done, and the horses quickened their pace, the downhill pull urging them forward. A handful of clanspeople spilled out the gates behind them, and the portcullis stayed open for the ebb and flow.

They were halfway down the temple mount when fire bloomed on the thatched roof of a cottage below. Another flame mushroomed in the hut beside it. Whoosh. Whoosh. Whoosh. Three more cottages were engulfed in fire.

Figures swarmed from the mouth of the village, rushing up the road toward them as though they fled the fire behind them.

"Those aren't villagers," Aidan shouted, drawing on his reins.

"Close the gates!" Lothgar roared, but Gudrun's men were already falling upon the confused clansmen, slashing and swinging. Benjie fell beneath an axe without ever coming fully awake. The dark swell rose up the hill, an army of Northmen who had been tucked inside the empty village.

"Scatter!" Alba screamed, and with all the power she possessed, she bade the horses buck and bolt, shedding their riders as though they too had caught fire. Gudrun's men were temporarily distracted with their rearing mounts, and Alba slid from her saddle as her horse shrieked and shot down the hill toward the approaching horde.

Her skirts clutched in her hands, she began running toward the gates, her arms pumping, screaming out in warning. No archers lined the palace walls, no watchmen called out the attack. The horns that had bugled in farewell had been quickly set aside for another round of drinks.

"To the gates!" Gudrun boomed, ordering his men back up the hill. He had managed to stay astride his horse, and she could feel him behind her, pushing the beast up the incline. She could not outrun them.

Halt, halt, halt, she begged the horse, willing him to resist the climb. Gudrun cursed, and the horse shrieked in protest. She looked back, gauging the distance between them, and saw Gudrun slap the horse's rump and dig his heels into its side, urging it on. The road behind her was strewn with bodies and splattered with blood. She thought she saw Aidan among the clansmen still standing, still fighting, but many of Gudrun's men had already begun to surge up the road behind her, abandoning the fight on the hill for the battle beyond the gates.

And then she saw him, several paces ahead of a swarm of Northmen, climbing the hill at a full run, an axe in each hand, his sword still strapped to his back.

"Bayr!" she screamed, both overjoyed and dismayed.

"Alba! Run!" he bellowed, and she obeyed, scrambling up the road that had never seemed so steep or so long, running for the walls that had never seemed so insufficient.

She heard the hoofbeats and the harsh breath of Gudrun's mount before he reached her, and she swerved and ducked, his hand glancing off the top of her head as she evaded him.

Then she was through the gates, tumbling into the courtyard that had been filled with carousing villagers and drunk clansmen for much of the day. The celebration had ended. The disembowelment of a string of the king's guard, slumped in a tidy row, had served to wake up the masses to the death that was upon them. The Northmen at the rear of the processional, and most likely a hidden contingent left on the mount, had already begun slaughtering every person in the square, regardless of age, gender, or size. Alba tripped over the legs of a woman sheltering a small boy in her arms. Both were dead.

Everywhere Alba looked were the slain and suffering. A toppled barrel of wine had been skewered by an axe, the sweet liquid gurgling out and spilling over the cobbles, mixing mayhem and merriment in a sea of red.

She wrenched the axe from the barrel, arming herself, and began searching for something to do, someone to help, or somewhere to hide. A handful of clansmen were racing toward the square, wielding swords and shields, and Alba recognized Bayr's grandfather and the warriors from Dolphys at the front. Then the horde from the village began spilling through the gates, and Alba began to run toward the temple, the only place she'd ever felt safe.

It was clear that others had sought sanctuary as well, but Gudrun's soldiers had followed behind, mowing them down as they fled toward the edifice. Some of the king's guard, posted outside the temple after the wedding, had begun to engage the attackers, but it was the sight of the keepers that drew Alba up short.

They ringed the temple, their backs to the stones, swords in hand, their purple hoods pulled back to reveal shorn heads and solemn eyes.

"Oh no," Alba mourned. "No, no, no." The keepers were not warriors. Many were old men whose rudimentary training in weapons would be no deterrent for battle-hardened Northmen. Her horror slowed her steps and stole her attention, and without warning, she was swept up by her hair and tossed over Gudrun's saddle.

⌒๑

Ghost had followed her daughter once before, trailing after her, not knowing where the journey would lead or how it would end. Seventeen years before, she'd walked from Berne to the temple mount, and she would walk back again.

If Dagmar discerned her thoughts, he didn't say. As soon as the ceremony ended, the king's men guarded the doors once more, herding in the people from the temple and barring the keepers from finding an audience with the chieftains. Just as they'd planned, Dagmar and the keepers hurried the refugees and the daughters into the sanctum tunnel that led to the east side of the mount. They'd waited until the ceremony was over, until the bells chimed and the temple doors were closed. The chaos on the mount would provide a diversion, and the long night ahead would give them time to put some distance between themselves and the king's guard, should he discover their absence. There were tears but no arguments. Ivo's death had illustrated the dire nature of their circumstance. The temple was no longer a sanctuary.

Ghost stepped into the tunnel last and steeled herself to leave without looking back, the way Alba had done when she left the sanctum on the arm of the North King. Ghost had watched from behind the wall, marveling at her daughter's iron control and vowing to face her future with the same courage. But now, just as she was leaving, Dagmar stepped into the darkness behind her, and Ghost could not walk away. She turned into his arms with a strangled sob. He kissed her lids and the tip of her nose, the hollows of her cheeks and the point of her chin before he settled his mouth on hers, his hands cradling her face as though she was infinitely precious to him. She clung to him for a moment, her lips lifted to his, her hands wrapped in his newly donned black robes. The keepers had hastily confirmed him Highest Keeper. No one else was willing to shoulder the mantle. He would be charged with protecting the runes and guarding the temple, even from a people and a king who no longer valued either.

When Dagmar ended the kiss and stepped away, she touched his face in farewell and felt the tears that coursed his cheeks. They did not say goodbye, and they did not lie to each other about a reunion. He clutched her hand a moment more, and then he was gone, ducking back into the channel of light from the sanctum and letting her go.

She walked through the darkness, the last in a long, single-file line of women who'd found a home in the temple only to be displaced once more. Of the three dozen females, only five were the daughters of the clans. The rest were refugees of foreign lands and war-torn clans. Some were old, some were young, and all were afraid. Each carried a small pouch—a little food, a change of clothes—to see them to Dolphys. Only Dalys had been to Dolphys before, but Juliah led the way.

When Ghost walked out of the darkness, squinting against the late-afternoon light, the others were waiting for her. She stepped forward and clutched Elayne and Juliah's hands, knowing her next words would not be welcome.

"I'm not going with you," she said, her voice firm, her heart pleading.

Bashti hissed and Juliah gaped, but Liis nodded slowly and Elayne squeezed her hand as though she'd expected as much.

"But . . . you cannot stay here," Dalys cried. "You are in more danger than all of us."

"No. I can't stay here," she agreed.

"You are going with Alba," Elayne murmured, and Ghost nodded, emphatic.

"She is my daughter, and she is alone," Ghost said, looking at each woman in turn.

"We have each other," Liis said, fierce. "Alba has no one, and today she sacrificed herself for us. We can do this for her."

"I want to fight," Juliah insisted suddenly, her impatience whipping around her. "I am staying here."

"No, Juliah. You are not," Ghost shot back. "You will fight for them!" She pointed at the women waiting on the hillside. "You will fight for each other. And you will live." Ghost balled her hands against the desire to pull them all close, to keep them with her. "Now go."

Juliah nodded, fighting back tears as the others broke down around her.

"Don't cry," Ghost begged, her voice shaking. "Please. We must all be strong. If the gods will it, we will see each other again."

She embraced them fiercely, kissing their cheeks and professing her love before she directed them toward the Temple Wood, willing them to hurry.

When they made it to the forest and disappeared into the trees, she set off, cutting across the hillside toward the northern entrance to the mount, the drab brown of her old shepherd's cloak covering her hair and shielding her face. She would wait for the bridal party at the base of the hill where the road that cut through the village became the way to Berne. She needn't rush, but she didn't want to be too far behind. The Northmen were on horseback and she was on foot. She didn't want to reach Berne after the longboats had sailed. She had her gold, and if she had to, she would purchase a horse in a village along the way.

The trumpets wailed, the sound sitting on the breeze, and Ghost quickened her pace. Minutes later, another sound rose in the wind, a sound Ghost could not immediately identify. It was a collective bellow bristling with shrieks and cries, like the sound of gulls caught in a gale or a frenzied crowd at a tournament. She couldn't see the front of the mount or the northernmost edge of the village, but the sound curled the hair on her nape and curdled the contents of her stomach.

She stopped to listen, eyes turned up to the temple walls, but nothing looked amiss. The sound swelled. Mayhaps it was only a game, another competition among the clans at the close of the king's tournament.

Then, from inside the walls, people began to scream.

It took Ghost several minutes to reach the north side of the mount and cross the sloped meadow to the road that rose from the village to the gates. Something terrible was happening—she could hear it, feel it—and her legs shook with exertion as she closed the final distance. She was not prepared for the sight before her, and she cried out in horror.

The wide entrance was littered with bodies. The Chieftain of Berne, his cloak made from the fur of a bear, was missing the top half of his head. An old woman who'd been Alba's maid in waiting for a dozen years lay staring at the purple sky, her eyes fixed and her chest gaping. Ghost scrambled from one body to the next, her hand clutched to her mouth, searching for Alba. There were Northmen among the dead, their matted hair and bone-studded clothing setting them apart from the clansmen crumpled around them, but Alba was not among them. Nor was the North King.

Someone had attempted to lower the portcullis, but there were bodies in the way, and it rested on the backs of two temple guards who'd been hewn down, one on top of the other. From inside the walls, screams and cries for mercy were interspersed with the clashing of shields and the grunts of men.

She had to go inside.

She took the blade still strapped to the Chieftain of Berne and walked to the gates, her stomach roiling. Stooping, she rolled beneath the dangling portcullis and rose to her feet in a brand-new hell.

The huge courtyard between the temple and the palace was a slaughterhouse, the slain so thick she had to bound between them, hopping from cobble to cobble as though she crossed an endless stream. In the center of the courtyard, stretching from the palace steps to the first arch of the temple, the battle raged, Northmen and clansmen locked in life and death, the tight braids of the clansmen the only distinguishing feature.

One man stood alone and entirely encircled, though he seemed to be holding his own against the warriors surrounding him. He was awash in blood and gore and armed with an axe in each hand. His hair was short and unadorned—no braid or bones—and for a moment, Ghost did not recognize him. Then he bellowed, bringing his axes together and felling three Northmen simultaneously, and Ghost realized it was Bayr. Her heart seized, and she bit back a cry of hope and horror.

A smattering of his clansmen fought nearby—Dred, Dakin, and Dystel—their braids swinging, their shields bearing the mark of the wolf. All were sorely outnumbered. Aidan of Adyar fought with the same madness that seemed to beset them all, back to back with a son of Lothgar, hacking and skewering, trying to withstand the assault of too many Northmen. Clusters of clansmen dotted the grounds, treading on their own dead as they battled to beat back the Northmen. A few archers were perched on the ramparts, seeking to even the numbers and turn the tide, but Saylok had suffered an overwhelming assault, and no one had anticipated it. No one but the keepers.

Ghost ran toward the temple, tripping over the dead and making note of the living, promising them she would return. She had to find Alba first. She wanted to scream her name but feared doing so would present a deadly distraction to the warrior who loved her.

She saw Keeper Amos fall, his skills no match for a powerful Northman. Bjorn was brought down beside him moments later. The exterior of the temple was lined with bodies in purple robes.

"Dagmar," Ghost moaned, eyes skittering frantically from one keeper to the next, searching for him, even as she resisted what she was seeing. And then she spotted Alba, bound to a temple pillar like a witch at the stake. Her hair was falling around her shoulders and her gown was torn from neck to navel, but she was standing, fighting against her bonds.

The North King had taken his axe to the temple door behind her, shredding the carved sections and obliterating the rune that had been painted in blood upon its surface. Ghost watched as the door split in two, the unhinged side falling outward with a mighty crash. Gudrun stepped inside, leaving Alba and the battle to carry on without him. A dozen of his men flooded the temple behind him, their minds on plunder, their victory assured.

Ghost fell only to rise again, stumbling toward the pillars where Alba was tied, terrified the North King would return before she could cut her free. She dropped her blade once and scooped it up with shaking hands, her palms slick and her heart pounding. And then she was at her daughter's side, sawing through the ropes as the ground began to rumble beneath her feet.

"Dagmar's going to bring down the temple," Alba panted, pointing toward the final two pillars where Dagmar stood, his hands braced between them, eyes clinging to Ghost, black robes billowing.

"Dagmar!" Ghost screamed.

"Run!" he roared. "Go!" His forearms were slick with blood, his legs planted between the pillars as though he needed them to stand. Almost immediately the walls of the temple began to tremble and shake, a monster within the mount, fighting to break free. The warriors in the courtyard stumbled back, the quaking beneath their feet causing some of them to fall and others to cease fighting, frightened more of the quaking earth than the swords in their enemies' hands.

Gudrun bellowed, cursing the gods, his voice echoing out through the entrance door, and Alba and Ghost ran, keeping each other upright as the temple continued to rumble and roil. Northmen began fleeing the mount, racing for the gates as the cobbles beneath them bucked and writhed, tossing the dead into the air and the living to their knees.

Ghost looked back, willing Dagmar to follow. The pillars where he braced his hands were shivering like stone snakes, brought alive by the blood runes painted on the rock surface. A groaning arose, inhuman and earsplitting, and the roof of the temple crashed down, abandoning the walls that had once supported it, a cloud of dust and debris mushrooming into the sky and coating the mount in white powder.

And then the world went still.

31

Bayr didn't know how many men he'd killed or how many friends he'd lost. He didn't know if Alba was safe or where she'd gone. He only knew he had to keep fighting, for if he fell, Saylok too would fall. Hundreds had been hewn down beneath the blades of the Northmen—villagers, clansmen, warriors, keepers—and they kept coming, mowing down the innocent and the unsuspecting with almost no resistance.

When the earth began to shake, he thought he'd taken a blow or sustained a wound that he couldn't yet feel, and still he fought, determined to battle until he could no longer stand. From the corner of his eye he saw Dred fall and Dakin stumble, and he roared in loss and outrage, tossing one man and burying his axe in the skull of another before he realized he was not wounded and his men were not lost. The Northmen reeled back, arms wheeling and legs buckling as though they walked the decks on a turbulent sea. Bayr staggered behind them, afraid they would gather and regroup, pursuing them with the single-minded focus of the last man standing.

He thought he heard Alba scream, but it was drowned out by a deafening groan, and he turned back to the temple just in time to watch it crumble, its dome disappearing behind a wall of white, the earth grinding in terrible torment.

And then the mount fell silent.

He could not see the living, if any living remained. Only the dead at his feet. The cloud of dust and powdered debris coated his skin, clinging to the blood on his clothes and the gore in his hair. The silence was almost worse than the screams.

Then Alba called his name.

"Bayr?"

Her voice came from his left, and he made his way toward the sound, tripping over splayed limbs and stepping on the slain.

"Bayr?" she called again, and he realized he'd failed to answer.

"Alba," he said, and the word rasped between his lips, so soft she shouldn't have heard. But she did. Through the whirling white, she appeared, Ghost beside her, and he staggered the final steps, sweeping her up against him, arms locked around her. Ghost immediately turned away, melding back into the fog as though she'd never been there.

"Chief?" Dred called. The air was beginning to clear, shapes and shadows shifting in the haze.

"I'm here," Bayr bellowed. "Dakin?"

"Aye, Dolphys. But Dystel is down."

"I'm down. Not dead," Dystel cried, strain making his voice sharp.

"Adyar?" Bayr called.

"I'm here," Aidan grunted. "Logan of Leok and Chief Josef too. Lothgar was slain on the hill."

"Dagmar," Bayr shouted. "Dagmar!" he called again, knowing it was futile but unable to help himself.

"Bayr," Ghost called, her voice thready in the murky light. "Bayr, help me."

Bayr ran toward her voice, Alba at his side, and found Ghost crouched in the rubble, attempting to shove the stones aside, tears streaming down her cheeks.

"He's here. I know he's here. I saw him fall when the pillars collapsed," she wept.

The temple pillars had split and toppled over each other, their jagged pieces creating a web of teetering stone. To move one could cause the others to come crashing down.

"Dagmar!" Bayr called, desperate.

"He is here!" Ghost insisted, pushing futilely at the massive pillar that rested atop the pile. Bayr pulled her down, wincing as she thrashed and resisted. His arms tightened around her, and he whispered assurance in her ear.

"I w-will find him," he promised. "I will f-find him. Now take Alba and m-move back."

"I thought I heard him, Bayr. I thought I heard him call out. He's there," she pled.

Voices began calling out from the cobbles and the corners, people emerging from their hiding places, gathering together and searching among the dead for those that yet lived. Bayr planted his feet and braced his legs, and with a plea to Odin and an appeal to Thor, he shoved the uppermost section from the top of the pile, freeing the columns below it. One by one, pushing the pillars this way and that, he cleared an opening in the intersecting beams.

He saw Dagmar's hand first, the scarred palm and the curled fingers tinged in blood. He reached down and grasped it, inching Dagmar toward him until he could get his arms beneath his shoulders and pull him free.

Dagmar was limp in his embrace, but his eyes fluttered, and Bayr felt a whisper of breath against his cheek as he lifted him in his arms and turned toward the silent onlookers.

"He is alive," Bayr said, but his voice cracked. Dagmar was alive, but his body was badly broken.

Ghost rushed forward and took Dagmar's dangling hand. Bayr searched, frantic, for a place to lay him down. Everywhere he looked, the earth was upturned, the soil dark against the worn cobbles, the blood of the dead seeping between the cracks.

"Lay him here, Chief," Dred demanded, hastily clearing a small patch of ground, moving the rocks and tamping the soil, his anguish streaming from his eyes and settling in the grooves that lined his trembling lips. Bayr knelt and laid Dagmar down. Dred shrugged off his tunic and folded it, inside out, to put beneath his son's head. His chest was as scarred as Dagmar's palms, the paths they'd each taken written on their skin.

"There is no pain. No pain at all," Dagmar murmured, his whisper faint. His eyes were open and his gaze aware, and Ghost knelt near his head, smoothing his brow, her tears dripping from her chin and spotting the dusty folds of her robe. For a moment, Dagmar gazed up at her, memorizing her face, but then his eyes sought Bayr.

"Help me draw the rune, Bayr."

Bayr shook his head, not understanding. He did not know the runes to promote healing.

"I can't feel my legs. I can't move my arms. You're going to have to help me," Dagmar continued, pleading weakly. "I tried to reverse it before, to draw a rune to change her curse, but I was never willing to die for it. And a blood rune demands lifeblood. Ivo tried, but he did not finish. And he did not understand. Not entirely. Ivo's blood would not break the curse. That is why he needed you."

Ghost moaned, anticipating what was to come, and Bayr stared down at the rune on his arm.

"But I share Desdemona's blood," Dagmar whispered. "And in the end, we can only sacrifice ourselves. To sacrifice others is no sacrifice at all."

"I will do it," Bayr said.

"Please . . . Bayr. You cannot save my life, so use my life to right a wrong."

Bayr lifted his gaze to his grandfather, to the shattered faces of his battle-weary clansmen. And finally, he looked at Alba and Ghost. It was the women—the girl children—who had suffered the most under Saylok's scourge.

"Lift the curse, Bayr," Dagmar said softly.

"Tell m-me what to do," Bayr choked.

Dagmar closed his eyes, as if the Norns were unraveling the final strands of the thread that kept him conscious.

"Open my wrist. We need lifeblood for the rune," he instructed.

Bayr shuddered, but he gritted his teeth and wrapped the blade in Dagmar's hand, curling his own around it to keep it in place.

"I feel no pain," Dagmar reminded him as he opened his eyes, compassion in his gaze, but Bayr still wept as he drew the sharp blade down his uncle's arm. Dagmar's heartbeat was weak, and his blood, its hue deep and dark, pulsed sluggishly before sinking into the ground. He had very little life left to give.

Bayr cut his own palms, adding his blood to the soil before wrapping them around Dagmar's once more. Then he began to carve his mother's rune, the rune Ivo had scored on his arm, the root of it all, the end of it all.

"The sign of the girl child," Dagmar murmured. "The wrath of a woman, the pride of men. It is all there in her rune, but we will add something new."

Bayr raised tormented eyes, the blade faltering.

"Trace the lines," Dagmar urged, "but where there is a serpent, we will draw the sun. Where there is hurt, we will draw hope. Man, woman, child, distinct but interdependent, and around them, life."

∽

There was no room for all the dead and no solace for the living. They all worked through the night, lighting torches and searching through the rubble, but they found no survivors in the ruins. The keepers were dead. Dagmar was dead.

They laid his body on the palace steps with so many others, sorting them in clans and families, trying to clear the courtyard and help the wounded. They piled the bodies of the Northmen on carts and moved them to the meadow beyond the walls where they could be burned. The villagers who survived the assault took their dead down the mount, returning to their homes if they were able. The people of the clans would be returning home too, leaving with their colored flags and their tattered lives. Their lost kin would remain on the temple mount, buried beside the keepers and the clanless. New graves already dotted the hillside.

Ghost moved in a sort of stupor, Alba beside her, ministering where she could, drawing runes of healing and saying words that soothed, numbing herself to the horror and blinding herself to the pain. It was the only way to go on. The sun rose and the surviving chieftains gathered for counsel around the Hearth of Kings. The torch was cold and the daughters were gone, and Ghost could only thank the gods that Dagmar had insisted they leave. Aidan of Adyar and Josef of Joran were present. Logan, the son of Lothgar of Leok, took his father's place among the chieftains, and a warrior from Berne stepped forward to speak for his clan until another leader could be chosen. Berne had a great deal to atone for; the traitorous warriors had paid with their lives, but so had many others.

No one had seen the king or the chieftain from Ebba since before the attack began. Someone claimed they had taken refuge in the temple with members of the guard when the battle broke out. If that was the case, Banruud had perished with the Northmen. It was a fitting end; the destruction of the mount was his fault. A young archer named Elijah, reportedly a nephew of the late Erskin, was brought forward to represent the Clan of the Boar. He'd been the first to scale the ramparts with his bow and had saved countless lives before the battle ended.

While the clansmen gathered, Ghost and Alba slipped out the east entrance and walked to the stream that trickled down the hillside and fed the river that ran through the Temple Wood, needing a few moments to wash and collect themselves. Alba had changed her gown—her trunks had been strewn across the hillside when the caravan was attacked and she'd retrieved most of their contents—and presented a dress for Ghost to wear, though it was several inches too long. It was clean and she was covered, and that was all that mattered. They scrubbed their faces and rewound their hair, searching for strength in the water and the soap. After a long silence, Alba spoke, her voice hoarse with unshed tears.

"Why did Dagmar bring down the temple?" she asked.

"To kill Gudrun," Ghost answered, and her hate for the North King surged in her chest. She welcomed the emotion. It was far easier than grief.

Alba was quiet, her brow furrowed as she tucked the wisps of her golden hair behind her ears. Ghost could see she was unconvinced, and Alba's dark eyes welled with grief even as she shook her head, resistant.

"He should have locked himself inside. He should have locked all the keepers inside the sanctum and sealed the doors with runes," Alba said. "He would still be alive. They all would."

Ghost could not let Dagmar bear such blame, and she reached out and took Alba's hand, lacing their cold fingers together.

"A keeper's job is to protect the temple and the runes from falling into the wrong hands," Ghost said, fighting her own agony.

"The hands of the Northmen?" Alba asked, her condemnation dissolving into sorrow.

"Or the hands of a wicked king," Ghost whispered. "The temple was full of things not meant to be found." Dagmar's tale of his childhood, of a far-off cave in Dolphys and an impressionable girl named Desdemona, flickered through her thoughts.

"Look," Alba whispered, rising, her eyes fixed over Ghost's head. "Ghost, look!"

Ghost turned, fearing the worst, and began to smile instead. A cluster of purple-robed women had emerged from the Temple Wood, a throng behind them.

"They came back," Alba cried, and she began running down the hill to greet them. Ghost was slower to follow, but no less exuberant. The Daughters of Freya had returned, and though the temple was destroyed and the future unknown, she could not feel anything but relief.

"We couldn't do it," Juliah said when Ghost reached her side. "We couldn't leave. We watched from the wood, and we heard the screams."

"We felt the earth quake and saw the dome of the temple fall," Liis added, her face grim.

"We waited all night. We didn't know what to do," Elayne said. "And then we saw you on the hillside and knew it was safe."

"Is it . . . safe?" Dalys asked, hesitant.

Ghost could not hold back her tears, and Alba clutched the girls to her, unable to speak. It was not safe; it never had been. It never would be, and the world was forever altered. But mayhaps they could make it better.

"Dagmar is gone. The keepers too," Ghost choked out, but she could only shake her head when the daughters peppered her with anguished questions and sought further explanation. There would be time for that when she was not so worn and the loss not so fresh.

"Come," Alba interjected. She turned back toward the eastern gate and began to climb. The group of girls and women followed, their steps slow and heavy, their thoughts unbearably loud.

"Where will we live?" a child asked from amid the tired group, voicing the fears of many. "The temple is gone."

"You will stay in the palace," Alba said, her shoulders set, eyes steady. "There is room enough for all of you. And we will take each day as it comes."

"And Bayr?" Juliah asked softly, fearfully. "What of Bayr?"

"He is here," Alba said, and Juliah's obvious relief rippled among the women, hope quickening the last leg of their climb. When they arrived within the walls, the destruction had them clinging to one another and weeping in disbelief.

As they walked through the courtyard, the chieftains gaped and the warriors clutched their braids. Aidan rushed forward, oblivious to everyone but Elayne, and pulled her into his arms, his composure destroyed.

"I thought you were gone," Aidan gasped. "I thought you were in the temple."

Bayr's face was lined with gratitude and grief, and he greeted the daughters one by one, clasping their hands and expressing his thanks. His gaze settled on Alba, and devastation rippled over his face before he bit it back. Ghost recoiled, realization dawning. He didn't know. Bayr didn't know.

"Bayr," Ghost said, her hand extended, desperate to explain, but he'd already turned away. And then he stilled, his broad back obscuring her view.

Dred cursed beside him, his voice trembling with loathing, and the men around him echoed his sentiments. Alba was carved in stone, and the women drew together. Ghost shifted, stepping around Bayr to see what had so upset the crowd.

King Banruud descended the palace steps, his clothes slightly rumpled but his shoulders back. He had taken refuge, clearly, but not inside the temple. He still wore his cloak and his crown, and he clutched the hilt of his sword. A handful of his clanless guard, all able-bodied and weapon-wielding, made a sloppy perimeter around him, their eyes skittering to the unclaimed dead and the ruin of the temple. The Chieftain of Ebba followed a few steps behind them, weaving as he went. He looked as though he'd barricaded himself in the cellar with a cask of the royal wine.

No one spoke as the king approached, but every chieftain turned to face him, their tattered clansmen—most still wearing the gore and grime of battle—falling in behind them. Alba stepped forward as well, her eyes grim and her chin lifted, claiming her place among the chieftains. After all, Banruud had made her a queen.

Ghost drew Benjie's dagger from the bodice of her borrowed gown.

"We've defeated the Northmen. Praise Odin. Praise Thor. Praise Father Saylok," the king boomed, unsheathing his sword and nodding at the chieftains as though he'd fought beside them. Banruud's retinue shook their swords at the autumn sky, shouting in celebration.

"Praise the Dolphys. Praise the keepers. Praise the clans," Dred shouted, his own sword lifted and his voice raised above the king's guard. Then he spit at Banruud's boots and wiped his chin.

"You were told to leave, Dred of Dolphys, under threat of death, as was your chieftain," Banruud said. His tone was mild, as though Dred caused him no real concern, but his eyes were on Bayr. He leveled his blade, and Bayr studied him with emotionless eyes. Alba reached out and clasped his hand, indicating where her loyalties lay.

"You severed your braid, Temple Boy. You're a traitor to your king, and yet you stand on my mount, eyeing my daughter and my crown."

"She is not your daughter," Ghost said, stepping forward. Banruud's face paled, and Ghost felt Bayr stiffen behind her. "And that is not your crown."

"The keepers made me king," Banruud hissed, his hand tightening on his sword. Ghost thought for a moment he would try to strike her down. She willed him to do it.

"You lied to the keepers. You lied to the clans. You lied to your son, and you lied to my daughter. We will take your crown, and we will choose a new king," she said, demanding he hear her. Demanding he see her.

"The keepers are gone," he sneered. "And you are a slave."

"The keepers are not gone," Juliah called, pushing her way through the crowd. Elayne, Bashti, Dalys, and Liis were right behind her, their purple robes attesting to Juliah's claim. "You made us supplicants. Master Ivo made us keepers. And you are no longer King of Saylok."

Banruud's face flushed, and his gaze jumped to the chieftains, as if gauging their support. Aidan of Adyar gripped his braid and sawed his knife across it. He tossed the thick blond plait at Banruud's feet. Logan of Leok and Josef of Joran did the same, their mouths twisted in disdain. One by one, every warrior cut his braid, throwing them down and severing their allegiance to the king. Elbor began to stumble back, and Banruud's men dropped their swords in surrender, unwilling to stand against the clans.

Banruud lunged toward Ghost and grabbed her, using her as a shield as he thrust his sword at Bayr's chest, knowing—as he'd always known—that it was Bayr who would replace him, Bayr who would take his power, and Bayr who would wear his crown. But it was Ghost who took his life.

And mayhaps he'd known that too.

She sank her blade into his belly as he held her to his chest, and she heard his sword clatter on the uneven stones. She ground her teeth and turned the blade, burying it deep, and Banruud toppled, staring up at her in odd resignation. She was the wraith who had haunted his dreams. She was the phantom he never forgot. And he was the man who had stolen her child. Yet he did not truly know her.

"Who are you?" he gasped, blood bubbling from his lips.

"I am Desdemona. I am Alannah. I am Ivo, and I am Bayr. I am the daughters of the clans, and the keepers of the temple. I am Alba's mother, and Dagmar's friend." Her voice broke on Dagmar's name, but she pressed on. "I am everyone you have wronged. And I am Ghost, the new Highest Keeper."

EPILOGUE

Bayr left the temple mount when his crown became too heavy. He never stayed away from the palace for long, and he always returned, restored by the solitude and the sense that Dagmar still walked in the Temple Wood. Sometimes Alba came with him. Sometimes they escaped to the falls and shed their clothes beneath the spray, their mouths silent as their bodies spoke. He loved his wife with an intensity that dulled the ache of Dagmar's death and soothed the strain of Saylok's expectations.

Alba was not with him today. Their child grew inside her, swelling her stomach and slowing her steps. She wanted a daughter—there had been many born to the clans in the first year of his reign—but Bayr wanted nothing more than a life by her side. He prayed only for the safe delivery of their child, daughter or son, and the health of its mother.

The scourge had ended, and the people of Saylok called him King and Savior, but Bayr knew he was naught but the Temple Boy, simple-minded and slow to speak. He no longer stuttered and stumbled through his words—Dagmar's rune had healed the land and untangled his tongue—but Bayr found he still had little to say. He listened and he labored, and when the day was done, he slept beside a woman who was far more adept at ruling a kingdom than he would ever be. He could not have endured it without her. There was no Bayr without Alba.

It had been a while since he'd visited Desdemona's tree. The whorls of grass and blackened earth had become part of the undergrowth, unlined and indistinguishable beside the stone that marked his mother's resting place. There was a stone for Dagmar too, and Bayr knelt to press his forehead against it, the length of his growing braid falling over his cheek. There was much to do, but he made himself be still. He'd not been idle since becoming king.

He had fortified the borders and defended the clans. He'd gathered a hundred men and razed the invaders on Ebba's shores, the new chieftain, Elijah, at his side; the same was done in Berne, though the Northmen had already fled, their numbers greatly reduced.

Dakin was chosen to lead the Clan of the Wolf, but Dred remained on the mount, committing himself to the service of his king. But he still called Bayr Chief. Bayr made him captain of the king's guard and defender of the mount. He could think of no one more qualified to train a new generation of warriors.

Unlike the palace, crowded and chaotic, the forest around him was blessedly hushed. Bayr breathed in the loamy air and curled his hands in the earth, the cold press of Dagmar's stone clearing his head. For many months the castle had been flooded with the injured and the indigent, but little by little, the wounded had gone home, and the King's Village had absorbed the others as new families were formed and cottages erected.

They'd begun to rebuild the temple too, re-forming the walls and shoring up the foundation. The altar stone had been moved to the palace and placed beside the throne, a reminder of the balance of power and the role of the king. Ghost had supervised the removal of every stone, careful to guard what should be hidden, eager to restore what had been lost. She had made herself Highest Keeper, and no one disagreed.

It was Ghost who had placed the crown on his head and the daughters who had named him king. They had all remained on the mount, but Bayr knew that the time would come when every one of them—Juliah, Elayne, Bashti, Liis, and Dalys—would have to choose her own path. They were afraid, and they did not want to leave—Bayr knew exactly how they felt—but they were not all keepers. The thought brought Dagmar's long-ago words rising in his memory.

"You must promise me that when the time comes, when you are grown, even if you do not want to be king, even if you are afraid, you will do what must be done."

"I have kept my promise, Uncle," Bayr murmured. "I have kept my promise, and I'm doing the best I can."

A branch cracked, and Bayr raised his head, abandoning his meditation. A wolf, his coat as black as Bayr's braid, stood several paces away, his blue gaze riveted on the kneeling king. Bayr had seen the wolf before, though it had never come this close. It didn't seem to have a pack, and it always kept its distance.

Bayr rose slowly, his knees numb and his palms tingling. The blood that had pooled in his forehead as he prayed rushed away, leaving him dizzy and his vision impaired. The wolf made no move to depart or approach, and after a steadying moment, Bayr turned to go. The wolf followed. Bayr halted and looked back, and the wolf stopped too. Bayr waited, gazing at the animal, who stared back at him. When he resumed walking, the wolf kept pace. It followed him through the Temple Wood, all the way to the base of the hill. When Bayr began climbing the eastern slope, the wolf watched for several seconds before bounding away, and Dagmar's voice rang in Bayr's mind once more.

"I am yours, Bayr. Always. My heart is yours. My spirit is yours, and even when I'm dead, I will refuse Valhalla, and I will follow at your heels, watching over you."

Bayr began to laugh, the sound echoing over the hillside. He threw back his head, and his laughter became a mournful howl, a salute to his clan and a call to the blue-eyed wolf. He was not the only one who had kept his promise.

AUTHOR'S NOTE

According to Norse mythology, Odin, the Allfather, had countless sons. Many were named and many were not; some, like Thor, are famed, and some are completely unknown. However, the god Saylok, son of Odin, as written about in *The First Girl Child*, is a figment of my imagination. I created him in the image of the gods of the time, gave him a story, and sent Loki, a well-known trickster in Norse mythology, to beset him. I thought about using one of the known sons of Odin as the father of my fictional land but liked the freedom that crafting a god of my own provided. If you haven't read Norse mythology, there is a wealth of adventure waiting for you there. May the Norns beneath Yggdrasil guide you in your journey.

ACKNOWLEDGMENTS

This book pushed me more than any of the thirteen books that came before it, and it would not have happened without my husband, Travis, who was a constant source of support when I didn't know how I was going to continue on. It also would not have happened without my agent, Jane Dystel—I even named a Dolphynian warrior after her—who makes me feel like I'm a big deal even though I'm just little old me.

Big thanks to my dear friend and assistant, Tamara Debbaut, and the rest of my team of editors and beta readers—Karey White, Amy Schmutz, Nicole Karlson, Stephanie Hockersmith, and Sue Adams—for reading and critiquing and helping me to make this story better than I could have on my own.

My gratitude to the team at 47North and Amazon Publishing for believing in me and making this adventure possible—Adrienne Procaccini and Jenna Free, in particular.

Finally, to my dad, who taught me early on what a good man was—Dagmar and Bayr are modeled after you. I hope there are many more stories set in Saylok.

ABOUT THE AUTHOR

Amy Harmon is a *Wall Street Journal, USA Today,* and *New York Times* bestselling author. Her books have been published in eighteen languages—truly a dream come true for a little country girl from Utah. Amy has written fourteen novels, including the *USA Today* bestsellers *Making Faces* and *Running Barefoot* and the Amazon #1 bestseller *From Sand and Ash.* She is also the author of *What the Wind Knows;* the *New York Times* bestseller *A Different Blue;* and *The Bird and the Sword,* a Goodreads Best Book of 2016 nominee. For more information, visit Amy at www.authoramyharmon.com.